Limited Edition
• FOR ELVIS FANS •
PUBLICATION JANUARY 8, 1996

To Mark —
Best Wishes!

Ly + Sue

RETURN TO SENDER

THE

SECRET

SON OF

ELVIS

PRESLEY

(Bettmann)

A NOVEL BY
LES AND SUE FOX

 WEST HIGHLAND PUBLISHING COMPANY, INC.

West Highland Publishing Company, Inc.

Publishers Since 1977

P.O. Box 4206
Tequesta, Florida 33469

© Copyright 1996 by Les and Sue Fox.

MANUFACTURED IN THE UNITED STATES OF AMERICA.

Library of Congress Card Catalog Number: 95—90418

FIRST EDITION
January, 1996

ISBN 0—9646986—0—9

Fox, Les.
   Return to sender : the secret son of Elvis Presley / Les & Sue Fox.
   p. cm.
   Preassigned LCCN: 95-90418.
   ISBN 0-9646986-0-9

   1. Presley, Elvis, 1935-1977--Fiction.   I. Fox, Sue.   II. Title.

PS3556.O69R48 1996   813'.54
                                       QBI95-20392

DEDICATION

It took eighteen years to write this book.

It took twenty-two years to have our first child. Congratulations to us, and to our beautiful daughter, Jamison.

This book is also dedicated to the most handsome dog in the world, Sir Randolph Edward Fox, age sixteen, and his recently departed companion, Lady Victoria.

Famous Elvis Quotes

"Elvis was the first and the best of the Rock 'N Roll era. He's my favorite." . . . **President Bill Clinton**

"Elvis Presley's death deprives our country of a part of itself. He was unique and irreplaceable." . . . **President Jimmy Carter**

"Without Elvis none of us could have made it." . . . **Buddy Holly**

"Before Elvis there was nothing." . . . **John Lennon**

"Elvis was the greatest entertainer who ever lived."
. . . **Eddie Murphy**

"There have been contenders but there is only one King."
. . . **Bruce Springsteen**

"Two thousand years from now they'll still be hearing about Elvis Presley." . . . **Wolfman Jack**

"Elvis Presley was an explorer of vast new landscapes of dream and illusion. He was a man who refused to be told that the best of his dreams would not come true, who refused to be defined by anyone else's perceptions." . . . **Dave Marsh, From his book,** *Elvis*

"I figure all any kid needs is hope and the feeling he or she belongs. If I could do or say anything that would give some kid that feeling, I would believe I had contributed something to the world."
. . . **Elvis Presley**

Chapter One

Memphis, 1979

"THE GOLDEN RULE"

*F*or the upper crust of Memphis, mourning the death of Elvis Presley did not quite take a year and a half. Thursday was still bridge night at the exquisite Germantown home of Charlotte Davis. Her friends began arriving at a quarter to eight, dropped off by their husbands or chauffeurs, to be retrieved at eleven. She did not expect to see her own husband until that time. Either he would be working in his office in the guest wing or he might spend an hour at the downtown gym. At least that's what he had told her. Hunter Davis was in great shape for a man in his late forties. Unfortunately, playing cards wasn't the kind of exercise or recreation he needed. A few greetings, a quick kiss, a wave goodbye and Presley's former confidant was off to his sanctuary at the far end of the hall: Do Not Disturb.

Charlotte and Hunter Davis shared a marvelous, enviable life in Memphis. To be in their elite circle of friends was considered an honor and a privilege. The first requirement, naturally, was to possess significant wealth passed on from at least two prior generations. It was better if your family had lost and regained a fortune during the Civil War and Reconstruction. But as long as your manners could be traced back to your grandparents, you had a good shot at finding your name on an engraved C & H Davis invitation for the big Christmas party. At the 1978 event, last month, there had been one hundred and eighty-six guests. It was a good thing the mansion contained nine and a half bathrooms.

To the public, the Davis marriage was perfect. Like his daddy, Hunter was a tall, husky, good-looking man who made time for his wife and children. He was busy, always in the thick of newsworthy legal battles, yet he managed to lunch with Charlotte at Le Jardin at least once a week. A superbly dressed couple, they were routinely seated at the center table, in view of the large cage of chirping canaries and where other socialites could observe them. Men were supremely jealous of Hunter Davis. He had it all: Money, power, freedom, a family and Charlotte, still one of the most beautiful women in town. He even had a perfect smile.

However, like many men of influence, it was never enough. Hunter Davis always desired another conquest. When he wasn't in court, trying to get around restrictive building codes for a greedy client, he was on a business trip looking for investment property. When he wasn't pushing his son, Hunter II, to work harder during his tennis lessons, he was challenging himself to play better golf. And when none of the above gave him the level of excitement and control he craved, he saw other women.

For Hunter Davis, bridge night read like a cheap romance novel. The big Southern lawyer liked the feel of fake fur on his bare ass. He also enjoyed watching the shapely young beauty bend over to pick up her clothes from the green shag carpet. Reaching down for a brown sock, he quickly straightened up and pointed his toe to avoid a charley-horse. In a moment the calf muscle softened and he stepped into his Jockey shorts. He remembered her long Flamingo Pink nails digging into his thick back. She had bit his ear, not hard enough to draw blood, only to leave teeth marks.

Her perfume was still in his nostrils. After he took a shower, all evidence of sin would be gone except the memory. If he had been too rough, she hadn't complained. Like most of the women he made love to, his partner on this chilly January evening was more interested in passion than comfort. Call it animal magnetism. Good looks or good luck. Call it whatever you want. Just don't let Charlotte find out. Like most rich wives in Memphis, or New York for that matter, she could suspect...as long as she didn't know.

How fitting that the room in which they had shared sex and sweat was decorated in a jungle motif by The King. The carved arms of the sofa and matching chair ended as open beaks. A stone waterfall splashed on tropical plants; an elephant sculpture here, a lion there. In this strange yet familiar place, Davis actually felt like the King of Beasts. Naked, uncivilized, taking whatever his appetite demanded. Walking away casually when he was finished with his prey. The difference, of course, was that she was just as satisfied.

As expected, the security lights came on when Davis' black Eldorado took the inclined curve of his driveway. He had nothing to worry about even if Charlotte or one of the girls saw him through the sheer drapes. His gym bag sat beside him, jammed with the same damp, smelly items of clothing he would have used exercising. His fresh, clean garments, brown pants, white shirt, tan sports jacket, were exactly what he normally wore home. He did not wear cologne, only anti-perspirant. That was his normal routine, and no use doing anything that might get Charlotte aroused.

Davis deliberately left the car outside the garage, where it had been, in case no one had noticed it gone; also, less noisy. Walking quickly to the door that led directly to his office, he tried not to slip on any of the half-ice puddles along the flagstone path. His key was out and he inserted it gently into the lock. Maybe he hadn't been missed. He usually wasn't. All of the answers he was prepared to give hardly ever met with questions.

As the heavy-duty brass deadlock clicked open, a voice behind him said, "Don't move." Just like in a detective story, complete with what felt like the barrel of a gun pressed into his side.

This was far from the first time Hunter Davis had been threatened with a deadly weapon. The most recent incident had occurred in the men's room of Cunningham's. There, just two months ago, a jealous husband had waved a pistol in his face and accused him of making love to his wife in Nashville. It was true, but Davis had denied it, talking the fellow into putting away his gun and then breaking his nose. There was no police report and after being escorted out of town, Davis never expected to hear from him again. Was this the same person? The voice sounded vaguely familiar.

"Who are you?" Davis asked, undaunted by the situation.

"Inside!" the voice ordered, trying to sound forceful.

Hunter Davis was a good talker. Although his heartbeat had jumped to 130, he remained calm and in control. He was a firm believer in waiting for the right time to act. Very little could be done with your back to a man. If he was going to kill you, that was that. But if he didn't do it immediately, a slight break in concentration would do him in. They entered the office.

"Don't turn around." The man closed the door with his foot.

There was a full moon out and it was possible to maneuver around the room in the dark. It was a bad sign when Davis saw the lights come on for that meant the man was not afraid of being seen. The lawyer was relieved when he was told to go to his safe. The light was needed to work the combination lock.

The wall safe was located behind a sixteen by twenty blow-up of his college reunion photo taken five years ago, back in 1974. Davis removed the framed picture slowly and leaned it against the wall. Without delay he opened the reinforced steel door and waited for instructions. It was important to act submissive for the time being. He breathed deeply, but nasally. The palms of his hands were moist, his fingers still outstretched.

"Listen to me, please," he said in his best courtroom manner. "There is money here, quite a bit, and some valuable jewelry. You can take it, I'm not going to try to stop you . . ."

"Give me the money."

Hunter reached in and removed a zippered canvas bank bag.

"Put it behind your back. Don't turn around."

He did what he was told. Enough time passed for the man to stuff the bag under his shirt after opening and closing the zipper. There were two hundred and twenty hundred-dollar bills in the bag. So far this seemed like a robbery but somehow Davis sensed another motive. It bothered him that the thief had waited for him to come home, had known about the safe.

"I'll take your wallet, too." Davis handed it to him. "And the jewelry."

Davis thought of another person it could be. That Gregory guy, Dawson Gregory, whom he had helped put away four years ago and who had vowed revenge when he got out of prison. It didn't sound like him, but he wasn't sure. "Open the file cabinet," the man said.

"There's nothing valuable in there."

"Just do it."

Hunter Davis sidestepped to a four-drawer 1920's raised panel tiger oak file cabinet. He found the key taped to the back, unlocked it and scratched his twitching right eye. The time was coming. He shifted his broad shoulders just enough to determine where the gunman was standing. The man was roughly 5'9".

"Open the second drawer down, then move to your left, put your hands on the wall and spread your legs."

Davis wrapped his wrestler-like fingers around the thick wooden handle and then, using all of his strength and both arms, pulled the drawer out furiously. Spinning to his right, the drawer flew completely out of its storage area like a cannonball and swung around in a wide arc until it collided with the uninvited guest. As it knocked the man backwards, injured and in pain, Davis heard the high-pitched tweet of a video game space weapon and felt a severe sting in his chest. He coughed, blinked his eyes and looked down at the handsome and muscular intruder sprawled out on his back, covered with file folders and papers. A small stream of blood was dripping from a triangular indentation in the center of his forehead, put there by the corner of the heavy wooden drawer. Next to his head was a dark blue German automatic, muzzled with a silencer.

The bullet in Hunter Davis' chest had not pierced his heart. It had come close, though, and he felt dizzy. Kneeling down before he fell, Davis ripped his shirt open to assess the damage. The shot had entered his upper right pectoral, just below his collarbone. It might have hit a lung. There was not a lot of bleeding yet, except perhaps internally. Davis had a short time to decide what to do. He could pick up the gun and make a phone call or he could sit down and try to yell for help. In such a big house with thick plaster walls, yelling might prove not only futile but dangerous if he lost consciousness. He began to crawl for the gun.

To his dismay, the man on the floor shook himself awake. Instinctively, Davis grabbed the man and pulled both of them to their feet. He had his hand around the man's throat and began choking the life out of him, the smaller man's feet off the ground. Don't pass out, this will only take a few seconds, Davis told himself, as his victim's chest heaved and he could not help spitting out saliva and his remaining air supply.

Then Davis felt a sharp pain somewhere, in his midsection, in his leg, he couldn't tell—and before he could kill the bastard his great physical power oozed from his body and he passed out.

⚜

"Mrs. Davis and her friend, Mrs. Cox over there, found the body about a half hour ago."

Detective Sergeant Darlene Flood stared at the deceased.

"Good looking guy," she said, her head turned at an angle to get a better look at his face. "Even with two bullet holes in his skull."

At 36, Detective Flood was already a veteran of the Memphis Police Department. Under the guidance of her father, now retired from the force, she had worked her way up as a rookie seventeen years ago to her present position strictly on her own merit. She had taken all the crap as a lady cop, finding few partners who respected her in her early career and not a whole lot more who did now. Especially since she always scored better on exams than the men, getting that last promotion in 1977 over the more popular Warren Pitt. And it certainly didn't help that she was good looking, her superiors always having to explain that she really was the most qualified, denying sexual payola. Well, who gives a damn? With overtime she was making almost thirty thousand a year,

6

owned her own home and wasn't divorced because she had never married.

"Where's the wife?" Flood asked one of the two police officers who had been called to the scene before midnight.

"I think she's in the kitchen with Officer Bradley and a doctor." The young man treated Detective Flood with more fear than respect. He had seen her chastise other cops for not doing their job correctly.

"You talked to her?"

"I talked to her," said the other police officer. He looked at his notes. "Mrs. Charlotte Davis, age forty-five. She was in the house all night, with three other women playing cards."

"Poker?"

The man looked at Flood. "No," he said. "Bridge."

"Get the details right." Darlene Flood looked at the dark holes above Davis' eyes. At a glance he appeared to have four eyes, two bloody. She had studied the room first thing. A large, opulent private office with twelve foot ceilings, like the rest of the house. A mess. Papers everywhere. A broken wood file drawer in the middle of the room. Why? An open safe, a possible robbery, now a homicide.

"Who turned the lights on?" Flood asked the cop with the pad.

"I don't know," he said, thinking about it. "They were on when we got here, right Jim?" The other cop agreed, admiring the bronze wall sconces.

"You're Mrs. Cox?" Flood turned to the woman on the couch. A man sat beside her, his arm around her, probably her husband. The woman looked up. "You were with Mrs. Davis when she entered this room tonight?"

"Yes," answered Linda Sue Cox meekly.

"What time?"

"After eleven," she said. "Ned got here a few minutes late and by the time we all said good night, I guess it was maybe twenty after."

The two cops had answers to some of her questions but they knew better than to interrupt or try to assist Detective Flood.

"Why were you with Mrs. Davis at eleven twenty? Why

hadn't you left?"

"Ned wanted to say hello to Hunter. Mr. Davis. I think he wanted to ask him a question."

"Did you?" she asked Mr. Cox. "What was the question?"

Ned Cox stood up. "I wanted to ask him about trading my car in for a new one. Hunter was really good at that."

Flood stepped closer to Ned Cox. She was about the same height as he was. "Did you speak to Mr. Davis earlier today?"

"No. I hadn't seen him for a couple of weeks."

"And you didn't arrive at the Davis house until after eleven?"

"That's right," Cox responded boldly. Was he a suspect?

"Did you see anyone outside you didn't know? Anything unusual?"

Cox relaxed. "No, I didn't. Just the ladies leaving."

"Thank you." Flood moved toward Mrs. Cox. "Do you remember, Mrs. Cox, if the lights were on in this room when you and Mrs. Davis came in?"

"As a matter of fact, they were." She tried to look away from the body of her dead friend. "We knew something was wrong as soon as we opened the door. It looked like a break-in."

"Thank you." Flood checked her watch. It was twelve-eighteen. She had come on duty at midnight and was sent to the crime scene instantly. She was still wearing the clothes she had worn all day, a flowery skirt, a white blouse, low heels and a lined corduroy jacket.

"You can go. Officer Degan, please show Mr. and Mrs. Cox out. Mrs. Cox, unless there is something you want to tell me that you think would be helpful, I'll be in touch with you later."

"It looks exactly the same as when we opened the door," she said.

"There was no one else here?"

"We didn't see anyone. We didn't hear a thing all night."

"That's what I was told. Well, good night. Thanks for your help."

"Can I see Charlotte on the way out?"

"Of course."

The remaining police officer watched Darlene Flood do her job. She tossed her jacket onto the couch, adjusted the holster behind her back and surveyed the disturbance. "No one's touched anything, right?"

"Nothing. We waited for you. Jim called Mrs. Davis' doctor — he lives a couple of streets down — and I called the medical examiner. They're supposed to be here by one the latest."

Flood picked up some of the file folders scattered about.

"This is crazy," said the detective. "I can see there was a struggle." She looked at the safe. "It's obvious that Mr. Davis was being robbed, but what I don't understand is why someone was looking through all these files on the floor."

"Who said anybody was looking through the files?"

"See this," Flood said, showing the cop a file with a bloody fingerprint on it. "Mr. Davis' hands are bloody, probably from that chest wound, but this print looks too small to be his. We're going to have to pick up all of this stuff carefully and re-assemble the files. If we can figure out what the killer was looking for, maybe we can come up with a suspect."

Officer Troy was a little impressed. He became a lot impressed when, after ten minutes, Detective Flood told him more. There was no forced entry. Davis' keys lay on his desk, suggesting that he might have opened the door at gunpoint. The hood of his car was still warm, indicating that he had come home in the last few hours. Most likely he had opened the safe. Any valuables had been removed. The shot to the chest had come first. You don't shoot someone in the chest after shooting him twice in the head. And if he were already dead, there was too much blood on his clothes for a post-mortem shot. He was probably still alive when the head wounds were made.

Which meant that murder was a probable motive. Otherwise, why wouldn't the assailant have left Davis lying on the floor bleeding, most likely unconscious, almost certainly helpless? This didn't feel like a robbery. And what about those teeth marks on the victim's ear?

"We don't have much to go on right now," Flood concluded. "There are no witnesses. We'll check for fingerprints tonight and look for footprints or any signs of an escape route in the morning. There's no use disturbing Mrs. Davis now. Her doctor has probably given her a sedative and she'll remember

more tomorrow. Let's check the hospitals for possible suspects. Let's ring a few doorbells, visit a few night spots. I don't
know what else we can do until we get more information. I'd
like you to help me on this case."

"Sure."

"That won't be necessary," said the fat man with the wet
fedora. "This case is mine."

Detective Curtis Debolle signalled the photographer to do
his thing. Flood put her hands on her hips. Her large brown
eyes pierced his beady little blue ones.

"Says who?"

"I got a call from Jackson," Debolle replied. "He was a good
friend of the deceased. The brass expects a lot of flak."

The photographer took three close-ups of Davis' fatal
wounds.

"Everyone was a friend of the deceased," said Flood. "What
kind of flak can't I handle?"

It was the same old story. They wanted a man to get the
credit. To talk to the reporters, who were probably mulling
around outside, hopefully behind the yellow tape, not de-
stroying evidence.

"I can see why no one heard the gunshots," said the fat
detective. "I almost got lost walking from the kitchen to here.
This is a big house."

"Don't touch the light switches or the back door," Flood
instructed the man with the big camera. Then to her
colleague: "No way were there loud gunshots, Curtis. You'd
hear that." Officer Troy was standing at ease, his hands
clasped at his spine, intrigued by the confrontation. "In my
opinion, the killer used a silencer. Now, what about the flak?"

Detective Debolle lit a cigarette. Dropped the match.

"Darlene," he said, taking a puff. "I don't have to tell you
that a situation like this is going to be highly sensitive."

"A situation like what?"

"Okay, it's very simple. Jackson happens to know that Mr.
Davis was not home this evening."

"Where was he?"

"At you-know-who's estate." Debolle coughed. "With a
woman."

"So?" Flood could see flashing red and yellow lights in the driveway.

"So? Mr. Davis is dead. That's a fact. We're not going to change that by turning this into a circus."

Flood felt her body heating up. She was a good detective. She had an excellent chance of solving this case if they would give her a free hand. But it wasn't going to happen that way, and she was angry.

"So there is going to be a cover-up?"

"See!" Debolle dragged deeply, coughed again. "That's the problem here, Darlene. You're just not a team player. No, there ain't gonna be a cover up. We'll find . . . *I'll* find the shooter. Don't worry about that. Hey, Troy, you can go. Wait in the hall a minute."

Darlene raised her right hand like a traffic cop. "You can stay," she said. "I want a cop in here at all times."

"You want! You want! You're off this god damn case, Flood!" Officer Troy stood his ground. "Okay, look Darlene. You want to pretend you're still in charge here, fine. I'm telling you, though. Jackson will personally advise you to get back to your other business."

"How are you going to handle this? You're not going to tell anyone that Davis was somewhere else? What about his car engine?"

She looked down at the man in the baggy pants.

"Darlene, listen to me. Forget the car engine. Forget about Mr. Davis' personal life. We're going to get all the evidence together and pursue it diligently. We've already got two suspects."

"Who?"

"We picked up a guy named Gregory. Davis represented his business partner a few years back. They were food importers. And this Gregory was juggling the books, embezzling a lot of money. He did some time, now he's out. Promised to get even with Davis. Maybe he did."

"Any proof?"

"I don't know yet. He lives about ten miles from here. Maybe he hired somebody. I'm just telling you we're investigating. We also have the names of two people Davis beat up recently. You know, this Hunter Davis was no angel. He had a lot of enemies as well as friends. But he had a certain reputation in Memphis. We don't want his wife or kids to suffer. Luckily, the kids are in Atlanta with their grandparents."

Darlene Flood was still mad, but she understood. Like her daddy had always told her, you can't fight City Hall. And that's what this was going to boil down to. Hunter Davis had been very connected politically. Apparently, there were certain relationships that were not going to be made public. If she was in charge of the case, everything would come out. If Curtis Debolle was assigned, maybe they would still find the killer, but nobody would rock the boat.

Darlene looked at Officer Troy. In his early twenties, he still had some youthful innocence left, but it was going fast. Which wasn't really bad, because a good cop had to think the worst of everybody. In court, it was innocent until proven guilty. On the street, it was guilty first, at least in a cop's mind. Then you eliminated the wrong suspects and, if you were lucky, ended up with one person who was guilty in and out of court.

Darlene studied the photos on Davis' desk. Mrs. Davis, too, was a looker. However, once you were in your forties you couldn't expect your husband's eyes not to wander. Maybe Mrs. Davis knew he was having an affair. Maybe he had been a womanizer for a while. Maybe poor Mrs. Davis, grieving in her kitchen the size of Darlene's whole house, had hired a hit man to take out the unfaithful Mr. Davis while the little woman played bridge with three alibis. Who knew? Let fat Curtis figure it out. If they didn't want her stirring up trouble, no problem. She had plenty of work. In three years, she would be eligible for a pension at 39 years old. She could still get married and have a kid. Who needed this bullshit anyway?

"I'm out of here," she said to Detective Curtis Debolle. "You want this, you got it."

Without another word, or another thought about who might have taken the life of a prominent local attorney with a lot of secrets, Darlene Flood left the room. On her way to the entrance she hardly noticed the costly French paintings, the family portraits, or the Persian runner. She could hear Mrs. Davis sobbing in another room — real tears or fake? — as she exited through the huge doors. She zipped her jacket and found her car keys.

In front of the Davis mansion it was turning into a zoo. Amazing how fast the TV people could be on the scene.

"Are you a member of the family?" asked a newsman, waving a microphone in her face. The cop assigned to the front door pushed the man away.

"I'm a cop," she said, walking to her car down on the street, off the grounds. "But I have no idea what happened."

The news people were trying their best to get into the house, or at least to get a statement. It was raining lightly. They would stand there in the wet moonlight, beneath leafless trees, until they got their story.

Chapter Two

❦

"THOU SHALT NOT KILL"

"I'd like another beer, please."

Mike Troy had pulled a double shift on account of the "Blue Flu" afflicting about a third of the Memphis police force. The issue raised by the union concerned benefits. Hospitalization, vacation time and retirement pay. This happened when contracts expired, and whenever a question of interpretation arose during an accepted contract. In other words, it happened all the time, proving that generals need wars and union leaders need labor disputes. It usually lasted about six weeks. That was how long it took for overtime to exceed the monetary value of the problem, and for cops to actually start getting sick from fatigue.

The unofficial strike was now in its seventh week, which meant it was just about over. Some cops had made a couple of thousand dollars extra since February, which they wouldn't have to report on their income tax returns until April 15, 1980, a year away. So no one was really unhappy yet, provided it all got settled by the end of the month.

The young police officer was drinking beer and whiskey sours with four of his buddies who had also been relieved of their duties at 8:00 PM. It was now ten to nine, and no one was drunk enough to start a fight yet. Jim Degan was playing the pinball machine, a tall one filled with Michelob on draft shaking and spilling on the glass top. The steel balls pinged and zinged, scoring 980,000 meaningless points, until finally a yellow light said "Tilt." Degan returned to the table with his

14

brew.

"Your turn, Mike."

Troy searched for a quarter to attempt to break the record on "Motorcycle Mania" when he noticed the tall, slim woman drinking alone at the end of the bar. She had apparently seated herself during the last five minutes, while Warren Pitt had been holding everyone's attention with a story involving a rabbi, a priest and a striptease artist.

"Whoops!" said Mike Troy, recognizing Detective Flood only when he was close enough to blow in her ear.

"Troy," said the tall, deep auburn- haired rogue cop. "If I didn't know better, I'd think you were trying to pick me up." Flood sipped her bourbon. It was too dark to see how red the man's ruggedly desirable features had turned.

"I knew it was you." Troy spoke in a confident voice, an amateur tactic to an experienced mind-game player.

Flood covered one ear with her hand, the ear visible to Troy.

"Since you couldn't see my face until the last second, you must have noticed my earrings." Her teeth flashed in a quick smile. She squinted a brown eye at him. "What do they look like?"

The man could not remember until she showed him. Each earring was half of a gold heart with an interlocking jagged edge.

"You broke my heart, detective," he said, eliciting a laugh and a longer smile. The ruse was over. She wasn't mad, and his normal color returned. It was hard to deceive Darlene Flood. Hard for anyone.

Troy glanced back at his table. The boys were teasing the waitress, who didn't seem to mind in this mostly cop-visited bar. The general public was welcome. Construction workers and older lawyers liked it, too. Very few women dropped by, as four-letter words flew freely across the oasis. More sophisticated night owls drank elsewhere, seeking better entertainment and a wider menu than ham and swiss on rye, or pretzels. Nor did most people consider framed Playmates-Of-The-Year and autographed pictures of the St. Louis Cardinals "atmosphere." But Earl Cunningham didn't give a damn. The ex-cop had taken over the place as his second career in 1969 and was honoring the first ten years by not hitting unruly patrons over the head with his baseball bat for a week. This was not a place you wanted to be unless you knew the owner or kept your hands to yourself. Mostly, this was a haven for local policemen.

"This is where Hunter Davis broke a guy's face on November 12th," said Darlene Flood.

"What?" Troy brought his gaze back to the pretty lady who was his boss.

"If your friends would rather you don't associate with me, maybe you should go back there."

"I don't care about that," said Troy. "What did you just say about Hunter Davis?"

Flood grabbed his arm, a powerful grip for a woman. "Come with me," she half ordered him. They moved to a booth out of earshot. Not that you could hear much with Johnny Cash at full volume. "I said, on November 12th, 1978, Mr. Hunter Davis, who then resided at 53 Old Poplar Pike, assaulted a car dealer from Nashville in Cunningham's Bar. Right here. In the bathroom."

"How do you know that? Was there a report?"

"Of course not. Mr. Davis was a regular. Plus, the guy pulled a gun on him first. The guy's name was Lance C. Goodner, and the truth is, he's lucky to be alive."

Detective Flood had managed to impress the less seasoned cop again. She gave Troy all of the lurid details.

"Where's the gun? And how did you find this out? I've typed up Detective DeBolle's paperwork. There's nothing in it about this Goodner."

"There's no gun," said Flood. "What I told you never happened here. Lance Goodner denies it. So would any of your friends who might have been witnesses. What can I say? Half the world is lying, and the other half believes them."

Troy shifted his eyes to see who was watching him. No one. They probably didn't know who was sitting with her back to them.

"You're telling me that Davis was murdered by a car dealer from Nashville..."

"A Lincoln dealer, to be specific. Elvis liked Lincolns and Cadillacs."

"Did he kill Davis?"

"No. He didn't. The slugs removed from Mr. Davis' body came from a German automatic. Mr. Goodner, on the other hand, is the registered owner of two Smith & Wesson 38 Specials. I assume he still has the other one."

Troy attempted to demonstrate his learning ability.

"That doesn't prove he didn't have a German gun, too."

"No, it doesn't. However, the fingerprint I reported on that file folder was not Mr. Goodner's. Which makes him an unlikely suspect. But that's not in the paperwork either. At least I doubt it."

"It's not," admitted Troy. "They did run the fingerprint through the FBI, though. I saw that. And they tried to match it to three other suspects."

"None of whom had anything to do with Hunter Davis' girlfriends."

"What does that mean?"

Flood chortled with disdain for the system. "It means that you're not gonna find word one in any police report about Mr. Davis' extra-curricular sex life."

"To protect his reputation?" Debolle's explanation.

"To avoid revealing the fact that the woman Hunter Davis was with the night he was murdered also knew police and elected officials. So it's been decided that the investigation can only go in other directions. Hunter Davis is dead. You heard fatso. Solving this crime won't bring him back. But looking for the killer by pursuing every possible lead might get lots of important people into hot water."

Officer Michael Troy was not a rookie. Maybe he didn't have the smarts of a pro detective at this point in time, but he found it hard to believe what Darlene Flood was suggesting.

"The investigation is closed?" he asked reluctantly. It would be harder to do his job if her answer was what he expected, and was true.

"It was never open," she replied, scraping up pretzel parts from a chipped glass bowl. "I've seen some of the reports. My father still has a little pull. There's no mention of where

Hunter Davis really was one hour before the murder."

"I heard he might have been at a gym."

"I heard he was having sex with a woman named Beth Schiller." Flood polished off her drink and waved it for a refill. "At Elvis Presley's house."

"You're not serious."

"Talk to the gardener," Flood advised. "He was putting down rock salt on the driveway that night. And he's got excellent vision."

Troy remembered the rainy evening. "It didn't snow," he said.

"Rarely does in Memphis. But rain turns to sleet." A fresh shot glass of alcohol was set down. "Ask him. Do you want his name?"

"No thanks." Troy started to rise. "I'd better get going."

Warren Pitt had stood up. Troy was not interested in sharing these exciting inside stories with anyone. Regardless of what was going on, he aspired to be a detective himself someday. Hanging around with Darlene Flood, whom he not only admired but found physically attractive - that low-cut white dress had not gone unnoticed - would hardly enhance his promotability. And if Pitt even remotely suspected that they were discussing the case Flood had been emphatically kicked off, his ass was grass. The tug of war between her figure and his future pulled the blond-haired Romeo to his feet and back to his peers. As it turned out, they never saw the lady's face. Nor did Detective Flood get to question him further about the gun. The weapon not written up in any report to date.

⚜

Charlotte Davis met Flood the next day for lunch. It was almost noon. If their get-together at Le Jardin, in the private party room, lasted less than fifteen minutes, there would be little chance of either of them being seen by the wrong people. They ordered house salads and Diet Coke.

"I haven't been able to identify the gun yet," Flood said.

18

"My feeling is that it's unusual enough that we can narrow it down to maybe a few hundred owners."

"A few hundred?" Mrs. Davis asked, hoping for better news. "How long will it take to check out that many people?"

Darlene forked a tiny Cherry Tomato into her mouth, scoffed it down.

"Months," she answered honestly. "I'm hoping that we only find a few located in Memphis, or in this state, or not far from Tennessee. If I have to search the whole country, it could take a long time."

Charlotte felt funny about this clandestine rendezvous. For starters, she wasn't convinced that Hunter had been murdered despite the police lady's expert analysis. Who could really understand the criminal mind? Maybe it had been a robbery - her husband kept large sums of money at home all the time - and Hunter's effort to foil the thief had cost him his life. After all, some of the blood belonged to the assailant, proving there had been a violent exchange. Why couldn't the man have shot Davis in the head - oh, those two gaping holes - and killed her beloved Hunter out of pure meanness? There were people, it was hard to regard them as human, who stabbed strangers to death, dismembered them and buried their bodies in their own back yards. Who said such an animal had not invaded their home, destroyed their life?

Detective Flood had an answer for everything. This was clearly not the work of a serial killer. And thieves were not murderers. If caught, they did not want to risk the death penalty. By the same token, this crime had been too sloppy for a hit man. Most likely, said Flood, it was someone the victim knew, perhaps casually. Probably not a cop. Not the right gun, no known motive, easier to have made it look like an accident under different circumstances. She wasn't ruling it out, but her gut feeling told her this had been about revenge. And sex.

Of course, Charlotte realized Flood might be wrong about that. By leaving no stone unturned, in the cop's words, they might find out it *was* an inside job involving the police. Then both their lives would be in danger. As well as the lives of her three young children, whom she was more worried about than her dead husband just now. Flood was certain there was a cover-up. How did she know how deep it went? Charlotte herself had confirmed that the "investigation" was at best going badly. When she called Detective Debolle to ask if he wanted a list of the stolen jewelry, his response was, " I guess so." Flood, through an intermediary, had already circulated descriptions of several readily identifiable costly pieces to pawn shops and jewelers. Debolle had not. This was not a sign of police diligence. It came closer to the gross incompetence Flood said she deplored not only in this case but in other "favored" situations.

"How about the gold jewelry?" asked Charlotte. "Has anything shown up?"

"It's only been two weeks." Flood crunched some sliced red onion and croutons, swallowed. "Very often these people hold onto valuables for a while before slipping up. My contacts are reliable. If any of it gets sold, we'll find out. Again, the farther away the jewelry is, the longer it will take."

Mrs. Davis was getting nervous. Nothing she was being told instilled great confidence in this whole private eye scenario. True, Darlene Flood was doing it at no charge. Which she appreciated, even though she still needed sleeping pills and was seeing a psychologist. But the fact of the matter was that Detective Flood, with all her energy and cleverness, was not doing much better than the police. Give me a month, she had requested. Don't tell anyone what we're doing, write down whatever you know even if it seems trivial, and trust me. Okay. She had trusted her. Met her every other day since the end of March without being followed. Now what?

"I can't keep doing this," said Charlotte, her hands trembling. "My therapist says I shouldn't dwell on the past, that I have to move on. She's right. Finding Hunter's murderer isn't going to replace my husband, or the father of my children. She says I should accept whatever the police say, even if they're lying."

Darlene Flood sympathized with her sorrow, and fears. "If that's what you want, I'll drop the whole thing." She looked at the society lady's red eyes. "I don't want to do anything to hurt you or your family. Or if you want, I'll continue to do this on my own. I won't bother you until I have the murderer. But with the department tying my hands, and without your help, I can't promise quick results. Tell me, Mrs. Davis, what do you want me to do?"

Charlotte Davis collected herself.

"I've already told you everything," she pleaded, as if being interrogated. Her hands were fists, her thumbs rubbing her fingers cricket-like. "You know Hunter was involved with lots of strange clients. I mentioned that he worked for the Presley family. He sometimes travelled with Elvis, I think. He flew to New York and Los Angeles all the time. He did business in Nashville and Atlanta. I went with him to New York at least twice a year. We stayed in Palm Beach in February...not this year, of course. I gave you all the names and dates I could remember. The police have his calendar, his telephone book, his cancelled checks. I'm supposed to get them back soon. You can have it. What else can I do?"

"Do you want me to drop it?"

"No. I just can't keep talking about it."

Flood understood. For her, this had become an obsession. For the victim's wife, it couldn't be that way or she would have a breakdown. She needed to play bridge on Thursdays again, if she could. To plan parties, especially birthday parties and other happy events. She had to get more interested in her kids' lives, take them to the zoo, play Monopoly with them, read books about dragons and rocket ships and cows that talk. She had to return to the way things had been before January, stop re-living that night. It was cruel to expect otherwise. She wasn't the district attorney. She was a woman, and a mother. Crime solving wasn't her occupation. Making peanut butter and jelly sandwiches, or asking the cook to make them, was her job.

"All right," said the investigator. "I hear what you're saying. And to tell you the truth, I can't spend my whole life on this case either. Maybe I'm wrong. Maybe the police are doing their job. I don't think so, but your husband was very tight with my superiors." She did not specify that this included affairs with women, although Mrs. Davis had made it clear she knew about that. Another factor in Charlotte's decision to limit her involvement. Like the police, she would rather the case remain unsolved than publicize and expose her children to Hunter's private life. "Maybe Detective Debolle and Chief Jackson are doing more than I think," she continued. "Maybe they've been to Graceland, spoken to other people about the things you've told me. I mean, we're not talking about jay-walking here. A good man was killed. In his own home, in the best part of town. It was in all the papers. They can't just ignore that, or forget about it."

Darlene Flood finished her salad, downed the Coke. Charlotte hadn't touched hers. There was no check to pay or sign for. The bill was mailed monthly.

"He was a good man," said the widow. "He really was. He loved to watch his son play tennis. And his two girls, Laura and Yvette, adored him. They miss him terribly. We all do. No matter what kind of crazy things he got himself involved in. He was a devoted lawyer. Went the whole nine yards for his clients. Yes, he made a lot of money, but he wasn't in it just to get richer. He gave back to the world."

"I was at the eulogy," Flood reminded Charlotte. She had been in the last row of the church. With a hidden camera and a hearing amplifier.

"I saw you." Charlotte restrained herself from remembering the day. "He was friends with Elvis Presley, you know. Oh, I told you that. But they really did things together. Like playing pool, and racquetball. Hunter loved to shop for automobiles."

"I've heard that," said Flood. "I wish I had known him."

"He was working on some kind of deal for Elvis," Charlotte said to the detective. "It was a secret. There was a lot of money at stake."

"What kind of deal?"

"Buying houses? For cash. I'm not sure. Would you like me to look into it? I could speak to our real estate broker. He might know."

"Give me his name," Flood decided. "I'll call him. Charlotte...may I call you Charlotte?"

"Sure." Charlotte's watch said ten after twelve.

"Charlotte, I think you should take your therapist's advice and forget about this police thing for a while. Let me handle it. If I don't come up with anything in a couple of weeks, I'll try to push Debolle. You know, embarrass him into doing his job better. I'm good at that."

"I'll bet you are."

"I won't be calling you. And don't call me. I've got plenty of evidence to follow up on. Someone is feeding me all the official reports. I'm not Richard Nixon. I can't bug the chief's office. But I promise you, I'll do my best."

Charlotte shook her hand and started for the rear exit.

"Talking about Richard Nixon," she said, looking back. "Did you know that my husband's college - Duke - turned down the Nixon Museum? That's where Nixon went to law school. Hunter and I were part of a committee in favor of the museum being at Duke. But we couldn't persuade the administration. They had to preserve their reputation." She smiled and left. Flood waited five minutes.

Spring was in the air in downtown Memphis. Robins sang in the budding branches of oak trees. Joggers in striped pants were stretching winterbound muscles. Walking briskly to her Honda parked two blocks away, Darlene had gotten the message: Preserve the Davis reputation. Or at least the public image of Hunter Davis. That was her intention. To investigate this case as far as possible short of inciting a sex scandal. To flush out the creep who had taken the life of Charlotte's philandering high-society husband without flushing her career down the toilet.

A slow moving dark Chevy with two big men in the front seat passed her, sped up and made a sharp left. She was too far from her vehicle to give chase, but the silhouettes looked like Debolle and Pitt. The license plate had two threes in it. Like the three years she had left before retiring at half pay.

Chapter Three

꧁꧂

"IN THE BEGINNING"

NOVEMBER, 1975
BEVERLY HILLS, CALIFORNIA

It was Hunter Davis' last stop before flying back to Memphis. His lack of success at the first clinic was hardly a surprise. The problem was, he just hated to hand over so much cash to a man he did not trust. Despite his qualifications, Dr. Ira Goldman might turn out to be a con artist. Although it wasn't his own money, Davis still treated $250,000 very seriously.

As he approached the entrance to the small grey building just around the corner from Rodeo Drive, he kept thinking of calling the whole thing off. But it was impossible to back out now, not after all the planning and all the promises made. In the end, it was his client's decision. Davis knew that this particular client would never change his mind. That the opportunity far outweighed the price.

The Memphis attorney was buzzed in through a pair of tall white heavy metal doors resembling a prison gate. On his way down the hall he observed two security cameras and some unidentified stainless steel devices. It was a very cold place, lacking not only such welcoming touches as flowers or pictures but windows as well. The total absence of California's abundant mid-morning sunshine helped to create the pervasive atmosphere of a below-grade vault. Nothing changed when he

24

took two steps up to the office door. Another electric release preceded his admission.

"Mr. Davis," said a cheerful young man, extending his hand. "Please come in. Dr. Goldman will see you in a minute."

"And you are . . .?"

"Oh, sorry." The man tucked in his 1970 Berkeley sweatshirt. "My name is Leonard Stein. I'm Dr. Goldman's assistant."

There was no other receptionist in the office.

"How come the doctor doesn't have a name plate outside?" asked Davis, more curious than suspicious.

"We're very discreet," Stein answered. "Many people don't want to be seen visiting a plastic surgeon."

Davis looked over this Stein character. He was short and chubby, with very fat fingers. His skin was terrible and he had a most unattractive face. He could use a dermatologist and a plastic surgeon, Davis thought. Still, he was articulate, polite and outgoing. If Goldman possessed the last two qualities, he had not revealed them at their recent meeting at a nearby restaurant. For a second, he thought about cracking that old joke: "Your father wasn't Frank N. Stein?" but Davis controlled himself. Humor wasn't called for under these circumstances, nor was Stein one of the good old boys.

Following a faint rumbling sound that Davis prayed wasn't an earthquake, a door to his right receded slowly into the wall. Dr. Ira Goldman, wearing running shoes and Levi jeans, emerged from the elevator. The slim 6'3" doctor was accustomed to looking down at most people. It still annoyed him that the imposing figure in the blue blazer and maroon and white pin-striped shirt was slightly taller. He quickly suggested they sit down, after a forced handshake, to talk business. Hunter Davis realized that this room was Goldman's office, not a reception area.

"Beverly Hills is certainly a beautiful town," said the visitor. "Maybe I'll try to do a little shopping before I go back. You know, pick up a tie and maybe a present for Mrs. Davis."

Dr. Goldman could not be bothered with aimless chit-chat. He had work to do, allowing no more than an hour to dispose of the Southern lawyer. He withdrew one of his monogrammed black Cross pens from its onyx launch pad and set it on a small notebook.

"If you're here, I take it we have a deal." He did not look Davis in the eye. Instead, he stared at the gold Confederate Flag cuff links. Just the right accessory for a jerk from Tennessee with a blond semi crew cut and navy blue loafers.

"We have a deal," Davis replied, tapping his attache case. "Provided that you answer all of my questions satisfactorily."

"I thought I did that last time," Goldman responded with some irritation. Then he stood up, adjusted his wire-rimmed glasses, squeezed his oversized Adam's Apple and sat back down. This was not the kind of guy you wanted to give a pile of money, thought Elvis' attorney.

"Leonard," said the doctor. "Wait upstairs for my call."

"Sure, Dr. Goldman."

"I hate to rush you, Mr. Davis, but I have a very busy schedule. What are the questions?"

Davis examined the scrawny scientist. His slender hands looked like a woman's, or a pianist's. Yet they seemed powerful. His own hands, in contrast, were as thick and beefy as his neck and chest, the result of three grueling sessions with weights at the health club every week. He could picture Goldman's bony arm struggling to escape from his superior grasp. He could feel himself pulling his victim over his own desk, knocking aside his fancy pens and banging his bushy-haired skull on the white tile floor. Instead, he removed a list from his jacket pocket.

"I have only forty-five minutes," Dr. Goldman warned.

"Fine. My initial question is the price."

"It's not negotiable."

"Why not? It's ten times what anyone else would charge."

"Why not?" Goldman repeated. "I'll tell you why not. Because first of all I could go to jail for doing this procedure. I'm sure you've checked out other sources before coming to me. No one else will do it, right?"

Hunter Davis massaged his chin with his thumb and forefinger. As he already knew, Ira Goldman was not a likable man. He refused to make eye contact and always spoke down to you. Obviously, he had an extremely high IQ, but it was wrong to treat people like servants. His beard covered half of his face and masked his expressions. It was like talking to a machine. His stark white office, also windowless, reflected his personality. On the other hand, he had something they wanted and had already agreed to pay a ridiculous price for. So the man from Memphis took a deep breath, smiled, and decided not to grab the California moron by his white lab coat.

"We still have some other options," Davis said coyly. "But you *are* our first choice. However, I don't understand why it's a million dollars."

"Okay, let me spell it out for you one last time and then you can leave if you want to. This is my own private lab. I don't get any grants and my funds right now are limited. I don't have the time or interest to do you any favors. The special equipment I need costs a ton of money . . ."

"Equipment you'll use again."

"True, but my only incentive to work for you is to foster my research. I'm sure you have some idea of how important my project is. If you and your client, whoever he may be, are not rich enough to support me for the next few years, frankly I don't need you."

Davis glanced at the doctor's wall plaques. His credentials were impeccable. Honors at Harvard Medical. An Army Major working directly with The White House for two years, Special commendations from Johns Hopkins and The Mayo Clinic. Photos with U.S. Senators and Hollywood legends. There was even a hand written thank-you note from The First Lady, and several from Royalty. Obviously, Goldman was capable of earning a big paycheck. There was just no way to know if he could deliver the goods. But they had no other option. His reputation had earned him the benefit of the doubt, at least for now.

"And incidentally, the price is *not* a million dollars, it's a million and a quarter. Two-fifty up front, another two-fifty when you receive the specimen, two-fifty at pregnancy and five hundred after a healthy baby is born."

"A baby boy."

"A boy, as agreed. I guarantee it."

To all the world, Dr. Ira Goldman was a top plastic surgeon.

Davis wondered if he planned to reveal his secret someday. They had spoken to a scientist in England who hoped to offer Goldman's services in a few years but who had never heard of the man.

"Okay," said Davis. "Let's do it. How long will it take?"

"Probably less than six months if I can get what I need. Maximum one year."

"How can we be sure this will work? I mean, it's all experimental."

"Don't worry, it'll work. I don't have time to waste on iffy side jobs. Plus, I need the money. As long as the mother is healthy — she can't use drugs or alcohol — there won't be a problem, I assure you."

"Did I tell you my client takes several prescription medications? His sperm count has been tested. It's very low."

"Makes no difference," said the scientist. "I filter everything. The only way we could have a birth defect is if the mother isn't healthy."

"No chance of that. What about getting you the sample?"

"Well, if your client won't come here, you can take the sample in Memphis and I'll send Stein to pick it up the same day. He'll bring a temperature-controlled container and I'll give you some sterile vials today. You've got a simple job to do. Don't contaminate the sample. That's your sole responsibility."

"We'll use a professional."

Goldman stood up and fidgeted with his pants. "Any more questions?"

"Yes, Please sit down." Reluctantly, Goldman sat. "About the surgery. How can we be sure our doctor knows what to do? The procedure is new. And will our doctor be able to tell what you've done?"

"I'll review the procedure with you and your doctor."

"I'm sorry. You can't talk to our doctor." Goldman frowned. His suspicious eyes almost looked up.

"Well, if you've got a qualified OB-GYN, I wouldn't be concerned. This will be very similar to other existing procedures. No one, by the way, with or without a microscope, will have the slightest idea what I've given you."

"Just one more thing," Davis said, laying his case on the desk. "I want to see the lab."

"All right," said Goldman, checking his watch. "Come with

me. I'll show you around. Believe me, once I get going this is a piece of cake. Have a little patience, we'll get the results. Hold on." He activated the intercom. "Stein!"

Instantly: "Yes, Dr. Goldman?"

"Stein, get down here. I need you to put something in the safe. And I want you to book a round-trip flight to Memphis around Christmas." He turned to Davis. "Is that soon enough?"

"Christmas is great."

⚜

Twenty minutes later Hunter Davis was on the phone to his client. Elvis Presley and a group of his friends, including Linda Thompson, were at the new ebony Story & Clark baby grand piano in the intimate music room. Elvis was playing, and singing religious hymns. Outside, although it was not yet December, the twinkling blue holiday lights were going up across the wide front of Graceland.

Vernon Presley crossed the white living room and stood in the recently installed stained glass peacock archway. He tapped his son on the shoulder when the song ended and whispered, "Phone call. It's Davis, on your private line."

"Thanks, Daddy." He pushed back the piano bench. "Excuse me, folks. This is important. I'll be right back. Take a break."

Elvis picked up the phone on Vernon's desk.

"Can you be at my house for Christmas?" asked the lawyer.

Sure. My Vegas concert ends December 15th. I don't have to be in Michigan until New Year's Eve."

Davis told his client everything Goldman had told him, including taking the sample in a month.

"This guy is a super jerk," Davis noted. "I have to be honest with you."

"Who else do we have?" Elvis tightened the belt of his karate uniform.

"No one. That's the only reason I gave him the money. It broke my heart."

"Don't worry about the money," said The King. "There's

more where that came from. The main thing is, you think he can do it. That's all I care about. After that, I'll go along with whatever you tell me."

Davis undid the top button of his shirt. He felt warm with his jacket on.

"How's the weather in Tennessee?" he inquired.

"It's a little chilly. I've got a fire going. How's it out there?"

"I could use some air conditioning." He loosened his tie, then pulled it off. "You sure you can raise that much cash in, say, nine months? He wants another two-fifty when he delivers."

"I told you. I've already cashed in some life insurance. The important thing is to get started on this. Christmas is perfect. After that, the Colonel has me booked solid. I don't know how I'm gonna keep up with his schedule. Oh well, I'm the one who wanted to make a comeback. Plus, I can use the money. Any luck trying to get me out of my deal with Parker?"

Davis had a copy of Elvis' contract in his valise. He had read it several times on the plane, and it still seemed ironclad.

"I'll find a loophole," he said. "Just give me some time. I've been concentrating on this baby thing. How's Lisa Marie?"

Elvis pictured the face of his beautiful daughter. His only child, so far. The little girl he loved and wanted to spend more time with.

"She's a doll," he told Davis. "Turns six in February. I'll get to be with her for the Holidays and if I'm lucky, on her birthday. Priscilla is doing a fine job of raising her. I know it's been two years, but I can't seem to shake off this divorce. I don't know how it happened. I guess it's my fault. I mean, I know it is. I've just got to make the best of it."

The singer ran his fingers through his thick dyed black hair. On and off, he had been feeling dizzy and nauseous lately. The break with his wife had taken its toll on him, though he hadn't been in the best of health before that. He popped two Rolaids into his mouth and chewed them up. He had been taking a lot of prescription drugs since his thirtieth birthday. Maybe it was time to see a holistic doctor and get more vitamins. He had read some books about Vitamin C last month, one by Linus Pauling. Another book had recommended mega-doses of Vitamin E and some of the B Vitamins, too.

Things had gone very well on the pop charts from 1969 to

1972. "Suspicious Minds" hit Number 1 in '69, and "In The Ghetto" made it to Number 3 that same year. In '72, "Burning Love" had gone to the Number 2 spot. A far cry from 1956 and 1957, when he had recorded five Number 1's a year, but not too shabby after his slowdown in the mid-sixties. . .the Beatles' years. He didn't hate the Beatles at all. Far from it. They had talent, a unique sound, and nothing but compliments for him. "Before Elvis, there was nothing," was a popular quote attributed to John Lennon. But since 1973, the year of the split with Priscilla, nothing had gone above Number 14 on the charts. "My Boy" was his only Top 20 song for 1975, rising no higher than to Number 20.

"Try to remain calm," Davis advised him. "Things are gonna get better. When I get back, we'll see how Mr. Picking is doing in New York. Once he finds the right couple, you'll feel like a new man." They both hoped it was true.

"How's the Hound Dog holding up?"

Elvis was referring to one of the two jets he had purchased in 1975 for about a million dollars apiece. Davis had used it for the trip. It was waiting at the airport for his call.

"The plane's great," reported the courier. "Of course, we had to taxi all the way into the far corner of the runway to avoid being noticed."

"Well, I have to get back to my guests. Then I'm gonna try to get in an hour or so of racquetball before dinner." It was later in the afternoon in Memphis.

"Don't work too hard," Davis said, joking.

"Ready for some more racquetball?" asked Elvis. One of Elvis' many activities in his non-stop life during 1974 had been the construction of a two-story racquetball building.

Davis answered affirmatively. He played everything. Hard.

"Let's get together on the court. I'd like to whip your ass."

"You can try," said the competitive attorney.

"H.D.," said Elvis, his voice resonating in that familiar Southern drawl. "You done well, boy. Real well. Thanks."

The deep voice sounded very optimistic, and grateful.

Hunter Davis smiled. Risking the man's money was hard to accept, but he knew there would be harder things to live with. Nevertheless, he would do whatever it took to please this client.

Chapter Four

⚜

"THE LORD GIVETH"

Traffic along Woodland Avenue was atypically congested due to all of the Jeeps and BMW's cluttering both sides of the street near the Randolph house. Some of the neighbors were dying to call the police about the incredibly loud music but Jack and Diane Randolph were members of too many public, religious and social organizations in Tenafly, New Jersey. Everyone owed them a favor. They deserved to celebrate their son's eighteenth birthday in peace, if you could call live Rap music peaceful.

The party was being held in the back yard of a lovely five bedroom, three-and-a-half bath Colonial set majestically on an acre and a half in one of the best sections of town. It was Saturday, May 13, 1995 and a crew had just finished repainting the house Manor white with Forest green shutters. Matching green urns around the pool overflowed with pink Geraniums and Vinca Ivy. The annual double row of pink and white Begonias and a patch of Impatiens lined the gray paver and Belgian block driveway.

Inside, the Randolphs had secluded themselves in a soundproof media room, seeking refuge from the noise which had assaulted them since late morning. It was now 2:45 and they were watching a video of *Casablanca* for the fourth or fifth time this year. As usual, the debate wore on over whether *Casablanca* or *Gone With The Wind* was the best film ever made. Jack's eternal vote was for Humphrey and Ingrid (Leonard Maltin agreed with him), Diane's for Clark and Vivian. Most people sided with Diane, claiming that *Gone*

With The Wind was a far more sophisticated and timeless story, not to mention the photography and romance. But Jack Randolph was obsessed. When it came to being romantic, according to Jack, "Frankly, my dear, I don't give a damn" was no match for "We'll always have Paris." To the New Jersey lawyer, life was basically a microcosm of *Casablanca*, not the other way around. So there was no use arguing with him.

A 60-inch screen flashed classic uncolorized cinema in a darkened room. Four smaller TV monitors were set into four lower cubicles. *Screen 1* showed a view of the pool. *Screen 2* the street from three feet above the front door. *Screen 3* scanned the kitchen and part of the family room. *Screen 4* the master bedroom. If any hanky-panky was going on elsewhere, they couldn't see it or record it.

"What a God forsaken place to live just because you can't get over a love affair," said Diane as the Moroccan police shot down a man in the street.

"Maybe today," Jack countered. "But not during World War II."

"Why? What was wrong with America?"

Diane shifted her bare feet from Jack's knees to his lap. He began to play with her toes while the action in Casablanca continued. A plane carrying German soldiers landed harshly at the airport.

"Nothing," Jack answered. "But what kind of story would it be if Rick Blaine had opened a diner in Teaneck? He wanted a gin joint, and he wanted it somewhere he'd be extremely unlikely to run into Ilsa."

"So she turns up in Morocco?" She stared at Jack. "Morocco?"

"Of course Morocco. She was married to the leader of the Resistance. He was in every country, for Pete's sake. They came to Casablanca because the French were still in control, not the Nazis. And Casablanca was how you got to Lisbon or America."

Diane loved to taunt Jack, to remind him that there were now two sequels to *Gone With The Wind* and none to *Casablanca* and watch him squirm. She could care less why Rick Blaine did anything, or what it all meant. Sure, it really was a terrific movie but my goodness Jack, grow up. The only reason she watched it with him once a month was to be alone and cuddled up with the man she loved. And to get a good foot massage.

"Ow," she said. "Not so hard."

"Why do you think Rick is neutral about everything?" Jack asked.

"To hold back his feelings."

"That's right. And that's why he's in Morocco. He doesn't want to be happy. Everyone else is trying to get out of Casablanca, but Rick wants to stay there."

The media room was a totally interior space sandwiched between Jack's home office (his main office was in downtown Hackensack, near the courthouse) and the butler's pantry. Its only egress was a doorway concealed as a locked closet. Jamie and Olivia called it "Dad's Bomb Shelter" after seeing a PBS documentary on the 1950's phenomenon. But the room was designed for personal privacy, a cozy retreat from a too busy and too demanding yet very happy life. All of the latest audio/video equipment was at hand, to be enjoyed via remote control from a super-comfortable soft leather sofa, two matching recliners and two English wing chairs Diane had upholstered in a bold Mario Buatta floral. The room could thus accommodate a total of seven music or film buffs.

Other appointments included an electronic compact wine cellar, an undercounter Sub-Zero, a microwave and a Capuccino maker. Above the coffee machine was a red Neon sign: "Rick's Café Americain." Finally, a miniature billiard table was angled into a corner. In the same area, a clever architect had managed to design the world's most luxurious brown granite three-by-six trapezoid shaped powder room. The $1,600 German made water closet in this room was so quiet that, according to the manufacturer, you needed a stethoscope to hear it flush. If necessary, the family probably could survive a nuclear attack (or Rap music) in here for at least a week.

The walls of the Randolph refuge were panelled in real walnut, the custom woodworking done by the prestigious Wohlner's of Englewood. A dozen recessed lights provided precise illumination to elements of the room, notably Jack's

Dartmouth and Cornell degrees and the spot reserved for Jamie's soon-to-arrive Tenafly High diploma. Exact reproductions of these family jewels would be found at the law offices of Randolph, Myers and Jacob. That morning, Jack had told his son: "Don't forget, I'm leaving room for *your* degree from Dartmouth." The smart aleck reply: "Right, Dad. In fact, why don't we get rid of your stuff to make more room for mine?" Not quite a joke, to be sure, as a shelf over the TV unit was lined with no less than 27 trophies Jamie had won in Little League (1989 State Finals), Football (1993 Most Valuable Player), Bowling (a 293 game in competition) and Varsity Wrestling. (Diane's college degree was hung in the library.)

At 6'1", the muscular 204-pound grappler might have gone Ivy League just on his ability to perform shoulder pinning reversals. In serious matches he had consistently excelled in this sometimes boring, sometimes thrilling sport where one mistake could put you in a wheelchair for life. Which was why Jack had convinced him, after first encouraging him to be a great athlete, to drop full contact sports in college and pursue academics. After all, scoring 1,420 on the SAT's with an A-minus average had been good enough to get into Dartmouth the hard way. Why risk your health trying to keep up the image of a high school hero? Even at his age, Jamie knew that football and wrestling triumphs would be long forgotten while friends, family and career achievements still remained.

Sister Olivia, 16 going on 32, was not athletic like "Big J." Nor did she do as well scholastically, running a borderline B (unlike her brother, she hated math and science) and trying much harder to be Best Liked or Best Dressed. She had always been the more beautiful child, modeling until she was eight, outshining Jamie until his pecs and biceps became the talk of Tenafly. Although slim, she was still well developed, especially in the revealing blue bikini she was wearing today. Her brother always kept his eye on her when she was around his buddies who had little on their minds except cars and girls. As she passed him and wrestling pal Steve McDermott, Jamie saw Mickdee turn and inspect her rear end.

"Touch her . . ."

" . . . and I'm dead meat! Chill out, Big J. I'm just looking."

Like Jamie, as well as Mom and Dad at her age, Olivia had dirty-blond hair (Diane's was still the blondest) and mysterious blue eyes. She was an inch taller than her mother at 5'8", with the same small space between her two front teeth, the same long neck, the classic Grace Kelly features. However, unlike her iron-pumping, hamburger-guzzling brother, Livvy was not into exercising and eating. A strict vegetarian, she preferred to hang with other lettuce lovers talking about boys (like Steve McDermott, Jamie's hunky friend), clothes and saving the environment. Occasionally the family was concerned about anorexia. True, she could pig out at Mrs. Fields in the Riverside Square Mall and then enjoy a large supper. But at only 108 pounds, they had to ask. In a frank discussion, Olivia swore that she did not have an eating disorder and insisted she was trying to gain a few pounds but it was hard on her healthy diet.

Everyone agreed Olivia looked a lot less like her father than Jamie, who explained that at least 50% of one's genes are inherited from past generations, not your parents. In his case, though, the resemblance of Jamie to Jack was remarkable. Regardless of who looked like who, Livvy felt part of a very close-knit family which totally supported her individuality and worried about her well-being.

As an example of the unselfish love found in the Randolph home, Livvy had offered to cook at Jamie's party. Unhappily, she found herself flipping medium rare burgers on this warm May afternoon, pretending they were really veggie-burgers despite the aroma of charred flesh. Her best friend, Lori, was assistant food server, but as a more ardent anti-meat person she refused to touch the "gross" hamburgers. Lori Bernstein was very cute, much shorter than Olivia with reddish brown hair and a customized pug nose. Kids teased her with the nickname "Tinkerbell" which was really a compliment because she was a dead ringer for Julia Roberts in Hook. Lori couldn't wait to leave for college so new friends would never call her Tink.

"How about Tinkerbell?" asked Steve McDermott, wolfing

down a half-pounder smothered in Heinz Ketchup. "Okay to look at *her* ass?"

"No problem, man," Jamie replied, grabbing Steve's feeding arm. "Just remember she's sixteen."

"Lori! Hand me two Diet Cokes, please," said Livvy.

Lori stopped staring at Jamie. "Coming up." As she reached into the ice-filled cooler Lori couldn't help wishing that he wasn't her best friend's brother. She had had a crush on Jamie since she was thirteen. Of course, every girl at the party felt the same. Though he dated, Jamie was far less interested in girls than other things. Like his coin collection. Like sports. Like how well he would do at Dartmouth. And he was an avid reader, his taste favoring the poetry of e.e. cummings, Ayn Rand, biographies of movie stars and UFO's. But he also loved MTV, rap music and 70's music. Lori hoped he would sing at his own party. She liked to hear songs by that old group, The Beatles, the way Jamie sang them. And she loved to watch him *sway* as he performed.

Behind the pool, in an oak-shaded part of the back yard, two young black men and two young white men, a band called The Racists, bellowed rhythmically about the police. They repeated ten times: "When I see 'em at night, I know I'm in for a fight. What they do to the brothers, well it just ain't right!" After a few more minutes they took a Coke and Chloraseptic break.

"Hey, looks like The Four Freshmen are calling it a day," Jack said, glancing at Screen 1 while the Moroccan police dragged off poor Peter Lorre.

"I doubt it, hon. But what do you care as long as we're in here watching the second greatest movie of all time?"

Jack put *Casablanca* on pause.

"Am I getting old, or does this music really stink?"

Diane wanted to change the subject but knew that she couldn't. She stood up and stretched her slender arms and legs. "Want a Diet Coke?"

"Yeah, okay. But answer me this, Diane. If Jamie can appreciate The Beatles and The Doors, how can he stand listening to 500 different songs with the exact same tune? Which is actually no tune at all."

"I don't think he sees it that way. "

"And no words either."

"Rap songs have words."

"But nobody can understand them."

"That's just what my parents said about rock'n'roll in 1958. Or as your son would put it, that's bogus!"

"Look, Diane, I know that kids need their own identity and their own music. Sociologically, it makes sense. That's why teenagers are now re-named Generation X. I understand that."

Diane handed Jack a can of soda with a straw in it, just the way he liked it. She loved her husband beyond words and would do anything to make him happy. Anything except agree with him when she had a different opinion.

"Then what is it you don't understand, sweetie? That Jamie is a member of Generation X, or whatever you want to call his peer group? That he can't be you, and like only your music and your movies? That he doesn't wear sideburns because no one else does? What don't you understand?"

Jack attempted to press *Stop* but accidentally pressed *Record.* The video-cassette automatically ejected. He put down the remote control and took a sip of Diet Coke. "Thanks, Diane."

It wasn't easy getting older. For Jack at 47, success was sweet. He had finally become a Senior Partner at the law firm. Unfortunately, he could no longer come home for lunch but that didn't bother him. He had two wonderful kids, neither of whom took drugs or embarrassed him, and a wife who had stood by him for 26 years. But his thick head of hair was now grey, his cholesterol stayed at 230 thanks to Edy's Chocolate Chip Ice Cream and his back got stiff for two days when he wrestled with Jamie for five minutes. He also worried about his parents in Florida. His father had retired seven years ago and loved playing golf every day. But he only saw his folks at Christmas and Spring Break. Soon they would arrive for Jamie's graduation, along with Diane's parents. Jack realized that in a few short years they could be gone and his own children might move away. Starting in September, Jamie would live mostly in New Hampshire. On top of everything else, there was finally a kind of music that he really, really hated. And his kids loved it. What a life. Jack remembered the good old days when he was a teenager in Tenafly. The days when he was called "Pretty Boy" by his close friends. The days when everyone wanted a '64 Ford Mustang just like the one in his 3-car garage purchased as an investment two years ago. The days when he dreamed of someday marrying a woman like his wife. Jack knew that his dreams had come true and that he really was happy. Even if he were the only person in town who understood the true greatness of *Casablanca.*

Diane Randolph was a mom's Mom. She loved to cook and bake. She cleaned her own house and planted her own garden (Jack did not mow the lawn. That was the job of Superior Landscaping.) She had always hoped to have at least five or six kids but fate had dealt her a weak hand and she felt blessed to have her two little ones. At 45, the baby factory was closed. Jamie, her first-born, had a special place in her heart, not because he had come first but because his conception was made possible by an experimental medical procedure. She had asked God if this was His will and He had said yes. Her kids were the greatest gift God could have given her and she was ecstatic over them and their wonderful father.

Like 1940's and 50's moms, Diane did not work and never had despite her B.A. in art history from New York University. She had grown up expecting to marry and take care of a successful man who would support her and her children. Jack and Diane shared the identical concept of family. The Randolphs would have fit in well during the Victorian Age. Or today, in many of the affluent towns of Bergen County, New Jersey, a bedroom community of New York City. In Bergen County there was still support for such old world values as no drinking or shopping on Sundays. Which didn't bother Jack or Diane Randolph, who both got headaches from beer and wine. They also preferred to stay home rather than to shop till they dropped at any of the 10,000 stores within thirty minutes of their front door.

Not to mention the two or more Cable TV shopping channels, one of which was now on Jack's TV screen offering him a $69 New York Giants Jacket for only $37.50. Apparently,

863 viewers had already gobbled up nearly half of the 2,000 jackets available but Jack was more interested in watching Humphrey Bogart manipulate the two German exit passes Peter Lorre had died for.

"I wouldn't wear a New York Giants jacket if you paid me $37.50," he told Diane, re-inserting *Casablanca*.

"Yes, I know. Because they're really the New Jersey Giants. What else is new?"

Diane gave Jack a light kiss on the cheek but before Jack could get the video back on he saw a Federal Express truck pull into the center of Screen 2.

"Who the hell is sending me legal papers on Saturday?" Jack rose to his feet, spilling a little Diet Coke on his pants and the couch. "Here, hold this. Let me get the door. I'm really pissed off. Unless it's life and death, this stuff is supposed to stay at the office."

"I hope it's not life and death," Diane said.

"Don't worry, it's not. Don't go anywhere. And don't watch the movie without me."

In less than thirty seconds, Jack was out the secret door, shouldering past a bunch of teenagers getting crumbs all over the carpets. He rushed down the brick steps to meet the Fed Ex lady. "I'm Jack Randolph," he spit out. "Who's this from?"

The slim, uniformed woman carrying a flat colorful package was startled as she did not expect to be met along the front walkway. "Whoa!" she said. "Don't kill the messenger."

Jack laughed. He still had a beautiful smile, and she laughed, too. Diane was watching all this on Screen 2. She realized that women still found Jack attractive and enjoyed the unjustified feeling of slight jealousy whenever she saw him with another woman. Jack read the label and then signed for the package.

"I'm sorry I yelled at you before," Jack said. "It's just that I'm trying to get through my son's eighteenth birthday party."

"I know what you mean. My daughter just graduated Junior High. Cost me an arm and a leg. We had to rent a place for sixty kids. How many you got back there? About a hundred?"

"Something like that."

"I figured. Look at all these cars. Looks like Beverly Hills. You're lucky I could find a place to park my truck."

"Yeah, well thanks again. But don't come back any more today."

"Don't worry. I won't. See ya."

Stanley Long from across the street was outside watering his lawn by hand, waiting for his seven zone sprinkler system to be repaired. "Hey, Jack!" he yelled over. "Could you make a little more noise?" It was a joke, but Jack couldn't hear him.

Diane waited for Jack's return but then she saw him on Screen 1. Jamie was lying on the grass arm-wrestling with another overly beefy school teammate, it looked like Eddie Silver with half his head shaved. She watched Jack come alongside Jamie and poke him in the ribs with the corner of the Fed Ex package. His arm was jerked to the right and the contest was over. Quickly, Jamie was standing up, ready to take down whoever had touched him.

"Dad," he said, surprised. "What are you doing out here? I didn't think we'd see you till tomorrow."

"Hi, Mr. Randolph," said Eddie, who was wearing his black and orange Tenafly Tigers football shirt.

"Hi, Eddie. How's it going?"

"Fine, Mr. R. This is a great party. Great food. Great music."

"You like rap, too?"

"You mean hip-hop?"

"Whatever, it's all great, right. Look, Eddie, I need to talk to Jamie for a minute. Okay?"

"Sure." Eddie looked around. "I promised my girl I'd go rollerblading with her for awhile."

Jamie was concerned, and his friends could see it in his expression.

"Everything all right, Dad?"

"As far as I know. This just came Federal Express. It's from Chemical Bank in New York. You have any idea what it is?"

"It's addressed to me?"

"Sure is. Here. Open it up. I just want to make sure this wasn't meant for me."

Jamie tore open the package and removed a smaller envelope which contained a letter. He read the letter, looked at his father with a puzzled face, read it again and then handed it to Jack.

"This is wild," he said. "The letter says I'm inheriting money. Is this for real? Who could be leaving me money?"

"Maybe it's a birthday gift."

"That's not what it says. Hey, Dad, I'm in the middle of things here." Two very pretty girls were trying to talk to Jamie. "Can you check this out and get back to me later?"

"I can do that."

Jack read the letter himself, twice, then disappeared from Screen 1. Diane intercepted him in the family room.

"Hi, Mr. R."

"Hi, Lori."

"Hi, Mrs. R."

"Hi, Lori. Jack, what is it?"

"Oh, hi, Diane. Sorry I took so long. Jamie got a letter from the bank."

"From our bank?" Diane didn't recognize the logo on the envelope.

"No, from the Trust Department of Chemical Bank in the city. Here, look. They say Jamie is entitled to an inheritance on his eighteenth birthday."

"Really? From who?"

"Doesn't say. Here, read it. The letter just says that Jamie and his parents should come to the bank at his earliest convenience. I guess we'll call them Monday."

"Who do we know that was rich?" Diane asked.

"Maybe it's not much money," Jack answered. "I can't think of anyone who would have left Jamie a lot of money. Can you?"

Jack and Diane returned to the media room where Diane removed her shoes so the foot masseur could get back to work. Until Monday, Jack was more concerned with Humphrey Bogart's letters than the one in his pocket. When Rick Blaine spoke, Jack moved his lips in synchronized speech. He knew every line in *Casablanca* by heart.

Chapter Five

ൟൟൟ

"THE STAR OF DAVID"

Getting ready for breakfast at the Randolph house was a big, healthy family project. The day began at 6:00 AM when Jack and Jamie stretched for a two-mile run. While they showered Livvy took Grover for a quick walk, then helped Mom cut up the fresh fruit. Apples, bananas, canteloupe, red seedless grapes, strawberries and soft dark apricots from the health food store.

The main course on Monday, Wednesday and Friday was organic oatmeal, topped with natural Canadian maple syrup. Lightly toasted seven-grain bread was spread with a little butter, now considered as good as margarine. Mom and Livvy drank herb tea. Father and son had Pero, a caffeine free coffee substitute made from barley, chicory and rye.

Jack and Jamie selected different vitamins and herbs daily, to be swallowed with delicious, fresh-squeezed orange juice. The staples were Vitamin C, Vitamin E, B-Complex, odorless garlic, ginseng and sarsaparilla, plus Acidophilus for digestion. Mom also took calcium and iron pills.

On Tuesday, Thursday and Saturday sugary supermarket cereals like Cheerios and Frosted Flakes were indulged in, along with Jamie's scrambled eggs once a week. On Sunday, Jack made Aunt Jemima pancakes.

Maybe eating right wouldn't keep you alive forever, but if breakfast was the most important meal of the day, at least they could beat the averages.

After breakfast at around 7:30, Jack played two moves of Chess in the living room (just like Humphrey Bogart) while the women folk cleaned up. It was an old-fashioned life in some respects but no one had any complaints. Everyone did his or her fair share of work over the long run.

It was Lori's Mom's day to drive. When Livvy heard two quick beeps of the horn she grabbed her books, brushed her hair for the twenty-seventh time, checked her perfect face for imperfections, kissed Mom and Dad good-bye, yelled "See ya" to Jamie, waited for "Bye, kid" and rushed out to join her chattering schoolmates.

Then Jack kissed his wife, a long semi-passionate kiss almost like when they were first married, straightened his tie and perused his kitchen. Jack truly missed leaving this comfortable, loving house, even to go to work which gave him great pleasure. He missed the smell of fresh, wholesome food, the old coffee tins and Americana they had collected over the years. In the living room, the patina of a rosewood Gentleman's Chair shone in the morning sun. He missed the whole thing. Jack checked his Rolex.

"Whoops, I'm running late, babe."

"Bye, hon. Call me when you get time. I'll be home till lunch, then I have to be at a fund-raiser at the church."

"Good luck. Oh," Jack said. "Where's Jamie's letter? I think I left it upstairs."

On cue, Jamie flew into the kitchen like Kramer on Seinfeld.

"Here," he said. "Let me know if we're rich. I'm home till ten." He stuffed the envelope into Jack's pocket.

"I'll call first thing. Then we'll make plans to go to the bank together, maybe later in the week."

"Thanks. Bye, Dad. I love you."

"Bye." Jack hugged his brawny son. "I love you, too."

Diane kissed her husband's smooth cheek.

"Bye, Jack. Drive carefully. Don't rush. There's nothing more important than coming home safe."

Jack got the same warning every day. "I know," he said, smiling. "Bye, Diane."

Diane Randolph spent a small part of the day reminding herself how lucky she was to have such a wonderful family. She rubbed her wedding ring, perhaps the most treasured material thing in her life, and tried to remember the last time it was off her finger. It had been there for both births, so tight Dr. Carrillo threatened to cut it off. It had travelled on every vacation, including scuba-diving in the Bahamas last year. And she wore it in the shower and bath. In fact, the only time it was definitely removed since September 2, 1968 was when she had that awful bout with poison ivy. To the best of her memory, Jack had never removed his wedding band.

She wandered slowly around the house day-dreaming, then drifted upstairs to see Jamie. His door was ajar but she still knocked.

"Mom?"

"It's me, honey. I just wanted to say hello."

"Hello." Jamie laughed. Mom was funny. "Are you all right?"

Jamie flipped his book onto the bed and propped himself up on an elbow. His room was shimmering with sunlight and he squinted to see his mother's face. Behind him was a color print of his favorite Van Gogh, "Starry Night."

"I'm fine. I just wanted to speak to you for a minute."

"About what?"

"About. . .Well, I was just thinking about how much your father and I love each other, and how much we love you and your sister."

This sounded familiar. "Livvy? You love Livvy, too?"

Diane chuckled. "No," she said. "We only love you."

"That's what I thought. Okay, now that we've cleared that up, can I go back to reading?"

"What are you reading?"

Jamie showed her the cover: "COMMUNION."

"What's it about? Religion?" Diane sat on the bed.

"No, it's about aliens. This guy from upstate New York claims he was abducted by little creatures from. . .somewhere. He says they performed exploratory surgery on his head and tortured him in their laboratory."

Diane winced. She did not believe these stories, but no one could absolutely discredit them. She pictured herself surrounded by little green men with disgusting surgical instruments.

"Jamie," she said. "I have a question for you."

"About the book?"

"No, about our family. You know I love kids, and sometimes I feel guilty that there's only two of you. I'm too old now to have any more kids. I did try when I was younger, and of course I could always look into adopting another baby. I don't know. What do you think?"

Jamie had no idea how to react. This subject was news to him.

"Shouldn't you be talking to Dad about this?" he said.

"I didn't say I was serious about adopting. I'm just telling you how I feel."

Jamie felt uncomfortable but he knew his mother needed his answer. "If you're asking me if I'd like another sister or brother, I could care less."

"Did you ever want a brother?"

"You know, Mom, it's funny you should ask me that."

"Why?"

Jamie remembered something from his early childhood. "Because I used to dream I had a brother," he said, surprising himself. "A twin brother. That's crazy, isn't it? I never told anyone. I haven't had that dream in years."

"Were you happy in the dream?"

Diane was slightly hurt that her son had never mentioned the dream before. She became very anxious but managed to contain her emotions. If they had been so close, for so long, why had he kept the dream a secret?

"I can't remember," he said. "It wasn't very important to me or I would have told you. It just happened. But I don't think I miss having a little brother. I'd have to give a lot of thought to having my own kids someday."

Now Diane was shocked.

"Are you serious?" she blurted out. "I can't believe you could say something like that. You mean, your father and I should not look forward to grandchildren until Livvy gets married?"

Jamie saw the hurt in her eyes. She felt betrayed. He should never have opened his big mouth.

"Come on, Mom," he said, touching her arm. "I'm only

eighteen. How do I know if I'm gonna have kids? I mean, I probably will. It's been great in our family. But it's not fair to ask me questions unless you want an honest answer. Suppose I marry someone I really, really love and she doesn't want children, or can't get pregnant?"

Diane looked into Jamie's moist eyes and realized the conversation had gone too far. She kissed his forehead and let her fingers slide tenderly from his temple to his chin. He was right. Here was a warm, intelligent young man with an open mind, to her the best son in the world, with his whole future ahead of him. Undoubtedly, he would make the right decision when the time came. Why was she worried that maybe he wouldn't want children when everyone else was concerned with teenage pregnancy? She was only forty-five years old. If Jamie had kids in fifteen years she would still be a young grandmother at sixty. Her own mother was fifty-two when Jamie was born, but people were living longer now, doing things at sixty they used to do at forty. She might even choose to begin a career as an art teacher when Livvy went to college. What was the rush?

"I'm sorry," Diane said, putting her hand on his and pressing it against her arm. "I'm just in a mood women get into. Forgive me?"

"Sure Mom," Jamie said, glad to change the subject. "You want to hear more about my book?"

The phone interrupted him. Jamie jumped up and grabbed the Sony portable, expecting it to be a friend calling on his number.

"Dad," he said. "What's happening?"

"Is your father okay?" asked Diane, still emotional.

Jamie nodded, then listened to Jack Randolph talk about the bank.

"It's about the letter, Mom. . .What? Yeah, Dad, I'm paying attention, Mom just asked me. . .Skip school today, why?"

Jack explained to Jamie what he had learned.

"Wow!" said Jamie. "That's awesome! Yeah, sure, I'll tell her. Okay, see ya."

Diane's focus began to shift.

"What's going on?" she asked.

"Dad called the bank." Jamie tossed the alien book onto his desk. "Mom, you're not going to believe this. Dad wants us to go into the city with him right now."

"How can I? I've got to be at the church by one. And you've got classes."

Jamie looked for a clean shirt.

"Dad said to change our plans. He spoke to this guy, Sawyer, at Chemical Bank. And this guy tells him about my inheritance. Dad said it's a real lot of money."

Diane was surprised. "How much is a real lot?"

"I don't know, Mom. Just a lot. The bank wouldn't tell Dad the exact amount on the phone. But they told him it was. . ." Jamie tried to remember the exact word. "Considerable."

Jack had called on the car phone and was already enroute to the house. Taking side streets off Route 4, the drive was less than twenty minutes. In twenty-five minutes, all three were in Jack's white Mercedes headed for the George Washington Bridge along the scenic Palisades Interstate Parkway. From the cliffs above the Hudson, the Manhattan skyline flickered between the passing trees.

About a week earlier Jamie had received his graduation and eighteenth birthday present from Mom and Dad. It was a nearly mint condition blue/green three year old Volvo 960. Previously leased by a client of Jack's, the car had only 21,000 miles on it and the leather still smelled new. Jamie had asked about driving it into the city today. After all, he had been driving legally for a year, illegally for two, and Jack had taught him to drive in the Berkshires when he was twelve. The discussion about who would drive was brief. "I'll drive," Dad said.

At the bridge there was the usual rush hour delay but they edged up to the toll booths in less than ten minutes, good for a Monday morning. The Port Authority had posted some new signs about closing the lower level for repairs but right now traffic was clear. As they crossed the bridge, Jack and Jamie noticed a few runners heading toward Jersey along the pedestrian walkway. Both thought that might be a neat thing to try sometime.

"Big decision," Jack announced as they approached Manhattan. "West Side Highway or F.D.R. Drive?"

Jamie had driven into New York with friends but never paid attention to highways. Neither did Diane. She was still trying to decide whether or not to wear the pearls she had brought with her.

"West Side Highway it is!" responded Jack to his own query, following the cloverleaf that seemed to twist in the wrong direction then veered back downtown. From the bridge the highway looked open all the way to midtown. Once on it, there was a slowdown. A taxi had sideswiped a new Lexus and two men were standing in the right lane arguing and pointing. Jack eased around them, too chipper to complain, and remained in the right lane until the 96th Street exit. He cut through Central Park to Fifth Avenue, passed the Met wishing he had time to stop, then headed straight down to the low 50's. They parked in a garage on 51st Street and walked the short distance to Chemical Bank's Rockefeller Center offices at the Avenue of The Americas.

"Tom Sawyer," said the big man with glasses. "And no jokes."

Jack shook hands with Chemical's Senior VP of Trusts and Estates, a wide-faced man of his age, an inch or two taller and weighing at least 350 pounds.

"I sometimes introduce myself as T. Leslie Sawyer," the banker explained. "But eventually people find out my first name is Thomas."

He motioned to one of the pretty young women seated in the large open office. She smiled and went for coffee. Jamie studied her rear musculature as she walked off. He thought he saw her staring at him from the coffee area hidden by three potted palms.

"Over here, let's use my office," Sawyer said, moving toward a pair of thick mahogany doors with etched glass panels. A floral design on one of the panels surrounded his name, indicating Mr. Sawyer's tenure.

"I've been in this place thirteen years," he volunteered. "I love it here. I'll probably die here someday."

Of a heart attack, Jack thought, looking at the triple chin.

The hefty banker really belonged in Houston or Dallas as everything around him was geared more toward Texan size than New York power. His desk had to be eight feet wide and his studded leather chair was proportionately too large. Basically, every object in his office was too large, including him. There was a humongous color photo of a Buffalo Nickel directly behind his desk.

"Where are you from?" asked Jack, translating Sawyer's hand movements to mean "sit down."

"Long Island," answered the big man. "And you people are from New Jersey. I see you live in Tenafly. Lovely town. I've got some good friends in Tenafly. Do you know the Rausches? Bill Rausch owns a BMW dealership in the city."

"I've heard of him. Don't know him," said Jack.

"I'd like to meet him," injected Jamie. "I have a Volvo to trade in."

"I don't think so," Jack responded.

"Well," said Sawyer, waving his hand to show the girl where to put the coffee, tea, juice and Perrier. "I guess now he can have any car he wants." Jamie smiled, but suddenly Jack was serious.

"Tom," he said. "Let's get down to business. I understand my son has inherited some money. Who's it from?"

The banker opened his file. "It's anonymous."

"Anonymous?"

"That's right. Even the bank doesn't know who the money is from. It's been with Chemical since 1977, all the taxes have been paid by the trust and the balance is free and clear. That's all we know."

"Who opened the trust?"

Sawyer shuffled through his papers. As his secretary left the room, she stopped behind Jamie to ask if that would be all. She placed her fingers on the top of Jamie's chair momentarily. He felt the static electricity on the back of his neck.

"Picking," he answered. "The attorney was Richard Picking. Have you ever heard that name?"

Jack looked at Diane, astonished. "Richard Picking?"

"I take it you know him."

"He was our family attorney. Actually, he was more of a friend. But Dick took care of certain specialized legal matters for us."

Diane put her hand on Jack's vibrating knee. She was nervous, too.

"Ask *him* where the money came from," Sawyer suggested. "Does he still practice in New York? Does he handle your own trust?"

"No. He passed away," Jack revealed.

"Oh, I'm sorry."

"It was a long time ago."

Jamie interrupted. "How much money do I get?"

His mother looked at him. "Jamie, mind your manners."

"I just want to know."

"It's okay," said Jack. "We all want to know. How much is involved?"

Sawyer adjusted his thick brown glasses and took a sip of Perrier. "Help yourself," he said, pointing to the refreshments. "Let's see. The exact amount is. . .Three million, eight hundred forty-six thousand, five hundred seventy dollars. . .and fifty-two cents."

No one moved. No one from Tenafly, New Jersey could believe what they had just heard. But it was not a mistake.

"Here's the check," Sawyer said, rotating his file so the Randolphs could read the amount on the extra large blue-and-white draft clipped to the corner of the file folder.

"I don't know who. . ." Jack began, leaving his sentence unfinished as he reached for a glass of orange juice.

"Why didn't Richard Picking ever. . ." Diane said, realizing she didn't know what she wanted to say. She took a cup of tea.

"Who's Richard Picking?" Jamie asked. "Did he know me?"

"Apparently, that's beside the point, Jamie," commented Tom Sawyer. "The money is yours. It's all legal, I assure you, and there are no strings attached. Except for the terms."

Jack the lawyer pulled himself together.

"What are the terms?" he demanded.

"I'll be happy to give you a copy of the agreement, Jack. The basic idea is that Jamie does not get the bulk of the money until he is 25, at which time he receives half, and the other half at 30. In the interim, he gets $25,000 a year. You, his parents are then authorized to withdraw from a new trust account, which you may keep here or transfer to another bank, whatever Jamie needs for college plus all medical and legal expenses. It's pretty straightforward."

"Anything else?"

"No, that's it."

"Okay, thanks." Unexpectedly, Jack bounced to his feet. "*Okay, thanks?* Hey, what am I saying? My God, Jamie, you're rich! This is fabulous!" He shook his son's hand. "I don't know who did this for you, but I guess it really doesn't matter."

"It *doesn't* matter," Diane said, wondering if this day was a turning point in life or just good luck. "But *I'd* like to know."

"Well, I'd like to know, too, honey. But I don't have the slightest idea how we're going to find out who Richard Picking represented in 1977."

"Did he have any partners?" asked the trust officer.

"No. And his wife died before he did. His family used to live in Charleston, but I don't know if we can locate anyone, or if they know anything."

"Could I ask you something, Jack?" The big man attempted to straighten out his wrinkled suit jacket.

"Certainly. For four million bucks, you can ask me anything."

"No, seriously. A thought just occurred to me, and I don't know if this makes any sense, but is it possible that the money belonged to Mr. Picking himself?"

Jack considered the possibility. "I don't think so," he said, turning to Diane who shook her head no.

"Why not?"

"Because Dick Picking was in very bad shape financially before his death. It was public knowledge. There was no way he had four million. . ."

"Excuse me. It wasn't four million dollars in 1977, Jack. It started out under one million."

"Even one million. If Dick Picking somehow had that kind of money in 1977, why would he leave it to my son?"

"Maybe he hated his whole family," Jamie said. Everyone ignored his comment.

"What's really interesting," said Jack, "is that we spent a great deal of time with Dick in the 70's. I never suspected a thing."

"If he set up the trust on behalf of a client," Sawyer noted, "he had to keep it confidential."

"That's true. I just can't figure out who the client could be. Or why he or she hasn't contacted us since."

"Maybe he's dead, too," said Diane.

"Maybe."

"I guess we'll never know."

As the Randolphs prepared to sign the papers and accept the check, Mr. Sawyer opened his desk.

"I forgot to give you this," he said, handing Jamie a small envelope. "This comes with your inheritance."

Jamie opened the envelope and a thin gold chain slithered out, followed by a gold Star Of David.

"What's this?" he asked. "I'm not Jewish."

"Maybe the mystery man is," Sawyer reasoned. "In any event, it's yours."

"Thanks," said Jamie, admiring the piece of jewelry. "Can I wear it, Dad? It's kind of cool."

"Be my guest." Jack continued to look over the documents, finding it all clear and precise, just the way Richard Picking always worked. Jack was a real estate attorney, but he knew enough about trusts and wills to understand they had nothing to lose by accepting the money.

"We'll be depositing the funds at our bank in Hackensack," Jack advised. "You've been very helpful, Tom, but we'll be more comfortable this way."

"As you wish. Let me know if we can be of further service."

From his expression, Jack knew that Chemical would be unhappy Sawyer couldn't keep the trust where it was. Such is life.

"And there's nothing else, nothing in your file that might help us identify Picking's client?"

"Nothing, Jack. No names or numbers. I'll be happy to ask around, of course, but I didn't handle the trust until 1982. In my opinion, the benefactor's name was meant to be kept a secret."

A half hour later the Randolphs were eating lunch at a classy cafe overlooking the Rockefeller Center skating rink. The rink was currently decorated with flowers and a sculpture display. Jamie excused himself to go to the men's room.

"What a day," Jack said, folding Jamie's check in half and slipping it behind the fifties in his green and red striped Gucci wallet.

"I wonder if we should tell him." Diane looked very upset.

"Tell him what?"

"About the in-vitro procedure. That Richard arranged it."

"Why?" asked Jack, pretending he didn't understand. But he couldn't suppress the thought they both held in their minds like a smoking gun. "I know why, Diane. You think I may not be Jamie's father, don't you?"

Diane looked around for Jamie.

"Who says I'm his mother?" she whispered to Jack. There were tears in her eyes but she was afraid to cry until they were alone at home.

The possibility that Diane might not be Jamie's mother had never crossed Jack's mind. Then he remembered who the boy looked like.

Chapter Six

❦

"REAP WHAT YOU SOW"

The black piano player is wearing a double-breasted satin dinner jacket with a black bow tie and matching handkerchief. He takes down his piano stool, adjusts his sheet music and begins to tickle the ivories.

"Leave him alone, Miss Ilsa," he tells the sophisticated woman sitting near him. "You're bad luck to him."

The attractive brunette in her early 30's is wearing a white V-neck dress and large sparkling earrings. She sips her champagne.

"Play it once, Sam," she insists. "For old times sake."

The piano player would rather not.

"Play it, Sam," she begs. "Play, *As Time Goes By.*"

As a very nice song is transformed into a classic, Rick suddenly enters the big room too quickly, then breaks his stride when he hears the tune. He approaches the musician.

"Sam, I thought I told you never to play. . . "

Diane Randolph noticed that Jack was asleep and nudged him.

"How can you sleep at a time like this?" She patted his cheek.

Jack opened his eyes too slowly to catch a glimpse of *Casablanca,* which had been playing for about a half hour. Diane clicked off the TV.

"What time is it?" Jack asked.

"It's almost eleven, Jack. Jamie's not asleep yet, I can hear him doing something. I'm not going to sleep at all tonight if we don't tell him about the in-vitro."

The room began to take shape and Jack forced himself to sit up so he wouldn't doze off. He knew that Diane was really going nuts over this inheritance thing. It was bothering him, too, but like most lawyers Jack avoided making hasty decisions.

"Can't we discuss this again in the morning?" he suggested.

"No," his wife answered. "We've got to do it right now."

Jack slipped off the bed and stretched in the scarecrow position.

"Can I brush my teeth first?"

"No, he might go to bed. Let's go in there now."

Jack figured she was probably right. This was an issue they hadn't wanted to deal with for many years, but they always knew the day would come. Now that day was here and long-forgotten memories would have to be rekindled. Like the day of Diane's baby shower, back in 1977, when Diane could not shake the strange feeling that something was wrong with the baby. Of course, as it turned out the baby was perfect, just like Olivia two years later. Or the fact that the whole procedure had been secretive, as though they might be committing a crime, which they weren't. But the medical records indicated that Diane Randolph had been artificially inseminated, which was not exactly true. Or maybe it really was.

"Okay, let's tell him," Jack said, taking Diane's cold hand.

Together they walked down the hall to their son's room. The walls along the way were covered with family photos. Baby pictures, including the one where Jamie's eyes were crossed. Group shots around the piano at Christmas, with aunts, uncles, cousins and grandparents all compressed into a hugging mass. Turn-of-the-century sepia tone photographs of young couples from both families, the Randolphs and the Smiths, several of whom had passed on as elderly people decades ago. More recent pictures of some of these same relatives with their children and grandchildren. School and church portraits. Photos at the lake by the summer cottage in Massachusetts. Pictures of Jamie and Dad as high school wrestlers. A shot of Mom and Olivia with Santa Claus in Macy's. Jack and Diane's wedding portrait. Lots and lots of pictures, all happy ones, all bringing back good memories.

Tonight, Jack and Diane Randolph did not look at any of

the pictures as they turned the corner to visit Jamie. He was already standing in his doorway, waiting for them. They both jumped.

"Hi," said Jamie. "I thought I heard you guys coming. What's up?"

"We have to talk to you," said Diane.

Jamie knew this was serious. "Is it about this morning?"

"What do you mean?"

"You know, about the baby thing. That I don't have a brother."

"What's he talking about?" Jack asked Diane.

"Oh no, it has nothing to do with that. We were talking about having children this morning, Jack. Well, actually, it's not totally unrelated. Can we go downstairs?"

In the kitchen, Diane put up a pot of hot water. It would be easier to break the news if she was doing something with her hands.

"I'll have some chocolate chip cookies," Jamie declared.

"No you won't," said Mom. "Sit down."

"Can I tell him?" Jack asked.

"Oh, boy. This is gonna be a mess. I can tell." Jamie folded his arms on the kitchen island.

Jack finally began the discussion.

"This is about your birth." Jamie looked interested. "I hope you're not going to be mad at us for not telling you sooner, but your mother and I were having a hard time conceiving and. . . "

"You're not going to tell me I'm adopted?"

"No, you're not adopted. How could you be adopted? We have snapshots of your mother pregnant with you. Isn't that ridiculous?"

"Well, I don't know, Dad. What is it then?"

"Just tell him, Jack!" Diane searched in the refrigerator for a suitable beverage.

"Okay, okay. Sorry I lost my temper." Jack clamped his hands together like he was going to give a sermon. "You're a test tube baby," he said.

"What? What are you talking about? In-vitro?"

"Yes, in-vitro. It's true. We were considering adoption

because we didn't think we had any other choice. In fact, Dick Picking was our adoption attorney. Jamie, please don't get upset about that part of it. We never wanted to adopt. I mean, we would have adopted because we wanted a child to love, but we really always wanted kids of our own. If it were possible, we would have had more kids, but we're really, really glad to have you and Livvy. Really, I mean it."

Jack was far more emotional than Jamie, and at this sensitive moment even more than Diane. Until now he hadn't realized how hard it had been not to talk about this for so long. Diane could see how Jack felt and she put her arm around her partner.

"It's all right, darling. Jamie knows how much we love him. I was telling him this morning how much we always wanted children."

"So what's the big deal?" asked the tall teenager. "I know you love me. I'm not mad. What am I supposed to be mad about? That you never told me about the in-vitro procedure? No offense, but I know like three or four people who had in-vitro done recently. One of my teachers did it last month, and she's pregnant. I was surprised she told the class but it's not something weird. Am I supposed to feel like the son of Frankenstein or something?"

Suddenly Jack didn't know what to feel. Here he was, on the verge of tears, releasing years and years of guilt telling his son something he thought might jeopardize their relationship, and now Jamie was saying it was no big deal. Well, that was one thing you could count on with your kids. They were always good for a surprise. Now Jack felt like an idiot. What *was* the big deal about in-vitro? They had waited so long to discuss it, they couldn't see that it had become commonplace.

"But there's more," Diane said.

"There is?" Jack was so relieved at Jamie's initial reaction that he forgot about the inheritance issue. "Oh yeah. There is."

"What else could there be?" Jamie asked. "So you lied to me my whole life. Who cares? I lie to you all the time."

The family had a good laugh. At this point in the conversation they needed one. Jack punched Jamie on the shoulder. Jamie gave him a shove. "Stop it," Diane said, kissing her two men.

"No, really," Jack continued. "There is more. It's about the money, the money we just found out about at the bank."

"What about it?" said Jamie. "Don't tell me it's from you."

"No, I don't think so," said Jack. "Are you kidding? Where do you think I'd get that kind of money?"

"I'm joking. What about it?"

Jack organized his thoughts and took a sip of hot chocolate. Diane had made three cups.

"It's about Dick Picking," Jack said. He pictured Dick Picking at the hospital when Jamie was born. If he had tricked them in some way, it never showed on his face. "Picking arranged for the in-vitro. I don't know if you figured this out yet, Jamie, but you are actually the world's first test tube baby."

"What?"

"That's right. In-vitro was a totally experimental procedure in 1976. Look it up. The first official test tube baby was named Louise Brown, and she was born in England in 1978. You were born the year before."

Now he had Jamie's attention.

"How is that possible?" Jamie asked.

"Of course, we can't prove it. We don't even know who did the in-vitro fertilization. Dr. Carrillo knew about it, but I don't think he knew who the doctor was either. The only person who knew everything was Dick Picking. He's the one who took your mother's eggs and my sperm and had them fertilized. He told us it had to be kept secret. I still don't know why. Maybe someone would have got in trouble for what he did. But this is why we're really upset. Whoever did the in-vitro had complete control over your life. It wasn't done in Englewood Hospital. They took the sperm and egg somewhere else, then they brought it back a couple of days later. We don't really know what happened. They could have switched the sperm. They could have switched the egg. Or both."

"Dad, you're paranoid. Why would anyone do that?"

Jack wished he was paranoid.

"I don't know," he answered, biting his lip. "All I know is, why would someone leave you all this money unless you were related to him? Don't forget, the trust was set up at the time of your birth."

Jamie accepted the chocolate chip cookie his mother held out to him. He took a good look at his father, then at Diane.

"I'm definitely your biological son," Jamie said. "I don't have any doubt about that."

"Then who left you the money? Dick Picking was *not* rich. We don't have any rich relatives. I know you're not Dick Picking's son, you don't look anything like him, but. . . "

"That's because I look like you."

"But you don't look like me," Diane added, ready to cry.

"Yes I do. I think I do. Don't you think I look like Mom, Dad? Hey, this is insane. Just because you had in-vitro, and just because I got lucky enough to inherit a lot of money doesn't mean I'm not your son. Come on, there has to be an explanation. Maybe we had a distant relative who was rich. Or maybe you did a really big favor for someone who was rich."

"We could do a DNA test," Jack said. Diane's heart stopped. It was bad enough to imagine that Jamie might not be hers or Jack's. What if there were scientific proof that he came from someone else?

"Oh my God," said Diane. "That would prove it."

"No it wouldn't," said Jamie. "Don't you guys watch TV? They argued about the blood tests in the O.J. Simpson trial. Some experts said the tests are conclusive, some said they could be wrong. It's not foolproof. And DNA tests are more controversial. Guys, get a grip on yourself! Nothing has changed around here. Really. Hey, wait. I've got an idea. Why don't we talk to the doctor who delivered me? Let's ask him who did the in-vitro. Maybe he knows."

"Sorry, Jamie," said Jack. "That won't work."

"Why not?"

"Because Dr. Carrillo has Alzheimer's disease. He's had it for several years and he doesn't practice anymore. He can't carry on a conversation."

"What about his records? What about his nurse?" asked Jamie.

"I told you. The in-vitro was a secret. No one knew

anything. . . "

"What about your lawyer, Picking? Didn't he have records? I can't believe no one knows the name of the doctor who did the in-vitro. What about the hospital?"

"Jamie, that was eighteen years ago. Richard Picking was the one who told us not to put anything in writing. I highly doubt that the hospital knew anything either, and who would we even contact now? Plus, I forgot to tell you something about Richard Picking."

"What?"

"He committed suicide. He was depressed about losing his wife and son. I guess it finally caught up with him because he killed himself a couple of years after you were born."

The truth was, Jamie found this entire matter tremendously exciting, rather than disturbing. This was the kind of story you only read about, or watched on *Murder, She Wrote*. But it was really happening, and it was happening to him. A story that involved millions of dollars, a family secret, a lawyer who had committed suicide and a doctor who couldn't tell them anything because he had lost his mind. It was too good to be true. The more he heard, the better it got!

If anything, his life had been a little too perfect, too routine. He wasn't complaining. It was nice to always be around people who liked you, who bragged about you, who told you how smart and wonderful you were. But it was also boring. Nothing really bad or controversial had ever affected him or his family, except maybe that time they thought Livvy had been kidnapped. Uneventfully, she turned out to be locked in a neighbor's attic playing with a kitten for six hours.

Here was his big chance to follow the road not taken, thought Jamie. To be a combination of Christopher Columbus and Sherlock Holmes, or at least Matlock. He had thought of a way to calm down his increasingly distraught parents while at the same time undertaking a long sought after challenge.

"I've got an idea," said Jamie in an authoritative tone. "Instead of jumping to conclusions, why don't I conduct a professional investigation?" Jack waited for his wife's reaction.

"When?" asked his mother. Jamie thought about it.

"This summer," Jamie replied correctly. He knew they

would never go for it until school was over. "What do you think, Dad?"

"I don't know." Jack did not know exactly what Jamie had in mind, and his son was supposed to start work at his office in July. "Jamie, you're *not* a professional. What do you want to do?"

Jamie had eaten three chocolate chip cookies so far. He snuck one more out of the package. "That's all," said Diane, taking the rest.

"Okay, here's my plan. By the way, Mom, what's your blood type?"

Diane tried to remember. A big smile crossed her face. "It's Type O," she said, "The same as yours."

"Okay," said the New Jersey junior detective. "That's a start. Now here's what we have to do."

Jack and Diane felt a sense of relief at Jamie's attitude. For while there was still every reason to believe that Jamie was 100% theirs, just in case he wasn't it appeared that he could handle that fact better than they could. And now that Jamie would receive $25,000 plus his first year's tuition, the money he would have made working was unimportant. Besides, how long would it take for him to admit he was at a dead end?

"First, I have to make a list. I mean, *we* have to make a list. We should really do everything together, as a family, like we always do."

"What kind of list?" asked Jack, thinking it would be a short one.

"Well, like the names of everyone I should interview."

"Like who?"

Jamie was excited about this detective thing. Maybe it would be good for him.

"Like Richard Picking's family. Or his close friends. Like Dr. Carrillo's wife. Like people at the hospital, and maybe somebody else at the bank who was there in 1977. And I want to check out our own relatives."

"I don't think you're going to find anyone who knows more than us."

"Maybe not, Dad, but what have I got to lose? I'll just keep the case open until I follow up all the leads. Then I'll drop it.

I promise."

"The case?" thought Jack.

Technically, there wasn't much they could do to stop him. He had enough money and he was old enough to drive and travel. Even if he wanted to visit Picking's family in South Carolina, assuming he could find someone, they couldn't tell him not to go. It was equally foolish to discourage him. They had nothing to hide, and they had always instilled in him the value of the truth. The bottom line was, he wanted to do the right thing. Nor would they be unhappy if he found the anonymous benefactor, and that person had nothing to do with the in-vitro procedure. Then they would all sleep better.

"You're still going to Dartmouth in September?" Jack asked.

"Damn right. I still need a good education. Although now I don't have to worry so much about getting a job. Just kidding, Dad. If there's one thing you taught me, it's self-respect. I didn't earn that money. I'm happy it's there, but I know I have to be something."

"We're proud to hear you say that," Jack said, meaning it.

"I'm not going to make this my lifetime ambition. I give you my word. If I can't track down the guy who left me the money. . . "

"Or the woman."

"Right, Mom. Or the woman. You see, I really do need you guys for my back up team."

"Let's not get carried away."

Jamie felt good. He felt like this was going to be the best year of his life, certainly the best summer. Which was really saying something considering his torrid affair with cheerleader Arlene Hanson last summer. But now he had been given the opportunity to prove himself. To apply his intelligence to a real life mystery. And if he was lucky, to eliminate his parents' unreasonable suspicions about his genetic heritage.

As Jamie lay in his bed making plans for his new summer job, he began to ask himself more and more questions. Should he tell any of his friends about this? Probably not. Should he buy a pocket tape recorder and a tiny camera? Maybe just the tape recorder. Did he need binoculars? Was it possible that the money was somehow illegal or given to him by mistake? If so, he was better off not searching for the truth.

His mother had one last question for him as she poked her head around the corner.

"Jamie?" she asked. "Did you brush your teeth again?"

He could taste the delicious bits of chocolate pasted to his gums. "Yes, Mom," he replied.

"Good night."

Chapter Seven

꧁❀꧂

"YIELD NOT TO TEMPTATION"

APRIL, 1974
MEMPHIS, TENNESSEE

It was a beautiful Spring day to celebrate your 20th anniversary college reunion at Graceland, the fourteen acre home of Elvis Presley. Provided, of course, that one of your dearest friends, Hunter Davis, just happened to be The King's personal attorney with permission to nail Duke Law banners to the towering oaks along the driveway.

Richard Picking felt a cool breeze on the back of his neck as a valet drove off with his $29 Hertz rental. Behind the house a high school marching band was attempting to play Duke's Alma Mater which reminded the New York attorney that he had never played football. Hunter Davis, who at this very moment was going out for a pass, had different memories. A big bruiser at 43, the same age as Picking, he hadn't lost a great deal of his strength and speed since that last game in 1954. Unfortunately, it was difficult to maneuver in fancy loafers and though he caught the ball well, down he went in Elvis' back yard as dozens of fellow Duke grads and their husbands and wives watched.

By the time someone had pointed him out to Richard Picking, Davis was already sidelined, sitting on a bench with his wife, Charlotte, one shoe off. The ankle hurt like hell, but it wasn't broken and it most likely wouldn't swell up until late that evening. He spotted Picking walking slowly toward him

65

in his usual methodical manner, stopping briefly to let two waiters pass with a cooler of Budweisers. Davis waved and Picking waved back, steadying his glasses with his free hand.

"Dick Picking, you old. . .whatever!" shouted Davis over the band. He tried to stand, wobbled, and sat back down before shaking hands. "Dick, this is my wife, Charlotte. I don't think you two have ever met. Charlotte, this here Yankee is Richard Ellis Picking. Dick and I were really tight at Duke. He used to help me cram for all the big tests. I owe Dick everything I am today, but I gotta tell you, boy, I ain't reimbursing you for your airfare."

Hunter's wife knew that Picking was not a native New Yorker. His Southern accent was intact, though he did pronounce a few words funny. The part about the studying, however, was true. In college, Hunter Davis had been pretty much a goof-off, with just enough smarts and the right connections to earn his degree in a timely manner. Without Picking, he would still have the certificate, but a year later and only after a few bribes.

"Wonderful to see you, Hunter. It's really been too long."

"Yes, it really has been. But maybe we can see each other a little more often in the future. I have something to talk to you about privately, in a little while. Business."

"Would you like me to leave?" Hunter's wife was used to his less than tactful behavior. It had gotten him ahead in his career, and sometimes it was actually an endearing quality.

"No, no, honey," said Davis. "But you know what? I sure could use some kind of ice pack for this ankle. It's starting to swell."

"Like your head," said Mrs. Davis, not kidding but in good spirit. "I'll be back in say ten or fifteen minutes. Is that all right? I have to pay a visit to the little girl's room."

"That'll be fine," said Davis, winking at her. As she turned to go, he lunged forward and pinched her derriere. "Sex maniac," she responded, also not kidding.

Richard Picking, shy and conservative, loosened his tie. He was one of the few lawyers wearing a Duke tie and he was visibly embarrassed at the rude way Hunter Davis had sent his wife off. But that was Hunter. Polite when he had to be, effective the rest of the time.

"I was awfully sorry to hear about your wife and son," Davis said, again embarrassing his friend who had no idea anyone kept track of his life. Over the years, the two had continued to exchange Christmas and birthday cards, but the notes had been fairly impersonal. They had written letters during the late 50's, but Picking hadn't married until 1966, and he hadn't had a child until 1968.

"Thank you," replied Picking. "It's been three years but it seems like yesterday."

"I'm sure it does. My oldest is eleven now. I can't even imagine."

As they spoke, a young man came over and handed them two beers, along with an ice pack. Davis dropped the ice pack on the bench, fitted on his shoe and stood up.

"Let's take a walk around to the front," Davis said, moving Picking in that direction with a powerful right arm. "It's quieter there."

Hunter and Dick Picking sat on the stone steps below the four 20-foot tall round columns on the porch, smaller versions of the huge Georgian columns at the Duke Library. By the time Picking drank half a bottle of Bud, Davis had finished off his bottle plus two more a valet brought him. "Man, am I thirsty," he said, and burped. With his short blond hair, Hunter Davis still appeared collegiate. He had very nice skin and virtually no blemishes on his face. In a way, he looked like the weight-lifting version of Pat Boone, his wide nose perhaps the only sure sign he wasn't Pat himself.

"So how have you been, Hunter?"

"Me? Great. I love this town. I doubt I'll ever live anywhere else. The Davises have been here forever. I love my work, too."

"You're on your own like me, right?" The beer helped Picking make conversation.

"Yes sir. Could never work for a big firm. I tried it for a while but they had too many rules. I do represent a few corporate clients, like Cox Industries. But more or less I'm a legal negotiator. People hire me to find a way to get ten pounds of shit in a five pound bag. You probably read about that situation with the DeWitt Brothers over in Arkansas."

Picking searched his memory bank. "Don't recall," he said candidly.

"Well, I guess it wasn't such a big deal," Davis laughed. "But I did get my picture in the New York papers again."

"What happened?" Picking was genuinely intrigued as to what local matter would be news up north.

"These two brothers, Clinton and Clyde DeWitt. . ."

"Oh, wait," interrupted Picking. "I did hear about that. That's the one where the U.S. Government condemned that little house on the river."

"That's the one." Hunter Davis was impressed. "Those two idiots actually turned down $475,000 for that shack near the bridge. Then they barricaded themselves inside and threatened to blow up the bridge if anyone tried to get them out."

"Yes, now I remember. You went into the house and convinced the brothers to take the deal."

"It was more than that," said Davis in a cocky pose, palms up. "The Feds had to agree to buy them a farm out west and to make part of the payment in cash. Do you know what it takes to get Uncle Sam to pay in cash?"

"How'd you do it?" Picking had always admired his friend's ingenuity.

"Simple. We just had the closing at the local bank where the DeWitts had done business all their lives. There were two checks. One was cashed by the bank manager, and he actually agreed to cash it before the papers were signed. I had to pay that guy a thousand bucks out of my own pocket that morning. But it was well worth it. The state paid me to represent them, and I wound up getting a 2% real estate broker's fee!"

"Very clever."

"Yeah, Dick, I get the job done. Whatever it takes. But I'll tell you, I really did feel good about that whole situation. And I'll tell you why. Do you believe those goddam DeWitt brothers really had dynamite in their house? They had fourteen sticks of dynamite in a kitchen cabinet."

"No kidding. Did you know that when you were in there?"

Picking saw himself trying to supervise this kind of situation by telephone.

"Hell no! But if the police, or the National Guard had tried to remove those two rednecks by force, I would have got the hell out of there. Cause I did know that Clyde had two pistols under his shirt and those two guys felt like they were in *Gone With The Wind* defending the whole South."

Davis signalled for some more beer.

"I get a lot of jobs like that around here," Davis went on. "That's how I got hooked up with Mr. Presley, well actually his father. But enough about me. Tell me what you've been doing these days."

"You work for Elvis Presley?" asked the New York adoption attorney.

Davis handed Picking some broken salt pretzels from his pocket. They came from Cunningham's bar.

"Known the family for quite awhile," bragged the big lawyer. "Needless to say, they've already got all the lawyers they can use, but sometimes they need a lawyer who doesn't mind taking some chances."

"If this involves anything incriminating, don't tell me." Davis laughed.

"You're a riot, Dick. No, I don't break the law. I got it too good to even think about doing time, plus I hear the prisons in Tennessee are the pits. Mostly, I buy things for Elvis. Otherwise, you know, people try to rip him off."

Talking to Hunter Davis was like reading The Enquirer. As he listened to Davis describe a deal involving four Cadillacs Picking was sorry he no longer lived in the South. The stories, and the people, were so colorful, so down to earth, unlike most New Yorkers. Which was why he decided to specialize in his particular area of law. The clients who came to him were truly desperate, they really needed him and they bared their souls. There was no way you could ever get that kind of satisfaction out of modifying escalation clauses in long term leases.

"I'll be honest with you," said Davis, completing his report on why Elvis was allowed to use firearms at Graceland. "I know all about your career as an adoption attorney: I think what you do is very admirable." After four beers, the word "admirable" came out as "ammerbull". Davis started on the fifth. "And so does Mr. Presley."

Picking didn't understand. "Is that a joke?" he asked. As he stood up, his knees creaked.

"No, it's not." Davis remained seated. "Dick, I have a little confession to make. Elvis Presley would like me to hire you."

"What?"

A friend of Hunter's trotted up to the pair, ignored Picking, and informed Davis that the reception was scheduled to begin in half an hour. "Mrs. Davis says she expects you to be there."

"Tell her I will." Davis did not introduce Richard Picking and the messenger walked off. "I'm serious, Dick. Elvis Presley would like to utilize your services to help him arrange for a second child."

When Picking had mentioned to a few acquaintances that he would be visiting Elvis Presley's house they had expressed mild interest. His secretary had been silly enough to ask for an autograph. However, he could not guess the reaction he would get to announcing that he was Elvis' adoption attorney.

"You're not kidding," said Picking.

"I'm not. But before you say anything, let me tell you what we have in mind. I don't know if this is something you would be able to do for us or not, but it must remain completely confidential." So much for the news release. "And Mr. Presley's name must be anonymous."

Richard Picking thought about that last condition.

"Oh," he whispered. "You mean the birth parents can't know."

"Nobody can know," Davis clarified. "Except you, me and Elvis."

"How is that possible?" Picking scraped a fingernail across his teeth. A small piece of pretzel got wedged under the nail and he flicked it away. "Under New York law, we've got to file the names of the adopting parents. As a divorced single man, it would be highly unlikely Mr. Presley would even be allowed to adopt. Aside from that, he's a resident of Tennessee, isn't he?"

Davis picked a small chunk of pretzel from between *his* teeth, and ate it.

"He's not going to adopt, Dick. I said we want to hire you to help Elvis have another child. Elvis wants a son."

Richard Picking was tempted to smile. He thought he detected a controlled smirk on his college pal's face. He decided to play along.

"I'm listening."

"Okay, this is what we'd like to do. As you know, Elvis already has a beautiful six year-old daughter, Lisa Marie. Before he gets too much older, he'd like to have a son as well. But, Elvis doesn't want to get married right now, and he's not sure he even has the time to raise a son. We could solve those two problems by having someone else bring up the boy. Of course, it would have to be the right mother and father."

"Pardon me," Picking cut him short. "I don't get it. I don't get this at all. You're telling me that Elvis Presley wants to have a son in New York, where he's not a resident. Then he wants someone else to take care of the boy for him. That is very, very strange, to say the least."

"I agree," said Davis.

"This is a joke, isn't it?"

Davis pointed a finger at Picking, pretending it was a gun, and shot him.

"This is definitely not a joke. See, there is a new medical procedure, it's being tested in Europe. It's not perfected yet, but we think we have a doctor here in the United States who can do this thing."

"What is it?"

"Are you ready? It's pretty unusual."

"I'm ready. What is it?" Picking asked, already knowing the answer.

"It's fertilization of the female egg with a male sperm completely outside of the womb. It's the conception of a natural baby, but in a laboratory."

At this point, Picking knew that what his friend was telling him was anything but a joke. As an adoption attorney, he kept abreast of all the latest scientific advances and he had read extensively about this procedure. In fact, it was something he expected to discuss with his clients in a few years, or whenever it really happened. At the present time artificial insemination was considered the most reasonable medical alternative to adoption. Many couples did both at the same time, and went with whichever came first. Often, after adopting, the wife later became pregnant, with or without medical intervention. Also, many of his female clients tried fertility drugs, as did some males.

"You're talking about a test tube baby," said Picking.

"That's what we're talking about."

Picking was confused. "Why?" he asked. "I'm sure Elvis Presley could have a baby with lots of women."

"I'm sure he could. But he doesn't want to."

"Why not?" Picking recalled all the pictures of Elvis with beautiful women he had seen in magazines.

"Because he wants a very specific mother. And he wants that mother to already be married to just the right man."

"I'm lost. You'll excuse me if I find this amusing, but I do."

"Look," said Davis, using his friend's arm as a handrail to pull himself to his slightly unsteady feet. "There's no reason why you should get this information second hand. Why don't we go straight to the top."

"What are you talking about?"

"Let's go see Elvis. He's in his father's office. I want you to hear it right from the horse's mouth." He tugged Picking up the stairs.

Vernon Presley's office was not fancy. A good sized room, it housed a few steel desks, some file and storage cabinets, a copying machine and a TV set. It had a low acoustical ceiling, cheap wall paneling and a speckled gold industrial carpet. Elvis sat behind Vernon's desk waiting for his guests. When they entered, he took down his feet and sat up straight.

"This here Yankee," repeated Hunter Davis, "is Richard Ellis Picking."

Elvis leaned forward and shook hands. "Richard Elvis?" he asked.

"No. Ellis." That broke the ice and they all had a chuckle.

"Hey," said Elvis Presley. "Aren't you gonna be late for that dinner party, H.D.?"

"Maybe. But this is important. Charlotte will be fine. Well, big guy, this is the man I told you about. We went to school together and I guarantee you we can trust him. I was just telling him about your desire to father a child. A son."

"That's true," Elvis confirmed. "I would really like to have a son, I wish it could be tomorrow but I can wait."

"Wait for what?" asked Picking.

"Didn't you tell him?"

"I started to, but I thought maybe it should come from you," said Davis.

Elvis picked up a pencil and began tapping it. "Okay, here goes. Mr. Picking, Richard — you can call me Elvis — I'm looking to see a little boy grow up the way I should have. I want him to have a real comfortable home, with a mama and papa who really love him, and some brothers and sisters. I don't want him to grow up poor or hungry. I don't want him to grow up in the South, although I love the South. And I don't want him to know anything about me. I mean, that we're related."

"Why not?"

Elvis smiled at the obvious question.

"Because I don't want his life to be anything like mine. I mean, I know his mother isn't going to be sickly and die young just because Gladys Presley did. But I don't think he should try to be a singer. Truth is, I think being an entertainer is a terrible life. You have to make too many promises and be too many places. He doesn't have to be a doctor or a lawyer either. He can be whatever he wants, as long as he gets a good education, goes to college, and doesn't need to worry about making money all his life. I just want him to be happy."

"I take it you feel that you're not happy." Picking knew the feeling well.

"No, Richard, I'm really not. I mean, I've *been* happy in my life. I loved my mother, and my daddy. I loved Priscilla. I still do. And I love my little girl, even though I don't see her nearly enough. I'm gonna try to do better in that department in the very near future. But overall, no, I have not really had a happy life. It seems like I was just getting my first hit record a couple of years ago, but I know it was more like twenty years. Where did the time go? I don't know. Where did my life go? I need to start over."

Richard Picking could see that Elvis was expressing his true feelings. However, he was not God, nor could he solve everyone's problems. In fact, he couldn't even cope with his own life.

"I tell my clients," he said, "that having a child will not make you happy. And you can't live your life through someone else."

"That's what you tell them?"

"Yup."

Elvis stood close to Davis' friend. The famous face did not look familiar to Picking, though he had seen it a thousand times.

"Well, let me tell you something, sir, and I mean this with all due respect. I have lived one hell of a life. I've had nothing, and I've had everything. I *have* everything! Fame and fortune, houses, cars, girls, jewelry. People all around the world say they love me. God knows they buy millions of my records and they watch my stupid movies. But I would give it all up in a New York minute if I could just start my life over as someone else. So don't tell me what makes me happy."

Picking was not offended. "And who would you be?" he asked.

"I'd be me," said Elvis, "but not as the little boy named Elvis Aron Presley who grew up in Tupelo. I know it's a fantasy," Elvis admitted. "But I don't care. That's what I want. And the only way I can do it is to create a new life. I already messed up Lisa Marie's life. I'm trying my best but she doesn't live in a real home and she's always going to be the daughter of Elvis Presley. I need for someone to be the me I never was." Elvis took a breath and looked at Hunter Davis. "Ask *him*, Richard. He knows this is the only way."

With that, Elvis left the office and disappeared into Graceland. Richard Picking felt like he would never see him again, not just on this pretty Spring day, but for the rest of his life. Yet he also felt that he could not simply dismiss Elvis' request.

"I'm still in the dark," Picking told Davis. "How can I help?"

"We're looking for a couple who would rather not adopt, who want their own child. A son, very, very badly."

"You just described everybody I see at work." Then Picking realized something that had been said more than once. "And what makes you think we can find a woman who only gives

74

birth to *boys*?"

"That's not a problem," said Davis inexplicably. "The problem is finding the right parents. Like Elvis said, we're not in a rush. We want this to happen in a year or two, so you won't be under any pressure." Davis picked up a framed photo of Elvis' ex-wife and daughter.

"Okay," said Richard Picking. "Tell me exactly what you think I can do, and I'll tell you if it's possible."

Davis slapped him on the back.

"Good. That's the way to go. Dick, what we would like you to do is to find us a fertile couple who are willing to try an experimental medical procedure in order to have a baby. Under hospital conditions. With the supervision and care of their own doctor. We want a couple who have a stable marriage, preferably not older than thirty, well off, where the husband holds down a good job. We don't want a bus driver or an airline pilot. We want a college professor, an engineer, a doctor or an architect, just to give you a better idea."

"That's the kind of people I see. But why no pilots?"

"Too dangerous, and they're away from home too much. We want a daddy who's going to be around."

Elvis and Davis had thought of everything.

"Go on."

"We need people who have already tried every conventional way to have a baby, including artificial insemination. There has to be no physical reason why they can't conceive, except bad luck. You have to be convinced before you recommend them to us that their only remaining option is to adopt."

"Why?"

"Because we don't want to stop someone from having their own child."

Picking searched in his pockets for his notebook. Davis handed him a pen and pad.

"And then what?"

"And then we hope that the reason they never conceived is the male sperm. We replace that sperm with the sperm of Elvis Presley. We fertilize the egg in a laboratory. We put it back inside the mother and we hope it takes."

Picking rubbed his eyes. This was a crazy idea, all right,

but it wasn't impossible. He wanted to know more.

"What if it doesn't work?" he asked.

"We can try it again. Or if the couple won't agree, we've failed. It's possible we could look for another couple, but by that time Elvis may want to call the whole thing off. I think he just wants one last chance."

"I don't know," said Picking, shaking his head. "I don't know if it makes sense. I don't know if it's ethical. I know it's not legal."

"Why not?"

"Because you're concealing the fact that it's Elvis' sperm from the parents."

Davis explained again that Elvis did not want the parents to consider this child anything but their own. That they might not raise the child the same way if they were told the truth. That they would certainly treat the child differently if they knew it was related to Elvis Presley.

"I could tell them the sperm is from a sperm bank."

"If you tell them that and they say no, then what do we do? They'll never trust you. And they won't really consider it their baby. That's not what Elvis wants. As far as being legal, this whole procedure is currently not regulated. I don't think there should be a written agreement. We want the hospital to think this is artificial insemination. Forget the law. This is something you can't do with legal permission. But I really think you need to deal with the ethical question. Is it right or wrong?"

"How can it be right?"

Davis put his hand on the back of Picking's thin neck. "It can be right," he answered, "if you believe you are giving people the baby they could *never* have. If you believe they would *adopt* a baby instead, but will never be happy it's not their own child. It can be right if you admit that the only way this couple could ever have a child through pregnancy would be to go to a sperm bank. And why would anyone else's child be superior to Elvis Presley's?"

These were questions no one, including Richard Picking, could answer without a great deal of contemplation.

"I don't know," he said.

"I don't know either," responded Hunter Davis.

The more he thought about it, the more it bothered Picking. And fascinated him. A few moments ago he had told himself he wasn't God. Now he tried to deny his wish to be just that. Perhaps his old friend was correct. How wrong could it be to give a childless couple the one thing they dreamed of? An adopted child wasn't theirs at all. At least one conceived from the mother's own egg was half theirs.

"The child will never look like the father," Picking said, concerned.

"Find a father who resembles Elvis," Davis proposed. "Lots of men do. New York is a big place. Run ads in The New York Times."

"Childless couples with Elvis look-a-like fathers seeking to adopt, please contact me?"

Davis laughed.

"I'm joking, Dick. You're creative. Look around. Maybe you won't find anybody. We've got some other options, but you're our first choice. What have you got to lose?"

"Time. I don't have enough of it now."

The phone rang. Davis picked it up. It was Elvis, telling him his wife was looking for him and asking Davis to apologize to his colleague for being rude. Davis hung up.

"That was Elvis," he acknowledged. "He wants me to apologize to you if you thought he wasn't polite before." Davis took a piece of paper out of his shirt pocket. He sat down at Vernon's desk and wrote out a check. It was payable to cash and it was for $7,500. He handed it to Richard Picking.

"What's this?" Picking looked at the check. He needed almost this much to balance his checkbook and pay some bills. Well, he didn't *necessarily* need the money. A number of clients would be getting the chance to adopt one of these days, maybe even this month, and he would collect his fees.

"It's a retainer." Davis stepped back so that Picking could not return the check easily. "It's a no-obligation retainer."

"What does that mean?"

"It means you don't have to take the job. All you have to do is agree to consider it. Go back home to New Jersey. Ask some questions. Talk to some clients. Think about what's right and wrong. Then get back to me. If you're not comfortable with the money, return it. Or just tear up the check and give me a call."

A thought struck the New York attorney.

"How can it be a boy?" Picking wanted to know. He wasn't refusing the money, at least not yet. Which made the big Tennessee lawyer feel just like he did when he had a big fish on the line. If he could get Dick Picking to take that check back home, he knew he would cash it. Once you took someone's money, you always felt obligated.

"It can be done. Believe me, it can."

"You have a doctor that can control the sex of an unborn child?"

"Dick, I'd rather not tell you, if you don't mind. The man would prefer not to divulge his name at this time. I can only inform you that he works at a major hospital right in New York and you will probably read about him one of these days."

"Is it Robert Loughlin at Columbia?"

"Dick, I can't tell you. And I'd have to ask you not to contact anyone in an attempt to find out who the doctor is. However, I can assure you he will be working closely with the mother's doctor." Davis was lying. The doctor they planned to use had yet to be selected and no one but he and Elvis would know who it was. The doctor would never know about Elvis and would not have the slightest idea where the baby was born. They had other options to explore first, but no matter who they used the entire matter would be a secret. There would be nothing in writing. No evidence.

"I don't know," said Picking half-heartedly. "Maybe I should give you back the check and call you soon."

"I told you. Don't cash the check. Remember, it's not money if you don't cash it." Davis did not look at the check. Instead, he added some additional specifications to the list. "We want an athletic father," he said, sucking in his stomach and flexing his muscles. "We need a six-footer, a guy like me who wants his son to play football. We want a family from England or France originally, not Germany or Russia. Write this down."

"Why England or France?" asked Picking, taking notes.

"Because that's where Elvis' mother's ancestors, the Mansells, came from." Davis smiled and ate some pretzels. "Jeez, I need to take a wicked piss," he said. "Oh, yeah. The mother has to remind Elvis of *his* mother, Gladys. She doesn't have to look like her, it's enough for the boy to look like his father. But Elvis needs to feel that the boy's mother will be devoted to her son."

"Like his mother? I thought he didn't want his son to grow up the same way he did?"

"He doesn't. He wants the boy's mother to have a college degree and be very involved in the community. But not a working mother."

"Anything else? Do they have to be right handed or left handed?"

"Don't make me laugh, I'll piss in my pants. Let's see. They have to be religious. It doesn't matter what religion, but they have to go to church. They have to want to have more children."

"How are we going to know that?"

"Ask them," said Davis. They just have to *say* they want more children."

"What if they can't have more children later on?"

"We'll cross that bridge when we come to it. But Elvis was an only child. He had a twin brother who died at birth, but he never had any other brothers or sisters. He feels that it is less likely the boy will be just like him if he has a brother or sister, or both. And the parents can't be from California."

Suddenly Richard Picking broke out laughing. He dropped the check, picked it up and stuffed it in his pants, but couldn't stop laughing. Hunter Davis rushed to the bathroom, and returned shortly. By then, Picking had composed himself.

"What were you laughing about?"

"This is insane," said Picking. How am I ever going to find a husband and wife that meet all of these requirements? There may not be anyone on the planet like the people you want."

"You'll find them. If not, keep the money. Figure it on an hourly rate and bill me when you go over. Oh, I forgot one other thing."

"Now what?"

"At least one of the parents has to have the same blood type as Elvis or his parents. He's Type O."

Picking jotted it down.

"Oh, naturally. And do they have to play the guitar? Wait, I'm sorry. They have to be *unable* to play the guitar, right? No, they have to *hate* to play the guitar!"

Now it was Hunter Davis' turn to crack up. That last remark really had him in stitches. While trying to recover, he made it even worse by saying: "Don't you want to know why the people can't be from California?"

"Yeah, why?" asked his college chum.

"Because Elvis thinks everyone in California is nuts!" Hunter Davis fell to the floor holding his stomach. After nearly passing out, he had one final incentive for Picking.

"If you do find us the right couple," he said, "the finder's fee is $75,000. That's a 10% deposit you're considering. Like I said, we'll pay you by the hour until you've had enough. But if you are successful, you get a nice bonus." The big man tucked in his shirt and tried to look more presentable. He had a lot of hands to shake at the reception, and he had to give a speech on why Americans need lawyers. "I'll see you in a few minutes," he said, shaking hands with the man he hoped would help make Elvis happy. "I just have to make one quick call."

"Don't tell Elvis I'll do it yet."

"That's not who I'm calling." Picking started to leave. "Hey, R.E.P.! Let's keep in touch. I'll be in New York in a couple of months. Let's get together." Davis lifted the receiver.

By the time Richard Picking's footsteps became inaudible, Hunter Davis was talking to Elvis.

"He's in," Davis said. "I guarantee it."

"How do you know?" Elvis was excited.

"I checked up on him. I love that boy, I really do. And he's very smart, otherwise we wouldn't need him. But he made some very bad investments last year and he can use the money. He can use a lot more than the check I just gave him."

"And you think he'll find the right people?"

"I think so. If they exist. But we can't bug him. Let him

get back to us. He's obsessive, like you and me. Once he puts his mind to something, he can't stop. I figure we'll hear from him in a week or two."

"And then?" asked Presley, taking a bite of a bologna sandwich.

"And then it'll take as long as it takes. Hey, bud, this ain't like making Jello. This is your life. We've got to do it right, we've got to do *everything* right. Now I have to start interviewing the doctors."

Hunter Davis had compiled a list of more than twenty names. All experts and specialists, some very unconventional.

"Try not to pick one from California. I hate Californians."

"I know."

Chapter 8

꒰ஓ꒱

"SOLOMON'S DECISION"

OCTOBER, 1975
NEW YORK CITY

After so many years of glamorous entertaining, The Plaza Hotel was showing its age. In another decade it would need major refurbishing. Like most aristocratic tourists, Mr. and Mrs. Hunter Davis still considered The Plaza the place to stay. It reminded them of Europe, and they enjoyed the southern style atmosphere of excess politeness. In a city renowned for its foul-mouthed cab drivers, garbage strikes and slums it was nice to come in contact with hands in clean white gloves.

"Where's Charlotte?" asked Richard Picking, setting down his four dollar cup of Hawaiian coffee and rising to greet his friend.

"Oh, she'll be here in a few minutes. I told her we needed to discuss something in private. Dick, I just want you to know how much Elvis appreciates the effort you've been making for him. Here's another check."

"Thank you," said Picking, accepting payment.

"I know you've been trying your best, Dick, and we're not upset at you. But it has been well over a year since we started this search. True, you have given us the names of several interesting couples. I really thought we had a winner with those two psychologists from Scarsdale, but then they went and got pregnant on us. I mean, God bless them, but now they're out and I don't see where any of the others. . ."

"Excuse me."

Hunter Davis picked up the coffee he had just been served.

"What?" he asked, taking a sip of the fresh black brew.

"I think I've found your birth parents."

"Really? Who are they?"

The New York lawyer looked over both shoulders. This whole affair made him edgy and he always felt like someone was watching him. The yellow envelope he handed Davis contained a photograph and a bio on a young couple from New Jersey. Picking acted like it contained top secret documents.

"This is Mr. and Mrs. Jack Randolph. They came to me over the summer looking to adopt. They've been married seven years, trying to have a baby since the wedding night."

Davis smiled at the photo.

"He looks a little like Elvis."

"In person, he looks quite a bit like Elvis," said Picking. He's heavy set, like you. And he has light hair. But I thought that's what you wanted."

"It is what we want. Elvis figures that's what he would have looked like if he didn't dye his hair and trained harder. He prefers the kid to look more like his father and less like him or the mother."

"Anyway," continued Picking, "Jack Randolph is a 28 year old lawyer and his wife, Diane, is 26. Except for the pregnancy problem, they are both in perfect health. He jogs and works out. She's a little sedentary these days, but it's understandable since she thinks she might be having a baby every month. You're going to love this, Hunter. Jack Randolph works in Hackensack. It's not far from home so he can have lunch with his wife about three or four days a week. And he's *dying* to have a son."

"That's good. What about their ability to conceive?" Davis reached for a croissant roll.

"They've done it all. Artificial insemination, drugs, having sex at certain medically determined times. Nothing has worked. All the tests show they should be able to have children. Their doctor thinks the problem is related to stress, but even he recommends adoption."

Today's news was really a pleasant surprise for the man

from Tennessee. Having made four previous trips to New York, he had become much more discouraged than he let on. And Elvis did not look too good lately. He really needed a rest and he needed some cheering up. This would do it.

"How about their blood type?"

"The mother has the same type as Elvis. The father doesn't."

"Perfect. So we would have a child who looks like daddy with a blood match to the mother. No one will be suspicious. Do they belong to a church?"

"Hunter, I'm telling you. The Randolphs are like a custom order. There's only one problem."

"What's wrong with them?" Davis grabbed a second roll.

Picking shrugged. "I'm the problem," he said apologetically. "I still don't know if I can go through with this."

Davis controlled himself. "Did you discuss it with them?"

The two lawyers looked each other straight in the eye. Picking scratched his head.

"I did. They're not opposed to the procedure. In fact, they're very excited about it."

"But you're still concerned about lying to them?"

"It's not just that. And I know that they would rather have a baby on their own. What's bothering me the most is, I know that this could be done with *Jack's* sperm. The baby could be his. If I knew who the doctor was, I could arrange for the procedure using their own sperm and egg."

Davis stopped smiling.

"No you couldn't," he said, emphatically.

"Why not?"

"Because the doctor is willing to do this for *Elvis Presley* as a personal favor. He would *not* do it for anyone else. There have been lawsuits."

"But in a few years. . ."

"In a few years we could all be dead." Davis spoke hastily. "I'm sorry, Dick, I didn't mean that. If this procedure becomes available to the public later on, the Randolphs can always use it to have more children. In fact, we would help them give the boy brothers and sisters."

That last comment made Picking less opposed to the plan.

"Let me ask you a question," suggested Davis. "You say these people are desperate for a child, a son if possible, which I guarantee you will be the case. I don't think you should ask Mr. Randolph this question, but I'd like *you* to answer it objectively. Knowing what they want, don't you think the Randolphs would go to a sperm bank rather than adopt?"

Picking pondered the question. He knew his friend was a very skilled manipulator, otherwise he would not be in such demand. The question was designed to convince him to go along with the experiment. Still, it was a valid issue. Would Jack Randolph rather have a child that was related to his wife, or would he choose a total unknown? He didn't know the answer. And he couldn't ask Jack without tipping him off. Instead, he asked himself what he would do. Instantly, he knew the answer. If he could have a child today that was even fifty per cent Patricia, it would be like he hadn't lost her completely. That was a major reason why most people wanted children, to still have part of their mate if catastrophe struck. In his own case, regrettably, God had chosen to take them both. But what wouldn't he give for a son or daughter with his wife's blood in its veins? He'd give anything.

"I'll do it," he said, quietly.

"You will? Hey, that's terrific." Hunter Davis' mood changed dramatically. He grabbed his pal's clenched fist and squeezed it. "Of course, I still have to run this by The King. He gets final approval."

"Of course." Richard Picking pictured his wife's face on the last day of her life. The day he had gone to work and kissed her good-bye, looking forward to seeing her and little Billy when they came home from the Bronx Zoo. It was too painful to remember more, and he still felt guilty that he had let them go without him. Why didn't he take the day off? Why?

"So let me take this file and get back to you tomorrow. As far as I'm concerned, this is a go. Is that all right?"

"Yes, fine."

"One more thing, Dick. Dick?" Picking was staring at the ceiling.

"Sorry, Hunter. I've got other problems on my mind. Go ahead."

"I was just thinking that if Elvis says okay, we have another legal matter for you to handle."

"Which is?"

"To set up a trust for Elvis' son. I know that the boy will be raised in a good family. The Randolphs do make enough money, don't they? Good. Even so, Elvis does not want to mention his son in his will. He wants to put aside the money now, and we're talking in the mid six figures, so the boy doesn't have to worry about college, or anything else of a financial nature. We don't have to do anything yet. I just wanted you to know."

Another consideration occurred to Richard Picking.

"Does Elvis plan to make any contact with his son?" he asked.

"No, he doesn't. He feels that the boy has to grow up without being part of his life in any way, unless there was an emergency."

"He doesn't want to see the boy at all?"

Davis re-sealed the envelope after taking a long look at Diane Randolph. Pretty lady.

"He does want to see him. He wants to see him the day he's born. And he wants to see him from time to time. We don't know how we're gonna do that yet. You may have to help us out with that. Send us photos. Tell us when the boy might be in a public place where we could get near him without being noticed."

"How can Elvis Presley go anywhere without being noticed?"

Davis smiled. "You hit the nail on the head, bud. That's exactly what we don't want to happen to his son. You see, you can't live a normal life when you're famous, or even if your daddy's famous. Elvis hates that. He can't even go to McDonald's for a cheeseburger and fries. We don't know how he can see the boy. Maybe he'll put on a beard and a wig."

As soon as Hunter caught a glimpse of his wife across the room the Elvis conversation ended.

"Don't you just love this hotel?" beamed Charlotte Davis. "The tall ceilings, the columns, the open air bistro. You know, some company in Rockefeller Center has a display in the lobby filled with real Silver Dollars. Don't you love Silver Dollars?

They're so big, and they have a picture of an Eagle on the back. Hunter, can we stop and pick some up?"

At 10:00 AM, it was hard for some people to muster the enthusiasm to order breakfast. But Charlotte, Hunter's whirlwind wife, was ready to dance, to lunch at the Whitney Museum and then, possibly to fly to Paris! That spark was what had attracted him to her originally, and vice versa. In a way, they were two of a kind, social butterflies, hard workers for different causes. They both had a gusto for life and neither could be at a party without being the center of attention. In Memphis, they were almost celebrities. In New York, Hunter became somewhat subdued. Charlotte remained flamboyant and you couldn't miss her in that tight pink dress. Even in The Big Apple.

"I'll have the fluffy French Toast," she announced as Hunter called a waiter to their table. "Good morning, Mr. Picking. How are you today?"

"I'm doing very well," replied the quiet man. Picking stood as a courtesy as the waiter pushed in Charlotte's chair. Charlotte's carefree friendliness was contagious. A smile crossed Picking's narrow face.

"Then how come you haven't eaten anything?"

"We were waiting for you, dear. I'll have the Eggs Benedict, some orange juice and maybe a couple of hot cakes. Dick?"

"I'll just have an English Muffin. And some more coffee."

"Anything with the French Toast, ma'am?"

"Just maple syrup and some decaf."

At 41 years old, Charlotte was more than simply attractive. She was still gorgeous, with naturally beautiful features, a curvaceous figure and stunning green-grey eyes. Her profile, especially, was striking and truthfully her only real flaw was wearing a bit too much make-up. Hardly anyone ever noticed that since they were too busy admiring her long legs.

"Is she still a knockout?" asked Hunter, blowing Charlotte a kiss.

"You're so sweet," she said. "But I really have to get back on that exercycle when we go home. I've eaten a truckload too much in New York."

The tasteless cold coffee swished against Picking's lips.

"And what have you boys accomplished today?"

"Just some routine business," said Hunter.

"Involving adoptions?"

Hunter answered affirmatively and Picking shook his head in agreement. Actually, in the past six months Hunter Davis had helped his friend arrange three adoptions involving unwed mothers from Tennessee and affluent couples in New York. This was the kind of service Richard Picking and his wife had provided in the sixties.

"Your late wife was an adoption lawyer, too, wasn't she, Richard?" asked Charlotte.

Picking nodded weakly, with sad eyes.

"Oh, I'm sorry. Should we talk about something else?"

"No, it's all right." He began playing with his teaspoon. "Yes, Patricia and I worked together for several years, even after she gave birth. She had an office at home and I came to Manhattan."

"Do you still live in the same house?"

Picking recalled the short amount of time the three of them had spent there together.

"For the time being. It's really way too big. When I met Patricia, she was doing extremely well. She owned her own home in Demarest, New Jersey. After we married we bought a place on a couple of acres in Alpine. It was an older home and we were dumb enough to renovate it while living there. That's the last time I would ever do that. But it turned out very nice and the grounds are spectacular. The previous owner was a landscape architect. We have some Weeping Hemlocks that are outstanding. The only problem is I'm going broke keeping up the place."

"Well, we're trying to fix that," injected Davis.

"I hope Hunter really is helping you," said Charlotte.

"Oh, indeed he is. I've been lost since Patricia passed away. Can't seem to drum up enough new business. I spend way too much time with my clients, and it's so hard to find babies in New York these days. Healthy, white babies, that is."

Davis took over. "He used to work for the state adoption agency in Charleston," he explained. "Was making what, like

$16,000 a year?"

"Yes, and Patricia was making about triple."

"He knew that because she hired him at a conference in New York," said Davis.

"It was a seminar on adoption law. I was required to attend."

"So listen to this, Charlotte. The two of them meet, right. And Dick tells her how many babies are being offered to him every month, plus all the babies he hears about in North Carolina and Georgia. His wife, well she wasn't his wife yet, can't believe it. Here, she's driving a thousand miles a week trying to locate women with unwanted pregnancies and all she has to do is pick up the phone and call Dick."

"Wasn't that illegal?" asked Charlotte astutely.

"Not after I quit my job," said Picking. "Which was Patricia's idea. She convinced me my career was going nowhere and why shouldn't I help myself as well as all those women with kids they didn't want. When we got married, we became partners, but initially she taught me how to make money as her assistant. At first I thought it was being greedy but Patricia proved that many of the so-called free adoptions were fixed. If you had a good lawyer and some money, you wound up at the head of the list."

"You mean if you knew a scoundrel like my husband?"

Picking laughed.

"Exactly," said Hunter, dead serious. "She also told Dick that in most cases the babies would be better off up north, away from their families, getting a better education with less chance of legal problems down the road."

"So I still had all my sources," Picking continued, "and we flew back and forth every couple of weeks. We made a lot of money and we made a lot of people happy. That's what I've tried to do on my own, but it's just not the same. For the first year, I could hardly function, so I lost contact. Then after I finally got organized the laws had changed. I didn't file some of the papers correctly and two adoptions were declared illegal. One of those couples sued me for negligence and won. Things weren't going well at all."

"Then he finds out his stock portfolio is in the toilet."

"You didn't keep track of it?" asked Charlotte, observing the waiter's approach.

"For a while I couldn't. Patricia's brother handled my account, but it turns out he made some serious errors of judgment. It wasn't his fault but I lost a lot of money."

At the next table sat two Middle Eastern couples wearing turbans and lavish jewelry. They were typical of the kind of exclusive clientele who stayed at The Plaza.

"The way I figure it," said Hunter, watching the food placed delicately in front of him, "in about a year or two he'll be rich again. Hey, you know what you ought to buy right now, Dick?"

"What?"

"A townhouse in Manhattan. They're dirt cheap. Everyone is convinced New York is going bankrupt, but that'll never happen. I'm telling you, now is the time to buy. I know a guy who picked up a three story house on 52nd Street, right around the corner from St. Patrick's Cathedral for about a hundred and a quarter. He showed me pictures. The place has a double spiral marble staircase in the foyer, huge French Doors and woodwork you can't believe. Used to bring double that, or more. I've got the inside scoop on this. A place like that is gonna be worth a million bucks when the market recovers, maybe five or ten years."

Picking grimaced. "Tell me about it," he said. "My office uptown is a converted apartment which I paid about double what it's now worth."

"Now's the time to be a buyer, I'm telling you."

"Where do I get the money?"

"Sell your house in Jersey. Can you make a profit on that?"

"Probably."

"Do it. You said it's too big anyway. Then sell your office in Manhattan and work from your new home. You can even rent part of it. You'll clean up."

"Leave him alone," Charlotte said. "If it's such a great deal, why don't we buy a townhouse in Manhattan?" She poured syrup over her French Toast.

"I've got a bid in on one as we speak."

"No kidding?" asked Charlotte. "Can we drive past it after breakfast?"

Hunter Davis was a wheeler-dealer. He didn't mention to Charlotte that the townhouse would be purchased by Elvis Presley even though he could use it whenever he came to New York. If it ever got sold, he would tell her the truth. He was in for 20% of the profit instead of a commission.

A short time after breakfast, while his wife was oohing and aahing at some old paintings on exhibit at the Whitney, Davis left a message for Elvis. Picking had found the right couple in New York. Next month they would travel to Beverly Hills together and try to find an alternative to the eccentric plastic surgeon. No need to call back. Elvis would see the dossier in a couple of days.

The secretary at Graceland had no idea what any of this meant.

"Don't worry about it," said Davis. "We're doing someone a favor. Just make sure he gets the message."

Chapter 9

⚜

"SEEK AND YE SHALL FIND"

The chill running down the young wrestler's spine had nothing to do with February weather. He was used to that, running four miles every morning up and down the icy hills of Bergen County. What concerned him was a 5'7" stack of muscle named Pete Brankofsky. Yes, he was the favorite going in, with his 19-0 senior year record and an impressive three years of 66 wins, 4 losses. But at 206, "Brank The Tank" looked worse than mean and nasty, which he was. He looked impossible to pin and Jamie had doubts about being able to lift this human fireplug off his feet and throw him down.

He remembered his dad's words: "When you wrestle, nothing else in the universe exists." It helped his confidence, even during the ritual staredown, and he concentrated on his basic goal: to keep the advantage of balance and speed. Strength, of course, was important in this sport but it wasn't paramount. He had beaten stronger opponents many times. As all good athletes know, but often forget at critical times, control is the key.

All of this philosophy fell by the wayside as his ribs met the right shoulder of Mr. Brankofsky and he tumbled backwards.

"Two points!" yelled the referee. "Takedown."

Luckily, control also involved good habits and Big J's gyrating hips immediately brought him on top of the tightly wrapped mound of flesh.

"Two points, reversal!" screamed Jack Randolph, standing up quickly and bumping into his wife.

"Sit down, Jack. It just started," complained Diane,

shifting her body out of range.

As Jamie dug the balls of his feet into the mat, head squeezed tightly against Brankofsky's left ear, chin buried in a bulging trapezius, he could feel their two heartbeats. His was beating faster. The Tank spread his legs wide apart but with one violent thrust Brankofsky was flat on his face. Error number one for the visitor: Poor balance. Now as he lay on top of this extra thick combatant, Jamie knew he had him. He didn't waste his time and energy trying to turn the wrestler over. That might come later. Instead, he let him up, they assumed the adversarial position and in a split-second Jamie's feint made Pete Brankofsky lunge too soon. Jamie had his opponent's arm bent backwards, and threw the man past him using the wrestler's own momentum to gain another two points.

Once again, he knew by feel that he wouldn't accomplish a turn yet. Instead, he released Brankofsy, then grabbed his left leg and forced him to hop to the line for safety. It was embarrassing to be caught in that position by surprise and the fellow arm-twister wanted revenge. Error number two: Emotion replaces reason.

Jamie let his leg get snatched by Brankofsy, but knowing what was happening, he slipped between his opponent's legs, rotated 180 degrees and used every ounce of power to stand up. No pain, no gain, thought Jamie. The crowd watched in amazement as Brankofsky held Jamie's neck while being lifted into the air on the taller man's back. Without warning, Jamie flung himself and Brankofsky onto their backs, tucking his chin so his head didn't break the other man's teeth. It was the kind of bold original move that made his coach and dad proud, and his mother a basket case.

Between the impact of his back slamming into the floor and Jamie's weight crushing his upper body, Brankofsky got the wind knocked out of him and was easily pinned. Incredibly, he got back to his feet, faked a smile, adjusted his headgear and was ready to continue. However, he had lost any advantage he might have enjoyed at the outset and he lost the match 16-6.

Five months later, as the match was vividly recreated in full color as a dream in the mind of the victor, Jamie Randolph felt exactly as he had at the time. His neck hurt, he was sweating profusely and his breathing was labored. When one eye opened, he discovered that he had nearly taken the life of one of his pillows. Next stop: the shower.

Finding himself alone, Jamie decided that an apple and Cheerios constituted a good breakfast. Dressed for July in shorts and a Grateful Dead tee shirt, he deposited his socks and sneakers by the door, then entered Dad's office. He removed a small notebook facetiously titled "Free Money Checklist" from the bottom desk drawer and opened it to hand-numbered page five. The first four pages had been left blank in case he needed them later on.

Tossing his bare feet up onto the desk top and easing back into Dad's green swivel recliner, Jamie studied his list of things to do:

(1) Call Sawyer at Chemical Bank. Ask to see files.
     Ask who made investment decisions.
(2) Call Mrs. Carrillo. Ask to see files.
(3) Call Charleston for phone numbers of Pickings.
(4) Go to Englewood Hospital. Ask to see files.
(5) Go to Bergen Record. Look up Picking.

Holding his black Pentel Superball pen between his orthodontically aligned teeth, Jamie prepared to make his first call. It was now Friday, and he had been putting this off since at least Monday. He had told himself he needed to think about what he would ask, but partly he had just been lazy. On Tuesday, his friend Steve had talked him into meeting some girls from Michigan visiting next door. On Wednesday, he read half of a book about space travel. The other part of procrastinating had to do with success and failure. If none of these leads panned out, the investigation was over.

He called Thomas Sawyer.

"Chemical Bank. Mr. Sawyer's office. Can I help you?"

"Yes, my name is Jamie Randolph." He sat up. "I was in to see Mr. Sawyer about a trust I inherited about two months ago."

"Please hold." Jamie listened to a recording of current rates. "Mr. Sawyer's office. Who are you holding for?"

"Mr. Sawyer, please. This is Jamie Randolph. I was. . ."

"Oh yes, hold on." It sounded like the hot babe. "Come see us again." It *was* her.

"Tom Sawyer," came the jovial introduction. "Mr. Randolph?"

"No, it's his son," replied Jamie. "I'm calling about the trust money I inherited. I have a question."

"Shoot." Jamie pictured a set of bison horns adorning the hood of Sawyer's Cadillac.

"Well, I'm still interested in finding out who left me the money, even though I don't know exactly how I'm going to do it."

"Good for you. How can I help?"

"Can I see your file on the trust?" the boy asked.

Sawyer hesitated. "No, Jamie, I'm afraid you can't. It's confidential. But I can try to get you information from the file. If you remember, we didn't see any other names."

"I know," he said, "but I was wondering if there were any letters from Mr. Picking that might tell me something. Anything, really."

"Nothing other than transmittal letters. And forms." Sawyer gave his secretary a note to bring him the file.

"You mean, you don't have to know where the money comes from? How do you know if it's legal, like maybe it's stolen or something?"

Sawyer laughed.

"If you're asking me where the money came from, all we know is Mr. Picking remitted by check and filled out all the government forms required. Where he got the money, or why he set up a trust for you, is not our concern. Of course, if anyone had claimed it wasn't legal, we would look into it. But in eighteen years, we never had an inquiry."

"Okay, then who made investment decisions?" Jamie was not ready to drop the matter.

"For the past thirteen years, young man, I did. However, I'll tell you this. Mostly the money stayed in Treasury Bonds. This was a very conservative trust. A small percentage, less than 10%, was in common stocks. If we had been given the discretion to buy more stocks, you'd probably have a lot more than four million dollars. But whoever funded the trust didn't want to lose money. Basically, you earned an average of 8% to 12% a year, nothing very exciting. One or two stocks did very well, though."

"Nobody else ever suggested what to do with the money?"

Sawyer opened the folder and thumbed through the pages.

"Not that I can see. Since we now know that Mr. Picking passed away quite a while ago, it's obvious why *he* never modified the agreement. If anyone else was involved, they never contacted us. Unless they died, too. So we just followed our instructions to contact you in 1995."

Jamie was disappointed, and frustrated.

"And you won't show me the file?"

"Sorry."

"What if I get a court order?" Jamie said, raising his voice.

"That's up to you," responded Sawyer. "But I don't think your Dad is going to do that."

"Why not?"

"Look, son, I know you want to know about the money, but that's not our job. I'd help you if I could, but there's nothing here. If you think we have mismanaged the funds, then by all means sue us in court. Like I said, talk to your Dad first. That's all I can tell you. Have a good day."

Sawyer hung up abruptly. Jamie shut off the phone. He knew that he wasn't going to get any more information from Chemical Bank and suspected he had been a bit rude. Well, like Dad said, you didn't get anywhere without stepping on a few toes. He called Mrs. Carrillo.

Anne Carrillo lived in Oradell. There was another listing for Dr. Gerald Carrillo at the same address. He dialed the first number.

After six rings. "Hello." An elderly voice.

"Hello, my name is Jamie Randolph. I live in Tenafly."

"Who are you?"

Jamie explained to a crotchety Mrs. Carrillo that he was the son of Jack and Diane Randolph and that her husband had delivered him at Englewood Hospital in 1977. He told her that he had just inherited a lot of money and that he was trying to find out who had left it to him. He spoke in a more pleasant, less demanding tone of voice than he had used with Sawyer. When she could control her coughing, the doctor's wife informed him that Dr. Carillo was in a nursing home. She went into great detail about what a fine physician he had been, as well as a good father and how he had loved to play ping-pong. Jamie knew that Alzheimer's disease was not communicable but trying to get to the point was a chore. When he finally asked about the medical files, Mrs. Carrillo began to describe what a mess her basement was. It sounded like there were hundreds of boxes down there. And mice.

"Could I possibly have the phone number of one of your sons or daughters?" Jamie asked cleverly.

Mrs. Carrillo hung up on him. So much for good manners.

Grover, the Randolphs' eleven year old Brown Lab (named for one of Jamie and Olivia's favorite Sesame Street puppets) began barking in the living room. Jamie scurried out of the office to find the old dog's head bobbing from side to side as two squirrels chased each other up and down a tree.

"Relax, Grover." Jamie stroked the back of Grover's thick neck, thicker than his own. Grover barked twice, then turned to lick his master. "That's a good boy. Here, lie down on the rug and I'll play for you." The young man patted his dog's big, round chest.

Jamie sat down at the piano, the beautiful Baldwin piano that had been in the Randolph family for more than half a century — yes, the same piano on which Dad made him play *As Time Goes By* on their anniversary every year — and began to play for his dog. In addition to his athletic ability Jamie had always shown superior musical talent, and the piano had come easily and naturally to him. He had started to play at the age of five or six, the same age at which his voice had begun to stand out at church. He hadn't pursued either seriously since sports was his first love, and his Dad's greatest source of pride.

To his surprise, learning the guitar was a different story. He had owned a guitar since his tenth birthday and he had practiced diligently for eight years. But it had never been like playing the piano. Which was perfectly fine with Grover, who had rolled over on his left side, let out a noisy and sputtery sigh and closed his large hazy eyes. The sound of Jamie's music, a kooky ad-lib blend of Ray Charles, Little Richard and Henry Mancini if such a thing were possible, always put the big Lab to sleep. Jamie was happy to see his friend at peace. He remembered the days of the powerful retriever leaping high into the air to bring down a Frisbee. It didn't seem so long ago that he and his sister had actually ridden on Grover's back, or been dragged across the room by a sock torn between mock snarling teeth. But time flies in a dog's life, and Grover no longer jumped the back yard fence to seek females in heat. Mostly he cared about taking naps now, and one of these dreaded days he wouldn't wake up, or they would have to bring him to the vet to end his pain. Jamie tried to put these morbid thoughts out of his youthful mind and when he was sure his canine pal was in dreamland, he stopped playing.

Before calling Charleston, Jamie called his father.

"You're in my office?" Jack said. "Keep those big clod-hoppers off my desk."

The guy has X-ray vision, thought Jamie. "They're not on your desk, Dad." To make that statement true, Jamie crossed his legs under him.

"So what have we got, Detective Columbo?"

"Well, I'm not exactly sure," said Peter Falk in that slow, slurred voice. Then, changing back to Jamie, "I called that big guy at the bank again."

"Tom Sawyer."

Jamie laughed. "Yeah, Tom Sawyer. He asked me if I wanted to pay four million dollars to paint his fence, but I told him I was busy. Seriously, though, I asked to see his file. . .actually, I told him we could get a court order if he wouldn't cooperate. . ."

"You didn't!" Jamie could tell Dad was miffed. He knew honesty wasn't always the best policy and moved ahead swiftly.

"Anyway, I won't be calling him anymore. Then I called Dr. Carrillo's wife. She sounded pretty old, didn't really know where his files were, told me he's in a nursing home."

Jack Randolph remembered the kindness of the doctor at the time of Jamie's birth.

"What's next? Oh, wait. Did I tell you your Mom and I called all of our cousins on that list?"

"When?"

"Last evening, when you were out with your friends. So far

we've contacted seventeen people and not one of them has inherited any money, or knows any other relative who did, or has any idea who in our family was rich."

"Did you tell them how much we got?" Jamie wondered.

"No, I just said it was a very large figure. I'm sure the whole family is going to be in a feud over this. My second cousin Alvin Edwards hung up on me."

"I know how you feel."

"Jamie, hold on a second." Jack Randolph was handed a note by his secretary. He read it and crushed it up. "You'll find this interesting," he said to his son. "I just heard from a man named John Perryman. He was a very wealthy client I did some work for before you were born. He invented some kind of oil filter that General Motors eventually bought for a lot of money. He was one of about a half dozen clients I helped in the seventies that I thought could have come up with a million dollars. The others couldn't even remember me, and one died."

"What about this guy?" Jamie's eyes lit up.

"He just left a message with Amy that he accidentally misplaced a couple of million dollars in 1977 and if we've found it he wants it back."

"Nerd."

"I guess that means you don't want me to return his call," Jack quipped. "Maybe he needs the money."

"Maybe I need the money. Hey, by the way, where's Mom? She was out when I woke up and didn't leave a note."

"She went shopping at Saks with your sister. This is when they buy Winter clothes."

"Okay, Dad, thanks. I'm going to call Charleston next."

"Great. Let me know if anything develops. Oh, Jamie. I just remembered something. Did you ever see re-runs of a TV show from the fifties called *The Millionaire*?"

"No, why?"

Jack pictured the small black and white television set in his parents' living room. "It was a weekly half-hour program where a billionaire named John Baresford Tipton gave away a million dollars to people who really needed it. People he didn't know."

"Who doesn't need a million dollars?"

"You know what I mean. Deserving people. A family with a child who needs an emergency operation, stuff like that. Anyway, the gift was given anonymously, and no one ever found out where it came from. I think the people had to sign an agreement that they wouldn't look for the benefactor."

At first Jamie didn't make the connection. "I get it, " he said, finally. "You're saying it's possible that this gift was so anonymous we could never find out who it came from."

"Especially since Richard Picking is dead."

"Well then, I guess this will be my last day on the case. See you tonight."

Jamie hoped his words would not be prophetic as he dialed area code 803. While waiting for *Information* to pick up in Charleston, he suddenly thought of a question he forgot to ask Mr. Sawyer. If the original trust officer could still be contacted, maybe that person had been told the name of the anonymous benefactor by Picking in confidence, and maybe it would now be passed on to him. He made a note in his book. Then he jotted down the phone number of the only person in Charleston named Picking: Daniel Picking. The phone rang twice and an answering machine began its spiel.

"You have reached the residence of Dan Picking. No one is here right now, but we'll get back to you. . ."

"I'm here!" shouted Dan Picking. Pause. "Sorry, I was in the bathroom, had to spray."

All right, said Jamie to himself. Now here is a man who is going to tell the truth, the whole truth and too much of the truth.

"Who is it?" asked Dan, buckling his belt.

"Is this Daniel Picking?"

"The one, the only. Who the hell am I talking to?"

"My name is Jamie Randolph. I'm calling from New Jersey."

"I can tell."

Like I can't tell you're from the South, thought Jamie. "Are you related to Richard Picking, the lawyer?"

"I'm his brother," came the reply. "Who are you?"

Jamie could hear country music playing on the radio in Charleston. It sounded like Willie Nelson. As they spoke, Jamie could hear the words of the song clearly: "You were always on my mind." He liked the Elvis version better.

"My Dad knew your brother."

"My brother died in 1978."

"I know. My Dad says he was a very good man," said Jamie diplomatically.

"He was," confirmed Picking's brother. "What do you want?"

From the sound of his voice, Jamie suspected that Daniel Picking had never totally recovered from his brother's death. It was bad enough to lose a loved one, but suicide was always the hardest. Friends and relatives couldn't shake the guilt of not seeing it coming and preventing it. Jamie knew a kid in school whose brother had shot himself. After that, he was never the same.

"When I was born, in 1977, your brother set up a trust account for me. About two months ago when I turned eighteen I got the money."

"Yeah, so?"

"It was a lot of money, and it was anonymous."

Dan Picking was confused. "What do you mean anonymous? Your father and my brother arranged it, right?"

"No, my Dad didn't do it. He didn't even know about it until my birthday this year. And we don't have the slightest idea who would leave me a million dollars. . ."

"*How* much?" Now he had Dan's attention. "What'd you say?"

"Well, my Dad said not to tell anyone but it's a million dollars." At least he hadn't said four million. It suddenly occurred to Jamie that the man in Charleston was not at work on a Friday morning. "How come you're not at work?" asked Jamie.

"Cause I'm a real estate agent. I work when I want to. Listen, Jeremy."

"Jamie."

"Whatever. You're telling me my brother gave you a million dollars? I didn't think he *had* a million dollars. When we settled his estate, which was a giant pain in the ass, I had to put up the money for his grave stone. By the way, he's buried somewhere near you. Paramus, New Jersey?"

"With his wife and son, I assume."

"Whatever." Dan popped a cigarette into his mouth and lit

it with a "Save Willie" lighter he had picked up at a local crafts show. "So how did my brother get all this money and why did he give it to you?"

"That's what I want to know."

Dan began pacing around the room, fanning smoke away from his unshaven face. "And why would you be stupid enough to call me and tell me about it? You know, I've got Dick's will. That money might belong to me. I hope this isn't a sick joke."

"It's not," Jamie said. "If the money's yours, I guess I'm screwed. But I don't think it was your brother's money."

"Give me your phone number," demanded Dan, writing it down. "And your father's number."

By now Jamie had come to the conclusion that this man was disturbed, and would probably be of little help.

"If the money *wasn't* your brother's, whose do you think it might have been?"

"You got me," remarked Dan Picking, who had not worked since he had broken his hip falling off a ladder. His fingertips were stained with nicotine and he smoked his filterless cigarettes until they were too hot to hold. A million dollar windfall was just what he needed, if it was for real. He tried to think of a way to get the kid to fly to Charleston.

"Maybe someone around here knows something," Picking baited him. "I've got some extra time next week. If you want to come to Charleston, I'll introduce you to some people." Then he blew it. "I'll only charge you a hundred bucks."

"Let me think about it." Finally, it was Jamie's turn to hang up.

"Wait!" said Picking. "I just thought of something."

"What's that?"

"My brother was very close with a lawyer from Tennessee he went to college with. Maybe he knows about this."

"What's his name?"

"I don't remember," said Picking. "But I could find out."

"Okay, thanks," said Jamie. "Sorry to bother you," and clicked off.

Well, there's another one down. Unless Daniel Picking really knew the Tennessee lawyer he had mentioned, which was doubtful. In any case, he now had enough motivation to want to know about the money himself, Jamie figured. If he discovered anything, he would call. Off to the hospital.

PART TWO

❧❧❧

The grass was wet, so Jamie sat in the driveway next to his Volvo, putting on his sneakers. Without warning, a red convertible BMW screeched to a tire-wearing halt inches from his bumper. In the front seat with Steve McDermott was a very tanned, very bosomy young lady in a halter top. In the back was her less stunning but still attractive friend.

"Hey, Big J!" announced Mickdee. "Remember Gloria and Jennifer?" The two girls smiled and waved. "I took them to the mall. We're headed for the beach. Hop in!"

Jamie was tempted. After all, his batting average as a private eye was zero and he was not optimistic about the rest of the day. The beach, of course, meant the Jersey shore, which would kill the whole day and beyond.

"Hi, Gloria. Hi, Jennifer." Jamie gripped the side of the car and leaned toward the trio. "I'm sorry," he said. "I'd really like to go with you guys but I have work to do."

"On a day like this?" Steve held his sunglasses and stared directly at the sun. "Don't be a dweeb. Do it tomorrow. Better still, wait for rain." The girls laughed. They had apparently not been chosen for intellect. Not that Jamie was too good for horsing around with Steve and a couple of good looking babes, but he had promised himself he would take care of business.

"I really can't."

"No problem," said Mickdee, shifting into reverse. "We've got a list of eager customers. Better luck next time." He turned up the CD player. "We're outa here!"

"Drive carefully!" Jamie called as the BMW skidded onto Woodland Avenue, made a U-turn and accelerated to fifty. None of the three young vacationers was wearing a seat belt. Steve would put his on when they got to the Garden State Parkway. He had already gotten a warning from the highway patrol. The odds were he would make it to twenty-one, in which case he would almost surely live to meet his grandchildren. If Jamie had decided to go, all four would be belted in their bucket seats, and he would probably be driving.

At Englewood Hospital, Jamie was directed to Medical Records where a well-mannered businesswoman type in a light grey suit named T. Adams handed him a form. In order to see any hospital records, she clarified, the form had to be filled out correctly, signed by his doctor and then reviewed by the hospital administrator. "We'll mail photostats to your doctor once the form is approved," advised Ms. Adams.

"But I just want to read about the day I was born," pleaded Jamie.

"I'm sorry. This isn't a public library," responded T. Adams, who looked like she could *eat* a librarian. Jamie imagined using the same moves on her as he did on Pete Brankofsky.

"But it's my file!" he said to the stoic paper pusher.

"No. It's your mother's file," Adams corrected him, the corners of her lip-glossed lips curling up like a Miniature Schnauzer's.

Jamie was really having trouble getting anyone to cooperate with him today. It was hard to pick a winner but of the four people he had spoken to so far, it was a close tie between Mrs. Carrillo and T. Adams for most annoying. Thinking what his father would do, Jamie heard himself utter "Thank you" and walked away.

As he was deciding between Coke and Pepsi from a vending machine, Jamie felt a pointy finger poke his ribs. He turned to see the pretty face of Donna Rosenberg, a former classmate. Donna was wearing a white uniform with the required name tag. She worked in the hospital.

"Hi, Jamie," she said cutely. "Did you come to see me? Don't answer, I'm kidding. How are you doing?"

"Not so good."

"Why not?" Donna touched the back of Jamie's hand for a second.

Before answering, Jamie thought about what he would say to enlist her help.

"I'm having a problem," he said. "My Mom was in Englewood Hospital in 1977 to give birth to me."

"I was born here, too. Guess we have something in common."

"Guess so." Jamie took Donna's elbow and whispered. "Something happened to my mother in the hospital. My Mom's had a medical problem for a long time and it might have something to do with the anesthesia."

"Your mother had a C-Section?" the girl asked.

"No. It's complicated. The problem is, they won't let us look at her file. We think they might have destroyed it."

"You just talked to Theresa Adams?"

"Yeah, why?"

"Don't expect any help from her. Everyone hates her. What's your mother's first name?"

"Diane."

"Okay," said Donna Rosenberg. "Meet me here in an hour," and she took off down the hall.

Jamie was not hungry yet, so he cruised over to Tenafly High School, passing the parks and playgrounds he visited as a child. He parked his car across the street from the school, lowered two windows and shut off the engine. Large shade trees and an occasional breeze saved him from needing the air conditioning as he sat thinking.

Tenafly held a lot of memories for Jamie Randolph. He saw himself and his little sister on the swings. He pictured Little League games, including one when he slid into home plate and broke his left ankle. He tried to recall who his friends were in sixth grade, whether any were still his friends and whose houses he used to go to after school. He saw the face of a boy named Jimmy Trice, who had moved to Seattle. They used to lift weights together, until Jimmy had tried to get him to smoke pot. He had never used drugs, had no intention of ever using them.

If there was anyone he had *ever* known, ever helped, ever talked to, who was capable of leaving him four million dollars, he couldn't think of that person. He couldn't think of any reason why *anyone*, even if he didn't know who it was, would want to leave him so much money. Everyone in town liked him. His friends, his teachers, storekeepers, the police, his neighbors (except during loud parties) but there was a big difference between liking someone and giving them millions of dollars.

And yet, there it was. *Somebody* had given him the money. Another idea struck him and he opened his notebook. "Look for government forms," he scribbled, referring to the forms Sawyer had told him Picking had filled out. Thank God for forms, he thought, even though he despised them. He had filled out enough forms applying for college to fill a garbage truck, which is where most of them probably ended up. Somewhere, however, Picking's trust forms might still exist, maybe giving a name. Even if Chemical Bank didn't know the name of the benefactor, maybe the U.S. Treasury did. God, that was going to be fun, requesting information from the government. It might take years.

By the time Jamie was done reminiscing and re-analyzing the case of the Randolph inheritance forty minutes had gone by. He drove back to the hospital. Standing nervously in the area where he had spoken to the young lady, he looked around for her. Other than a woman struggling to use the pay phone while holding a little girl's hand there was no one in sight. It was just about an hour. He hoped Donna hadn't gotten into trouble trying to assist him, if that was what she was doing.

Again surprised by the jabbing finger of the charming and peppy Miss Rosenberg, Jamie followed her to an empty lounge. There she handed him a large brown envelope with a chemical odor.

"I made photostats of your mother's file," giggled Donna, making eyes at him. "Now will you marry me, or at least take me to the movies?"

Girls were always like this with Jamie. He certainly didn't mind being found desirable but they acted like they wanted to get too serious. Making a commitment was not on his agenda.

"Let's see," he said. "Marriage or the movies? I guess I'll take you to the movies."

"When?" she asked.

"I'll call you. Donna, listen. This is really important to me."

"That's why I did it. I could lose my job."

"I know. You're great. In fact, you're the only good thing that's happened to me today." Donna flashed a lovely smile.

"But I can't stay here now. I have to see this file right away."

"But it's my lunch break. Can't we grab a sandwich in the cafeteria and talk for like a half hour? I wanted to show you the nursery."

"Where I was born?"

She took his arm and started for the cafeteria, then turned left.

"Well, almost. The whole baby wing has been renovated. All the rooms have changed, it's much nicer now, but it's still the Englewood Hospital nursery. The babies are so adorable. A woman from Bergenfield just had a little boy who weighs over eleven pounds. And there are two sets of twins. Come on, take a quick look. Then we'll eat. You've got time. Come on!"

Unlike Donna, who seemed like she wouldn't mind getting pregnant during her lunch break, Jamie had lots of things on his mind before babies. However, he was curious to see the newborn infants. Maybe he would get a flashback, or a brainstorm, from the experience. It was the least he could do for someone who had just saved him possibly weeks of aggravation.

At the nursery window Jamie found the babies more interesting than he expected. Some lay motionless, sleeping peacefully, some were flailing their tiny arms and legs, their bodies tightly bundled, screaming and hyper-ventilating. Handwritten cards taped to their see-through containers identified the children by name, date of birth and weight. Jamie found it weird to imagine these helpless little people as adults, or even as toddlers. One young couple proudly pointed out their new son to him.

"Oh, there's the big one," said Donna. "And the twins."

Jamie found himself mesmerized by the twins. While many of the newborns looked alike at a glance, twins really were alike. And would stay that way. "Are they identical?" he asked.

"Both pairs."

"Awesome!"

"Really."

"Okay, I'm hungry." The cute couple shared a grilled cheese sandwich and fries.

After lunch, Jamie drove to the newspaper building about

fifteen minutes away. There he was directed to the morgue where a middle-aged bookworm type sat at a microfilm machine. He looked up, refocusing his eyes.

"Can I help you?" asked the guardian of the printed word.

"I hope so." Jamie popped two Tic Tacs into his mouth. "I'm trying to get whatever information you have on a lawyer named Richard Picking."

Jamie wasn't sure if he was in the right place. After all, once again this was not the library.

"Spell it," said the man. Jamie's luck was improving.

"Picking. P-I-C-K-I-N-G. Richard Picking. He lived in Alpine. He died in 1978."

When the file manager stood up, Jamie made him shake hands. "My name is Jamie," he said. "This would really help me out."

"Bob Otterson. Let me get to my computer."

Jamie followed the man around some large oak library tables past several sizable accumulations of newspapers. The papers were arranged neatly on tall frame metal shelves.

"I didn't know you stored newspapers," Jamie commented.

"It's only temporary. Once they're put on disk we dump them."

"Oh."

When Otterson reached his desk in the center of the room, he began typing fiendishly on his terminal. "This is going to take about ten minutes," he advised the young man. "Why don't you sit down?"

Jamie parked himself on the hard maroon cushion of an old wooden chair. He crossed his right leg over his left and balanced the envelope on his calf. Removing the scotch tape, he pulled out a pack of hospital forms and began to sift through them. Some of the writing was hard to decipher: doctor-ese. He didn't really know what he was looking for as he worked his way from top to bottom. A typewritten letter from Richard Picking stared at him. It was dated July 27, 1976. *It read:*

This is to confirm that my clients, Mr. and Mrs. J. Randolph, will be utilizing the facilities of Englewood Hospital from August 17, 1976 to August 21, 1976

*for the following purposes: (1) To conduct exploratory
surgery on Mrs. Diane Randolph in the hope of
determining and correcting certain reproductive
problems diagnosed by Dr. Gerald Carrillo; and (2)
To effect an artificial insemination of Mrs. Randolph
with her husband's sperm if Dr. Carrillo deems
appropriate and safe.*

*Enclosed please find completed forms and
medical backup to protect the Hospital and its
employees in the event that any serious complica-
tions arise, or should Mrs. Randolph die during
these procedures.*

After reading the letter twice, it struck Jamie as odd that
it would be an attorney, rather than the family doctor, to make
arrangements for surgery. Obviously, as he knew, what was
considered to be routine surgery was in truth anything but.
From what he had studied about in-vitro in biology, he
guessed that the "corrective" procedure was secretly the
harvesting of eggs. Since the Randolphs did not want the
hospital to know about this, the best thing to do would be to
use only Dr. Carrillo's medical staff. If so, the hospital would
want a release from full responsibility due to the absence of
hospital supervision. In essence, this was what Mom and Dad
had told him that night in May. Here was the proof.

Further verification that outside people had been used
exclusively was a report and invoice from an anesthesiologist
from Chicago. Why else hadn't they used someone local?

There was not much more of value. Blood and urine tests,
lists of prescribed medications, hospital bills, the phone bill.
The phone bill? Maybe a call had been made, knowingly or
not, to the mystery person. Jamie began to review the calls.
There were over sixty calls made in a few days, mostly, he
assumed, business calls made by his father who had stayed
with his wife during the ordeal. He didn't recognize any of the
phone numbers or destinations. They might be worth checking
out tonight with Mom and Dad.

"I've got two stories on Richard Picking," said the morgue-
keeper. "How far back did you want to go?"

"I don't know. When are they from?"

"1974 and 1978. Do you want to know the captions?"

"Sure." Jamie crossed his fingers.

"The 1978 story is called *Bankrupt Attorney, 48, Kills Self.*"

"And the other one?"

Bob Otterson looked at Jamie. "This is funny," he said. "The other story is *Alpine Lawyer Parties With Elvis.*"

"Come again." A phrase his Dad used frequently.

"That's what it says," repeated Otterson. "Lawyer Parties With Elvis."

"Is that a joke?"

"I don't know, son. We'll have to fish out the hard copy."

Jamie followed the man back to his microfilm machine. On the way, Otterson explained that older material would remain on film indefinitely. It was too costly to transfer everything to digital.

It took a few minutes for Otterson to locate the old reels and find the stories in question. Jamie observed patiently, waiting for the process to be complete. While he was reading a printout of the suicide story, Otterson handed him the earlier one. Yes, indeed, it seems that our never-to-be-famous friend and attorney, Richard Picking, did manage to get his Warholian fifteen minutes. For there he was on Page 3 of The Bergen Record (not Page 1 but certainly not Page 36) at Elvis Presley's home, "Graceland," in Memphis Tennessee, just one person removed from direct physical contact with The King! It was April, 1974, at a college reunion, Picking surrounded by a rather large group of stuffy forty-something lawyers. To the left of Picking was a tall, husky man with light hair, his arm draped around Picking's shoulders. And to the left of that man (identified as Hunter Davis) was Mr. Jailhouse Rock himself, Elvis Aron Presley, his arm around Mr. Davis' shoulders.

"I also found a 1971 story on a Patricia Picking," Otterson noted . "I can retrieve that one for you if you want. It's called *Mother And Son, 2, Die In Collision.* Do you want it?"

"That was his wife," said Jamie. "I heard about the accident. Yes, I'd like to see that one also."

Just for kicks, Jamie looked over the hospital phone bill again. Maybe there *was* a call to Memphis! Maybe this Davis guy knew something. After all, if he had managed to get his photo taken with Elvis, and if he happened to know Richard Picking. . .Oh my God! There was a call to Memphis.

Jamie could hardly wait to get home and try calling the number. He did not realize that the call had been made nineteen years earlier and that it might not be traceable. He did thank Bob Otterson profusely for his help and waited for a copy of the last article.

"You're a big guy, aren't you?" the diminutive man asked rhetorically. "And you know, you actually do look a little like Elvis."

"Everybody tells me that. My Dad looks like him, too."

"Okay, here it is. Good luck."

Jamie smiled, saluted and hustled out to his car, very excited.

Twenty minutes later he pressed "Talk" and dialed the Memphis number. A lady's voice answered: "Law offices. How may I direct your call?"

This was too good to be true. "Hunter Davis, please," he replied.

"Hold on."

More country music. He seemed to be listening to a lot of it on the phone these days.

"Mr. Davis' secretary. Mr. Davis is in conference. May I help you?"

Was this really the same person in the news photo? Did this Hunter Davis know Richard Picking? Jamie started to speak in a cracking high-pitched voice, cleared his throat and said: "Yes, I'd like to speak to Mr. Davis about an article about him in The Bergen Record. In New Jersey."

"What is this in reference to?"

"It's confidential," Jamie said. "Please ask him to call collect."

Ten minutes later the phone rang. It was Hunter Davis. He did not reverse the charges.

"Jamie Randolph, please." There was something strange about the voice.

"This is Jamie Randolph."

"Mr. Randolph, I understand you wish to discuss a confidential matter with me?"

"Yes." Jamie tried to picture the man on the phone. He

didn't sound like he was sixty years old. "I recently inherited a large sum of money, over a million dollars, from a trust set up for me in 1977 by Richard Picking."

Silence. "Hello?" Davis said. "I'm waiting. What does this matter have to do with me?"

"You don't know Richard Picking?"

"No. I don't. Who is Richard Picking?"

"That's very interesting, Mr. Davis. You don't know Richard Picking, but I'm looking at a picture of you with your arm on his shoulder at Elvis Presley's house. In 1974."

"In 1974?" Davis laughed. "You mean, when I was eleven?"

"You were only eleven years old in 1974? But how could you. . ."

Davis cleared up the confusion. "I know the picture you're referring to, Mr. Randolph. The Duke reunion. I've got an original photo at home. The man you're inquiring about isn't me. It's my father."

Jamie shrugged off his embarrassment, or his stupidity. "Can I speak to your father?" he asked.

"My father died sixteen years ago."

Oh, boy. More bad news. "Shit."

"Would you like to explain to me, Mr. Randolph, why you just said 'shit' when I told you my father is dead?"

Jamie apologized. "Got a minute?"

As a very busy attorney who had taken over his father's practice with the help of his mother and his Uncle Phil, Hunter Davis Jr. answered honestly: "That's about all the spare time I've got today."

"Okay, I'll make it quick. Somebody left me a lot of money. The inheritance is anonymous, which means that I have no one to ask about the money."

"Except Richard Picking," said Davis.

"He died in 1978. Committed suicide."

"I see. And you think my father knew who gave Mr. Picking the money?

"I don't have any idea," Jamie confided. "So I'm asking you. Could you find out if your father knew Richard Picking? Are there any old files you could go through?"

Hunter Davis looked at his workload. He had to be in court

tomorrow at 9:00 AM. He had a deposition scheduled in his office in a half hour. And he had to re-write a nine page Answer in a messy divorce case. There was more.

"Send me a letter," he said. "I'll consider your request."

"You don't believe me."

"It's not that. I'm really busy," Davis explained. "A lot of people with serious problems pay me to help them. I'm not sure I have time to look for files. Besides which. . ." Davis knew that all of his father's records were in his home file cabinet. ". . .there is no reason to believe my father did business with this Mr. Picking. What does one picture prove?"

Jamie was stumped. "Maybe nothing. But I'll tell you this. Someone dialed this phone number, *your* number, from my mother's hospital room in New Jersey *in 1976*. My mother was in the hospital for surgery, arranged once again by Mr. Picking, not her doctor. I say Richard Picking called your father. That was almost a year before I was born." Jamie changed course. "How about your mother?" he inquired. "Can I talk to *her* about this?"

Hunter Davis covered the phone with his hand and whispered to his secretary, "I'll be off in a second." Then to Jamie: "I'd rather you don't talk to my mother. She's gets very upset if anyone asks about my father. Please, Mr. Randolph, I'll try to help you if you write to me. I give you my word."

After they hung up, Jamie called his father's travel agent. He was not about to give up his first and only lead in the case. It was just a two hour flight to Memphis.

Chapter Ten

❦

"THE LORD'S PATH"

A close encounter of the third kind.

Cruising above the smoky white clouds at 540 miles per hour, Jamie couldn't get it off his mind. Isolated somewhere over the Blue Ridge Mountains, invisible from the ground 31,000 feet below, this was a perfect opportunity for "them" to examine a varied cross-section of over two hundred humans. Of course, all of the passengers would have to be brainwashed into believing they had experienced a mass hallucination. And the film in their cameras destroyed. He could hear the familiar voice of Robert Stack narrating the Sunday Night Special: "Did it really happen? A plane enroute from New York to Memphis, the one-time home of Elvis Presley, mysteriously disappears for six hours. Hundreds of people swear they were abducted by aliens, including an honor student from New Jersey. But not one photograph or video exists to prove the story. Now let's listen to some first hand accounts of this — possible — interface with outer space."

When Jamie felt the tiny hand moving around under his rear end he literally jumped out of his seat. He turned to find a very frightened little boy who squeezed past the coffee cart and ran to his mother.

"I was just looking for my Power Ranger missile," he said. "That man was going to hit me!"

The woman stretched her neck to make eye contact with Jamie over the obstruction in the aisle.

"I'm sorry. He's got a vivid imagination."

"So do I," Jamie replied, readjusting himself into his seat.

Back to reality. The clouds were thinning and in ten or fifteen minutes American Flight 262 would begin its descent. It was becoming increasingly unlikely that they would be hijacked by an 1,800-MPH UFO this morning.

Actually, as far as Charlotte Davis was concerned, Jamie Randolph himself was an unidentified flying object headed directly toward her. At first, Jack and Diane Randolph were not sure they could agree with Jamie's strategy of a surprise visit. After a long discussion, they finally gave their approval, at which point their resourceful son informed them that he had already booked a round trip.

Jamie had called the Davis residence the day before leaving. He was told by the housekeeper that yes, Mrs. Davis would be home tomorrow to receive the flowers Jamie wanted to deliver. That part was true, as was the statement that the flowers were from a stranger. Mrs. Davis might not come to the door, the person advised, but she would be there.

Once he was at the house handing someone a beautiful bouquet, Jamie figured he could charm his way in. That theory was about to be tested as the taxi drove off, leaving him standing on Old Poplar Pike at the foot of a hill leading up to a mansion. There were two pairs of cut stone columns at both ends of the winding circular driveway. On the one closest to him was a bronze plaque with the name "Magnolias" in relief in script. The property, much larger than his parents' yard, was entirely surrounded by a fence made of tall black twisted wrought iron spears. Where the fence met a column, there was a small square mail drop. Each pair of columns was connected by a locked double gate. Jamie looked up to see at least two cameras in the trees (had Jack Randolph designed this?) and then noticed signs on the fence. One gave the name of an alarm company, the other said "Beware Of Dog." Getting to the front door of this house was not going to be easy.

Eventually, Jamie noticed a black speaker-phone protruding from a rhododendron on the right side of the driveway. He walked across the cobblestones, held the flowers behind him like a suitor about to meet his blind date, and pressed the button. He waited.

"Yes, who is it?" came the garbled voice of someone uphill.

"Flower delivery," Jamie answered.

"Where's your truck?"

"What?" Jamie looked around, realizing quickly that he was being watched on a TV monitor. "Oh. My truck? They dropped me off while they're making another delivery. I called on the phone yesterday."

"Who did you speak to?"

"You, I guess. Don't you remember? I asked if Mrs. Davis was going to be home."

There was a long silence, during which Jamie became very nervous. Up to now, he had been confident, a recently appointed millionaire on a jaunt to Memphis to track down the truth. But really, he was just a big kid from New Jersey standing by himself, uninvited, outside the home of some very rich lady who had no idea who he was. And whose son was a lawyer. Was she calling the police? Was she about to set the dog on him? He considered running away. That was stupid. Where would he go?

"This is Mrs. Davis," the voice said, to his relief. "You obviously spoke to Marna yesterday. She got sick. Wait there."

About two minutes went by. A very attractive lady in her fifties or sixties was coming down the long driveway, passing dozens of no longer flowering Magnolia trees. At her side were two large Rottweilers, twin brothers of the killer dog from *The Omen*. Charlotte Davis was wearing a pair of white Liz Claiborne slacks and a solid yellow tailored shirt with matching slip-ons. Compared to Jamie, she was dressed to the hilt.

"Are the flowers for me?" she asked. "Who sent them?"

Extending his arm through the gate far enough to give her the pink and white roses, but not within biting distance of the dark brown beasts, he answered: "I sent them."

Charlotte looked at the roses, smelled their fragrance, and considered this handsome young man in jeans and a Duke tee shirt. He was built like her husband, muscular in all the right places, a little shorter than Hunter, not quite as broad.

"*You* sent them?" She was curious. "Do you attend Duke?"

"No. I picked this shirt up at the airport."

"Are you asking me for a date?" she said with a straight

face. Jamie blushed, caught himself and replied politely, "Maybe."

The two dogs were pacing back and forth, not growling, but Jamie didn't trust them. He was not anxious to be inside the gate, yet that was still his plan. "Do they bite?" he asked, like a jerk.

"Only if I tell them to. Sit, boys!"

Like trained marines, the killers came to canine attention.

"My name is Jamie Randolph. I'm from New Jersey. I came to Memphis to see you. I spoke to your son and he told me not to bother you."

"You came to see me? Do we know each other?"

Jamie looked at her face. In the moving shadows of the rustling oak branches any serious wrinkles were hidden. Whatever her skin was like in brighter light, the woman looked great for her age. She must have been *dynamite* twenty years ago.

"No. This is the first time I've ever seen you."

"Then why did you bring me flowers?"

"Because I need your help."

"With what?"

"It's a long story," Jamie began. "I'd really like to talk to you in the house. It's pretty hot out here. I think you'll be safe with your little buddies there." Charlotte found him amusing.

"Tell me more," she said, her eyes widening.

"Okay. Basically, I just inherited some money, a lot of money, over a million dollars in fact. But I don't know who left it to me." The young man looked up to catch a glimpse of a plane flying by.

"That's interesting, if it's true. I don't know who left it to you either." She shifted her weight to one leg for better balance. Her green eyes were beautiful.

"But you might have a clue."

"Oh, really? Well, it wasn't me. Or if it was, I want it back."

Jamie laughed. "Everybody thinks I'm kidding, but I'm not."

"Let me see some identification," said Charlotte.

Jamie moved his left arm backwards for his wallet. The dogs stood up without command. One jumped on the gate, his jaws at neck level.

"Sit!" They retreated.

"Here." Jamie gave Mrs. Davis his New Jersey driver's license.

"Tenafly, New Jersey. That sounds familiar. Where is it?"

"About five miles from the George Washington Bridge."

She returned his license.

"All right, Jamie R. Randolph, now tell me why you think I know about your inheritance."

"Can we go inside? I'm dying." Beads of perspiration dotted his forehead.

"No, but we can sit out on the veranda in the back yard. I've got some fresh lemonade. Would you like a glass?"

Jamie nodded. Mrs. Davis activated a keypad on the inside of the gate and both doors opened slowly. "Follow me." The dogs trotted alongside Mrs. Davis, nipping at each other playfully. Jamie stayed on her other side.

"This house was constructed in 1928," Charlotte informed him. "My husband's father built it for his second wife. It's an exact reproduction of a Charleston plantation house. Some of the magnolias are old, most have been replaced. They're beautiful in bloom, in April or May."

As they approached the house, it got even bigger. The exterior was painted pale pink with white trim, and every window was bordered with large black shutters. Mrs. Davis led him around the right side of the house, which featured a four car garage and several rooms that were not part of the main structure. Around back, the visitor from New Jersey felt like he had been transported back in time. There was no pool or tennis court like most newer homes of this magnitude. Instead, wooden swings suspended from giant tree limbs, a croquet court, a carriage house, a pond and an enormous veranda.

All of the furniture was antique green or white wicker, including more than a dozen large chairs, several rockers, two day beds and four tables. Jamie could picture the governor of Tennessee sipping lemonade on the Davis porch. Or gulping down shot glasses of Jack Daniels. He could picture himself *dead* on the Davis veranda, torn to pieces by the manic-depressive Rottweilers, while Mrs. Davis fetched the lemonade, and put her roses in a vase. The guest sat down as requested, selecting a chair with its back against the house. At least the dogs would have to come at him in full view. At least he could guard his neck. He felt better when they darted down the steps, leapt across some rocks and chased each other around the pond. Kicking up turf as they ran, halted, bit and ran again, Jamie admired their powerful physiques and acknowledged that they could effortlessly outrun him. He could never score two points wrestling either of them, and attempting to pin their massive shoulders was out of the question!

Mrs. Davis returned with a tray holding a light green Depression Glass lemonade set, a pitcher and four glasses. Jamie was glad to see her.

"Where are you staying?" she asked.

"Days Inn. Over by Graceland."

"The place with the swimming pool shaped like a guitar?"

"That's it. And 24-hour Elvis movies in every room."

"You're joking. How tacky." Charlotte filled two glasses. He didn't ask why there were two more.

"You might think all this Elvis stuff is tacky, but I was reading those Graceland brochures. Did you know over 650,000 people a year visit Elvis' home? The only private residence seen by more people is The White House."

Charlotte grimaced. "Don't tell me about Elvis Presley," she whined. "We hear too much about him already. I guess you know they opened up his kitchen to the public for the first time in March."

"Yeah, I saw it on Entertainment Tonight."

"Terrific. Now people can actually see where Mary Jenkins made his fried peanut butter and banana sandwiches."

"I guess you didn't like Elvis," Jamie suggested.

Charlotte recalled Elvis and Hunter skimming stones across the pond and eating cheeseburgers.

"I loved his music. Him, I wasn't too crazy about." They both sipped their ice cold drinks. "But I guess I shouldn't be too hard on Elvis. After all, he grew up dirt poor, which would explain his atrocious decorating. Did you ever see his hideous

Jungle Room? Or his pool room? My God. But he did love his mother, God rest her soul. And I honestly believe he wanted to be a good father to that beautiful little girl who married Michael Jackson." She shook her head. "Michael Jackson. Can you believe it? Oh well, that's the price you pay for fame."

"I talked to your son, Mrs. Davis. Is he your only child?"

Charlotte crossed her long legs and gazed into the boy's fascinating, sexy eyes.

"No, Jamie. I have two wonderful daughters. They're a few years younger than Hunter and they live in Memphis, too. Enough about me and Elvis. Let's get back to you. Why did you speak to Hunter?"

Jamie knew this next part was going to be tricky. He wanted to find out about Richard Picking but he was afraid to come right out and say that name. What if he was a taboo subject? The conversation might be over.

"I found this picture in a New Jersey newspaper." He showed Charlotte the story about the Duke reunion at Graceland. The headline was folded back.

"Wasn't that picture taken before you were born?" she asked.

"It was. Three years before." Jamie took in some extra breath. "That is your husband standing right next to Elvis, isn't it?"

"It certainly is," she answered. "I have an original of that photo hanging in my husband's office. I was there in 1974. Of course, no one wanted me in the picture since I didn't go to Duke." She stared at the young man's Duke shirt. So that's why he bought it, to impress her. "And next to Hunter was his good friend Richard Picking, who flew down from New York for the party."

She'd said it first. "Richard Picking was my family's attorney," he revealed.

Charlotte caught on. "Oh, really," she said. "So that's the connection."

"That's right," Jamie confirmed, pulling his chair closer. "It seems that in 1977, the year I was born, Richard Picking set up a trust for me. Since Picking was sort of broke, and since I don't think I'm related to him in any way, my parents and I believe he represented an anonymous client."

Charlotte looked around. She thought she heard a car door slam. The dogs' ears perked up.

"And you think my husband was that client? You think Hunter Davis left you a million dollars? No way, José!" Suddenly her demeanor changed. "Why do you think he would do that? Because you're secretly his son?"

Jamie felt very uncomfortable. Somehow he had managed to be offensive.

"I'm *not* his son. I'm *not adopted.* My parents are Jack and Diane Randolph. I was born in Englewood Hospital in New Jersey," he protested. "If I've said something wrong . . ."

Charlotte calmed down. "Oh," she said. "For a minute there I thought we were going to have a problem. Then what do you want from me?"

The dogs took off like torpedoes as the real son of Hunter and Charlotte Davis came around the corner of the house. Hunter, Jr., looking very agitated, pushed away the two face-licking killers without breaking his stride. He was wearing a grey pin-striped suit with a light blue shirt, no tie. Sweat dripped from his collar. He looked a lot like his father, except much slimmer, and he had inherited someone else's pattern baldness genes.

"I thought we agreed that you would write to me!" Davis shouted at Jamie. He put down his pocket phone, kissed his mother on the cheek and poured himself some lemonade. "I thought I asked you nicely not to bother my mother."

"It's a free country," said the eighteen-year-old.

"It's a free country? Would you like me to call the police and find out if they think trespassing is legal in a free country?" The overheated attorney guzzled down the full glass. "I want you out of here. Now!"

"Sit down, Hunter. I'm perfectly okay," said his mother.

"Where's Marna?" asked the lanky six-footer.

"She's not feeling well. Hunter, relax. I'm fine. I just called you so you would know what was going on. I didn't ask you to leave the office. I know how busy you are. And it's so hot today. Here, drink some more."

"If I'm trespassing, how come the dogs didn't attack me?"

asked Jamie.

"Don't antagonize him. Hunter, he's only a boy. Look at him. I know he's a big fellow, but he's no match for Amos 'n Andy."

You can say that again, thought Jamie.

"Let's go," Davis said, shaking the back of Jamie's chair.

"Hunter, stop it. Let him finish. He came here to ask me something and he might as well get it out before he goes home."

Jamie tried to think of the most important single question he could ask Charlotte Davis, in case it was his last.

"My mother had a special operation in 1976 in order to get pregnant," he told her. "The surgery was arranged by Richard Picking, who was at the hospital when it was performed. Richard Picking called your husband from my mother's room in the hospital. Can you tell me, or could there possibly be a file on Richard Picking that would explain why he would make that phone call?"

Charlotte Davis knew there had never been a file on Richard Picking, before or after Hunter's untimely death. She also knew that her husband's arrangements with Picking involving interstate adoptions had been strictly confidential. Whether any of it had been illegal she didn't know or care. It was all in the past now, where it belonged. There was no use bringing it up just to satisfy this boy's curiosity. He had admitted he was not adopted, which meant he knew who his parents were. All he was interested in was the name of the person who had left him a lot of money. Since that wasn't really a problem, why delve into matters that could only complicate her life? Why get her son any more upset than he already was?

"I'm afraid I can't help you," she said. "I hardly knew Richard Picking and like I said, he was only an old friend. As far as I know, Hunter did not do business with him. There isn't any file, that's for sure."

"How would you know that?" asked Jamie the detective. "You've looked for a file on Richard Picking?"

Hunter Jr. came to her defense like a Rottweiler. "*I've* looked for that file," he interjected. "Okay, Mr. Randolph, it's time for us to leave. I don't see a car, so I guess I'll drop you off wherever you're staying."

"Just take my phone number." Jamie handed Mrs. Davis his father's business card. It had his own number written in pen. "I appreciate your seeing me, Mrs. Davis, I really do. I'm sorry if I disturbed you." The aggressive Hunter, Jr. had his elbow.

"You didn't disturb me," she said. "I'm sorry I couldn't help you. Just be grateful for the money. Somebody must have cared about you."

"I wish I knew who," Jamie commented, wishing he could have stayed longer.

"Okay, good luck," said Charlotte. "Maybe you'll get your answer someday. I hope so. It was nice meeting you. Hunter, you'd better get going. It's getting a little cloudy. Drive carefully. I'll see you for dinner on Friday. I miss my little grandchildren. Tell them grandma has chocolate for them."

"Just what they need. All right, mother, take care." Jamie pulled his arm free.

On the way back to the motel, Hunter Davis apologized for his behavior. The air-conditioned Cadillac had cooled him down in more ways than one and he offered Jamie a deal.

"I really don't want you asking my mother any more questions," he said, politely but firmly.

"I don't plan to." It had begun to rain.

"I mean it," Davis said. "If you promise me that you will never call her again, I'll give you a name."

"Whose name?"

"The name of someone, a lawyer, who worked very closely with my father in the 1970's. He's still a lawyer in town, and he might have known this Richard Picking you keep asking about. No guarantees."

"Who is it? I promise." Maybe it wasn't the end of the line yet.

"The reason I don't want you talking to my mother has to do with my father's death," Davis explained, changing the wiper from intermittent to normal.

"But it was sixteen years ago."

"You're going to find this out sooner or later, nosy as you

are. My father did not die of natural causes." The Cadillac hit a pothole. "Damn," said Davis.

"He was killed in an accident?"

"He was murdered. In our house. In his office."

"Oh my God!" This was definitely not the end of the line.

"The police said it was a robbery. Money was missing from my father's safe. But the way he was shot." Hunter paused. It hurt him to talk about it, too. "I was only sixteen. I never saw the body. Except at the funeral. I wasn't even home when it happened. But I know everything."

"Oh my God. I didn't know. No one told me. I'm really sorry. Jeez, I didn't mean to get your mother upset. Really."

"It's okay. You didn't get her upset. Yet."

Jamie noticed a sign on the side of the road: *Visit Graceland.*

"I won't talk to her anymore."

"Thank you."

Jamie couldn't help asking Davis about his father. "You said your father was murdered. How do you know?"

"Because he was shot three times. Twice in the head. That's not just a robbery."

"They never found the guy who . . .?"

Davis jammed a stick of gum in his mouth, offered one to Jamie, who declined.

"Well, they picked up this guy. Gregory. My father had investigated an illegal business matter that put him in jail. Supposedly, he wanted to get back at my father. But the police didn't have enough evidence. Then the guy left town, he disappeared. They never found out who did it, or why. There was this lady detective who kept calling us for awhile, she was trying to help, but they pulled her off the case. End of story. I don't know, I've been tempted to re-open the investigation myself, but I think it would only harm my mother. I think the police were incompetent, but look, it's been so many years, my father is dead, we're not going to bring him back. You know what I mean?"

Jamie understood. "I know it's not the same thing," he said. "But if I don't make every effort to find out who gave me all this money now, then I think someday, I'm going to wish I did."

"You're not wrong," Davis agreed, turning onto Elvis Presley Boulevard. "The lawyer's name is John Porter. I'll call him right now, tell him you want to see him. He does licensing and claims work for the Presley estate. He knows me, and he knew my father. Hang on." Davis pressed Autodial. "Ginger? Hi, it's Hunter, I'm in my car. Is John there? No. Where is he?" He held on. "He's where? Oh great, we're right in the neighborhood. Can you call him for me? Yes, tell him I'm sending someone over to see him. Write this down. The young man's name is Jamie Randolph. He wants to talk to John about a legal matter involving a large sum of money. This has to do with my father." He held again. "No, I can't come with him. Ask John to call me later. Thanks."

"Where am I going?" asked Jamie.

"I'm dropping you off at Graceland. John Porter is there now. His secretary is telling him to expect you. I've got to get back to my office for a conference or I'd go with you. Call me later."

For the second time in as many hours, Jamie Randolph found himself standing in the street in front of a mansion in Memphis wondering if he should run away. It had stopped raining. He decided to find John Porter.

At the same time, Charlotte Davis sat at her husband's desk in the very office where he had been murdered while she played cards. She had her head in her hands and was crying. She still missed him as much as the day he died. Even with the fences, the alarms and the killer dogs, she was still frightened. She would never remarry. She would never sleep the way she used to. And she had absolutely no inkling of whether or not to give Jamie Randolph the safe deposit key. The key she had found taped under Hunter's upstairs desk drawer in 1990. The key in the red cardboard envelope imprinted "Merchant's Bank Of Memphis." The envelope marked in black ink, in her husband's handwriting: "J. Randolph 5/13/77." The same date on the driver's license she had just seen.

Chapter 11

"A VISIT TO THE HOLY LAND"

"This lawyer is at the gates of heaven, trying to get in," the joke began. For John Porter, spending the day at Graceland with his staff was more fun than work.

"We heard that one already," said the girl making photostats.

"I didn't hear it, Marsha," said the other lawyer.

"Thanks," said Porter, sitting with a leg draped over the corner of Vernon Presley's desk, his left hand holding his right wrist. "It's funny even if you heard it before. Plus, it's not polite to tell someone you heard their joke, especially when that person is your boss's boss."

"That's right, Marsha," confirmed the claims assistant, his eyes glued to the secretary's exquisitely rounded derriere. She wore a slightly snug flared charcoal pants suit, which clearly defined both cheeks and her panties when she bent over. Porter's eyes were in the same place, neither man having any interest in assisting the girl juggling an armful of fourteen inch legal documents at the copy machine.

"Okay, tell the joke. I'll pretend like I never heard it."

The intercom buzzed. Porter lifted the receiver, still watching Marsha's ass. It was hard to find competent help these days, harder to keep girls with good figures who didn't mind mild sexual harassment. Porter was informed that the young man referred to him by Hunter Davis was being escorted to the office. Normally, he would be downtown in his own building but this was his monthly quality control inspection.

"This lawyer is trying to get into heaven," he repeated at a faster pace. "And Saint Peter says to him, we don't let lawyers in unless they're honest. How old are you?" Porter started laughing at his own joke. "I'm sixty-three, the lawyer answered. Are you sure? said Saint Peter. Yeah, I'm sure, the guy goes. Okay, sixty-three and a half. Is that better? Afraid not, says Saint Peter. According to these papers, you're a hundred and forty-six. But I was born in 1932, the lawyer says. Don't you have my birth certificate? No, Saint Peter says. We went by your time sheets!"

Had the punch line not been funny Porter's assistant would have laughed anyway. But he really thought it was humorous.

"I've got one," said Marsha, removing staples with her fingernails. A uniformed guard leaned through the doorway and knocked on the jamb.

"Got a Jamie Randolph here."

"Thanks, Ed. You can go."

The girl making copies looked over her shoulder, did a double-take.

"Wow, this guy looks like Elvis!" she remarked, dropping some papers.

"Everybody looks like Elvis," observed Porter. The boy from New Jersey took two steps into the room, waited for directions. The senior attorney wriggled off Vernon's desk and approached him. Jamie noticed that the two men were wearing identical wing tip shoes.

"John Porter," he said, shaking hands. What a grip this kid had.

"Jamie Randolph. Mr. Davis said I could talk to you."

"About your inheritance?" queried the lawyer. The other two had stopped what they were doing to see what the kid wanted.

"Oh, Mr. Davis' secretary told you about me?"

"No, I just figured if you're here about a large sum of money, and you look the way you look, you're another heir to the throne."

Jamie was puzzled. "I'm here to ask you about Mr. Davis' father," he explained. "And a lawyer from New York that he

127

knew named Richard Picking."

"I suppose you're not going to tell me you're Elvis Presley's long lost son? Because if you are, let me clarify the position of the Presley estate. Elvis Presley had only one child, Lisa Marie. Books have been written about people who claim to be the son or daughter of Elvis, but I can assure you that not one person has ever extorted a penny from the estate. And as long as I'm around, they never will."

"That's not what I want," said Jamie. "When you mentioned my inheritance, I thought you knew."

"Knew what?" The faces of the assistant lawyer and his secretary echoed the question.

"Knew that I just inherited a million dollars."

"Is this a joke? That dirty . . . " Porter asked. "Did Hunter Davis put you up to this?"

"No, I'm serious," Jamie insisted. A couple of months ago, on my eighteenth birthday, I received an anonymous gift, arranged by Richard Picking, in 1977, the year I was born."

"The year Elvis died," Marsha muttered. Porter gave her a stern gaze.

"And I'd like to know who left me the money." Jamie's eyes scanned the room quickly. He had a feeling of Dejá Vu as he looked over the 1970's decor. Had he been here in a previous life? Had aliens brought him here? Maybe he needed to take a nap.

"Paul," said the older man. "You and Marsha finish up here. I'm going to walk this pleasant young man outside." He put his arm gently around Jamie's big shoulders and guided him away from the office. "Jamie, you seem like a very honest, bright young man, and since you were sent to me by a friend, I will try to help you. But don't bullshit me. If you're looking for money, don't tell me this is about something else."

"I'm not." Jamie felt himself leaving the premises. Lawyers in Memphis were very good at that.

"And if you really think you're Elvis Presley's son, I suggest you look up some back issues of The Enquirer. They've done stories about people like that for years. They probably know more about Elvis Presley than I do. And I know quite a bit, since I've been here for fifteen years and I've watched this place grow. Do you know, we have over 650,000 visitors a year at Graceland, and we license Elvis' name, and products with his picture on them, around the world? This is a big business, Jamie, and I protect it."

"Did you know Richard Picking?" asked Jamie.

Porter stopped to make sure a No Smoking sign and a fire extinguisher were in view. Insurance companies were very particular about fire safety. Maybe it wasn't his job to check on such trivial matters but an ounce of prevention. And it would be his job, after the fire, to explain why they should collect an insurance settlement, when the nearest fire extinguisher was upstairs.

"Yes, I knew him. But I only met him once or twice, briefly."

The lawyer tapped two fingers on the extinguisher's small glass gauge. The indicator pointed to green, Full.

"Do you know much about his relationship to Hunter Davis in 1977?"

"Not really. Hunter was involved in just about everything. He put himself into dangerous situations for publicity, and for a nice fee. People knew if you needed a fearless lawyer, Hunter was your man. I heard about a few cases where individuals got punched out. Hunter was a big guy, bigger than you. Not too many lawyers or cops messed with him. You know he was shot and killed?"

"His son told me."

Jamie watched the well dressed sixtyish attorney stoop to delicately remove a wad of chewing gum from the floor with a Kleenex.

"You can get killed with this crap," Porter warned, depositing the waste in a can. "What did Richard Picking and Hunter Davis have in common?" he asked himself. "I know they went to Duke at the same time. Oh, wait. I remember something. Hunter bought Richard Picking a Cadillac in Memphis. Picking paid for it. But Hunter got him a deal. That was one of Hunter Davis' specialities. He loved to bargain."

So there it was:The Big Breakthrough! Davis and Picking both loved Cadillacs. That explained everything. Because he had purchased a Cadillac for Picking, Hunter Davis had decided to give him a million dollar rebate! And Picking had put it in a trust for his friend's newborn son. That made sense. (Not!) Jamie gathered his thoughts. So far nothing made any sense. "Let me ask you a question, Mr. Porter." Jamie cracked his knuckles. "If you were me, how would you go about finding out who left you the money?"

Porter took a good look at the Elvis look-alike with muscles.

"You're telling me the truth," he said, smiling through a set of too-perfect teeth.

"I really am. If you don't believe me, ask my dad. He's a lawyer, too. I have absolutely no interest in Elvis Presley's money."

Jamie handed Porter his father's business card.

"How would I find out who gave you the money?" said Porter. "Well, I assume the trustee doesn't know."

"They don't. It's Chemical Bank in New York."

"Okay, then the only person who would know is either the attorney who set up the trust, or whoever gave him the money. I take it you've spoken to Richard Picking."

"He died a long time ago."

"I didn't know that," said the Graceland lawyer. "Well, if the bank doesn't know, whoever gave Mr. Picking the money must have bequeathed it to him as a gift."

"What does that mean?"

Now Porter was in his element. "It means that in order for the money to remain *anonymous*, the giver of the gift had to pay a tax on the money when it was given to your attorney. In other words, if your attorney received, let's say a million dollars, the donor had to pay another quarter million or more in taxes."

"That's wild," said Jamie. "So the original gift was even larger?"

"Correct. But if that is what actually happened, you're never going to find the gift-giver unless he wants you to find him. Or her. That's the whole point of an anonymous gift."

Jamie was not thrilled.

"Or I can talk to everyone who knew Richard Picking. The money had to come from someone he knew if it didn't come from him."

"You can't talk to Hunter Davis Senior, either," Porter

reminded him.

"Then I need to talk to his old clients. Maybe the money came from one of them. I mean, it came from somebody!"

John Porter stopped walking. They had reached the front door.

"Well, boy, now we're getting back into this sticky area again," he said. "Because *Elvis Presley* was one of Hunter Davis' clients. And I can guaran-damn-tee you Elvis didn't leave you no million dollars."

"Hunter Davis worked for Elvis?"

Jamie was surprised and enlightened. He had seen the photo of Hunter Davis with Elvis in the paper, but it didn't click. The story had mentioned something about Elvis visiting Duke to try The Rice Diet; with Hunter Davis being from Memphis, it figured that the party at Graceland had just been a social event. But obviously it had been more than that. Presley had allowed his lawyer (his business associate? his friend?) to use Graceland to host a personal gathering. To impress his friends and fellow alumni with his power and influence. After all, how many lawyers could boast that they could have a get-together at Elvis Presley's house?

"That's how I came to work for the Presley estate," explained Porter. "When Hunter was alive, I never worked for Elvis."

"Did you meet him?" Jamie had almost forgotten where he was standing. He looked up at the huge columns on the front porch of Presley's house.

"Once. At a local fund-raiser. Elvis was very civic minded. He worked closely with social and religious groups. The time I met him, he was doing something with the Memphis Police."

"And after Elvis died?"

Porter closed his eyes, remembering days gone by.

"After he died, Hunter Davis was still alive. For about a year or so. There was a lot of commotion in 1977 and 1978. All kinds of people claimed that Elvis had promised them money, or personal possessions. This nut from West Virginia said she was entitled to all of Elvis' Gold Records! Had a letter signed by Elvis to prove it. Of course, the letter was a forgery. So, thanks to Hunter Davis, I got my foot in the door helping him get rid of a couple of hundred false claims. Meanwhile, the real will was probated."

Jamie Randolph found all of this new information exciting, even if it wasn't getting him any closer to the truth.

"I take it I wasn't in the will," he suggested, grinning.

"All the money went to Lisa Marie," Porter told him. "But she didn't get it till she was twenty-five. And this is what *you* get." Porter handed him a leaflet about the Graceland tours. "It's getting late. I've got to go."

As they walked down the seven front steps to the driveway, Jamie turned to the attorney.

"Mr. Porter," he said. "You've been very helpful to me. I don't know if I'll ever find what I'm looking for, and maybe it doesn't matter. But I really appreciate your taking the time to see me."

"No problem. As long as you're straight with me. Now, I'm not going to hear from your father, the attorney, next week, am I? Telling me that you'd like a little of our money."

"No way." They shook hands, Porter squeezing tightly to show macho. "But I do have a favor to ask you."

"Uh-oh, here it comes."

Jamie lowered his voice. "Is there any way I can get back into the office where I met you, just for a minute?"

"Why? You liked the girl? I could see she liked you."

"No. This is funny. I know you're not going to believe me, but I had a very strange feeling in that room." Jamie raised his eyebrows, and so did the listener, unconsciously. "I felt like something once happened in that room that had to do with me."

"Yes, son of Elvis."

Jamie laughed. "I'm not the son of Elvis. I just felt something. . . weird. I just wanted to take another look. A quick one."

"I don't think so. Maybe some other time."

Jamie was disappointed but he had lost his will to argue.

"Hey, Mr. Porter!" shouted a black gardener trimming shrubs in the circular patio across the driveway. "Who's that over there with you?"

"Just another Elvis!" returned the lawyer, embarrassing Jamie.

"Looks like we could put this one on Wheaties," the man joshed. He set down his shears and walked over to Porter and the boy. Jamie admired the expansive lawn. There were bare spots here and there, perhaps caused by the roots of the stately oaks. As he came closer the man's age showed. He was at least in his seventies, his white shirt spotted by sweat, or the recent rain. His bald head was wrinkled.

"How are you, Duncan?" said Porter, not even thinking about shaking hands.

"Fine." The gardener sat down on a white cast iron bench. Behind him was a pair of four foot high white concrete lions, one with its mouth open. Elvis had liked these majestic figures since his acquisition of Graceland in 1957. "You looking at the lions?"

"They're nice," Jamie said, his upper lip curling as he spoke.

The gardener's face twitched.

"Goddam," he said. "This boy don't look as much like him as he acts like him."

"Ignore him," Porter said to Jamie. "He sees Elvis in his sleep. Mr. Johnston, here, has worked for the Presley family for thirty-eight years. All this beautifully kept landscaping is his doing."

This guy would never make it in Bergen County, thought Jamie. The plantings were too sparse. No weeping specimens, no red-leafed trees, just a bunch of straggly azaleas. Perhaps Elvis didn't appreciate horticulture.

"Elvis *loved* the lions," said Johnston. I guess cause they're the king of beasts and he was The King." A Tennessee landscaper's one-liner. Jamie smiled.

"Did you know Hunter Davis?" the boy asked. Porter checked his Rolex.

"I have to get back to work," said the attorney, tapping Jamie's shoulder and shuffling back into the house. "Good luck." Jamie waved to an empty doorway.

"Hunter Davis. Hunter Davis." More Alzheimers? "Oh, *Hunter* Davis. The big guy that used to buy Elvis' Cadillacs."

"That's him. Did you know him?"

The gardener studied Jamie curiously. "That was a long

133

time ago," he said, wondering if this boy was distantly related to Elvis. "You couldn't have known him."

"I didn't."

"That's the man got his head shot up over in Germantown. Yeah, I knew him. He used to come here at night, and sometimes in the afternoon, even after Mr. Presley was dead." The man stepped closer. "Married, but he used to bring young women here. Nobody said anything, but everybody knew."

"Even his wife?" If nothing else, Jamie was learning a great deal about the seedy side of rich folks in Memphis.

"Probably. Everybody else knew. Somebody must have told her."

Jamie felt sorry for Charlotte Davis, and maybe Hunter's son, too. This explained why Mrs. Davis hadn't had anything nice to say about Elvis. And why she hadn't elaborated on her husband's work for the Presleys. Besides buying cars, what other things had Hunter Davis engaged in? A lawyer who, in the words of John Porter, wasn't afraid to punch people out if necessary. He had promised Hunter, Jr. he would not talk to Charlotte again, and he wouldn't.

"Anything else you can tell me about Mr. Davis?"

"Not really. But I did see him kick a taxi driver's ass once. And," added the man. "His wife was a *piece* of ass!"

Duncan Johnston got to his feet. "Are you a cousin of Elvis Presley, I mean, are you the son of a cousin or something? You sure do remind me of the man. You don't sound like you're from Tennessee or Mississippi."

"I'm from New Jersey." Jamie waited for a joke, but it didn't come. Apparently, Mr. Johnston had never driven the New Jersey Turnpike.

"I knew you weren't from the South. I've never been to New Jersey. In fact, I've only been out of Tennessee three times. Twice to North Carolina and once to Florida, all by airplane. I was born in Memphis."

"I was born in New Jersey. I'm not a cousin of Elvis Presley." Jamie couldn't resist. "Do you think Elvis is really dead?" he asked.

"You're right," said the gardener. "You ain't no cousin."

Jamie surmised that he had just insulted someone, or

something. The memory of Elvis? Duncan Johnston's intelligence? The man left in a huff.

"No wonder he reminded me of Elvis," Duncan said to himself as the boy danced down to the famous Musical Gates. "White people look alike." He laughed at the unoriginal joke.

❧

The answering machine was on. Dad wasn't home yet and Mom didn't feel like talking. Livvy was over Lori's house, for a change, unable to peel her eyes off the life-size color posters of Luke Perry and Brad Pitt. Jamie would leave a message, take a late afternoon snooze and wait for a callback. He was also hungry. For some strange reason, as "nourishing" as they were, two Yodels didn't quite fill him up. But he was too lazy to shower again and walk to the coffee shop. Dad still had the same greeting on his tape.

"This is Humphrey Bogart. I'm in Morocco, but if you leave a message we'll get back to you as soon as we get our exit visas. Do it, Sam."

Beeee-eeeeee-eep!

"Hi, Mr. and Mrs. Randolph, and your little beauty queen. I'm at the Days Inn in Memphis and I've had a very interesting day. If you'd like to hear about it, call me after six at Area Code 901 - 346 - 5500, room 116. Don't wake me up before that. Hope everyone is feeling good. I'll probably be coming home tomorrow. Bye!"

Jamie took off his clothes and struck a bodybuilder's pose in the mirror over a dresser. In the bathroom, he hit a different pose. As he splashed water on his face, the phone rang. He grabbed a hand towel, unfolded it as he ran, dripped across the room, picked up on the third ring.

"I told you not to call till six."

The Southern voice on the other end said, "Excuse me?"

"Who is this?" asked Jamie, combing his hair with his fingers.

"Hunter Davis."

"Oh, I'm sorry. I thought you were someone else."

Davis was calling from his car. Jamie could hear the honking traffic.

"I'm headed for the airport," Davis informed him. "How did it go with John Porter?"

Jamie lay back on the bed. A TV catty-cornered by the door was playing *G.I. Blues*. Juliet Prowse was dancing circles around The King. Elvis was snapping his fingers in his perfectly pressed army uniform.

"He was very polite, and he tried to help me."

"That's good. Hang on. Hey, you! Move over, you son of a bitch!"

Like father, like son.

"Mr. Davis?"

"I'm here. What did Porter tell you?"

"Not much. He knew Richard Picking, but he had no idea if Picking and your father did business together. He said some very nice things about your father. He said your father got him his job at the Presley estate."

"Anything else?" It sounded like Davis had slammed on the brakes.

"No. Oh yeah, he told me that if my inheritance came from an anonymous trust, and the lawyer was dead — Picking, I mean — that there was no way I could find the gift-giver unless he wanted me to. You think that's true?"

Davis was trying to pay attention to Jamie.

"Sounds right. But you have no idea who would have a reason to leave you money?"

"No. I don't. No one has any idea."

"I'm entering the parking garage," Davis said. "My phone's going to break up in a minute. I just have one last thought for you. But you have to promise me again that you won't call Mrs. Davis while I'm out of town."

"I promise." For God's sake, why doesn't the guy give me a lie detector test?

"Okay. Here's my tip of the day. Did you ever think that maybe the guy who left you the money had a *reason* to keep it a secret?"

"Like what?" asked Jamie.

The transmission was starting to fade.

"Like maybe the money was stolen and you'd have to give it back. Like maybe the guy was a murderer and you wouldn't keep the money if you knew. I don't know. I'm just saying. . ."

Hunter Davis, Jr. was gone. Swallowed up by the mysterious sound-wave-eating-walls of the airport structure. Jamie fell asleep. The phone was still in his hand.

When he woke up, the room was dark, he was starving to death and it was a quarter after ten. The digital clock was flashing "12:00" and the TV could not turn itself back on. After a temporary power failure, the air-conditioning was still working, thank God.

Jack Randolph answered the phone on the very first ring.

"Randolph and Randolph," he said, rubbing his eyes. He had been reading the Wall Street Journal. Most of his recent stock picks were doing well, Intel and Compaq Computer in particular. The problem was, he really couldn't read the quotes without glasses, so maybe he wasn't doing as well as he thought. He could not find the listing for Ameridata, a hot tip.

"Dad? Were you calling?" Jamie cleared his throat and blinked his eyes. Both Randolphs had blurry vision. Jamie's would be 20-20 in a minute.

"We called you around seven. The phone was busy. We tried every ten minutes, so we figured you took it off the hook."

"I did, by accident. I fell asleep. I just got up. I have to get out of here and find the nearest McDonald's."

Olivia picked up the phone. "Is it for me?"

"No, cute face, it's for me. It's your brother."

"Hi, Jamie."

"Hi, Liv. How's Brad?"

"Brad?"

"Pitt."

"Talk to Dad," she said. "I'll find out everything from him." Click.

"So what happened?" asked Jack.

"Not much. I met Mrs. Davis today, and her son. He was kind of pissed off that I went to see her. But I was very polite. Eventually, he referred me to a lawyer who works for Graceland who knew Hunter Davis twenty years ago. He also knew Richard Picking, but had no idea what the two of them did together, or why it had anything to do with me. Mostly, he was worried that I was pretending to be the son of Elvis Presley."

"Were you?" Oh, to be young and in Memphis, Jack thought, slightly envious of his son's adventure.

"No. They said I look like him a little. And they get all these people who come around asking for money. . . Anyway, this other lawyer told me something interesting."

"I'm listening."

Jamie told his father what Porter had explained to him about the anonymous source of the inheritance. That the name of the gift-giver might have gone to the grave with Picking.

"I suspected that, but I didn't want to discourage you from making a thorough search," Jack said.

Jamie then related the stories he had heard about Hunter Davis and his relationship to Elvis Presley. How they might have been involved in all kinds of deals that no one knew about but them.

"All everyone remembers about Davis and Presley is that they bought a lot of cars together. But Hunter Davis was known as a lawyer who would do anything for a buck. He had a lot of pull at Graceland. So he must have done more for Elvis than help him price Cadillacs."

Finally, Jamie revealed Hunter Davis, Jr.'s insight about the possible secret agenda of the benefactor. That if he had something to hide, he might not want Jamie or Chemical Bank to know his name.

"That doesn't make much sense," said Jack Randolph. "Why the hell would a thief or a murderer leave you a million dollars?"

"I don't know."

Suddenly Jack got a brainstorm. It came to him like the proverbial bolt-out-of-the-blue and he felt like a new character in *Casablanca.*

"The mystery is solved," he said to his son. "But you're not going to like the solution."

It was getting late and Jamie's stomach was growling. Why

hadn't he brought food with him from the airport? He looked around for a scrap to eat, like a smoker without cigarettes searches for a butt.

"What's the answer?" asked Jamie. "Who left me the money?"

"I don't know *who*. I just know *why*."

"Why?"

"Whoever put the money in a trust for you wanted it back."

Jamie tried to understand.

"I don't get it."

"All right, here's my theory," said Jack. Suppose someone who knew Richard Picking wanted to launder illegal cash, or just wanted to keep a totally confidential account with a million dollars for future use. What would he do?"

How to hide cash? That was an easy one.

"Buy diamonds or gold," answered Jamie.

"Possibly. Or, if he didn't want to speculate, he might put the funds into an interest bearing trust account."

"In my name?"

"In the name of a newborn child," Dad explained. "Not to be turned over to that baby for eighteen years. Then, during all that time when the child has no knowledge of the money, the trust can always revert back to the benefactor."

Jamie became more intrigued than hungry.

"Is that legal?" he asked Dad.

"As long as the attorney who set up the trust remains alive." Jack's theory was legally sound.

"He can just take the money back?"

"Sure. He would have the authority to amend the trust as he sees fit as long as the child is not of legal age. It's just like changing your will. I can put you in or I can cut you out. Until I die. Then the will stands the last way I wrote it."

"And Richard Picking died a year later."

"So he could no longer amend the trust."

Jamie opened the drawer beside his bed. He looked under the Bible and located a sheet of paper. There was a pen next to the phone. He drew some circles, wrote names in them, connected the circles with arrows. The big circle in the middle was labelled "Me — $4,000,000." While he was doing this,

Jack refined his concept.

"Next, assume that a second party, Hunter Davis or Elvis, found out that Picking had passed away. What would he do?"

Jamie was writing dates in the circles, then question marks next to some of the names. He had drawn eleven circles so far. In one of them he wrote the name "Elvis Presley — Died 1977."

"That person would be very concerned about how he was ever going to get his money back," the boy responded.

"But he would have eighteen years, no, seventeen from the time Picking died, to devise a plan. He would certainly hire another attorney."

Jamie looked at the circle marked "Hunter Davis — Died 1979."

"Except if it was Elvis Presley," said Jamie.

"What are you talking about?"

Jamie had an idea of his own.

"Elvis Presley died before Richard Picking died. If *he* had given Picking a million dollars, tax free, to hide in an account in 1977, he wouldn't have cared about it in 1978 because he wasn't alive. And if it was arranged by Hunter Davis, his attorney, *he* too was dead by 1979."

Jack summed it up. "Which means that the only three people who knew about this crazy deal would all be dead sixteen years before the money was inherited. So the money would be managed for the full eighteen years by Chemical Bank before it was legally yours in 1995."

"And no one would know or care. It was all perfectly legal."

Jack and Jamie had turned into Holmes and Watson.

"But it still doesn't make sense," said Jack.

"Why not?"

"Okay, I understand that if Richard Picking was hired to set up this trust, let's say for argument's sake by Elvis Presley through his lawyer, the procedure is logical. Picking selects a newborn baby he can keep track of, and specifically instructs the bank not to contact the child, you, until this year. But why doesn't he just keep the money in his own name? Or why doesn't Presley stick the money in a Swiss bank account? Then he wouldn't have to pay the gift tax."

They were stumped, again.

"It's a good theory, Dad." Jamie yawned, waking up. Jack yawned, falling asleep.

"And how do we know it *was* Elvis Presley?" wondered Jack.

"Who else could it be? Indirectly, he was connected to Richard Picking. He had millions of dollars. He was eccentric enough to be involved in some kind of crazy scheme invented by his crazy lawyer. You know how crazy lawyers are, right, Dad?"

No response.

"And I know how we can check it out," Jamie concluded.
"How?"

"There's only one place to go if you want to know everything there is to know about Elvis Presley."

"Graceland?" asked his father.

"No. The National Enquirer."

Chapter 12

❧

"THE SACRED TRUTH"

The directions from Palm Beach International Airport were easy to follow. Take I-95 South to the Lantana Road exit and head east, toward the ocean. At Federal Highway, turn right and drive south again for about a mile. And there it was: Burger King. Home of the Whopper. As usual, Jamie Randolph was ready for a hamburger.

First, he wanted to see exactly where The National Enquirer was located in Lantana, Florida. About a quarter mile to the right, just over the railroad tracks, he spotted the red, white and blue plastic billlboard. The Enquirer's sign was supported by large, red upside-down McDonald's arches. On second thought, he would eat first.

Wiping ketchup off his face in the car mirror, Jamie waited for the long train to go by. He counted the cars. One-hundred and twenty-seven open top freight cars, all ruddy brown, identified with the letters "F.E.C." over a five digit number. The young man from New Jersey wondered what, if anything, was in the cars, why there were so many and where the train was going. Miami or Fort Lauderdale, he supposed, since there was less than a hundred miles of the east coast left as the train moved south. "F.E.C."? Florida's East Coast? Later, someone would confirm that, indeed, that was what the letters stood for. The Florida East Coast railroad dated back to the turn of the century when Henry Flagler, John D. Rockefeller's oil partner, had decided to develop the area. The freight cars carried gravel on the trip north.

Except for new automobiles, like Jamie's not very exciting blue Buick Regal (arranged by the travel agent), Federal Highway could have been a 1950's set from The Twilight Zone. Cheap motels, outdated restaurants. Good thing he at least had the smarts to tell the agent to book him the most expensive room at the most expensive hotel in town. "Money is no object," he had said, figuring to pay double the $45 per night rate at Days Inn. For $90, you should get a pretty good room in Florida in July, when rates were way down.

Jamie made a quick right at a blank white building called "Finland House" and looked for a sign. He found himself in a cheap neighborhood of pink, orange and turquoise one-story houses in desperate need of renovation. Continuing along, he was led down a winding, narrow asphalt roadway that appeared to be going nowhere. Dense tropical foliage blocked his view until he emerged into a parking lot adjacent to a small baseball field. He pulled into a spot and stared at two low orange-roofed buildings, their exteriors faced with large pebbles.

A green and orange striped awning supported by flimsy aluminum poles covered a walking path to the front entrance of the building on the left. As he took a few steps toward the door, Jamie noticed a small American flag on a thin flagpole. Despite a large circular planting of Chinese Fan Palms and native Florida greenery, it was hard to believe that this was the *headquarters* of America's self-proclaimed widest circulation newspaper. If you could believe anything The Enquirer printed, three million people a week bought a copy and allegedly eighteen million people read it. That last part sounded right. For every person dumb enough to pay for The Enquirer, five other people just borrowed the rag. It was only fitting that its building should look as chintzy as its reputation.

It was Friday, July 28th. Jamie doubted that anyone would be anxious to help him on the last day of work but he had nothing to lose. If he had to come back on Monday, that was okay. He would do a little sun-bathing, maybe go surfing, see *Forrest Gump* a second time if it was still playing. If nothing materialized on Monday, he would call it quits. Return home convinced that he and Dad had found as much of the truth as possible, be happy that he had inherited $4 Million never intended for him. He wasn't giving it back, that's for sure. He wasn't giving it to Picking's brother. Lisa Marie Presley certainly didn't need it, if it were hers. Finally, the Davis family was already rich as sin, and money couldn't erase their tragedy. So it was his, no matter what.

Just outside the building, in the circular driveway, a white station wagon was parked with its cargo door wide open. A group of Enquirer employees, mostly women, were buying carnations and roses from a small-time entrepreneur. On the vehicle's rear bumper was a Confederate Flag decal. Jamie reminded himself that he was still in the South. However, maybe people would be more receptive in this laid back atmosphere.

He entered the lobby through one of the glass doors and walked up to the receptionist. A rectangular General Electric clock on the wall to her right had to be worth at least ten dollars.

"I'd like to talk to a reporter," he said to the attentive young lady.

"I love your hair. It's totally cool." The girl fluffed the back of her own hair. "Why do you want to see a reporter?"

Jamie had concocted his story on the flight from Memphis this morning.

"I think I could be the son of Elvis Presley," he said seriously, effecting the kind of swagger that might have impressed Duncan the gardener.

"That's a good one," she responded with a seen-it-all attitude. "Hold on a minute."

A phone call was coming in from someone claiming to have broken the Guinness Book Of World Records' official rope-skipping record. The receptionist put him through to the sports department.

"My name is Melissa," the girl said, checking out Jamie's physique on her tip-toes. At least she wasn't shy. "What's yours?"

"Jamie. Jamie Randolph."

"Not Jamie Presley?" she said, toying with him, flirting.

Quick-witted, Jamie replied, "Oh, don't be cruel to a heart

that's true."

The girl didn't get it. She was too young. Actually, so was he but his father was always listening to oldies tapes in the car.

"That's an Elvis song," he explained.

"Oh." The girl showed him her red and jeweled fingernails. "What do you think?"

Jamie nodded. "Beautiful."

A short oriental man with short black hair in a black suit popped around the corner. "I'm taking lunch, Melissa," he advised in a superior voice, no accent. His eyes darted to Jamie. "Are you being helped?"

"He's Elvis' son."

The man looked Jamie up and down. Boy, they were really a bunch of nosy bastards at The Enquirer.

"Could be," the man said, raising his forefinger for emphasis. "We haven't done a story on Elvis recently. Come with me." Melissa kissed her palm, backhanded a wave good-bye.

Jamie glanced at several wall plaques honoring The Enquirer for humanitarian news coverage. One was from PETA, the animal rights group. Before he was directed past the employee food area down a hall of offices, he also noticed the person who had come in behind him. Seated in one of the Scandinavian oak chairs in the lobby was a large woman with a bag over her head. She peered at him through two eye holes and shuffled her red boots on the blue/grey carpet. Jamie wondered what her story was.

"Where are we going?" he asked, a steady hand guiding him.

"Don't worry. You're going to like her."

A ring of thirteen silver plated stars encircled the hand lettered name on the door: Sid Morrison, THE SUPERSTAR. Without knocking, the oriental man walked in, beckoning Jamie to follow with two quick tilts of the head. Seated behind a cluttered desk was a blond haired young lady with her back to them typing at a computer.

"We have an open door policy," the man explained.

"Hi, Lonnie." The girl continued her work undisturbed.

"Hi, Delaney. I'd like you to meet the son of Elvis Presley."

When Delaney Morrison spun around Jamie thought he was looking at a young Cybill Shepherd. Truly, this perfectly shaped face with wispy blond bangs, china blue eyes, light freckles and a small turned-up nose was the cover-girl image for "Seventeen" magazine. The All-American girl next door, complete with spotless white teeth and a fresh smile, a look made even more dramatic by her black Guess tee-shirt and white Guess jeans.

Instantly, Jamie Randolph was in love, and the last person in the world he wanted to be was the son of Elvis Presley. But it was too late.

"How do you do, Mr. Presley," she said in a businesslike tone. "I'm Delaney Morrison."

"I'm Jamie Randolph," he said, shaking her delicate little hand.

"Well, I'll leave you two to get acquainted," said Lonnie. "Do your thing. I'll be back later." He was out the door in a flash.

"That was Lonnie Manners," said Delaney. "I don't think that's his real name, but it's cool. He's the staff coordinator. Please, sit down."

Jamie removed two books about The Beatles from a chair and sat. He admired the small gold hoop earrings adorning her cute ears. On her left wrist she wore a pink cloth headband and a pink Swatch watch. Jamie looked at her skin.

"I see you don't have much of a Florida tan," he said.

"That's because I'm a real Floridian. Only tourists are stupid enough to sit in the sun until they get skin cancer."

"Where are you from?" Jamie cancelled his plans to bake on the beach.

"Fort Lauderdale, but it got too crowded. Where are you from?"

"New Jersey."

"Where in New Jersey?"

"You've never heard of it. Tenafly."

"A girl in my English Lit class at Boston lives in Tenafly."

Jamie put his hands on the edge of the desk and brought his face closer to hers. His heart was racing. He inhaled oxygen to slow it down.

"You go to Boston University?"

"Entering my sophomore year in September. I'll be majoring in journalism."

"I start at Dartmouth in September. I wrestled in high school, but I got in strictly on my grades."

"I guess you're a lot smarter than your father," said the perky coed.

"My father went to Dartmouth and then Cornell Law."

"Elvis Presley was an attorney?" she joked.

"Not Elvis Presley." Jamie laughed. "Jack Randolph. My . . . adopted father." Jamie recalled the name on the door. "Who's Sid Morrison?"

"Oh," she said. "You mean The Superstar? That's *my* dad. He's been with The Enquirer since high school. They send him all over the world to do stories on Michael Jackson, Madonna, Cindy Crawford. . . people like that. Lisa Marie Presley. Elvis Presley. Right now he's in Beverly Hills covering O.J. Simpson. He got me this job as a summer intern, pulled some strings with the big boys, thought I could use the experience."

"Are you any good?" asked the Elvis impersonator.

"I think so." She smiled again, looking directly into his magnetic eyes. "Here's a story I did on The Beatles getting back together. Without John Lennon, of course." Delaney handed him a newspaper showing Paul McCartney, George Harrison and Ringo Starr in 1965 and 1995. "It's terrible," she said. "That's what's going to happen to us in thirty years."

Jamie studied the young and old faces. It *was* terrible.

"Elvis would have been sixty this year," he told Delaney.

"That's not news." She clasped her hands and leaned forward, eager to learn something. "So tell me about your real father. Elvis."

Jamie couldn't go through with it.

"I've got a confession to make." He wanted to touch her hands but he kept his on the desk, tapping the wood top. "I told the girl out front that I *might* be the son of Elvis Presley, and I might. But I'm not sure."

"When will you know?" It was a sarcastic question.

"Well, that's where you come in. See, I need your help

doing some research on Elvis Presley, and anything that involves an attorney named Hunter Davis. This would be back in 1977, or maybe a year or two earlier. It could prove if I'm really Elvis' son or not. Can you look it up?"

"Are you serious? Do you know how many stories we've done on Elvis?"

"How many?"

"Watch this."

Delaney went back to the keyboard and punched in "Search — Elvis." A few seconds later the encyclopedia of the life of Elvis Presley began to appear on the screen.

"Well, I've got a few years with nothing else to do, how about you?"

The girl had a great sense of humor. Not to mention a great figure.

"Can you look up Hunter Davis?" Jamie asked.

She tried. "Nothing." Damn.

"How about Richard Picking?" Nothing.

"Who's Richard Picking?"

Jamie told her the whole story, from the beginning. He watched her eyes as he spoke. She was not only interested in the story, she was interested in him. He could tell. And he was definitely interested in her. This was his lucky day, whether he found out about Elvis and Davis or not.

"There are lots of crazy stories about Elvis," said the junior reporter. "You want me to print some? Here's one about Elvis' twin sons. Did you know that Elvis was a twin?"

"Was he?"

"His twin brother died at birth. Oh, look. We did a story on Elvis being kidnapped by aliens. I love UFO stories."

"So do I. I'm a UFO freak. Did you read Communion?"

"I did a book report on it. Oh, wait. I've got one. Elvis and his mother are both still alive. They've had plastic surgery and they perform together in Las Vegas."

"Who wrote that?"

Delaney turned around and made a goofy face. "Who else? My father. He used to have an investigator that followed Elvis around in California and Las Vegas. Elvis owned houses in Los Angeles and this guy's job was to take pictures of Elvis wherever he went. Poor Elvis. His life wasn't his own. I could see why he never made it to fifty. My dad's fifty-four and he looks better than Elvis did at thirty." Delaney checked the screen. "There are even worse stories," she said.

A private eye who followed Elvis around with a camera?

"Hold it," said Jamie, before his new friend could overwhelm him with Elvis trivia. "Did you say your father paid someone to take photos of Elvis during the day, when he wasn't performing?"

Delaney pictured the cameraman's face. He looked a little like Tony Danza from *Who's The Boss.*

"On the West Coast. His name was Alonzo X. A very nice man, silly name. I met him three years ago. He's retired in Hawaii, but my father made him come to Florida to take pictures at my Sweet Sixteen. Sid told me his whole life story. He's photographed everybody, and I mean every-body."

"Did your father save the photos?" asked Jamie. "Of Elvis, I mean."

"Yeah, I guess so. They would be the property of The Enquirer."

Maybe this wasn't the end of the information highway yet.

"Could I see them?"

"That's a good question," said Delaney. "Let's ask Mr. Computer." She entered a few commands, shook her head. Tried something else. "Yes, yes. Here it is. Confidential Elvis Photo File. Uh-oh."

"What?" Jamie strained to read the tiny letters on the screen.

"The files are in this room," she said. "See those locked cabinets? Only my dad knows where the key is. I'd have to call Sid to get them."

"Can you do it?"

"For the son of Elvis?" They giggled. "I'll try. Where are you staying?"

"At the Ritz-Carlton."

"Very nice. Right on the ocean. We live on the ocean too. About four miles north of your hotel on A1A. Did you just check in?"

"No, I'm supposed to check in today," Jamie said. "Maybe

I should go do that now before they give away my room."

"Oh, I doubt that. Not in July. But you never know. "

They agreed that Delaney would try to get her father's photos of Elvis and bring them over to Jamie at the hotel. When he left, she called Sid Morrison's pocket phone.

"9-0-2-1-0. Morrison."

"Daddy? It's me."

"Little Superstar! How's it going, sweet pea? Everything OK?"

It always felt good to hear his voice. Confident. Happy. Even during the divorce, which was as amicable as a split can be after fifteen years of marriage, Sid had been jovial.

"I'm doing good," she answered. "They published my story on The Beatles — I forgot, I told you that last week. Mom says hello. I had dinner with her on Wednesday. She sold another house in Palm Beach, a million dollar home not far from Mar-A-Lago, to a business associate of Donald Trump. How's the O. J. situation?"

"Exciting. Boring. You know. It's all been said. I've been playing tennis more than working. That's where I'm off to right now. You just called because you're a devoted daughter?" His only child, the love of his life.

"No, actually, I'm working on a new story. It just walked into your office a little while ago. A guy who might be the son of Elvis Presley. I mean, I'm sure he isn't, but you told me that appearances can be just as good as the truth. And you should see him, Daddy. He's tall, built like a brick shithouse — pardon my French — and he really does resemble Elvis, except he's got blond hair and he's from New Jersey."

"I'm paying attention," said Sid. "Don't get mad if I drop the phone. I'm tying my shoes with the phone under my chin. I'm going biking . . . Oops."

They were disconnected. Delaney pressed Redial. Sid clicked on.

"Sounds like you like him. How old is this. . . Elvis?"

"His name is Jamie and he's my age. Maybe younger." She told Sid the story. "I'm supposed to bring your Elvis photos over to his hotel. I told him I didn't know where the key was, but I just wanted to see if you think this is worth the time."

"Sure. Why not? Go for it," her father advised. "If the rest of the story is true I can get you a Page Three. It's not a headliner, unless of course he *is* the son of Elvis, but it could put you on the map."

Delaney was proud of herself. "How do you want me to handle it?"

"You're doing good." Sid massaged her ego. "Bring him the photos, see if it helps him. You've got to gain his confidence. Everyone else probably thinks he's nuts, and maybe he is."

"He isn't, Daddy. He's very normal. That's why it's such a good story. He's a high school wrestling champion with an A-average. He's going to Dartmouth in the Fall. His father's a lawyer. I think he's telling me the truth."

Sid called to someone waiting for him, a woman. "Gotta beat it," he said. "Keep in touch. Bring him out to California if you want to. I'll get photos of him looking like Elvis' twin brother for you. If not, we'll touch them up! I'm not very busy next week. Maybe we can get the paper to pay for a two-day trip. Tell them I want to do it. They've got the money."

"Bye, Daddy."

"Bye, sugar. Let me know what happens. Just be careful."

⚜

The Ritz-Carlton Hotel in Manalapan, an oceanfront strip of prime real estate bordering east Lantana, was only a few years old. An elegant, Spanish style building, it reflected the popular genre of Palm Beach architect Addison Mizner. Its orange barrel tile roof basked defiantly in the hot summer sun of South Florida.

Jamie noticed a restaurant in the exclusive little mall across the street from the Ritz. *Plaza La Mer* was the name of the shopping area.

A valet waved him down and commandeered his vehicle. Based on the value of the rental car and Jamie's clothes, the hotel employee assumed the guest would occupy a $135 per night garden room. That was the lowest priced room, even in July. The valet was not insulted by the one dollar tip. The

151

Buick drove away slowly, like a Rolls Royce.

Inside, Jamie declined handing over his black Samsonite valise and proceeded to the marble lobby. He crossed several exotic carpets on a browser's route to the Registration desk. The room was three stories high, filled with beautiful paintings, art plates and antique furnishings. Real wood seemed to be burning in the lobby fireplace. Nearby sat a piano.

"I'll be playing here tonight," said a man dressed for a wedding, dusting the piano top with a white handkerchief. An enormous black vase displayed a striking flower arrangement. Jamie recognized only the chartreuse orchids.

"What are those orangey flowers?" he asked the desk clerk. "The ones shaped like a Macaw's beak."

"Bird of Paradise, sir," the man replied.

"That's some bouquet," said Jamie, dropping his luggage with an echo. "I just gave someone flowers. Compared to yours, I gave her weeds!"

The clerk feigned a laugh.

"May I have your name, please. And your credit card."

A reservation was found for Mr. J. Randolph. "Oh!" said the man, straightening up. He rapped his knuckles three times on the counter, a sound which carried across the lobby. "Johnny!" he called loudly. "Please take Mr. Randolph's bag and show him to his room." Jamie heard quick footsteps. A bellhop was at his side holding his Samsonite.

An impression was taken of his American Express Card; it was Jack's account. The card was re-inserted into its wallet slot. Jamie had a feeling his room was going to cost more than $90.

"You can sign later." The clerk was radiant, like someone had just informed him that Jamie was famous. "Welcome to the Ritz-Carlton. We hope you will enjoy your stay, sir. John will take you up. There is champagne waiting for you. Let us know what you need. Today's specials are on the menu in the dining room." Jamie felt like Elvis. Or Bill Clinton. "At what time will the rest of your party be arriving, sir?"

This was getting ridiculous. "It's just me," said Jamie.

"Very good, sir."

"Oh. I am expecting a young lady, Miss Morrison. She's

supposed to be here shortly."

"Excellent, Mr. Randolph. We'll announce her and send her up. Would that be Miss Morrison from The Enquirer?"

"You know her?" Jamie asked.

"I've seen her with her father. Will he be joining you for dinner?"

This was starting to be fun. Like a game.

"No, he can't," said the special guest. "I'm afraid he's stuck in Beverly Hills, having dinner with O.J."

"I see," said the clerk, not knowing if it was a joke.

"I'm ready, sir," said the bellhop.

"We hope you will enjoy your stay," repeated the desk clerk, like a trained talking monkey. "My name is Steven." Jamie wondered why Steven hadn't summoned the other man by ringing the bell near his hand. Jamie rang it once, ignored the stares, and walked to the elevator.

When the two young men entered the *Presidential Suite* of the Ritz Carlton in Manalapan, it all made sense. Yes, he had asked for the best room in town, at any price. A slight miscalculation. He was afraid to ask how much this room — these rooms — cost per night. Even with the July discount.

After he was escorted to the Master Bedroom with its Italian Marble Jacuzzi and back to the Living Room, with its working fireplace, Jamie thanked the bellhop ("My name is John"), palmed him five dollars and slapped himself hard on his forehead. What had he done? He shuffled through all of the papers and brochures on the large desk. No rate sheets. He wandered into the dining room and found only a hotel menu and the champagne. He popped it and poured himself a few ounces. Then he remembered that Delaney was coming over and tried to get the cork back in. No luck. Champagne spilled on the fine dining room table. He sopped it up with a monogrammed linen napkin, hid the napkin in the drawer of a buffet.

He just about had time to take a shower, shave and change his clothes when the phone rang. Looking out across the terrace to the blue and white ocean, Jamie told Steven downstairs to delay Miss Morrison for five minutes. He splashed on some extra Jovan Musk, threw all his clothes into the jumbo closet and put on a Harry Connick, Jr. CD. Boy, this place had everything.

As she walked into the dramatic hotel suite, Delaney remarked: "I always wondered what a $2,600 room looked like."

"Me too," said Jamie, dying. "Welcome to my world."

She scrutinized the expression on his face.

"You didn't know this room cost that much," she scolded him, in a nice way.

Jamie blushed. "You're right," he admitted. "I told my travel agent to get me the best hotel room. I had no idea. . . How the hell could she make a reservation for such an expensive room? They must have told her the price."

"You can cancel it. Unless someone else wanted the room while they were holding it for you." Delaney smiled. "No one will blame you."

He thought about it. Dad was going to give birth to kittens when he got his American Express bill in August. No one had to know before then. On the other hand, it was his money, at least until he was stupid enough to prove it wasn't his money. But legally, it was still his. What was a couple of thousand out of four million? Even at eight per cent, the lowest interest rate Mr. Sawyer had mentioned, he was earning almost a thousand dollars a day. In three years, he would have five million. Oh, what the hell! You only live once. Live like a king, he decided, if only for one day. Tomorrow he would check out and find a cheaper room, that is if he wasn't flying home.

"I'll just stay tonight," he said to Delaney. "I'm already here."

"It's your money."

"Would you like to look around?"

She saw the Steinway Grand Piano. "Yes, I would," she said.

After the tour, Jamie poured them two glasses of champagne.

"You know, you can probably get this room for free," said the devious Miss Morrison.

"How?"

"Because the hotel has served you an alcoholic beverage

illegally. You have to be twenty-one to drink in Florida. But I guess when you stay in the Presidential Suite, it's okay to break a few rules."

"Did you hear the joke about the guy who can't get a room at a hotel?" asked Jamie.

Delaney knew the punchline.

"The President's not coming. I'll take his room," she said.

She was too smart.

"I'm sorry," said Delaney. "Girls aren't supposed to do that." She batted her eyelashes and made a dainty hand movement.

"I play the piano," Jamie volunteered.

"Play it." Oh God, please don't say the words, Jamie thought. Don't say Play It, Sam.

He sat at the piano and loosened up his fingers. Harry Connick, Jr. was doing a rendition of "Misty" and Jamie accompanied him beautifully. Vocally, as well as instrumentally.

"You've got a lot of talent," Delaney complimented him. "You're not Elvis, but you do have talent."

"Sit down next to me. I'll teach you."

Delaney placed the thick envelope on the sofa. Jamie slid over and she joined him at the piano.

Unexpectedly, even more to himself than to the pretty girl with the faint scent of perfume, Jamie turned and kissed her. The kiss lingered, but suddenly Delaney was on her feet.

"See this?" she said, a wicked look on her face.

Jamie tried to identify the small black object in her right hand. It was held like a perfume atomizer. "Is it Red Door?"

"It's pepper spray," she said. "One dose and you'll be on the floor crying like a baby."

Jamie laughed, pretended to cringe with one hand up, protecting his eyes.

"For kissing you?" he said. "I didn't know that was a crime in Florida."

Delaney lowered her weapon. Replaced it into the back pocket of her jeans.

"Who says that's all you wanted?"

Jamie's eyes met hers. "Who says that's all *you* wanted?"

"Take a look at the photos," Delaney barked. "My card's in the envelope. Call me when you're done. I'll have someone pick them up."

"Okay, wait." Jamie extended his hand. "I'm sorry. I shouldn't have done that. I apologize. Can we be friends? You're really trying to help me out and I didn't mean to offend you, or scare you."

Delaney hesitated, then shook the wrestler's mitt. It was very powerful, but she could feel the gentleness inside.

"I'll forget it if you'll forget it," she proposed.

"Done. Let's see the pictures."

She unclasped the envelope. Inside were well over a hundred eight-by-ten glossy photos, all of Elvis. Many had magic marker notations right on the picture: arrows pointing at people, circles around faces, names and dates.

"These are from 1970 to 1977," explained Delaney.

Jamie was fascinated by the candid camera view of Elvis' life. The first photo showed Elvis with some sexy showgirls in Las Vegas. Behind them was a group of people including bodyguards and casino managers. Elvis was dressed in a flashy white jumpsuit and wore extra wide sideburns. By the mid-70's Elvis Presley looked like he was fading fast. There was no one in the picture that Jamie recognized except The King.

Other shots caught Elvis getting in or out of elevators, walking around backstage, buying jewelry, shaking hands.

There was a photo of Elvis talking to Paul McCartney at the airport.

"That one's got to be worth some money, right?" Jamie inquired.

"Hey, look. Here's one with his shirt off at the pool."

Jamie checked out Elvis' muscle tone. He was practicing karate with a smaller man with his back to the camera. Elvis was chubby.

"That's Chuck Norris," Jamie said. "I can tell."

Delaney turned the photo over. A handwritten note by Alonzo X identified Elvis' partner as Chuck Norris. Elvis wanted to make a movie with him, it said.

"Pretty good," Delaney said. "Do you know karate?"

"No, just wrestling. If someone tries to use karate on me, he'd better kill me with the first karate chop. Otherwise, I'm going to bend his arm around his back like a pretzel. Karate is very over-rated. So is boxing. My dad told me that for self-defense, nothing beats wrestling."

It occurred to Jamie that the young lady might not be interested in the martial arts, or his abilities as a violent person, so he continued sorting through the photos.

Elvis had been photographed entering a rare coin and stamp establishment in Beverly Hills. Somewhere else, he had agreed to pose with a high school football team. In a bizarre never-published photo, Alonzo X's notes said that the police were arresting two bald headed young men for throwing something at Elvis. And in perhaps the craziest picture of all, Elvis was captured in the lobby of the historic Beverly Wilshire Hotel, holding Clint Eastwood at gunpoint with a 44 Magnum.

"The gun couldn't be loaded," said Delaney. "I hope."

After reviewing more than half the stack of black and whites, it was beginning to look like just another day in the life. When there he was, leaning against a big 1973 Cadillac Eldorado. Parked in front of a building with tall white metal doors resembling a prison gate. Elvis was hiding in the car, you could see his face clearly, wearing sunglasses. And the big man talking to Elvis, with short blond hair and dressed in a business suit, was without a doubt, Mr. Hunter Davis.

"That's him!" said Jamie, his voice filled with emotion. "I can't believe it. That's Hunter Davis, the lawyer from Memphis."

"Are you sure?" asked the girl. "How do you know?"

"That's him. Definitely. Here, look at this."

Jamie removed a folded photostat of a newsclip from his wallet.

"See the man next to Elvis Presley? That's Hunter Davis. Next to him is the other lawyer I'm interested in, Richard Picking. They were both at Graceland in April, 1974 for their college reunion. When was *this* picture taken? Where was it taken?"

Delaney read the notes on the back. The driver of the car, Davis, was unidentified. The man inside the Cadillac was Elvis. The date was November 16, 1975, a year and a half before Jamie's birth. The location was at the office of Dr. Ira Goldman, a Beverly Hills plastic surgeon. An interesting comment by Alonzo X appeared: "Earlier in the day I followed Elvis and friend to the Beverly Hills Fertility Clinic. Is Elvis trying to have a baby? Elvis stayed in the car the whole time."

Jamie was elated. At long last, a break. A true lead that could be followed up.

"So why was Elvis seeing a plastic surgeon?" Jamie asked.

"Inquiring minds want to know," said Delaney, friendly again.

"Or maybe it wasn't Elvis. Maybe it was Davis seeing the doctor."

"From what I've read about him, Elvis Presley saw a lot of doctors in the seventies. Too many. He was taking a lot of pills. Maybe the doctor was writing him prescriptions."

"He never had a face lift, did he?" asked Jamie.

"Not that I know of. And he never had another child. Except if it's you."

Jamie was no longer putting on an act.

"How could it be me? I know who my parents are. I'm not really adopted. My mother gave birth to me physically."

Delaney agreed. "And if my father had thought this was news, you can bet he would have followed up on it. He wasn't married in 1975. He was —he still is — the most aggressive reporter I've ever met. He'll do anything to get a story."

"Are you Jewish?" Jamie saw the gold Star Of David Delaney wore.

"Half-Jewish. Sid is Jewish. My mom isn't. I wear a cross, too." She showed him.

"I wear a Jewish Star and a cross." Jamie showed her his. "I got the star from whoever left me the money. This is a weird coincidence."

"I don't think Elvis was Jewish," said Delaney.

"Hunter Davis either," he added.

They finished looking through the photos and Delaney agreed that Jamie could borrow them overnight. Maybe he had missed something. Before she left, Jamie called Beverly Hills information and asked for the phone numbers of the two doctors' offices. Both still existed. Jamie wanted to call them but didn't know what to ask. The photo was twenty years old. Who was going to remember Hunter Davis from 1975? With Elvis it was a different story, but the note said that he had waited outside. Even if Elvis had gone in, would anyone remember why? Would anyone talk to him about it?

"I'll ask Sid what to do next. I'll call him tonight."

"Speaking of tonight, can we get together for dinner or something?"

"Sorry, I have other plans." Shot down. A new experience for him. "But I'm free tomorrow. It's Saturday, remember?"

"Great. Can we hang out? I've never seen Palm Beach."

"Sure," Delaney said, happy to oblige. For a girl of nineteen she knew a lot about Palm Beach. Her father had been keeping track of Palm Beachers for over thirty years. Her mother lived in the North End of town. Together, they covered the waterfront: the Atlantic Ocean, Lake Worth and everything in-between.

She would like to know as much about Jamie Randolph, whoever he turned out to be, as she knew about Palm Beach.

Chapter 13

❧

"ADAM & EVE"

If he had jogged north and she had jogged south, Jamie and Delaney would have met near the Lake Worth bridge. Since both had taken their morning runs south, contact was not made until after seven.

"Am I calling too early?" the young man asked.

"No, I'm up before six on Saturday. I sleep late on Sunday." Delaney did not like over-sleeping, ever since she had read that the average person sleeps away twenty years of his life.

After jogging by the ocean-to-lake mansions of Manalapan, Jamie understood why The Ritz-Carlton had been constructed nearby on an empty dune. It was a gold mine on The Gold Coast, one of several hotels catering to the rich and the very rich.

"What time can I pick you up?"

"Be here at eight. But *I'm* driving." No problem. Her car had to be more comfortable than his. "We're going out for breakfast. Did you sleep good?"

"I'm more comfortable in a $45 room," Jamie answered honestly. "Did you call your father?"

"Yes. He's supposed to call me back later with some ideas."

"Great."

"Dress casual," she said. We're eating outdoors."

"That's how I always dress."

Delaney gave him directions. She was ten minutes away. Plenty of time to shower, and pack. He was checking out this morning. Jamie made a mental list of all the goodies he could have bought for $2,600. A new VCR. A couple of Prince tennis rackets. A mountain bike. A dozen pairs of shoes. Instead of just one night in a gigantic hotel suite, which was already over. He put it out of his mind. Let's move on, he told himself. I'm still rich enough to buy all that other stuff.

He had spoken to Mom last night. The overpriced room was not discussed. All he had said was, he was making a little progress and he might stay in Florida for another day or two. Mom had guessed he met a girl. He told her Delaney's name but he didn't mention The Enquirer.

Jamie watched himself towel off his muscular body in the wall size mirror. He liked looking at his own physique, he admitted it. The only thing that puzzled him was why Dad's chest was covered with hair and his was bare. Other than that, they had the same mesomorphic build. In less than ten minutes, he was dressed and in the car. Out another ten dollars in tips for the bellhop and valet, Jamie turned right onto A1A and began driving the scenic route to Sloan's Curve.

On his right, along the ocean, were a variety of six-story luxury condos with alluring names like "Emeraude," "The Meridian" and "The Enclave." The places had a similar look but each had its own personality, as well as its own private beach. Jamie had tried to run along the beach this morning, but couldn't do it in his Nikes. He loved the smell of the clean salty air, the feel of the near-hurricane-strength "ocean breezes" in your face. It amazed him to watch seagulls and pelicans use the bold wind to glide gently over the water without getting their wings torn off.

A view of the ocean was hindered most of the way to Delaney's house. To his left was the half-mile wide Intracoastal Waterway, and the pleasure boaters were up and at it. Speedboats, yachts and fishing trawlers of all sizes went by in both directions. Water-skiers were flying and skipping their way to nowhere. He wished he was one of them. Maybe he would be, in seven years, when he collected his first big installment. The Florida lifestyle had a way of making you feel like not working. As in California, people here seemed to define the world as a place to eat, boat, fish, golf, play tennis and party.

The curve at Sloan's Curve came up quickly, and suddenly

Jamie found himself past Delaney's house, hugging the shoulder of the road overlooking the foamy blue Atlantic. Traffic was light. A tight turnaround and he was back on the curve southbound. He found the entrance.

The Morrison residence was large and expensive, like all direct oceanfront homes, especially in Palm Beach. Less lavish than the Ritz-Carlton, it dwarfed his suite in size. And the upstairs balcony had an equally magnificent view of the isolated sandy shore whose nearest eastern neighbors lived three thousand miles away.

"You're rich," Jamie told Delaney, his hair flying loose out on the breezy terrace.

"My dad makes like two-fifty a year," she replied. "Is that rich?" Her hair was tied back.

"If you live here, it is."

"He made a lot more in the eighties." Delaney felt the refreshing wind in her face. She closed her eyes for a moment. "This place cost less than a million new. Trump paid ten million for his house. Of course, it's about twenty times as big. But we're happy here. I love the ocean."

"I can see why." Jamie observed a large vessel far out on the horizon.

"Come on, let's go. I'll show you the rest of the house later. We've got to be at Harpoon Louie's by eight-thirty. Sometimes it's busy. Plus, we've got a lot to see."

They left the Elvis photos sitting on the kitchen island and took her black Porsche convertible. Sid's car, that she was allowed to use over the summer if she didn't strip the gears and parked only in the deserted section of lots. The engine roared as she took Sloan's Curve at what felt like a hundred. She drove like his pal, Steve McDermott. However, she was wearing her seat belt. So was Jamie.

Now all the mansions were on the left, their docks on the Intracoastal, their beach cabanas across the road in front. Some of the homes had underground tunnels which permitted ocean access without crossing the street. This was the "Estate Section" of Palm Beach featuring many of the town's largest houses. The architecture ranged from Spanish Mizner to Imitation Versailles to Ultra-Modern to Sprawling Japanese

Pagoda. Right now the beach didn't look too bad. Occasionally, a storm washed pieces of it away, including the road itself, and Palm Beachers grudgingly chipped in to restore everything. They called it "maintenance of the erosion problem."

Delaney pointed out famous homes. The pinkish grey Coquina Stone mansion where John Lennon and Yoko Ono had lived. Donald Trump's 122-room castle, formerly the Merriweather Post estate "Mar-A-Lago" (ocean to lake), recently converted by the enterprising and manipulative Mr. Trump into a social club. Closer to town, Ms. Estée Lauder's white-columned Georgian residence, an armed guard stationed at the gate when she was visiting Palm Beach.

"We'll be back here for lunch," advised the tour guide, passing The Breakers Hotel, turning left onto Royal Poinciana and shooting over the drawbridge toward the highway.

In twenty minutes they were in the town of Jupiter, still known mainly as the home of Burt Reynolds, but rapidly expanding into a prestigious suburban metropolis. The Porsche sped across another bridge, seconds before flashing red lights signalled that the road was opening up to allow large boats passage. Delaney turned right, then left, then into the parking lot of Harpoon Louie's, a popular waterfront café facing the bright red Jupiter Lighthouse. The lighthouse had been a landmark since the Civil War and needed a new coat of paint badly.

"Who's side was Florida on?" asked Jamie. "The North or The South?"

"Who do you think, Yankee?" came the southern-accented reply.

They ate on the extended wood dock overlooking Jupiter Bay, a veranda only slightly larger than the one at Mrs. Davis' home in Memphis.

"See that house across the water? The one with the cedar shake roof. That's Perry Como's house, if he's still alive."

"Who's Perry Como?" asked Jamie.

"I'm not sure. I think he used to have a TV show."

A waitress in beige shorts and a white top brought them two bowls of Irish Porridge, with heavy cream and thick syrup.

They had been sipping fresh-squeezed Florida orange juice.

"This place is really neat," said Jamie, watching a brown pelican alight on a wood piling. There was a light breeze off Jupiter Bay, nothing like the ocean.

"You have to know when they're serving breakfast. Usually they don't open until lunch. I know the manager."

Jamie gazed at Delaney as she spooned a small portion of cereal into her mouth, testing its hotness. She was wearing a blue and white striped sundress, he a blue and white striped Ralph Lauren Polo Shirt.

"Hey, we're dressed like twins," he said.

"You're right," she said, noticing the stripes for the first time. "Should I put on a pair of dungaree shorts and tuck in my dress?"

Jamie couldn't help looking at her shapely legs when she asked the question. He had been trying not to ogle them in the car, but the dress was short and rode up whenever she moved. She had the faintest trace of blond baby hair on her calves and above her crossed knee.

"I don't shave my legs, if that's what your wondering."

He had shovelled in a heaping spoonful of hot porridge. Without thinking, he swallowed it, choked and washed it down with cold juice.

"Was I staring at your legs?" Two quick, raspy coughs. He was better.

"I think so. In the car, too." She ran a finger, slowly across her lips, removing a trace of food. "I don't mind, Jamie. I like you." Her forwardness was a pleasant surprise. "I like you, too," he said.

"I like your hair," she said, touching it.

His thick, dirty-blond hair was straight, medium length and combed back. Women would kill for his hair. "Where's your pepper spray?" he asked before making any advances.

She patted her purse. "It's here if I need it."

"You won't," he assured her, sliding his fingertips down the back of her arm.

She put her hand over his, left it there for a few seconds. "That gave me a chill."

"I have that effect on women," he joked, immodestly.

"So did your father."

"Jack or Elvis?"

"Elvis," she said. The fresh brewed coffee was delicious. Jamie did not drink regular coffee at home. It made him drowsy. Just the opposite of Mom and Dad.

On the way out, Delaney began telling him about the nouveau riche flocking to Jupiter. To "gated communities" like Admiral's Cove and Frenchman's Creek, thousand acre sanctuaries with private marinas and waterways, multi-million dollar clubhouses and world class golf courses.

"Of course, Palm Beach is still the place for Old Money," she clarified. "Admirals Cove is for doctors, lawyers and astronauts. Oh, there is a place called Jupiter Island for people who want Palm Beach without all the glitz. It's just over the bridge. The landscaping is so dense you can hardly see the houses. And all the rich people have these little bitty signs stuck in their front lawns with their name on them, like: The Vanderbilts."

"Is it too early to call your father?" Jamie followed her through the long parking lot to the Porsche. Across the street, a new museum was under construction.

Delaney turned her wrist. A quarter to ten. A quarter to seven on the West Coast.

"No, he's up," she said, jumping back into the car, showing off her white panties for a split second. She grabbed the car phone. "Daddy? Good morning. I'm with Jamie Randolph, we're at Harpoon Louie's. Yes, I'm parked way back in the corner. No, I'm not driving too fast." She rolled her eyes for Jamie's benefit. "Yes, he's a very nice young man. No, he doesn't take drugs. No, I didn't ask him. Come on Daddy, please. I'm not a baby. Yes, he's right here. Would you like to talk to him? Fine."

She pouted and gave Jamie the phone.

"Mr. Morrison. Hi. It's Jamie Randolph." He listened. "I'm eighteen. No, I'm not driving the car, your daughter is. Yes, she's a very good driver. Excellent. Yes, my father really is a lawyer. Randolph, Myers and Jacob. In Hackensack. Yes, I would really appreciate it if you could check out those two medical offices. Oh, right. Saturday. Okay, well, it's not really an emergency." Jamie looked at Delaney. He didn't expect this kind of cross examination, but she just shrugged her shoulders. This guy was pushier than he was. "Yes, okay. So if we don't hear from you today, we'll talk to you on Monday. Am I busy this week? No, why? Would I like to come to California? I don't know."

"I can't believe he asked you that."

"I've never been to Beverly Hills. Yeah, sure, I watch it on TV every Wednesday. Yes, I'd love to see it in person. It must be outrageous. Would I come if The Enquirer paid for it? Well, yeah, I guess so. I'm not sure. I'd have to call my parents. Okay, I will. Yes, today. Would you like to talk to Delaney?" His jaw dropped. "He hung up."

"That's Sid."

Delaney drove to the north end of Jupiter Island, also known as Hobe Sound, playing the part of Robin Leach. She then took U.S. 1 south to Singer Island, showed him another luxury community called "Lost Tree Village" and the second wildlife preserve of the day named for deceased billionaire John D. MacArthur. Back in the fifties, MacArthur had purchased much of northern Palm Beach County for a song. It remained largely undeveloped until after the insurance magnate's death. Even now, in the nineties, huge parcels of land were just being subdivided, subject to environmental concerns. In Jupiter, the Atlanta Braves were planning to move to a new spring training stadium and it was rumored that Ted Turner might relocate his whole corporate headquarters there. Ted Turner, the man who also owned the rights to thirteen Elvis movies, Delaney informed him. She had read it in TV Guide.

After criss-crossing Singer Island, Delaney drove west on PGA Boulevard to the fairly new Gardens Mall. A two-story extravaganza paved with millions of square feet of marble and highlighted by an eighty foot tall center atrium, promoters had hired Lauren Hutton to invite the public to the Gardens Mall in local TV ads. During the winter business was booming. Like most activities in Florida, shopping at The Gardens slowed in July. Two little girls stuck their tongues out at them from a glass elevator rising to the mezzanine.

"I have to pick up my mother's ring at the jewelry store," Delaney explained. "They adjusted it for her. I promised I'd get it on the way."

"On the way to where?"

"On the way to shopping for myself in the mall, silly," she said.

At which time the enthusiastic young lady embarked on a whirlwind tour of six clothing shops, two women's accessories, Sam Goody's, two shoe stores, Sak's Fifth Avenue and ended up at the jeweler's holding her mother's ring. All in less than an hour and a half. Enroute to the car with Jamie carrying four fat white bags and two thin ones, Delaney picked up a pair of teddy bear lollipops at The Chocolate Factory.

"We need to restore our energy before meeting Claire," she said, unwrapping a pop.

"Who's Claire?"

"Claire Montgomery. My mother. We're meeting her for lunch." She bit the head off her teddy bear. "By the way, you weren't peeking when I was trying on clothes, were you?"

"I wish I was," he answered truthfully. "Those were pretty hot outfits. Especially that red bathing suit with all the holes. You did buy that one, right?"

"Twenty-three dollars," recalled Delaney. "On sale. I also bought that black negligee. Not that *you'll* ever see me wear it again. Come on, can't you walk any faster?"

Jamie had never taken much of an interest in shopping. But this wasn't like accompanying his sister, his mother or girls he knew. Shopping with Delaney Morrison had been exhilarating, fun, interesting, maybe even educational — or did it only seem that way because he enjoyed being with her so much? Was he infatuated with her, or was he falling in love? It didn't matter. All he knew was he would not be back in Tenafly on Monday, and maybe he would take her father up on that trip to California if it meant they could be together. Besides, this was his summer job.

"Where's lunch?" Jamie asked, slamming the trunk.

"In Palm Beach. At Chuck and Harold's. We passed it before. Remember I said we'll be back here for lunch, by The Breakers?"

Jamie could barely remember his social security number.

"Mom's a broker," Delaney continued. "She just sold a house and we're celebrating. Lunch is on her."

"Where does she live?"

"On Garden Road, in Palm Beach. About three miles north of the restaurant. If she has time we can stop at her house after lunch. It's nothing great, a renovated sixties house with a giant living room and a nice pool. Mom bought it after the divorce four years ago. She's very independent. She had her own money before, during and after the marriage. When Grandma Montgomery dies, she'll really be rich. Her family owns like half of New Hampshire. In the summer, they all live in a place called Wolfeboro. On the lake, of course."

"Why did they get divorced? Do you mind if I ask?"

"You can ask me anything. Sid and Claire just need their own space, it's as simple as that. Dad's life is too exciting. He can't sit still. They met at a wedding in Palm Beach and fell in love. Got married, she moved to Fort Lauderdale, I was born, we all hated it there, moved back to Palm Beach when I was seven." Delaney caught her breath. "The house is big enough, well you know. But Sid can't keep normal hours, always has to travel, meet new people. Especially young women. I lived with Mom until last year when I turned eighteen. Then I moved into the dorm at Boston. I'm only living with Dad temporarily. He thinks I'm going to be a reporter like him. I want to *teach* journalism, but don't tell him. Mom knows. She always loved real estate. She liked being a mother but Sid wouldn't give her a break. He always wanted more kids, but without being there. She always wanted a more active social life."

They were on the highway, doing about seventy. They passed Blue Heron Boulevard going south.

"What's a blue heron?" the New Jerseyite inquired.

"A big bird. I'll show you one. Anyway, the shit hit the fan in 1991 when Mom demanded to have a career. Dad told her to wait a few more years. She told him she had waited too long already. She told Sid she wasn't asking, she was telling. I was there." Delaney remembered the day. "There wasn't a lot of fighting. They just made some kind of deal, Dad got the house,

Mom got me. I'm not mad at Sid. He really loves me. And he still loves Claire. He's just nuts. And she couldn't take all the crazy people Sid has to associate with. You know, they're pretty low key in Palm Beach, and deep down Mom is a Palm Beacher. Sid's not. He could care less if he writes a story about someone living around the corner. Like the Trumps, or the Pulitzers. It bothers Mom. She's really a nicer person. Sid knows it too."

"I don't get it," said Jamie. "Your father seems like a very open minded guy. He goes where he wants. Your mother didn't object for fifteen years. . . "

"She objected. She just lived with it."

"Oh. But why couldn't he give her a little more freedom? I mean, if they really loved each other."

"Because Dad's really a traditionalist, in his private life. The man gets to do what he wants, the wife stays home. Sid wanted her to stay home until I went to college." That was the precise relationship *his* father and mother had. Except Jack stuck around and Diane didn't want a career until her kids were grown up. But Delaney was right. Her father's idea of marriage and family was too domineering.

"What about you?" Delaney asked.

"My Mom and Dad? They're both traditionalists, so the marriage works."

"No, you. What about you?"

Jamie thought about it as a police car passed them on the other side of the highway. Delaney slowed to fifty-five.

"Me? Well, first of all I don't plan to get married for a while. My Mom got real upset when I told her I wasn't sure I would have kids."

Delaney understood.

"I'm not sure either," she said.

They approached the Okeechobee Boulevard exit. There seemed to be a lot of boulevards in Palm Beach County.

"What's an Okeechobee?" asked the Northerner.

"An Indian name. There's a town called Okeechobee sixty miles north. Finish answering my question. I answered yours."

Jamie would have liked to change the subject. This was

too serious for . . . a first date.

"If I get married," said Jamie, "And I expect to someday. If I get married, I want to know everything about that person before we say 'I do.' I don't believe in divorce. I mean, if it happens, it happens. But I believe in fate. When you meet the right person, you know it. But then you still have to be sure that you can always love each other. Don't get mad, but if your parents were honest, they might not have married."

"My mother was pregnant."

Jamie extended his arms to the dashboard, stretched his muscles.

"I'm not shocked. But that's not a good reason to get married."

Delaney scowled at him.

"You mean, if you got me pregnant, you wouldn't marry me?"

"I wouldn't get you pregnant," he replied.

"But what if you did?"

Jamie didn't know the answer to that question.

"Okay," he said. "I guess if I got you pregnant, which could only happen with someone I knew I was going to marry. . . "

Delaney cut him off.

"Are you saying you're a virgin?" she asked with anticipation.

"I've done lots of stuff with girls," Jamie said defensively.

"But you're a virgin," she repeated. "I can't believe it!"

"If I got you pregnant," Jamie said, ignoring the issue, "I would marry you. I would marry you because I believe that every life is too important to be careless with. Every child deserves his natural mother and father if possible. And then we would work it out so it was fair for both of us. I don't think the man is superior. I don't see anything wrong if the man stays home and the woman works. Or they take turns. I don't know. But there always has to be a way. I really believe that." Then Jamie remembered why he was in Florida in the first place. "Of course," he said, "now that I'm a millionaire . . . "

"To be continued," Delaney said, wiping her eyes.

"Did I get you upset? Are you crying?" Jamie asked.

"No, dummy," said Delaney. "The wind blew something

into my face. Hey, see that big round building, the one that looks like a space station? That's the new Kravis Center. It's like Lincoln Center in New York."

As the couple drove through the new West Palm Beach downtown, they could feel the revitalization process. A decaying business section had been demolished and new streets and structures were taking its place. In a few years, many planners envisioned a marvelous new city in Florida.

"Does Donald Trump have anything to do with this?" asked Jamie.

"Donald Trump wants to rebuild the whole world," Delaney answered. "For thirty percent."

ॐ

There was no wait for a table at Chuck and Harold's. And when there was, it didn't apply to Claire Montgomery. Claire waved to Delaney from her vantage point on the streetside patio. Her daughter returned the greeting from the huge flower decorated lawn separating opposing lanes of traffic. They had parked across the street between a new Mercedes and another Porsche. Jamie held her hand until she skipped onto the curb and rushed to her mother.

After the perfunctory double kiss, she made the formal introduction.

"This is my friend, Jamie Randolph. He's on vacation from New Jersey. He's staying in the Presidential Suite at the Ritz-Carlton."

"At twenty-six hundred dollars a night?" remarked Claire. "You must be rich. Can I show your parents a house?"

Jamie smiled.

"He's not with his parents, Claire. He's here by himself."

"In the Presidential Suite? Are you a rock star, or an actor? Oh my goodness. Delaney, he looks just like . . . a little too young . . . "

"Don't say it, Mom."

"Kurt Russell!" Claire shouted, and some heads turned.

Jamie laughed and offered to shake hands. She pulled

171

him toward her and kissed his cheek.

"Nice to meet you, Mrs. Montgomery." Jamie could feel her lipstick on his face.

"Call me Claire, please. So tell me, who are you, Mr. Ritz-Carlton?" Jamie looked at Delaney before answering.

"Jamie will be attending Dartmouth in September," said the girl.

"I'm impressed. Your grandfather went to Dartmouth, rest his soul."

"Jamie's doing research on investigative publications. It's a summer project. The National Enquirer falls into that category."

"Barely," said Claire, tongue in cheek. "Too bad your father's not around. He could give Jamie some pointers. On second thought, maybe it's better that he's not."

No one mentioned the possible trip to Beverly Hills. Jamie realized that Delaney did not want to discuss everything with her mother at this time. After providing Claire with a brief biography of Jamie, Delaney was ready to order. Paddle fans revolved silently on the outdoor painted beam ceiling. The summer sun was already overhead at one in the afternoon, but it was still hot. The fans and an awning helped. The noisy street reminded Jamie of the Village in Manhattan, except for the Royal Palm trees.

"I'd like the Linguini Primavera," said Delaney. She shook open her napkin.

"The Oriental Honey Mustard Dolphin with sunshine rice and vegetables," Claire told the waitress.

"I'll have the barbecued rib sandwich." Delaney nudged him with her elbow. "Not in this heat," she suggested.

"Make that two Linguinis," said Jamie.

The drinks had arrived, two Evians and a large Coke. Claire had previously ordered a white wine, but she wasn't really drinking it. Occasionally , she wet her fingertips and licked them off. A covered basket of the bistro's mouth-watering light and dark hot rolls was also served. A two inch square of butter was stamped with a bee hive design.

"Walk me to the wash room," said Delaney. "Back in a minute, Mom."

On the way, they passed the bar. A glass case displayed Chuck and Harold's caps for sale. The caps showed hot red peppers and jungle parrots on a black background. Overhead was a tremendous color blow-up of two middle aged men, arms outstretched, dressed as waiters.

"I take it that's Chuck and Harold." Jamie guessed Chuck was on the left, alphabetically.

"Yes. Unfortunately, Chuck passed away a couple of years ago. Terrible accident. Chuck and his wife took their boat to the Bahamas and didn't hear the weather report. They were lost at sea in a hurricane. The family searched for them for months."

"That's awful." Jamie looked past the bar to an interior courtyard dining room protected by a blue and yellow tarp.

"Don't tell her about this Elvis thing, okay?" requested Delaney. "And don't say anything about Beverly Hills either. It's not a secret, I just don't feel like arguing with Claire today. She's happy."

"No problem. I only have one question. Why is your mother eating porpoise for lunch? Isn't that illegal?"

Delaney put her hand on Jamie's shoulder and vibrated with girlish laughter.

"She's eating *dolphin*, not porpoise. In Florida, dolphin is the name of a popular fish. Don't worry, she's not eating Flipper!"

After lunch, Delaney gave Claire the ring. The very pretty woman, who closely resembled her daughter, slipped it on her pinky.

"Perfect," she said. "I designed it myself." The ring was shaped like the state of Florida. Its granular surface depicted sand. In the sand was a tiny "Claire" the way it might be written with a big toe. They kissed goodbye. Claire kissed Jamie, who had removed the lipstick from her earlier kiss. Luckily, she hadn't put more on after lunch.

⚜

According to Delaney Morrison, world authority on the

173

finest streets in America, Worth Avenue in Palm Beach was "classier" than Rodeo Drive in Beverly Hills. Both featured exclusive stores like Gucci and Cartier. And both were very expensive places to shop. On Worth Avenue, for example, you could have a museum quality family photo taken for two thousand dollars. The difference, Delaney explained, was the "old world ambience" in Palm Beach. The European style alleys leading to hidden courtyards. The predominant older architecture, the flowering vines of clematis and bougainvillas climbing romantic archways . . .

"Is that a drinking fountain for dogs?" asked Jamie, looking down.

A few seconds later the question was answered when a tall lady in white high heels allowed her Bijon Friese to quench his thirst. After imbibing, Jacques (or Fifi) felt a tug on its rhinestone and red leather collar. He shook himself and haughtily continued his Worth Avenue excursion.

"I see what you mean about high class," Jamie jokingly commented. At the corner, a white Rolls Royce was waiting. An overdressed chauffeur held the door while the lady in white and her matching doggie entered the rear seat.

"What? You don't think that a slobbering dog is classy?" said Delaney.

They laughed together, then did a little window shopping in one of the alleyways named "Via Parigi." The young lady purchased a wide-brimmed straw hat.

"Oh, I forgot. Did you want this?" Delaney asked, offering Jamie a half melted chocolate teddy bear. She unwrapped it and once again bit the head off. "Here," she said. "You can have the rest."

The saleswoman chuckled, not taking her eyes off the young man. She was trying to decide which she liked better: his face or his body. He was her junior by at least twenty years, but she still fantasized going to bed with him. Jamie hardly noticed her. She tingled when he took Delaney's hand and inserted her fingers into his mouth along with the chocolate. Brown streaked fingers came out. The rest of the bear had been devoured. The attractive woman had to figure the bill three times before getting it right. When they left she drew in her breath, let it out, said "Oh, my," and placed an ice cube behind her left ear for ten seconds. Like his father, Jamie did have that effect on women. They returned to the car.

"Why are there chalk marks on your tires?" asked Jamie.

"The Palm Beach police check your car in an hour," Delaney explained. If you park on Worth Avenue for more than that, they give you a ticket."

He looked around. "In the summer? There's no one here."

"Don't mess around with the Palm Beach police. They have very good manners but they follow the letter of the law."

Jamie wondered whether it would be the same in Beverly Hills. He pictured Eddie Murphy giving him a ticket, sucking in his crazy laugh.

In the car, Jamie told Delaney about something he had overheard in the restaurant.

"The people sitting in the corner were talking about buying a house in Palm Beach. They were visiting from Maine. The guy was a publisher from New York. They heard the summer was a good time to buy. She said she wanted a small house in town, near the ocean. I meant to tell your mother."

"You heard all that while we were talking?"

"Yeah, I can listen to two conversations at the same time."

Delaney didn't know whether to tell him or not. She had done a little homework on Elvis last night, skimmed a book or two. In one she had read that Elvis Presley's innate musical ability was related to his wonderful hearing. He had perfect pitch. And he could listen to two conversations at the same time. Just a coincidence, she decided. Why bring it up?

The Porsche careened into the driveway at Sloan's Curve. It just missed Jamie's rent-a-car and came to a stop at the rising garage door. She pulled in and closed the door behind them.

"Are you going back to the hotel?" Delaney asked. "Would you help me carry my things in first? We can call Sid again if you want, go through the photos one more time." She didn't want him to leave.

"Where's the nearest Holiday Inn?" Jamie asked matter-of-factly.

"You checked out?"

"My bag's in the trunk. I may be rich," he said, tapping his temple, "but I'm not crazy."

"Stay here with me," Delaney suggested, a little too quickly.

"No, I don't think so."

She touched his arm. "Look, I'm sorry about the pepper spray thing," she said, hoping he wasn't mad. "I over-reacted. I know it was just an innocent kiss. I realize I'm so attractive, you couldn't resist." She tickled him. "I trust you. I can see what kind of guy you are. Stay here."

Jamie looked at her mouth. Her soft, sensuous lips were tempting.

"That's the problem. I'm still a guy. I don't want anything to happen. Delaney, you're really beautiful. And you're a very nice person. I'd like to get to know you better. In fact, I don't even want to go back to New Jersey."

She held his thick arm.

"Then don't. We have separate guest accommodations. Don't get too big a head. I'm not asking you to marry me! All I'm saying is why go anywhere else when I've got this big house to share with you? For one night."

The weather was perfect, not a cloud in the sky. Jamie was dying to feel the hot sand through a blanket and the hot sun on his skin. He wasn't going to get cancer in one hour. The beach was only a hundred feet away.

"Can I think about it? I'd really like to lie on the beach for a while, like the stupid tourists do."

"And I can tell you something I know about Elvis," Delaney promised.

So much for the Holiday Inn, thought the young man.

By a quarter to five, Jamie had been broiling for over an hour, first lying on his back, then on his chest. His tender skin did not look as red outdoors as it would in the house. The strong sun protector Delaney had rubbed on his body helped but sunbathing in Florida in July was brutal. The girl with untanned skin sat wisely under an umbrella.

"I think you've had enough for today," she told Jamie. Obediently, he rose to his feet, feeling the heat mostly behind his knees, and picked up his stuff. Sunglasses, lotion, a towel, his watch and his wallet. His keys were inside. He carried everything, including the blankets and the umbrella, back to the house.

"What did you want to tell me about Elvis?" he asked, grimacing as his red shoulder scraped against a door frame. Delaney suppressed a snicker. Maybe sunburn wasn't fatal, but it sure hurt like hell.

"Oh, it's about that theory you and your father came up with. Where Elvis and his lawyer were transferring money, using your name, only they died before they could get it back." Delaney removed her sandals. Set them neatly next to the slider facing the pool, toes out, left shoe left. "Your theory makes sense, because from what I read Elvis was very pro-America."

"What do you mean?"

Delaney closed the door behind them to keep the air-conditioning in.

"He would never have put his money in a Swiss Bank. Even to avoid taxes. Elvis took pride in paying his taxes. I also checked rates. As a long-term investment, the lower interest rate you get in Switzerland, plus the risk of currency changes, makes it smarter to keep the money here. At least that's what my financial planner says."

The girl really had a brain.

"And he wouldn't have set up a trust in his lawyer's name either."

"Why not?"

Delaney turned up the thermostat so they could shower.

"Because if the lawyer died, which in this case he did, the lawyer's *family* might have a claim to the trust."

"That's true," said Jamie. "You made some good points. Where can I take a shower?"

"In the guest bath." Delaney pointed. "It's down that hall, make a right, up the stairs. One more thing," she said. He looked back, holding his suitcase. "None of this proves a thing. It's just a theory. You could come up with other theories that make sense."

"That's why I'm trying to find out more about Hunter Davis. Maybe I should go to Beverly Hills. Maybe your dad can help."

"You mean *we*? We should go to Beverly Hills?"

"That's what I said."

She punched him in the stomach, hurting her wrist.

"No, you didn't. You said *I*. I should go to Beverly Hills."

"Well, I meant we. Same thing. I'm gonna take a shower. See ya."

After showering and changing into shorts and tee shirts, Jamie and Delaney agreed to call for a pizza. They watched TV while they waited. The Black Crowes were jamming in a new video. Jack hated this group. Jamie and Delaney loved them.

"I've got plenty of beer," she said. "What kind do you like?"

"I don't drink."

"Just testing. I don't have any beer anyway."

Delaney dug her fingers into his rock hard abdominals.

"I'm not ticklish," Jamie said, reaching for her underarm. "Are you?"

"Yes! Don't touch me!" she screamed, twisting away. He caught her by the wrist, released it when the doorbell rang. The Pizza man was five minutes early.

He ate three slices, she, one. Then they watched Delaney's favorite movie of all time: "Sleepless In Seattle." He had never seen it before. He liked the movie, too. Meg Ryan was pretty cute for an older woman. And that Tom Hanks. How did he get all these great parts?

They were in the entertainment room, on Sid Morrison's gigantic leather couch, a stone fireplace soaring to the vaulted ceiling. In the corner was the largest wide screen television Jamie had ever seen. Yet the picture quality was incredible. Delaney explained that this was High Density T.V., a gift to Sid from some big shot in Japan. Jamie put that down on his shopping list for May, 2002. When he tried to slide his arm around Delaney, the sunburnt skin chafed by the door forced him to pull it back.

"What's the matter?"

"My shoulder hurts," he said. "I guess you were right about the sun."

"Take off your shirt," she said, helping him lift it over his head. She turned him around to assess the damage.

"Want me to kiss it?" Delaney asked. "It might feel better if I give it a medicine kiss. That's what my mother used to do for my boo-boos."

"I'm sure it would."

Delaney touched her lips lightly to the red skin. The heat warmed her face. "It's hot," she said, running two fingers down his spine. The medicine kiss was definitely working.

"Can I kiss you?" he asked politely.

"I don't know," she said. "Can you?"

His arm was under her tee shirt, around back, holding her waist. As they kissed, tongues touching, he could smell her skin. If she was wearing perfume, he couldn't sense it. He moved his mouth to her neck and then to a bare shoulder. All he could inhale, and taste, was the scent and salty flavor of the clean surface of her body. He took a little nip at her neck, then kissed it softly. The purring sound in her throat indicated that she approved.

"Let me undress *you*," she said to his surprise, after a few minutes.

He stood up and felt the metal snap below his navel pop open. His pants and underpants went down in a quick movement. Delaney was kissing his chest. He bent his head to smell her hair, ran his fingers around both of her ears, then brought a hand under her chin so they could kiss again.

"Now let me undress you," he said, carefully removing her shirt. He unclipped the front-opening bra and kissed her breasts.

"Don't stop," she said breathlessly, and Jamie Randolph wondered how it had gone so far so fast. He had been with many young women before, done just about everything whenever he wanted, but it had never felt like this. He wondered, too, whether she had done this with many men before him. Could she have given herself so willingly, so easily, to others? He wanted to know, but he really didn't care. He couldn't ask, and it really didn't matter. All he knew was fate had brought him here, to this warm and attractive young lady who seemed to be a missing piece of the puzzle that was now his life. . . his obsession. . .

He took her in his arms, and as easily as most men would hold a small child, he carried her to the rug in front of the fireplace. They embraced and kissed deeply while Jamie slipped off her shorts and panties with one hand. Her thigh was narrow in his massive grasp. His fingers crawled up gently stroking her flat tummy, then down to her knee. He kissed her ankles, then her legs.

She watched him, opening and closing her eyes as he touched and kissed her everywhere, trying to say things to him with her eyes and her body language that words could never express. She thought he understood. And he did.

Afterwards, Tom Hanks and Meg Ryan were finally meeting each other on the top floor of The Empire State Building. Delaney and Jamie were still naked, but covered by a small blanket taken from a chair, their heads on throw pillows. When Jamie tried to tell her how happy he was, she kissed him and said, "Don't talk now." She buried her head in his chest and cuddled up against him, feeling his great strength.

The next time Jamie tried to say something to her, he realized that she was asleep. He decided to take a short nap, too. They woke up at eight-thirty Sunday morning, watching violent cartoons, in the same position they had fallen asleep.

"Good morning," whispered Delaney, smiling at Jamie, touching his nose with a fingertip. "How's your shoulder?"

"It's fine," said Jamie. "Magic cure. Shall we try it again?"

And they did, lazing away a Sunday in Palm Beach.

Chapter 14

❦

"MEET THY MAKER"

Sid Morrison's stretch limo driver was an expert at negotiating the traffic from L.A.X. to Rodeo Drive. He made the trip in less than half an hour. Sitting beside Delaney on a bench seat facing the rear, Jamie tried to size up the good looking man holding hands with the dark-haired model. He was sure Mr. Morrison was doing the same. A fold-up imitation wood cocktail table separated the two couples. Four glasses of Evian water rattled in their plastic holders. Elton John's "Circle Of Life" seeped quietly from hidden speakers.

"So you're the son of Elvis Presley," Sid spouted out abashedly.

"Daddy!"

"I didn't say it. He did."

"He is very good looking," said Sid's escort. Her name was Yvonne. She spoke with a Spanish accent, but looked Asian. "Is he really the son of Elvis Presley?"

"Ask him," Sid coaxed.

There was silence for about a minute.

"I'm not the son of Elvis," said Jamie. The model sat back, drooped her shoulders unprofessionally, placed her hand on Sid Morrison's leg.

"Then who is?" Sid asked.

Jamie laughed. "You're a good kidder, Mr. Morrison."

"Call me Sid."

"I'm not saying it's absolutely impossible that I'm the son of Elvis." Jamie looked at Delaney. "Well, maybe I am saying that."

"What are you saying?" asked Sid. "I'm a busy man. My daughter is a busy woman. This is a busy town."

"I'm busy, too," added Yvonne. It was all in good humor.

"All I'm saying is that there seems to be a connection between me and Elvis Presley's lawyer. That's what I want to check out. If by some miracle it turns out I'm Elvis, Jr., then I guess you've got a good story."

"A very good story," said The Superstar. "That's why I asked the paper to put up the money for your trip. They know it doesn't always happen, but if it's there, I'll find it. You can bet the farm."

Delaney stared at Yvonne's wandering hand.

"Even if he's not related to Elvis, the inheritance mystery is a good story. Right, Dad? Page three, right?"

"Well, maybe page five." Sid lifted Yvonne's hand, held it in his. He wasn't shy, but the model's behavior was becoming just a tad inappropriate.

When the car let them off at Rick's Place on Beverly Drive, Jamie was ready for "the best hamburger in Beverly Hills." What he never expected was that it would be served in an eatery designed after Rick's Café Americain in *Casablanca.* Exact details had been duplicated right down to the standing piano and an elegant satin-jacketed black pianist who had just arrived via time machine from 1942.

"My dad would think he died and went to heaven," Jamie said, gaping at Humphrey Bogart across the room. He remembered a synthesized TV ad for Coke where Elton John and Bogart are in the same room. "It looks so . . . real!"

"It's supposed to," said Sid Morrison. "That's why Sylvester Stallone and Arnold Schwarzenegger just spent two million bucks on a hamburger joint. They even cook authentic Moroccan cuisine, not that anyone would know if it wasn't. And I doubt that many people order it. But it's fun. Excuse me. I left Yvonne in the car, she's not having lunch with us."

"Why not?" asked Delaney. "Can she stand not touching you for an hour?"

The remark was in bad taste, but her father ignored it.

"She doesn't eat lunch," he explained. "And she's got a

photo shoot outside of town. I'm picking her up for dinner at eight." While the couple was shown to the only empty table, Sid left to say goodbye to his girl friend. A "Reserved" sign was removed, and they were given menus.

It was just after noon and almost as hot in California as it had been in Palm Beach. Barring an earthquake, the air-conditioning was a life saver. It was about seventy-five degrees in the restaurant. Two Nazi officers in full dress and mustaches, hopefully actors, drank faux martinis at the bar. "Sam" was playing a forties number; it wasn't "As Time Goes By." A few witty patrons said, "Play it again, Sam." The piano player smiled like it wasn't the ninety-ninth time he'd heard it this week.

During lunch (Jamie and Sid ate hamburgers; Delaney ordered a salad), plans were made to visit the Beverly Hills Fertility Clinic first. It was located on Little Santa Monica Boulevard off Beverly and Sid had called. He made a one-thirty appointment with Marcia Havermeyer, the director, who had no idea who he was. The name of a biologist at Cal Tech had been mentioned, a friend of his who was a candidate for the Nobel Prize. Nothing had been said of The National Enquirer, Elvis Presley or Jamie Randolph. Sid knew how to open doors, and how not to close them.

Their second stop would be Dr. Goldman's office. It wasn't far away, just around the corner from the center of Rodeo Drive, an opportunistic spot for a plastic surgeon. Unfortunately, Morrison had been informed that Dr. Goldman was out of town. In his place, they would be meeting with Leonard Stein, the doctor's assistant. He had sounded pleasant on the phone. Stein was told that the caller knew a very satisfied former client and wished to discuss having the same procedure done. Anything to get in the door. Jamie could appreciate Sid's techniques. He was taking notes.

"You guys are staying with me," Sid informed them. "My condo is over on Burton Way and Third, near Cedar Sinai Hospital. We rented a three bedroom for a year, so we each have our own room. And three baths, too. It's nice."

Delaney considered provoking him with a request that she and Jamie share a room, but skipped it. Even if he was planning to prance around naked with the long-legged mixed breed Cindy Crawford hanging on his neck, she would not be allowed to cohabitate. And if he had any notion of what had transpired at Sloan's Curve she would be banished to her mother's house forever.

"By the way, how's the Simpson deal?" Jamie asked.

"Don't ask." So much for making conversation. So far, he had learned much more about O.J. Simpson from Geraldo Rivera than from Delaney's old man.

"Oh, Daddy, I know what I wanted to ask you. Jamie and I would like to take a celebrity tour of Beverly Hills."

"Already booked for tomorrow morning." Sid handed them the Gray Lines brochure. "This is a special route, off the beaten path so to speak. You'll see Stephen Spielberg's house, if you want to call it that; Madonna's, and of course Mr. Simpson's home in Brentwood. And a couple of dozen more."

"That's great, Daddy. Thanks." Delaney reached across the table to give him a hug. Her chair tilted back at precisely the same time two tall costumed waiters were rushing to the kitchen. One slipped, dropping his tray. The other stepped on the tray.

Approximately two milliseconds after the first waiter grabbed Delaney's arm in a non-friendly manner, Jamie had him by the throat. Eyes bulging, the oxygen starved man observed his fellow server's wrist wrenched into an unnatural shape and the two were pressed back-to-back. It happened so fast that Delaney was only half seated when she noticed the waiter's face turning blue-red. Sid Morrison was in a state of shock, which didn't happen very often.

Before she could say anything, the human guard-dog had already released his two victims, shoving them backwards.

"What the hell was that?" said the second waiter, massaging his arm, keeping his distance.

"Are you paranoid?" the first waiter sputtered, leaning on a table to maintain his balance. "Who do you think you are? The Terminator?"

Jamie eyeballed them cautiously, detecting no aggressive momentum.

"You keep your hands to yourself, you won't have a

problem, shithead!" the wrestler warned. Without looking away, he asked Delaney if she was all right.

"I'm fine," she said, as the manager hurried to the scene.

"What happened, boys?" asked the Moroccan Police Chief.

"The girl tripped me with her chair," one responded. "Josh was right behind me. He saw it. Then this nut grabs us, starts choking me . . . "

"Don't say anything," Sid instructed Jamie. He called the manager aside. "We've had a little misunderstanding. My daughter's fiancé thought that one of your waiters was attacking us. The man did grab Delaney's arm. I think we've had an over-reaction here." Sid shoved some bills into the man's jacket pocket. "Why don't we all apologize and forget the whole thing?"

The manager agreed.

"Let's go, fellas. People are beating down the doors to get in here. Let's get some food on the tables." *Casablanca* played on twenty TV monitors around the room.

Taking the long way around, the waiters returned to the kitchen. Sid explained to Jamie that self-defense or not, lawsuits don't pay. He threw some more money on the table and suggested they leave immediately. People really were clamoring to eat at Rick's; the line went halfway down the street. A photographer had captured the whole thing with a telephoto lens for his boss, Sid Morrison. Great shots for The Enquirer — "Son Of Elvis Kicks Butt In Casablanca" — should the Elvis angle turn out to be a good story.

⚜

The Beverly Hills Fertility Clinic ("Established 1965") was a cheery place to come with a dismal problem. Its tall Palladian windows splashed daylight against spacious white walls humanized by prints of Botero's fat people and their fat pets. Realistic cat pictures by folk artist Susan Powers complemented the mood. Roman columns flanked the reception desk surrounded by cozy chairs, Laura Ashley love seats and an artistically selected variety of terra cotta flower pots. Only one other young couple was in the large room. She didn't appear to be pregnant, but they looked hopeful as the man's finger traced the path of a luminous blue tropical fish across the window wall of a two hundred gallon tank.

Jamie and his new friends smiled at the couple who turned their heads to see who else needed help today.

"Mr. and Mrs. Eckert, Dr. Jaffe will see you now."

A door had opened and the young hopefuls followed a nurse.

"Can we help you?" asked the lady behind the columns. She looked like a young grandmother from a sitcom. A show like "Growing Pains."

"Morrison," said Sid. "We have an appointment with Ms. Havermeyer."

"You're here early."

(Okay, we'll have some fresh baked oatmeal cookies. Where's the jar?)

"We'll wait."

"Sure. Just fill out these forms if you're a new client. You can use the table over there." She handed Morrison a white sheet and a yellow sheet, plus a Mont Blanc pen. No Bics here. "Is this your daughter?"

"Yes." Delaney only slightly resembled her daddy, but since Jamie looked nothing like Sid, it was still an easy guess.

"Let me ring Ms. Havermeyer. She usually eats in."

Five minutes passed.

Marcia Havermeyer also looked like a young grandmother. She was in her fifties, reasonably tall and slim, a brunette with grey edges, wearing round glasses and a string of small pearls. Her grey and pink checked dress was ultra-conservative. Matching grey low heels, grey stockings. A dark grey belt was hooked in the tightest position. She was somewhere between "not very laid back" and downright staid.

"I'm Marcia Havermeyer," she introduced herself with a bright business smile.

"Sid Morrison. And this is my daughter, Delaney, and her fiancé, Jamie."

They all shook hands and said pleased to meet you, etc. Then Marcia Havermeyer led them through a door to her private office. Once seated, Sid took control of the conversation.

"You mentioned Dr. Bartow," she asked. "Are you just a name-dropper?"

"No," said Sid, handing her Dr. Bartow's card. "Simon is a very good friend of mine. If you ever need his help, please call me. But that's not the reason we're here today." He returned the partially completed medical forms and the pen.

"All right. Why are you here?" Jamie caught a glimpse of a McDonald's Quarter-Pounder-With-Cheese wrapper crushed in the wastebasket behind her. "I assume that your daughter is not trying to get pregnant at this time. Should I assume that?"

Delaney laughed. Jamie did not, recalling their discussion on Saturday, and their subsequent activities.

"No, actually we're here about young Mr. Randolph, Jamie."

Jamie looked up. "I'm not having a physical problem," he explained.

Marcia Havermeyer evaluated the two men. The girl's father was not a bad looking man. In fact, a very well preserved specimen for, what was his age, oh here it is, fifty-four. A full head of Phil Donahue grey hair. A cute nose, though not nearly as nice as the daughter's. He was probably an inch or two shorter than her own height but in today's world that mattered less. Nice and trim. He probably worked out, maybe biked.

Now, the young man. He was *very* attractive. Of course, even in an open minded society the age difference was substantial: thirty years or so. But that didn't mean she was blind, or had lost her appreciation of the opposite sex. She knew it was impossible, but wished she could find an excuse to run her fingers through that thick hair, to touch his sultry lips. At least she could enjoy gazing into those sparkling Paul Newman eyes without fear of reprisal.

"We believe that Jamie's attorney, that is the attorney who represented his mother and father before he was born, did business with you in the mid seventies. Maybe 1975 or 1976."

"What kind of business?" asked the tall lady. She diverted her glance back to Sid.

"Well, we don't exactly know that. But Jamie is concerned that perhaps his mother or father is not his biological parent."

The director of the clinic acted surprised.

"Was your mother artificially inseminated? There was no such thing as an-egg donor in 1976."

Jamie had not told Delaney about the in-vitro. All he had revealed was that his mother had been subjected to some kind of experimental treatment.

"She might have been," the boy answered. Havermeyer looked at Sid.

"And you suspect that the family attorney may have purchased *semen* from us? It isn't done that way. We're not in the mail order business, you know. Our clients must visit the clinic personally, at which time we do a psychological profile and a battery of physical tests. We don't just say, 'Oh, you need a little sperm, here it is!' Is that what you're implying?"

"Please, calm down," said Morrison. She had lost her composure.

"Don't get mad," added Jamie, placing his hand on the desk, near hers. "I've been losing sleep over this thing, and I just need your help to put my mind at rest." He was taking lessons from Sid in just two hours.

"What was the attorney's name?" she asked. Maybe you're in the wrong place." She wanted to touch Jamie's fingers.

Havermeyer punched up the name of Hunter Davis. The computer screen faced her.

"He *was* here," she reported. "In 1975. However, I don't see *your* family's name in our files. I'm afraid I won't be able to give you any information without Mr. Davis' permission. Our files are confidential."

"Mr. Davis is dead," Jamie informed her, keeping his hand on the lady executive's desk.

"That's the problem," said Sid. "You see, Jamie recently received a large inheritance arranged as an anonymous trust by Mr. Davis. In 1977. The family never knew about this trust, and they're very upset about it. The money comes from outside of the family, which means that Jamie's true biological father might have left it to him. Since Mr. Davis passed away many years ago . . . "

"When?"

"In 1979," Jamie answered.

"Since Mr. Davis died in 1979, the family can't ask him about it," explained Sid.

"I see," said the director, scratching her warm neck under the pearls. "Well, I understand your predicament. This is why we are so careful about screening our clients. We really discourage any form of deception or misinformation. We don't see what we do as sinful or embarrassing in any way, and we believe strongly that all family members should receive full disclosure. Of course, it's always up to the client, and I'm not saying to announce your personal affairs to the whole neighborhood. But this is what happens when people try to hide something. The truth always comes out."

I hope so, thought Jamie.

"Well, that's all we're after," said Morrison. "The truth."

Marcia Havermeyer pressed the top of the chubby pen into her cheek. This was a delicate situation. She had been with The Clinic for nine years and valued her high paying position. Whatever might have happened here twenty years ago did not reflect personally on her. There was no reason to open a can of worms by discussing confidential matters with these strangers. On the other hand, adeptly answering a few simple questions might help avoid a scandal. All of these cases were sensitive and potential time bombs. Last month the board had authorized a large out-of-court settlement involving an interracial error.

A few seconds before Sid could show her his I.D. card, which might have ended the meeting altogether, Ms. Havermeyer relented.

"I don't really know who you people are," she said firmly. "I could be in hot water giving out confidential information. But I will try to answer a few brief questions for Mr. Randolph."

She exchanged glances with the handsome young man. What a body.

"Why was Mr. Davis here?" Jamie asked. She perused the report.

"His semen was tested. Mr. Davis claimed that he and his

wife were trying to have a baby. They were both in their forties. He told us that he had never fathered any children, and that if the problem was with him, there was no reason to test his wife for blocked tubes or whatever. Apparently, they did not wish to consider artificial insemination."

"What happened?"

"Unfortunately, Mr. Davis had a very low sperm count. His semen was considered 'Not Viable.' That was the last we ever heard from him."

Jamie sat up. "What about in-vitro?" he asked. "Did they consider that?"

"Not possible until the eighties," said Havermeyer. It was done a few years before that, but we didn't do it until we felt it was completely safe. That I know because we have testified in court."

"Who was Mr. Davis' doctor? Does he still work here?" Sid Morrison violated the Jamie-must-ask-the-questions rule.

"The doctor was Dr. Joseph Rosenthal. Yes, he still works here and you can make an appointment to see him if you wish. But I assure you, he will not answer any more questions about the case. In fact, I will deny answering your questions. I'll say you already knew the answers."

"Can I ask one more question?" Jamie pleaded. Those blue eyes.

"One more," said the reserved lady.

"How do you know if it was Hunter Davis' sperm?" Jamie inquired. "I mean, the sperm you tested."

"Whose sperm would it be?" she asked.

"A client's? My father's? I need to know. Is anyone else's name in the file?"

She took a look.

"No. Just his. As far as whether Mr. Davis actually gave us his own semen sample, I have no idea how we could determine that in 1995."

"Just one more question."

"No. I've given you all of the information you're going to get without a formal written request from a doctor."

"Was the test completed on November 16, 1975?" Jamie asked, hoping for one final answer.

"I told you . . . " Ms. Havermeyer checked the file, straightened her glasses, looked up at Jamie. "How did you know that?" she wondered.

"I've got E.S.P.," said Jamie.

❧

On the way to Dr. Goldman's office, Sid examined the 1975 Elvis photo. That Alonzo X did good work, he thought to himself, noting the sharp contrast and crisp details of the black and white image. With a magnifying glass, you could probably tell what time it was on Davis' watch.

"I wonder why this guy was seeing a plastic surgeon," Morrison commented as the limousine sped up Olympic Boulevard toward Beverly Hills High. "Turn before Century City," he told the driver.

Delaney, who had been conspicuously silent at the fertility clinic, snatched the photo from her father.

"He seemed to be pretty handsome," she said, "for his age. I don't see where he needed a face lift or a nose job. Maybe he just wanted to feel better about himself. You know, middle age crisis."

"We'll soon find out," said Jamie, putting his arm around Delaney and scrutinizing Hunter Davis' appearance. "Of course, his wife would know if he had anything done but I'm not supposed to talk to her."

"Delaney," said Sid, watching Jamie's hand caress her shoulder. "Did you trust that broad at the clinic?"

"She looked like she was telling the truth. Did you, Jamie?"

"She wasn't lying. She was really shocked when I told her the exact date."

"Well, if we don't get any answers about infertility from this Stein character — and I don't see how we will unless he's also a gynecologist — we'll be paying a little visit to Dr. Rosenthal." Sid saw the school coming up. "Slow down."

Beverly Hills High School looked basically like it did on television. Without the excitement of Jason and his friends.

"What makes you think he'll tell you anything, Daddy?"

Sid reached into his front pants pocket and pulled out a wad of hundreds.

"This!" said The Superstar. "You'd be surprised what people will tell you for $5,000 in cash."

"That's how much you pay for information?" asked Jamie, unsure of the amount of money in his own wallet. He needed to stop at an A.T.M. soon.

"I have a pay scale," Sid told him. "I'm authorized to spend up to $10,000 for a scoop. Of course we've paid a lot more."

"Who gets $10,000, Daddy?"

Sid stuffed the money back into his pocket.

"Usually, nobody. But doctors and lawyers are in the top echelon. They generally settle for $2,000 or so. Politicians get around $1,000. Cops are happy with $500. And the average person spills his guts for $50 or less."

They parked in the same spot Hunter Davis had taken in 1975.

A voice asked who was there, a buzzer let them in. The hall to the office was stark, well lit by fluorescents but totally devoid of personality. When the gated doors locked behind them, they felt trapped.

Inside, a charming man in his mid-forties offered three chairs. Beneath his loose-fitting smock, the man appeared to be powerfully built. His neck was as thick as Jamie's and he was only a few inches shorter. Other than his slight skin problem, he was fairly attractive, spoke well and had one hell of a handshake.

"Leonard Stein."

"Sidney Morrison."

So much for formalities.

"We don't get a lot of referrals," said Stein. "Who sent you here?"

"Does the name Hunter Davis mean anything to you?"

The man squeezed his jaw with two fingers, stared at the white tile floor, avoided direct eye contact. The three visitors observed a palpable recognition of the name by Leonard Stein.

"No, I'm sorry. It doesn't ring a bell."

Downstairs, Goldman, who was recording the conference

between Stein and his suspicious guests, broke into a cold sweat. No one had asked about that schmuck from Tennessee in twenty years. How did these people know? He videotaped a close-up of the three new faces. The older man looked familiar. So did the younger man, for that matter.

Ask him who he was, Goldman whispered to Stein's earphone.

"Who was Hunter Davis?" asked Stein.

Morrison glanced at the blank walls. The place was like a government research facility. Where were the doctor's credentials, or even a family photo? Why was there no sign outside, or inside? If they had removed items to paint the walls, where were the nail holes? Weird place. But then again, so was California.

"Hunter's a friend of mine," said Sid. "Claims you did a face lift for him."

"When?"

"Oh, it was quite a while ago. In the late seventies, I think. He's probably due for another one by now. Were you here in the seventies?"

Don't be too specific, whispered Goldman.

"I've been with Dr. Goldman since he began his practice. But let's see if we can be of assistance to you. I take it you're interested in a face lift."

"Are you a doctor?"

"No, I'm not. But as I'm sure you know, Dr. Goldman is one of the best surgeons in the country. I will convey what you tell me to Dr. Goldman as soon as he returns. Is it a face lift that you want?"

"Where did you say the doctor is right now?" asked Jamie. Stein turned to him. For the first time he noticed what a handsome young man sat before him. What he wouldn't give for that face, and the rest of it. He, too, was muscular but it didn't look the same.

"I didn't say," replied Stein. "He's out of town, on vacation, and is not expected back until mid-August. I should also inform you that we have about a six to nine month wait for new patients. Is that a problem?"

"No, it isn't," said Sid. Stein was still eying Jamie.

"Good. Then let me give you some forms, and our rates — we're not cheap by any means — and here is a brochure about facelifts." Stein opened a drawer and removed one of several booklets plus two applications. "You'll have to sign this consent form and have it notarized before we even consider you. The doctor does excellent work but some people just expect too much. Please read this over carefully. Then call us in about a month. Here's the doctor's card."

Ask him more about Davis, Goldman ordered.

"Thank you," said Sid Morrison. "I'll get back to you."

"Very good." Stein stood up. "Tell me a little about this Hunter Davis," he said. "What did he look like? Dr. Goldman might have seen him at a hospital, or perhaps he was here when I was out and the doctor will remember him."

"Do you have a photographic memory?" asked Morrison.

"Actually, I do. Why do you ask?"

"Because you didn't look up the name. Could you see if Mr. Davis is in your card file, or your computer?"

There was no file cabinet or computer in the room.

"I'm sorry. You'll have to ask the doctor about that. I'm only trying to be helpful while he's away."

"Do you still want me to describe Hunter Davis?" asked Sid.

"Please."

He's a reporter, Goldman warned. I've seen him somewhere.

"Hunter Davis. Five foot five. Bald. New York accent. Big scar under one eye, fell off a bike when he was a kid. He was a toy manufacturer. Used to give away Davis & Company key rings. I'm sure you'd remember him."

"Sounds hard to forget," commented Stein. "You're right. If he was ever here, I'm sure I'd remember him. But I'll still ask Dr. Goldman."

"Great. Well, thanks for your time."

Ask him who the kids are!

"Is this your son?" asked Stein, playing dumb. They shook hands again.

"No, this is my daughter, Sherry. And her friend, Nick. They go to school together in Virginia. They're just visiting California for a few days. I made them tag along just to bug them. You know how kids are. You have to keep an eye on them."

Leonard Stein couldn't keep his eyes off Jamie.

"And what did you say you do?" Stein asked. "Can I have your business card?"

"I'm a police detective." He felt Stein's hand pull away abruptly. Stein smiled. "I'll retire in about two years. That is, if we can ever get finished with this damn O.J. Simpson mess."

Without further ado, they left the office and walked down the hall.

The electric door slammed shut. It was hot in the street.

"He was lying, Daddy! I could tell."

"No doubt about it."

"I watched his face when you described Hunter Davis," said Jamie. "He knew what Davis looked like."

"And he had a bug in his ear."

"What?"

"A bug," Morrison repeated. "An electronic listening device. I'm sure Dr. Goldman was in the building. The whole thing is very strange. They're hiding something. I'm going to put a P.I. on the case. We'll find out who his clients are, where he lives, how much he makes . . . what he eats for breakfast. I hate to say it, son, but this could be more interesting than your story."

"It's all connected, Mr. Morrison."

⚶

The elevator door opened and Goldman stepped out.

"It was probably a mistake to let them come here," he said. Goldman had aged considerably since the days of Hunter Davis. His skin was pallid and he looked anorexic. "If they start snooping around, I'll never be able to work on the project in peace." Goldman took his assistant by the arm.

"I don't understand, Ira. Is that guy a reporter or a cop?"

"A reporter. By tomorrow, I'll know everything about him."

"Why do you think he's interested in Hunter Davis, after all these years?"

195

"Beats me." Goldman hammered his fist on the desk. "I can't believe we were stupid enough to talk to him."

"I didn't tell him a thing," said Stein. "How could they even know he was here?"

Goldman shook his head.

"That's what we have to check out. Davis didn't keep records of anything. I'm positive. How the hell did they trace him to me?"

"I have no idea," said the muscular assistant. "Uh-oh."

"What?" Goldman had already lost what little appetite he had. "What's the matter now?"

"What if that guy finds out you haven't seen a patient since 1980?"

"It's a problem," the doctor agreed, pulling up his pants.

"Maybe it's a different Hunter Davis. The description . . . "

"Don't be a fool, Leonard. There's no mistake. Morrison lied about the description. I don't know how but they know. They may not know what he was doing here yet, but they know we did business with him."

"What does that prove?" Both men were pacing around, like caged dogs.

"It proves they could be dangerous. At the very least, I never declared any of that cash. Do you know how much we would owe the I.R.S. with interest and penalties? Or what if they contact the American Medical Association? They could yank my license. Then how do I get supplies?"

A thought occurred to Stein.

"They talked to Mrs. Davis," he said. "It's the only way."

"You're right."

Stein pictured Charlotte Davis, the statuesque socialite from Memphis.

"It's the only way they could know anything." Stein looked puzzled. "But why would she wait till now? Why would she wait . . . eighteen . . . years . . . "

"That's him!" Goldman screamed. "The boy . . . "

"Eighteen years. *He just turned eighteen!* He just found out."

"And *she* told him."

Stein was relieved. "So there is nothing to worry about.

The kid just wanted to see where he came from. We can relax. It's over."

"I don't think so," said the older man. "If he wanted to confirm that we assisted in his birth, why didn't he ask?"

"Maybe they want to ask you directly, face to face."

"And why bring along a reporter? He's looking for publicity. If he knows he was the first test tube baby, he's got what? A book? A movie? All the talk shows. It could be worth millions."

"If that's what he's after," said Stein, "then it's too late. He's told other people. It's only a matter of time before everyone finds out what we've really been doing in the lab."

Goldman tried to straighten his aching neck and shoulders. He was out of shape in every way. One of these days, in a year or two if all went well, he would be able to take better care of himself. He would start injecting himself with Human Growth Hormone, undergo surgery, try some of the radical procedures on his own body. Up to now, he had not been willing to risk the possible side effects. His work was too important.

"Or he might not have told anybody. Who would believe him? I'm a plastic surgeon, remember?"

"Some people know better," said Stein. "Hunter Davis could have told anybody. His client knew."

The unknown client Stein was referring to was Elvis Presley.

"Yet we've never heard from his client, have we? Unless this Sid Morrison is the client." The doctor pictured Morrison's face. "And the boy is his son. They don't have to look alike if the boy isn't genetically related to him. I know he said the girl is his daughter, but the man is a liar."

Stein opened the bottom drawer of the desk and took out a portable chess set. He arranged the magnetic pieces on the small board.

"We'll have to figure this thing out." Stein moved the King's Pawn two spaces. His opponent did the same.

"Yes," said the scientist. "And we'll have to do something about it before we go down the tubes."

Queen's Knight to center.

Chapter 15

"AN IMMACULATE CONCEPTION"

It was March 14, 1977. The baby was due in two months.

Diane Randolph sat alone in the king size wicker rocker, looking around at her beautiful nursery. The room she had always dreamed of. The room she and her sister, Ellen, had furnished and decorated in February, when she was sure the life inside of her was strong and healthy. But now she wasn't so certain.

Dr. Carrillo, of course, said not to worry. Doctors always told you that, even when there was something to worry about. Jack, too, never stopped trying to convince her that the pregnancy books were right. A mother's natural state of mind was to worry about her baby, even before birth. Combined with her berserk hormones, Diane's undue concern for what was promised to be a *son*, was understandable, even predictable. After so many years of trying to get pregnant, why shouldn't she be upset every time she thought of a miscarriage, a stillbirth or a deformed infant? Whether it was a boy or a girl was really irrelevant. As long as the baby was normal.

The only person she could really talk about this with, besides Jack, was her sister. Dr. Carrillo was a man. What did he know about carrying a baby? They had agreed that Ellen would not be informed about the in-vitro. However, the bond shared by Diane and Ellen was in some ways as important as anything she had with her husband. So she told her sister that she had undergone a brand new, untested medical procedure which even she did not quite comprehend. One which still made her nervous and worried even in her eighth month.

A few weeks ago, while Diane painted the moon, sun and stars on one side of the nursery, Ellen was painting trees and horses on the adjacent wall. As they talked, Ellen tried to comfort her with the reminder that there had never been a single complication of pregnancy or childbirth in their family, or in Jack's, for the past thirty years.

Diane remembered that day as she rocked back and forth on this dreary Winter afternoon. A lonely afternoon which looked like it might snow as she stared out the nursery window of her beautiful new home. The mother-to-be tried to focus on what it would be like in this room in May, when they were a real family. She pictured a loud, happy little boy in the simple white crib. Tucked securely in place, surrounded by white bedding and sheets with blue and yellow stars. Trying to touch his rainbow mobile. The books had said to use black and white for newborns, but she wanted color. Unless he were blind, in which case it wouldn't make any difference. Oh, my God! What would she do if the baby were born blind!

"That is so crazy," said Ellen, when her sister called to tell her what she was thinking, "that I can't even tell you how crazy it is." Ellen was a Kindergarten teacher with two children who was used to comforting confused five-year-olds. When kids told her their pet hamster had died, or they were afraid of monsters, she knew exactly what to say. She had no idea what to tell Diane. "Just hold on for fifty seven more days," she begged.

"Fifty six." Diane was sobbing.

"Diane, please. Listen to me. The baby is fine. I talked to your doctor last Friday. He's never seen a healthier mother. You've gained the right amount of weight, you eat good, you get proper rest. You take vitamins. There hasn't been any bleeding. Your pregnancy is identical to both of mine in every way."

Diane wiped her runny nose. "Not in *every* way," she said. "We don't even know exactly how this baby was conceived, or what they put back inside of me."

"What are you talking about?"

Diane had said too much, but she couldn't explain further.

"I thought this was some kind of artificial insemination with special drugs or something. What did they do to you?"

"Nothing."

"Tell me."

"Nothing. I promised Jack." She was waiting for Jack to come home. He had assured her he would be home early today. Where was he? "I've got to call Jack."

"Is this Jack's baby?" asked Ellen.

"What do you mean?" How was she going to avoid telling her sister about the in-vitro?

"I mean, did you get artificially inseminated with someone else's sperm? Like from a sperm bank? I know you didn't go to bed with anyone else."

"Are you out of your mind?" Diane was infuriated. "Do you think I would stoop to that? Do you think Jack would let me? I can't believe you had the nerve to ask me that." She was regaining her sanity, and her self-control.

"Then what the hell are you worried about?"

"I guess it's just the whole experience. I never thought it would be so difficult to get pregnant, and now I can't manage my feelings."

Diane remembered all the tests, the drugs, the repeated sadness of being unsuccessful at conceiving.

"It's perfectly normal, Diane. I felt that way. Everyone does. Even the women who tell you they're calm and never worry about the baby. Liars. They're all liars!"

"You felt this way? I don't remember that."

Ellen was exaggerating a little, to make her sister feel better, which seemed to be working. During her own pregnancies, she had acted strangely at times, worried, had bad dreams. But nothing like this. Her husband's dry cleaning business was just getting off the ground in 1987 when she was carrying Brad.

"I drove Dennis nuts," she told Diane. "Ask him. Meanwhile, I just got home. I've got food to put away. I've got a seven year old and a four year old who want snacks right before dinner. And I've got to get everything ready for tonight. Oops."

"What's tonight?" asked Diane.

Ellen had slipped up. The baby shower was supposed to

be a surprise. Her finished basement was filled with balloons, ribbons and gifts. Fifteen people were invited.

"Nothing. I'm just having a little party."

"For who?"

"For no one. Just some neighbors." She put the phone down and yelled into the other room. "Bradley! Stop fighting with your brother. And don't open any of the snacks." Back to Diane. "Look, Diane, I know you're in a state and you want to talk, but you caught me at a bad time. Can I call you back later? Stuff is melting. I mean, you're not on the verge of suicide, right?"

"No. But if your party turns out to be a baby shower. . . "

Damn! What a big mouth!

"A baby shower? For you? Tonight? Good luck. I'll be happy if I get to *take* a shower tonight." Nice going, Ellen. "But I do want to make you a baby shower. I figured next month, when the weather gets nicer. I have a list of names that I need to go over with you."

"Okay, go. We'll talk about it. I'll call you later, or else tomorrow. Thanks for talking to me. I love you."

"I love you, too. Tell Jack to take you out to dinner."

"Well, I'm not cooking tonight."

"Good. See ya."

It was twenty to five. It was getting dark and Jack wasn't home. The last part of the conversation with Ellen had distracted her. If she was going to eat out with her husband, she'd better change. The phone rang. She knew it. He was going to be late.

"Mrs. Randolph? This is Jean in Mr. Randolph's office. Is he there? We have to tell him about a meeting that's come up for the morning."

The front door opened and in waltzed Jack Randolph. The big, happy go-lucky junior attorney from Hackensack, brushing a few snowflakes off his shoulders. "Hi, honey!" he called upstairs. "Sorry I'm a little late."

"You're not late, Jack. Jean? Hold on, he just walked in. Jack, your office is on the phone." The day was getting better for the Tenafly housewife.

"I'll take it in the kitchen."

Three minutes later, his coat draped over a couch, Jack bounded up the stairs, grabbed his rotund wife from a safe angle, and kissed her. He placed his hand gently on her belly, hoping to feel his son kick.

"We're going out," he said. "How are you feeling?"

"To be honest, not so good until I talked to Ellen. But now that you're home. . . "

"How is Ellen?" They would be seeing her in less than an hour.

"She's okay. *Her* kids are healthy."

"Oh, God. You're imagining things again. What is it this time? The Bubonic Plague? Or does the baby have three eyeballs?"

She punched his arm, hurting her wrist. "It's not funny, Jack. For all you know, the baby really does have three eyes! No one knows about these things. Suppose the temperature wasn't right when they did the in-vitro. Or, God forbid, somebody dropped the test tube. Or whatever it was. And I don't have to remind you about those horrendous Thalidomide babies. Who knows what chemicals were used in this procedure?"

They were standing in the nursery.

"Please. Come into *our* room. I get an eerie feeling in here. Not because there is anything wrong with Jamie Richard — he's fine, I can feel it. But I don't like being in a baby room without the baby."

"You see!"

"I mean, without being able to *see* the baby. Didn't I tell you this would happen if you set up the nursery too early? I'll bet you've been sitting in that rocker all day."

Diane put her hands in the small of her back and tried to arch her spine.

"Only since two o'clock. And don't be surprised if the baby turns out to be Olivia Ilsa. If you think I believe a word that Dr. Carrillo tells me, or that idiot lawyer from Georgia. . . "

"South Carolina." Jack had just spoken to Dick Picking this morning. Picking's baby shower gift was in the trunk of the car. "Oh, now he's an idiot. Before you were pregnant, he was the miracle worker. I'll do anything to have a baby. That's what you told him. Isn't that what you said?"

Diane remembered everything. The plans to adopt. The long delay. The lawyer's "crazy idea" about trying a new method of conception. Truly, it had seemed like a miracle, but right now she felt like she was carrying Rosemary's Baby. If the little tyke came out with three sixes tattooed across his forehead, she wouldn't be surprised. She would deserve it!

"I was desperate to give you a child," she whined.

"What?" Jack said, genuinely hurt. "I'm the only one in this family who wanted a child? I thought we both wanted one. I thought we were both desperate! That's not fair. It's really not." Jack sat down on the big rocking chair next to the crib. "It's not fair," he said, crying into his hands.

Headline: Pregnant Wife Turns Happy Lawyer Into Wreck In Five Minutes.

Diane sat down in the middle of the room, on the fluffy white rug, and began crying, too. What had she done? Jack was the only one who really, really loved her. She knew that. He would give his life for her in a heartbeat, without thinking twice. And this was how she repaid him for his love and loyalty? By making him feel guilty about wanting a child? It was wrong. But she couldn't help herself.

"Can I ask you a question?" said Jack, tears subsiding. She didn't answer, but she was listening. "Here's the question. How can this be bad, if it's God's will?"

Diane sniffled. "Who says it's God's will?"

"Don't you remember when we asked God if it was the right thing to do?"

He was right. That morning in church.

"You mean last summer, when you had the broken finger from playing racquetball?" They laughed. Jack's middle finger had been taped in an obscene gesture for six weeks.

"And we both agreed that if you got pregnant the first time, we would be happy, and would consider it a true miracle? Even though you had to take drugs to produce as many eggs as possible." Jack waited. "Do you remember?"

"I remember."

Jack sat next to her and held her hand.

"And we decided that no matter how it happened, as long

as it was my sperm and your egg, the baby was ours. We wouldn't have to worry about giving back an adopted baby, or raising a sick child because we didn't know enough about the parents. And when the doctor told us it could be a boy. . . "

She corrected him. "Dr. Carrillo didn't tell us that. The lawyer did. That's what worries me."

He didn't understand. "But Dr. Carrillo confirmed everything."

"Dr. Carrillo said that to the best of his knowledge there was no reason to doubt what Richard Picking told us. I don't think Dr. Carrillo even knows where the in-vitro was done. It wasn't at Englewood Hospital."

Jack tried to reassure her by pointing out how difficult it was to accomplish what they had done. They had broken new ground.

"Doctors are afraid to do this publicly right now. It's not illegal, but the National Institute of Health urges extreme caution. There's a lawsuit in progress in New York for over a million dollars because hospitals can't agree on what to do."

That seemed to calm her down for the moment.

Jack helped Diane up and they walked to their bedroom.

"Don't turn off the light in the nursery," she said. "Well, Jack, if the experts are so mixed up, why didn't we wait? Why did we have to be first? We're the guinea pigs. If something goes wrong, we can't even sue anybody because we can't prove what they did."

At least she was trying to be logical.

"Nothing is going wrong. Everything is perfect. The baby is perfect. You're perfect." Jack made her laugh, finally. "The new house is perfect. The nursery is perfect. The problem with waiting, Diane, is this might be the only chance we ever get. Hopefully, we can have more children, but we don't know. It's up to God."

Jack was right. Why hadn't she been able to get pregnant for years? They were both healthy. All the tests said it should have happened by last summer.

"I promise you," Jack said, kissing his wife's naked back, then her round belly as she searched in her closet for the right maternity dress. "After this baby, we'll try again. We'll try to have another child the natural way. But let's just have faith in this pregnancy the way it is. Let's just wait until May to see what happens. I know in my heart we've done the right thing. I couldn't live with myself if I didn't believe that."

They embraced and kissed again, passionately. "I love you," Jack whispered, playing with her ear. "I love you, too," said his wife.

About two inches of snow had fallen by the time they reached Ellen's house.

"I knew it," said Diane, recognizing all of her friends' cars.

Chapter 16

❧

"A CHILD IS BORN"

MAY 13, 1977
ENGLEWOOD, NEW JERSEY

Jack pulled the new Ford station wagon into the Englewood Hospital parking lot, turning too sharply.

"Jack! Please! I'm having a baby!"

"Not till we're inside. I mean it, Diane!"

Humor did not ease Diane's pain. "Jack, this is killing me! Get me up to my room. Hurry!"

The car stopped at the familiar front entrance and Mrs. Randolph was helped into a wheelchair.

"Can I leave the car here a minute?" Jack asked a hospital employee. "My wife needs me."

"Fine with me," the man replied. "This isn't New York. I doubt if they'll tow you away for at least an hour."

Diane was rolled into Admissions where several last minute papers had to be signed.

"Why couldn't we do this last week?" asked the husky young lawyer.

"Hospital rules, Mr. Randolph." More accurately, red tape.

After ten minutes, which seemed more like ten hours, a flexible plastic name tag was secured to Diane's wrist. Another was stapled to a file folder, later to be wrapped around the baby's wrist.

"Okay, let's head upstairs, Mr. and Mrs. Randolph. Your room is ready." Jack noticed the woman's ID card: Ann

Wallace / Hospital Aide. "Are you a nurse?" he asked her.

"No, I'm just your escort. Don't worry. Everything is fine. I take care of women in labor every day. We've got it all under control."

"Well, I don't do this every day. Let's get Mrs. Randolph to her room. And be careful with her." Diane moaned, her beautiful eyes squeezed shut, tears and mascara etching wavy black lines down her cheeks. Jack knew he had to be strong for her, to pretend he was even stronger than he really was so she wouldn't be frightened.

"Where's Dr. Carrillo?" he demanded to know.

"Who's he?"

"He's her obstetrician, Miss Wallace. And he's supposed to be here. We called him two hours ago and he promised to meet us."

"I'm sure he's in your room," said the aide, having no idea where he was.

It was an older hospital but still considered by many the best in Bergen County. In an emergency, people asked to be brought to Englewood. The halls were clean and even in this pre-AIDS era, the hospital staff went out of its way to promote a sterile environment. But catching a disease was not on Jack or Diane's mind. They merely wanted to be taken to a private room and to see the face of Dr. Gerald Carrillo.

When they got off the elevator, a nurse behind the security station extended her arm: "Passes, please." Ann Wallace handed her two pink cards.

"See," Jack remarked. "Everything is like *Casablanca.* You can't even have your baby without a pass."

Aside from Diane's agony, it was a nice room. A large window overlooked some trees rising above air-conditioning units. Someone had already sent a vase of mixed flowers. Thank God there was a private bath. A remote control color television was suspended from the ceiling. Jack had paid extra for a small refrigerator-freezer which was being set in place. Down the hall a woman was screaming hysterically. A baby was crying on the other side of the wall. It wasn't the Ritz, but it was the best they could afford.

As soon as Diane donned a hospital gown, a nurse

examined her and announced that she was not fully dilated yet. A messenger then told them Dr. Carrillo had called. He was delayed by an emergency for about an hour, not to worry because Diane's labor was likely to last several more hours based on her contractions. It was now 5:00 PM. Jack sat on the edge of the adjustable bed, holding his wife's tense hand, wiping the perspiration from her forehead with a washcloth from home.

When the phone rang again at a quarter to six, Jack was prepared to threaten Dr. Carrillo's life, emergency or not. Instead, it was Richard Picking.

"Dick," he said, relieved. "Where are you?"

"I just got your message at my office. If I'm lucky I'll make it to the hospital in an hour. How's Diane?"

"She's in pain." On cue, Diane let out a mournful wail. "I'm here, honey. Oh, Dick, she's really suffering. I know it's normal but I hate to see her like this." Diane began breathing quickly, as she had done in Lamaze class.

"Are they giving her anything? She should get a shot."

"Forget it," Jack said. "She made me promise not to let them give her any drugs. I mean, I would if it's life and death but you know Diane. She considers this a religious experience. She swore to God this would be a natural childbirth unless the baby's life were in danger."

"How is he doing?"

"Who?"

Picking cleared his throat. "The baby. How is the baby doing?"

"Oh, the baby. Yes, the baby's fine. It's in the right position and the heartbeat is strong. It's just a question of when the little bugger is coming out!"

"When does Carrillo think that will be?"

Jack gritted his teeth. "Dick, that son-of-a-bitch isn't here yet!"

"Yes, he is."

"Oh, shit." Jack felt a firm hand on his right shoulder.

"It's okay," said Dr. Gerald Carrillo. "I've been called worse. How's the Mrs.?"

"Dick, I gotta go. Hurry up and get here. See ya." Jack

blushed.

At 62, the doctor still had the proverbial patience of a saint. Dressed in white, the short, stocky obstetrician looked like he had just left his post at the gates of Heaven. Except for his thick mustache. He wriggled himself between Jack and his patient, touched her hand gently, felt her head and smiled. She tried to smile back. Dr. Carrillo, when he was actually at your side, was the kind of doctor all women wanted. When you needed him, he was genuinely, personally concerned about you. It was no act.

The doctor took Diane's pulse, then her blood pressure.

"How do you feel, my dear?" he asked, knowing the answer.

"Terrible!"

"I know. Let's see how close we are." He looked at her chart. "The nurse has been timing your contractions and I must tell you. You are not ready to deliver." Dr. Carrillo examined her thoroughly, estimated that the birth was possibly three hours away, then left for coffee. "I've had a rough day," he said, rubbing the back of his neck on the way out.

"So have I," murmured Diane.

"This really is like *Casablanca*," said Jack. "Only better." He returned to Diane's bedside.

"Back in ten minutes," Dr. Carrillo called from the corridor.

For Diane Randolph, this was the day she had waited for her whole life. Her very first child was about to be welcomed into the world, and if she kept faith that the baby was healthy, she knew she could bear the pain. She recalled the needlepoint her mother had stitched for her as a child: "The Lord Does Not Give Us A Burden We Cannot Endure." As the contractions became stronger, she continued to visualize the beautiful gift, now hanging in the nursery, and her mother's face. She was a second child but still could imagine her mother's joy giving birth to her twenty-eight years ago. They would call the family as soon as the baby was born. She missed her mother, who was anxious to be a grandmother for the third time.

Though completely conscious, Diane was experiencing the unearthly sensation of floating around the room. She could feel Jack's hand but sometimes she couldn't see his face clearly. Suddenly, she found herself staring at the diffused light entering the window and felt that it was exerting a magnetic force on her. She tightened her grip on Jack. Then the intense pain overshadowed everything and the walls of the room began to close in and crush her. A temporary release was followed by the kind of radiating warmth one feels when she sits too close to a fireplace. Then a chill, so cold she thought she might be dead. But Jack's warm fingers took away the shivers. Now she was getting very hot, and thirsty.

"Give me some ice cubes!" Jack told the nurse. He applied one lovingly to her temple, then dabbed it behind her ears. He gave her another to suck on.

⁂

The phone at Graceland rang nine times.

"Pick up, you rich hillbilly," Hunter Davis said to the receiver. Everything was falling into place.

Finally, a voice answered: "Hullo."

"Where the hell you been?" asked the lawyer. "I told you to stick close to the phone tonight. She's having the baby."

"Right now?" asked Elvis.

"As we speak. Picking just called me from the hospital. She's in the delivery room. I hope the flowers arrived. Hold on, it's my other line. This could be it."

Elvis rolled off the big bed and pulled on his boots. He stood unsteadily, waiting in his underwear. His heart was pounding. He picked up the glass of water next to the bed and took two capsules. One stuck in his throat. He drank more water and it went down. Where were his eye drops?

"Eight pounds, three ounces!" yelled Hunter Davis. "Goddam! We did it, boy. That asshole in Beverly Hills just earned his money."

"It's a boy, right?"

"Of course it's a boy. Jamie Richard Randolph. Born 10:26 PM, May 13, 1977. Not that that shithead Goldman really knew it would be a boy. I mean, he did have a fifty-fifty chance. But we'll give him the benefit of the doubt."

"He's healthy? Perfect?"

Hunter Davis took a slug of beer. "That's what I'm told. He's supposedly beautiful, just like you." Just like I used to be, thought Elvis. "I'll bet they're jumping for joy in New Jersey tonight!"

"That's great. When can I see him?"

"Tomorrow morning. You ain't busy tomorrow, are you?" Davis had obviously been slugging beer for quite a while. He burped. "Excuse me! Yeah, tomorrow. I've got a private plane all fueled up for a six a.m. flight. We can't take the Lisa Marie. I guess you knew that."

Elvis felt a little dizzy and sat down. He had some special vitamins for energy downstairs. B-12 or something. He would try a few of those. He was still recuperating from his thirteen day concert tour in late April.

"I figured I would have to fly back and forth without being seen."

"Incognito," said the beer-drinking lawyer.

"Yeah, right. But how are we going to do it, H.D.? Once I get off the plane, people are going to follow me. Do I wear a beard or what?"

"Better than that. A make-up artist will be on the plane."

Elvis was excited. If he had to see the baby disguised as The Hunchback Of Notre Dame, he would do it. He rubbed his eyes. He was waking up.

"I don't know what I'd do without you."

"I just hope you've got plenty of cash," Davis said, in his usual forthright manner. "I don't spare any expense when I do this crazy stuff. You know, if you underpay people, they don't keep their mouths shut. Loof lips sink ships." He tried it again. "Loose lips sink ships."

"Hunter," said the rock star. "I hope you're gonna be sober tomorrow."

"Hell, yes, I will!"

"Well, then don't worry about the damn money. That's not a problem. I told you that. Has it been a problem up to now?"

"No."

"Well, it's not gonna be a problem later on. I got you the two hundred grand for that townhouse in New York City, didn't I?

In twenty-four hours. Other than the mafia, who do you think can raise that kind of money? Not too many people. I just happen to be one of them, you jerk."

"Okay, okay." Elvis was giving him a headache. This had been a hectic day, making all those arrangements for his client to travel around without being recognized. Fortunately, they both had lots of friends in the Memphis Police Department, of which Elvis Presley was an honorary member.

"So how are we going to work it?"

"I'll pick you up at five," Davis instructed him. That was fine. Elvis did not plan to sleep until the next night. "We'll be in the air at six, up north by eight or nine. The hospital allows visitors after ten, so we've got plenty of leeway. I always like to be early."

"Me, too. But what am I going to look like?"

Hunter Davis laughed. "Don't ask. You're gonna love it. You'll be wearing a costume." Davis laughed again. "This is a riot," he said. "No one's gonna recognize you in a million years. Oh. You're gonna have to disguise your voice. Like they do in the movies. And you're gonna need to do a better acting job."

"That won't be difficult," said the singer-actor.

At ten the next morning, a six foot tall priest dressed in black entered Englewood Hospital in New Jersey. The man of the cloth appeared to be in his sixties, with a wide, bumpy nose and a ruddy complexion. His piercing blue eyes searched for a sign to the elevators.

"Can I help you, Father?"

The police officer did not act in the slightest way suspicious. And why should he? Enrico Delgado was the same make-up man who turned actors like Dustin Hoffman into believable, grossly distorted characters. And Delgado had an Oscar — a real Oscar — on his mantel to prove it. No wonder he charged four hundred dollars an hour, to ply his unique talents.

"I'm looking for the baby nursery," said Elvis in an Irish brogue.

"That's where *I'm* going," said a delivery man wheeling a hand truck loaded with boxes of something from Gerber. "Follow me."

"Do I need a pass?" the priest asked.

The policeman looked over at the crowded Admissions office.

"Nah," he said. "Go on up. They'll take your name at the nurse's station."

"Thank you, kindly." The visitor pushed his ID card from The Church Of The Good Shepherd down into the deep pocket of his tunic.

Upstairs, it was assumed that the priest had checked in downstairs and Father Elvis made his way to the nursery.

"The babies are right around that corner," a nurse told him.

The big entertainer from Memphis was in seventh heaven. He was not used to being treated like a normal human being. The special consideration afforded him as a priest was patronizing, but quite modest compared to the way he was "worshipped" as The King Of Rock 'N Roll. Unless he was the Pope, or at least a Bishop, no one would even think of kissing his gold and ruby ring. Nor would they attempt to tear pieces of his garments (and in the process, his flesh) as trophies. He liked it that he could meander around the floor without bodyguards, without signing autographs . . . without being prodded and touched and . . . violated. Except for Graceland, where he could be pampered and fed on his own terms, there was almost no place he could go where people respected his privacy.

To say that he was nervous about seeing the first male in his progeny was an understatement. Elvis felt like an innocent schoolboy again, with the same tensions and self-doubts he had experienced when asked to sing in class. Until today, it had all been theoretical. Watching videos of the pregnant Mrs. Randolph had been real and yet, like pregnancy itself, nothing was real until the baby actually took its first breath of air. He had seen so many photographs of Jack and Diane Randolph, he felt like he knew them. The way people who saw his movies, listened to his music and blew him kisses from the front row of his concerts probably felt they knew him. From the reports sent by Richard Picking through his Memphis attorney, he knew Diane's medical condition as well as Dr.

Carrillo.

But now all that theory was about to be transformed into three-dimensional flesh and blood. Jesse Randolph, that is, *Jamie* Randolph, was just a few feet beyond the thick plate glass window panels. It was an awesome moment.

"Excuse me, Father," said the tall, muscular young man brushing shoulders with Elvis. It was Jack Randolph. "There's my son," he told his brother, who had walked up to the window with him. "Two rows back. See him, Paul. The one with the blue cap and mittens. Diane's sister knitted them." Elvis recognized Jack's brother, Paul. Twenty-five years old. Unmarried. A mechanical engineer currently residing in Montclair, New Jersey. His picture was in the file. The file Hunter would put in the safe deposit box with the letter, the coin, the comic book and the wooden box. Elvis stared at the baby.

"Is that your first son?" he asked Jack.

Jack smiled proudly, the kind of smile you find on newly crowned boxing champions. And new fathers. "It sure is," he said. Elvis had the same look under his mask of make-up.

"He's a good looking lad. I wish him and his family a lifetime of joy and health." Elvis the priest raised his arm in a sweeping circular motion, as if bestowing a blessing. "In fact, I wish this for all of God's children, young and old, especially these brand new babies that have just come into the world. May the Lord grant them a pleasant journey."

Jack and Paul Randolph took a good look at Elvis. The singer winced. He had overdone it. They were going to see through the disguise. How could he have been dumb enough to . . .

"What a beautiful blessing," said the new father. "I wish my wife had heard it. She was so worried about this baby when it was inside of her."

"I know," said Elvis.

"You do?"

Elvis adjusted his holy collar.

"Yes, of course. All expectant mothers feel that way."

Paul whispered something to his brother. ("Ask him if he would come back to the room when they bring in the baby.") Elvis heard every word.

"Hey, that's a great idea!" Jack said. He turned to the priest.

"Father?" he said. "Could I ask you a favor?" (I'll be happy to do it, thought Elvis.) The Priest offered an ear. "Would you mind coming to my room for a few minutes? They're just about to bring in the baby for nursing. I wonder if you would hold him a second and make that blessing again. My wife is still a little depressed."

"It would be my pleasure," said the man of God. Elvis was delirious. Never in his wildest dreams did he imagine that he would be able to hold his own son the day after his birth. Not even if he paid a million dollars.

Diane Randolph's room was almost directly across from the nursery. That was why the Randolph brothers had appeared so suddenly. Together, they returned to the room, which was overflowing with brothers and sisters, grandparents, aunts and uncles, nurses, flowers and . . . Richard Picking. Jack introduced Elvis to Diane.

"This is Father . . . "

"McDuff."

Jack patted Elvis on the back with his strong arms. Arms that would protect Elvis' son.

"This is Father McDuff, Diane. We met him at the nursery. He was blessing all of the new babies." Everyone shook hands with Elvis, saying things like How Nice, God Is Always Watching, and so on.

"He's going to bless Jamie again, just for you," said Paul.

"Oh, that's wonderful," said Ellen. Her mother was holding hands with both daughters at the same time. "Isn't that wonderful, Diane?"

The new mom had barely slept in thirty hours. The doctor had let her sip a little coffee, so she would be able to entertain visitors for an hour. But then no more, because the caffeine would go directly into her breast milk and because she needed to sleep between baby feedings.

"What's that thing on the floor?" Father McDuff asked Jack.

"That's my sleeping bag." Someone turned off the TV. "As long as my wife is in the hospital, I don't go anywhere. They couldn't find me a cot, so I brought my own bed."

We could never have found a better father, Elvis thought. He glanced at Picking, who was staring out the window. There had been no reaction when they shook hands. Picking hardly noticed him. He was in some kind of trance.

"And you should see Jack with the baby," said Diane's sister. "He doesn't let that kid out of his sight. Diane told me he stayed with little Jamie at the warmer until his temperature got to ninety-eight and they moved him to the nursery. Luckily this room is right near the nursery."

"Well, you must be a right proud mother." They did say "right proud" in Ireland as well as Tennessee, didn't they? Elvis took the liberty of holding Diane's hand. Boy, they let priests get away with murder.

Diane summoned up her strength to speak.

"This is the happiest day of my life." She caught Jack's eye. "Except for the day I married *him*," she added. Elvis remembered the day he and Priscilla were joined in holy matrimony in Las Vegas. Their tenth anniversary would have been exactly two weeks ago.

When little Jamie was carried in, family and friends parted like the Red Sea. The nurse walked toward Diane.

"No," she said. "Please give him to Father McDuff."

The old man's eyes were irresistible, thought the nurse, handing the baby to Elvis. He kissed Jamie's forehead.

After the unofficial religious ceremony — Elvis wanted to sing Amazing Grace but refrained — the baby was returned to the mother and all were asked to leave.

"Are you hungry, Father?," asked Jack, remembering the stocked refrigerator. "We've got some yogurt, apples . . . peanut butter and jelly sandwiches for a quick pick-me-up."

"No, thank you," said Elvis, sweat pouring down his chest from under his stiff collar, just the way he perspired on stage.

When Father McDuff explained to the nurse that he was in the hospital to bless babies ("God's messengers have to make our rounds, too."), she decided to accompany him to all of the new mothers. In the early afternoon, Elvis was picked up by a taxi. He had blessed all thirty-one children, one at a time, including the Jewish babies. When it came to God, no one was taking any chances.

Chapter 17

❧

"AND THE FATHER IS THE SON"

The billiard balls scattered explosively in all directions, slowly but surely coming to rest in their predestined spots on the blue felt. Not a single ball was sunk; the red three-ball spun indecisively in the corner but ultimately chose not to drop in.

"Nice break, Captain," said Hunter Davis, chalking the tip of his two-piece pool cue. "I'll take the lowballs. Three in the corner."

The first shot was a freebee. Lisa Marie could have made that one with her eyes closed, and she was only nine. The next one wasn't so easy. Davis stroked the seven ball off the short cushion and back down the length of the table. It, too, fell into a corner pocket. Big deal. The game had just begun. There was plenty of time for a comeback even if Davis ran the table. They would be playing eightball for hours. Or until Elvis was ahead. "Nice shot," he said to his beefy pal. "Now what?"

The yellow ball was surrounded by stripes. "Watch this," said Hunter, recalling a trick shot he had seen on Wide World Of Sports. He angled his stick up sharply. The idea was to dig under the cue ball so that it would jump over the stripes and land on the yellow one-ball. Instead, it flew off the entire thirty-two square foot playing surface and hit Davis in the eye. "Oh, shit!" he said, and fell back into the orange armchair, banging the back of his head on the wall.

Elvis was cracking up. "Watch this?" he laughed. "I don't think so."

His pride was hurt more than his eye. It was tearing and his vision was blurry. The real damage was to the pool table. A six-inch "V" shaped rip in the felt was now the prominent feature of Elvis' red and blue table.

"Get me some ice, or a steak or something."

"Look what you did!" shouted The King. "You ruined my pool table."

"I'm gonna sue," warned Davis, holding his eye open with two fingers. "If I go blind, this is gonna cost you millions."

Elvis got some ice from the bar of the TV room next door. Davis wrapped it in his handkerchief and held it in place.

"I guess it's my turn," said the owner of Graceland. "Oh, by the way, Dr. Nick is now suing me."

"For what?"

"That business deal. We've been losing money. He's not happy."

"I can't believe it," said Davis, blinking his cold eye. "Let me look over the papers. This suing-your-friend crap ain't right. I'm gonna talk to him."

Elvis Presley's pool room was, in a word, dazzling. The sofas and walls were covered with multi-colored Op Art patchwork quilt material, also used on the ceiling in a pleated form. A stained glass lamp fixture hung over the pool table. The chair in which Hunter slumped, recovering, was one of a pair, its mate on the other side of a brass and black iron baker's rack. Three red reproduction Louis XV chairs were arranged in a semi-circle, for conversation. About a dozen prints, mostly modern art, hung on all the walls. There was a stone fireplace above which a brass framed mirror was firmly affixed.

Along with the basement TV room, Elvis and his girlfriend Linda Thompson had redecorated the pool room in 1974, using Memphis interior designer Bill Eubanks. The style was definitely "Elvis."

"I don't think your wife likes my taste," said the singer, lining up his next shot. The eleven-ball was in line with the side pocket. Elvis moved the cue ball a little too close.

"I saw that," said Hunter Davis. "Move it back." Elvis did.

"I said, Charlotte doesn't like my furniture and stuff." The striped ball rolled casually into the pocket. "And if we're playing strictly by the rules, one of your balls should come out."

"Don't touch my balls!" said the humorous attorney, refusing to discuss his wife's likes or dislikes. "Talking about balls, that reminds me. I've been analyzing your contract, and the Colonel seems to have you by the short hairs. There's just no way to break that contract."

Elvis bit his lip. The nine-ball missed its mark, but knocked in one of Hunter's solids.

"Thank you," said Davis, using his pool cue to stand up.

"There's got to be a way. Like they say, rules are made to be broken. God knows, you break them all the time."

"So do you." Davis over-chalked his tip.

"What if you were to get twenty per cent of the money I save getting rid of the Colonel for the first year," suggested Elvis.

"In that case, I could break the contract," came the response.

"How?" asked the boss.

"I'd kill him." Davis deposited his soggy handkerchief in the ice bucket on the top shelf of the baker's rack. "And while I was at it, I'd kill that greedy bastard, Goldman. And the little shrimp who works for him."

"It's a deal," agreed Elvis, only half kidding. "Hunter, you're a trip!"

"When did you sign that contract originally?" asked Davis.

"In 1956. I was twenty-one years old. Now I'm twice that. What did I know? I wanted to be a star. I figured 25% of nothing is nothing. If Parker was good enough to make me millions, what did I care if he got a quarter? You must admit, the guy is one hell of a promoter."

"I'll give him that," said Davis, removing his damp shirt. "But I still think the guy took advantage of you. If your mother and father hadn't approved the contract, we could claim you didn't understand what an open-ended agreement was. I mean, we could take it to court. A judge might be sympathetic to Elvis Presley, especially since you kept up your part of the bargain for twenty years. Or, your name might work against you. It's a tough call. And you'd have to be up to testifying in person."

Davis leaned across the table, stressing his lower back while he steadied his right hand. "No more trick shots, okay?" said the host. "Be cool, man."

"Hey, you broke my concentration," said the lawyer. "That isn't fair." Then he sunk the five and six balls with a single movement of pure luck.

"That's amazing," complimented Elvis. "Accidental. But amazing." He took a drink of Coke. "No, I can't go to court right now. Maybe next year, after my tour slows down a little. You know, I'm booked for like a hundred shows a year. Fourteen concerts in fourteen days, starting next week. I can't keep up the pace. I need a rest."

Davis missed his next attempt.

"Yeah, you don't look so good these days. Sorry, but I have to be honest with you. Not that I'm the healthiest guy in the world — I need to slow down myself — but you really ought to take some time off. Right now. Go to one of those private retreats. You know, where they put you on a diet, get you to eat better and exercise, give you a massage every day, basket weaving, whatever."

Hunter Davis wasn't the only person recommending a break. All of his friends, if anyone was really a friend, said the same thing constantly. Even Priscilla, when she called about visitation, told him how badly he needed to attend to his physical well being. But what the hell did they know about the pressure he was under? It was easy to give advice to someone else. Meanwhile, if he could just lose ten or fifteen pounds, that would be a start. He had to stop eating so much. Those diet pills had been more helpful a few years ago. And he loved to eat. Maybe a hypnotist . . .

"When do I have to come up with the rest of the money?" Elvis asked, adding to the pressure.

"Your shot."

Elvis laid his pool cue across the table.

"No, really. Isn't that guy bugging your ass for the money? How much do we owe him?"

"Five hundred grand. But don't worry about it. I've got a plan."

The phone rang. It was Ann-Margret. Elvis was happy to hear from her, it had been a while. Talking about friends, he had forgotten about the lady who had just called. She had always been a true friend, never wanting anything from him, genuinely concerned for his welfare. She was calling to say hello, to see how he was — oh here we go — to suggest taking it easy for a while. He'd like to, he told her, but he had obligations. He was fine, he said. A little fatigued, maybe, but he'd survive. Can I get back to you in a few days, there's an emergency. Thanks.

Elvis was exhausted. He had slept less than three hours last night, still high from the exciting reunion with Jesse at the hospital. But he needed to take care of business.

"What's the plan, H.D.?"

Davis slapped him on the back and Elvis pretended to make a karate chop to his friend's neck. He sang a bar of "Kung Fu Fighting."

"Well, I figure we already paid the jerk seven-fifty, in cash. All legal, for you. But probably not for him. I don't know what Dr. Frankenstein is doing in his little lab out there in fantasy land, but I doubt that it's kosher. And I doubt that he's declaring our payments to the IRS."

Elvis knew how Hunter's mind worked.

"So you don't think we should pay him the rest? But we agreed."

"Let me finish." Davis popped a can of beer.

He still remembered the first day he had paid Goldman in cash. A quarter of a million dollars in crisp hundreds. No receipt. No contract. No nothing. Just the word of a plastic surgeon that he could create test tube babies. Which was what they needed at the time, but now he had located two other doctors who would do the same thing for a hundred thousand. Too bad he hadn't found these guys earlier, he would have saved Elvis a bundle. And they were just as qualified. He had been in too much of a rush because Elvis was always worried about dying.

"I'm not saying we shouldn't pay him," the wheeler-dealer went on. "I'm merely pointing out that what he's already received amounts to what he asked for after taxes. So, in a sense, he's paid in full. Do you think it's right that you pay your taxes, but he doesn't?"

Elvis could see it coming. Hunter Davis was going to finagle a way to avoid paying off Dr. Goldman by confusing the issue. Well, it didn't matter to him. Goldman didn't know who *he* was. However, he knew exactly where to find Davis. Of course, he couldn't sue. And what could he do from Beverly Hills?

"You can't prove he didn't pay his taxes," Elvis argued weakly.

"That's true," Davis replied. "But what do you think? I say if we suggest that there's an IRS audit here in Memphis, he'll crawl under a rock."

"For how long?" Elvis drank more Coke. He had twenty-four 10-ounce bottles in a tray of ice sitting on the bar next door.

"Well, here's my plan. I think we ought to give Goldman fifty thousand dollars now, and fifty thousand a year for the next five years. That should satisfy him. Maybe he'll be in jail by that time."

"He's gonna go for that?"

Davis waved his shirt up and down, trying to dry it.

"The art of negotiating," explained Dale Carnegie, "is to make the other party accept the lowest amount. Now, I'll admit, technically Goldman may be entitled to the five hundred. But fifty thousand is better than zero. And that will be true next year, and the year after. And even if you eventually decide you can't live with yourself unless you give him all the money, at least you've bought time. Don't forget, the only reason he asked for so much money — he really overcharged you — is because he had you over a barrel. If we had waited, he would have done it for less. And I'll tell you something else. How do we know we got what we paid for?"

That got Elvis' attention.

"What are you talking about? I saw the baby. He was healthy. I told you I held him in my arms. He's fine. What's the matter with him?"

"Nothing," Davis said. "But here's what we tell Goldman. First, how do we know the baby's gonna *stay* healthy? The deal was for a healthy baby. So we say that means healthy for a couple of years."

Elvis thought about it. That part of the agreement was vague. And unlike his contract with the Colonel, interpretation wasn't up to a judge.

"Okay, I can see your point."

"There's more," said Davis. "We need to check out the baby thoroughly. How do we know Jamie Randolph is related to you? We only have Goldman's word. Don't get frazzled. I think it's your baby, but there's a lot of tests to do. We've got to check blood type, footprints, fingerprints, eye color, hair color, height . . . you name it. We want to see the kid start looking like you, and that's not gonna happen the first year, right? In time, they'll have even better tests."

"You're making me nervous, Hunter."

Davis put his shirt back on. It was still wet. His eye felt better.

"Don't be nervous. I mean, there's every reason to believe Jamie Randolph is who we think he is. He's certainly not the son of Jack and Diane Randolph because we disposed of their . . . stuff. He's not my son. And he doesn't look like either of those ugly plastic surgery shitheads. Who else could he possibly be? Don't sweat it, Captain. He's yours. The problem for Goldman is, he can't prove it. So he'll have to wait."

Elvis was relieved.

"Yeah, you're right. Who else could he be? Goldman knew if the baby came out looking like somebody else he wouldn't get the money. Of course, now you're not going to give it to him anyway, but he didn't know that." Elvis had convinced himself not to worry about the baby. "Plus, when I was with him in the hospital I could tell."

"You could tell what?"

"I could tell that he was mine. I could feel it." Elvis crossed his heart. "But you don't think anyone else knows, do you?"

Hunter Davis hated this part, coddling his clients. But it was all included in the fee. He reassured Elvis that indeed, it was impossible for the secret to go beyond the two of them. Dr. Carrillo had given the Randolphs' sperm and eggs to Richard

Picking. Picking, in turn, had handed over the specimens to Davis, believing that Davis was flying back and forth to the Beverly Hills Fertility Clinic to combine Mrs. Randolph's egg with Elvis' sperm. What actually happened during the next few days was unknown to Picking.

"You told him about the clinic in California?"

"I had to. All along, he thought a New York doctor would do it. Then he refused to go through with the procedure unless he could follow me to the hospital. I said that the doctor was flying with me to Beverly Hills secretly. I showed him a cancelled check I gave the clinic. He bought it. Don't worry, he's satisfied. Picking won't call the clinic. And if he does, they won't tell him anything. Take my word for it. It's too late for anybody to figure out what happened. He was happy we went to a reputable place. This whole thing is very disturbing to him. He's glad it's over with."

"Me, too."

All of a sudden, Elvis was hungry. He called to the kitchen and ordered some sandwiches. Hunter said he would eat whatever they sent down. The phone rang again. It was Dr. Nick's attorney.

"Give me the phone," ordered Davis. "Hello. No, this isn't Mr. Presley. This is his attorney, Hunter Davis. That's right, I represent Mr. Presley in this matter. And let me tell you something. I don't think too highly of this kind of crap. It's wrong to sue your friends. Yes, I know what happened. Doesn't mean shit to me. You win some, you lose some. Listen, you twirp, do you know who you're talking to? Hunter Davis. That's right. The DeWitt brothers. Now, I want you to set up a meeting with your client as soon as possible, and I want to get this thing settled. Out of court. Right away. And there ain't gonna be much in it except a real good fee for you. Got it? Good. Call Dr. Nick. Today." He hung up.

While they waited for the food to arrive, Elvis needed to talk.

"You remember why I wanted this baby, don't you?" he asked Hunter.

The radio was playing "Pretty Woman" by Roy Orbison. Davis tapped his foot.

"To have a son," he answered. "And to watch him grow up in a good home."

"I want him to be me, or my twin brother," said Elvis. "In the spiritual sense. Do you believe in reincarnation?"

"Never gave it any thought," said the winner of the first game. The black eightball bypassed the torn felt and plopped into the corner pocket. "I guess you do."

"Very much so. Rack 'em up!"

"No, you rack 'em up. Winner breaks."

Elvis began filling up the triangle with the fifteen colored balls.

"In fact," he said, "not long ago I met a woman visiting Graceland I'm convinced is the reincarnation of my mother, Gladys. I gave her my ring."

"Which one?"

"The ring my mother gave me when I was a young man."

Elvis and Hunter had never spoken about the Presley family. Davis was aware of Elvis' intense grief and sense of loss over Gladys. He assumed that this was a subject not to be broached lightly, that the man generally preferred to talk about music, sports or Bruce Lee. Since Elvis had brought it up, he would be happy to listen. Not many people were accorded the privilege. Elvis was, after all, one of the most famous men in the world.

"You'd do anything to be with your mother again."

"I will be with her someday," asserted Elvis. "When the Lord is ready to take me. Meanwhile, I'm hoping that her spirit will share the body of Diane Randolph, and Jesse's spirit has been reincarnated into the baby."

As everyone close to Elvis Presley knew, Jesse Garon Presley was the twin brother of Elvis who had died at birth on January 8, 1935. What was not as well known was the guilt that the surviving twin had felt all of his life. His mother had told him that when one twin dies, the one who lives gets the strength of both. But Elvis could never forget the story of the tiny corpse his father had placed in a shoebox, and buried in an unmarked grave.

"You think that's really what's happening?" Davis was curious now.

"I'm sure of it. The only problem is, I don't know how I'm going to stay away from the Randolph family. I have to, though, because, I owe it to Jesse. It's his turn to have a family, to grow up happy — happier than I did — to make something of himself, to fall in love, get married . . . "

"Hey, the kid's only two days old. Lighten up."

Elvis smiled. "H.D., you don't know how happy I am about this. Really. I owe you . . . a lot. You know I don't worry about money. If you want to screw this Goldman guy, I don't care. Or if you think he cheated us, fine, I trust your judgment. Just tell me what you want me to do. I just want you to know how much I appreciate what you-all have done for me. There's nobody else that would have gone to this much aggravation for any amount of money."

Tears were running down Elvis' cheeks. Hunter Davis was touched, and he felt a little guilty himself. The truth was, he had done it mostly for the money, not just to make Elvis happy. As the two big men patted each other's backs, Davis realized for the first time that Elvis Presley had become a friend. That he wanted to do what was right for his friend's son.

"Okay," said the friend of Elvis. "Let's discuss what we're gonna do so Jamie Randolph grows up happy. Should we try to make him a doctor?"

"He can be anything." Elvis picked up a sandwich from the plateful that had been placed on the pool table. "Except a celebrity. That's what's really killing me. I never have any peace and quiet."

"What about today?" asked Davis.

"Sure. As long as I hide in my house, or dress up like a priest, I can live a normal life. But how long does it last? Next week, I'll be back on the road, getting attacked by fans, singing my heart out, eating Kentucky Fried Chicken for breakfast, trying like hell to stay on top. Which I know I can't do forever." Elvis took a deep breath, chomped off a crescent of peanut butter sandwich. "And you know what the worst thing is? The worst thing is, I love it! I'm addicted to fame!"

When Hunter Davis bit into his sandwich, he didn't know whether to chew it or spit it out.

"What the hell is in this peanut butter sandwich?" he asked, making a face.

"That's my special combination," said Elvis. "Just eat it. After a while, you won't want anything else." Elvis washed it down with Coke. "So as long as my son doesn't want to be on stage, I'll be satisfied. Jack Randolph is a lawyer. He's not like Vernon. He'll guide the kid. But we'll be watching, just in case. And I want to leave him enough money so he can choose his occupation based on what really matters to him, not the salary."

Davis swallowed another mouthful of the Elvis special. It was tasting better. "I thought you liked acting," he said. "Some of your movies were pretty good. Would you be upset if the kid decided to be an actor?"

Elvis saw himself on the set of the more than thirty films he had made. It had been a drag most of the time.

"I'd rather he didn't. In the end, it's up to him. I just don't want him to be influenced by who his daddy is. Don't get me wrong. I love Vernon. I know it isn't his fault he grew up poor, like me. That he went to jail when I was a baby. Deep down, he's a good man. But you can't help following in your father's footsteps."

"I didn't know Vernon Presley was a rock star."

Elvis laughed, picturing his father on stage. "He's not. But like me, he lets people use him. He became nothing and I became a star. That's just dumb luck. Under the right circumstances, he would have been the star and me, nothing."

"You don't really believe that."

"Yeah. I do believe it. Life is a comedy, and a tragedy. And truth really is stranger than fiction. Did you see my movie, *Follow That Dream*? I imagined that me and Vernon were the real life characters who just happen to run out of gas in the right place. Oh, I've got musical talent, I don't deny it. But there's ten thousand other Elvis Presleys out there who have it, too. They're all nothing. Why? Just luck. And I don't want Jamie Randolph's life to be luck. Who knows what I might have been with the right upbringing. And a college degree."

Hunter Davis remembered the 1962 film Elvis had mentioned. A father and son accidentally wind up homesteading on a deserted beach. They build a local fishing and entertainment business which grows into a big success. After gangsters are warded off by the Army-learned judo of Toby (Elvis), the son falls in love with his adopted sister. They live happily ever after.

"Didn't you do a movie with Ann-Margret?" Hunter asked.

"*Viva Las Vegas*," Elvis recalled. "In 1964. It was a typical Elvis Presley movie — that's what the critics call them — but I met one of the nicest people I've ever known. Have you seen this book?"

Elvis showed Davis a copy of a profusely illustrated coffee table book called "Elvis In Hollywood" written by one of his biggest fans. Its author in 1975, thirty-two year old Paul Lichter of Pennsylvania, had documented all of Elvis' movies from "Love Me Tender" in 1956 to "Elvis On Tour" in 1972. The book contained six pages of facts and photos about the Elvis Presley-Ann Margret film, as well as a full-page color reproduction of every movie poster used during Elvis' screen career.

Hunter Davis thumbed through the book, pleasantly surprised.

"You did movies with a lot of famous actors and actresses," Hunter said. "And you always got top billing."

"That's one reason I didn't get the male lead in *A Star Is Born*," Elvis explained. "The studio insisted that Barbra Streisand was the star of the movie, something the Colonel couldn't tolerate. So Kris Kristoferson got my part."

"Were you pissed?"

"Damn right I was pissed. That role was my big chance to prove how good an actor I could be. It was a true dramatic part, not like *Girls! Girls! Girls!* or any of the others. *King Creole* in '58 wasn't bad, but this was better. *Flaming Star* wasn't too bad either. Marlon Brando was supposed to get the part of Pacer but they gave it to me. But there's only so much credit you're gonna get for a cowboy movie. I always wanted to be the new James Dean. Did you know I memorized the whole script for 'Rebel Without A Cause'? I watched it a hundred times. I'm still mad about *A Star Is Born*."

Davis found the book extremely interesting.

"Mind if I borrow this?" he asked, amazed at all the stars whose names appeared below Presley's: Richard Egan, Debra Paget, Walter Matthau, Barbara Eden, Hope Lange, Angela Lansbury, Gig Young, Charles Bronson, Stella Stevens, Ursula Andress, Barbara Stanwyck, Burgess Meredith, Nancy Sinatra, Mary Tyler Moore, Vincent Price, John Carradine . . .

"You can hold onto the book," said Elvis. "I want to put it in the safe deposit box with the letter I'm gonna write in a couple of days."

Davis took one last look at the book. Like millions of Americans, male and female, the author was obsessed with Elvis. He owned every Elvis record made, offering duplicates mail order through his own record club. He claimed to have met Elvis many times, to have attended 600 performances by The King and to be the owner of the red "Burning Love" jumpsuit. This treasure, he wrote, was obtained in Nashville in March, 1974 during the Cerebral Palsy Telethon in which he donated $5,000 and an original Sun record. A month before The Duke reunion at Graceland.

"This guy, Paul Lichter, really loves you."

"Who doesn't?" Elvis sneered. "Now let's finish some serious business. How much money do you think I should put in the trust for Jamie?"

Davis tried to remember the numbers he had calculated with his accountant. "I think we came up with something like eight hundred thousand," he advised. "I've got the exact figure at home. I'll let you know."

"That's close enough," said the secret benefactor. "He'll have a couple of million in eighteen years?"

"No question," answered Elvis' attorney. "The money will at least triple, even after taxes. But in order for this to remain anonymous, you've got to pay gift taxes on it now. That's another couple of hundred thousand. Picking is getting all of the papers from Chemical Bank in New York. He'll be listed as the trustee. My name won't be known, but I'll have a power-of-attorney signed by Picking giving me authority to take over the trust at will. I'll sign a similar document giving you authority over me, and we'll keep everything in the same box. How many keys do you want?"

229

"Just one. You hold onto it."

Davis pictured his house. "Okay. I'll leave the second key in the box for the time being. I'll tape my key under my desk, just so you know."

"That's fine. I'll write you a check in one week."

"Make it a cashier's check," said Davis. "I don't want your name associated with so much money. By the way, where are you getting it all?"

Elvis shrugged his shoulders, then smiled. "I told you. I cashed in some life insurance policies. I'm also selling some jewelry." He removed a gold chain with a Star Of David from around his neck. "Put this in the box, too. Better still, give it to the kid with the money. We'll both meet him in . . . what year will it be?" Elvis counted on his fingers. "In 1995. Let's see if he can guess whose it is."

The big lawyer had not anticipated Elvis' desire to meet his son in eighteen years. It was his belief that the superstar was making all of these arrangements so that he could remain at a distance indefinitely.

"You expect to talk to him when he grows up? I thought you didn't want to be part of his life?"

"Well, let's see how it goes."

Davis looked into his crystal ball. "I don't know how happy the kid is gonna be when he finds out you tricked him."

"How did I trick him?" Elvis wiped his face with a cloth napkin and ran his tongue across his front teeth to remove the sticky peanut butter.

"He's gonna think *the Randolphs* are his parents," Davis said. "Then, after eighteen years, you're gonna tell him *you are*? I don't know. If it was me, I'd want to kick your ass. Let's put it this way. After trying to let the kid have his own life for all those years, why would you risk screwing it up by telling him he's the son of Elvis Presley? Then he might decide to be a rock and roll singer, just to get even with you."

Davis was right. "I said we'll see." Elvis looked at his face in the mirror. It was downright pudgy. Why in the hell had he just eaten three and a half sandwiches? He pressed on his stomach. It was not flat and muscular like Hunter's. He tried to dwell on the baby. Its skin was so soft and pink, its blue eyes clear as a Summer sky in Mississippi.

"I know it's a long time, but I'm just mentioning it so you don't do something stupid. We've gone to a lot of trouble to set this up just the way you wanted it." Davis picked up another sandwich.

"Point taken," said Elvis. He could still smell the baby's untainted scent. Feel its pliable little bones. It was innocent. It was free to be itself . . . himself. It was a part of him. It *was* him, without the problems, the deadlines, the appointments, the expectations, the weaknesses, the fears. It was Elvis Presley, or Jesse Presley, without the whole mess that was pre-destined to shape and ruin his life. The baby was hope, forgiveness, salvation, redemption, a Golden Opportunity for the health and happiness *he* might have had, a second chance for greatness. But greatness defined as personal fulfillment, not the ability to sell records or to project the image of the handsome, rich and powerful sex symbol. Hunter Davis was right. This was all part of God's plan, as well as his own. There was no possible way he could simply show up in Jamie Randolph's life without altering the future.

Davis could see the disappointment in his eyes.

"You're doing a noble thing," he assured Elvis. "And maybe it will be possible for you to meet the boy one day. Not necessarily when he's eighteen, but maybe after he's married and has his own children. He'll be a lot more mature at thirty or thirty-five."

"I'm convinced." The King began rebuilding his dream. "But we've still got to work out all the details now. Like a will. Just in case."

"That's right. Like a will," Davis agreed.

Elvis thought about his will, which he had re-written only two months ago. He would like to add his son's name to the will, but that was stupid. What good would it do? The important thing was to set up the trust. In a few years, it could all be changed.

"Ready for game two?" Elvis held his pool stick over his head with two hands.

"I'm ready. Are you?" Davis circled around to the front of the pool table.

"Be careful, H.D., I don't need any more holes in my table."

"Do you mind getting the food out of my way?"

Elvis cleared the surface.

"About Dr. Goldman . . . "

"What about him?" asked Davis.

"I've been thinking about it, and I'd rather we just give him the money. I know we don't have to. That we could threaten him, report him to the A.M.A., whatever. But he still did what he said. I can get the rest of the money together in a month or two. Ask him to have a little patience. This is one more thing I don't need hanging over my head. If I'm gonna clean up my life, I don't want any loose ends."

"No problem," said the pool shark. "It's your money."

Chapter 18

"BY HIS OWN HAND"

Fourteen stories below the 86th Street office of Richard Picking, Manhattan had been tamed into a peaceful Sunday afternoon. Except for tourists taking photos on the steps of the Metropolitan Museum Of Art, the eighties were as empty as downtown Charleston, Picking's true home. Upstairs, the lawyer gazed down at a dog walker across the street with a pooper-scooper. Outside his door, it was absolutely silent. The polished marble corridor was free of cigarette butts, gum wrappers and the distinctive smell of New York commerce. There was no one else in the building besides the doorman, who was napping.

His small law office consisted of a ten by twelve waiting room, the same size conference room/library and a twelve by sixteen personal chamber. There was also a tidy little powder room and a tiny kitchenette, used mostly for making coffee. All in all, the Picking headquarters compensated in elegance what it lacked in size. Its furnishings featured three genuine American Federal pieces, thick antique Persian rugs, Bloomingdale's sofas and chairs and an incredible carved mahogany desk. The desk had been inherited from, and actually made by, his father's Great Uncle Clarence in 1896. All of the walls were painted light beige with the identical Greek Key border paper trimming every room. Grander apartments with tall ceilings had real crown moldings.

Clients generally felt extremely comfortable visiting the genteel New York adoption attorney. When they noticed his ten-shade Tiffany Lily Lamp, the more knowledgeable ones might have even been impressed. The walls were hung with original watercolors of Charleston, South Carolina. Landmarks rendered very nicely by a local artist who would never become famous. Picking loved these reminders of his earlier life, before he had met, married and later lost Patricia Jensen-Picking of Demarest, New Jersey.

A color five-by-seven of Pat and his adorable son, William, who had his mother's eyes, stared at him from Uncle Clarence's desk. It had been taken in January, 1971, six months before their tragic deaths. In a few days, the picture would be eight years old. Eight years. It didn't seem that long. Was it really so many years ago the phone had rung, bringing him the awful news that his two reasons for living had perished in a head-on collision on the Bronx River Parkway? Once more, he regurgitated the vivid details, blaming himself for not taking the day off to go to the zoo with his family. What the hell was so important at work that he couldn't afford the time? His last chance, ever, to see little Billy delighted by the antics of chimpanzees, the astonishing girth of smelly elephants, the fearsome writhing of a twenty foot boa. It was all on film, he supposed, when they recovered the camera from the glove box of the wreck. Unlike the car's occupants, the camera was unharmed, showing ten shots taken on the roll he had loaded that morning. He had never had the nerve to develop them. The film was still at home, in his closet, in a memory shoe box.

Just one more kiss. He had touched his lips to their restored but lifeless forms at the funeral. Their cheeks felt like soft mannequins, real but not real. Now he would cherish even that. He missed them. He longed to be with them. He couldn't go on without them any more. Especially after learning of the birth of Jack and Diane Randolph's second child, a healthy girl.

He picked up the phone and called Hunter Davis, shuffling the file folders laying on his desk waiting for Monday morning. Davis was home, said the housekeeper. Thank God. He had to talk to someone. He had to tell his friend his problems. The big Southern lawyer took the call in his office.

"Everyone gets depressed around the Holidays," said

Davis, anxious to get back to his kids. His wife had them all week. Charlotte was grateful that he loved to be with them on the weekend. She was taking a bubble bath on this delicious, tranquil Sunday afternoon. Chicken was baking in the oven, its aroma permeating the entire house.

"It's not just Christmas," replied Picking. "It's my whole life. I can't seem to do anything right."

"But business is booming. I've got some new leads for you. Two babies due in March. Unwed mothers, and we've got the fathers' permission to give up the infants. In writing. You'll make two families very happy. And collect two big paychecks. What could be better?"

Picking was still in debt. He had no idea how much. All he knew was the bank in New Jersey had mailed him a foreclosure notice which he had declined to respond to. And Merrill Lynch claimed he owed them over three hundred thousand dollars. He had no idea why the figure was so high. He no longer carried malpractice insurance, against the advice of Hunter Davis who constantly warned him of the huge risk. One more judgment and he would be disbarred. But why? He was a good lawyer who cared about his clients. He wasn't a shyster. He didn't drink or gamble. How could this be happening? What kind of world was he in? And why was his new mortgage rate double what it used to be? Inflation?

"That's very nice," he said to Davis. "But it doesn't bring back my wife and son. And I need a lot more money than that to pay my bills."

"I told you," said his friend. "Send me all your legal papers and I'll straighten it out for you. That house is way too big. You need to get rid of it and combine your home and your office. Let me take care of it."

It was a pleasant thought. Just give all your problems to someone else. Do whatever Hunter Davis told him. That's what he had been doing for the past four years anyway.

"I sent you a letter about the new Randolph baby," said Picking.

"Yes, I got it. Thanks. That was great news. If Elvis was alive, he'd be thrilled. Jamie has a sister now. What's her name again?"

"Olivia."

"Right. Olivia. That's a beautiful name. Have you seen her?"

Davis wished that he could see the two tots, especially the boy, but he had pledged to stay away for at least eighteen years.

"Yes. She's wonderful. The Randolphs are very pleased."

"Pleased?" questioned Davis. "I would think they're in ecstacy."

"They are," said Picking. "But I'm not."

"Why?"

Picking stapled Davis' business card to the top folder, removed the staple with a jawlike device, re-stapled the card to the file. Did it again.

"Because," he explained, taking a deep breath, "the baby was conceived *naturally*. They just informed me of this fact the other day."

"So what? That's good news." Davis signalled to Hunter, Jr. that he would return to the game room in five minutes. The youngster smiled and left.

"No it's not." Picking dropped the bent staples into his wastebasket. "It means that I cheated two lovely people, my friends, out of their first child."

"What are you talking about, Dick?"

Picking wavered unpredictably between irateness and depression.

"I'm talking about the immoral and unconscionable scheme we perpetrated on Jack and Diane Randolph," he said. "The evil plan concocted by you and Mr. Elvis Presley, the so-called King of Rock 'N Roll, to deprive the Randolphs of their own child. And now the rich bastard isn't even around to see his . . . creation." Suddenly, he was depressed. "It's really my fault, isn't it?" he whimpered. "I'm the one who found them for you. I talked them into it, not you. I arranged for their sperm and egg to be removed from the hospital." Richard Picking started to sob. "I promised my wife and child," he said, mainly to himself, "at the cemetery. And I broke my promise. For money. For my own sense of immortality. As if what I did was what God really wanted. And Elvis never even saw his son!"

"Yes he did!" shouted Davis.

Picking was surprised.

"He saw Jamie Randolph? When?"

"At the hospital. The day after he was born."

Picking rubbed his eyes. "I don't remember that," he said. "You told me that Elvis would come to the hospital, in diguise, after I called you. But . . ."

"He was the priest," explained Davis. "Father McDuff. The big priest with the accent. Elvis told me you were in the same room with him when he blessed the baby."

Picking laughed. "That was Elvis?" he said. "I can't believe it."

"He was made up by a top Hollywood guy," Davis said, holding up two fingers to Hunter, Jr. His son ran back into the hall and down to the playroom.

"Well, I'll be damned." Picking shook his head. This guy was good.

"Does that make you feel better, I hope?"

Picking touched the photo of Pat and Billy.

"It doesn't change anything. The Randolphs still have a son that is only half theirs."

"And a daughter that is all theirs. Dick, if you or I don't tell them, they're never gonna know about the boy. Do they love him?"

"They're crazy about him. But if they had just waited a little longer, they would have conceived on their own."

"You don't know that." Davis meant what he said. "How do you know if they ever would have had a child without the in-vitro? Psychologically, they were impotent. It was only after we allowed them to have their first child . . ."

Picking flew into a rage. "We *allowed* them?" he screamed, at the top of his lungs. "We . . . allowed . . . them . . . ? Do you hear what you're saying, Hunter? We didn't allow them. We manipulated them! We lied to them! We played God with their lives! Jesus, Joseph and Mary, Hunter. What have we done? How can I ever forgive myself for this act of betrayal? How can I go on?"

It was useless trying to reason with him in his present state of mind. Hunter Davis was a patient man when it came to problem solving. He hated making the wrong moves, and he knew only one thing about dealing with Richard Picking this afternoon. Picking was dynamite and he might be the spark. So he let the man rant and rave for another few minutes and then suggested they continue their conversation after dinner. That chicken smelled good.

"Where are you now?" he asked Picking.

"In my office in the city. Why?"

"Don't stay there. And don't go home either. I don't think you should be alone right now. Can you visit some friends for a while?"

"Which friends?" Picking snarled. "The Randolphs? Should I go visit my friends with one real baby and one fake baby? I can't even look them in the eye."

Davis used psychology.

"How about someone you recently arranged an adoption for? You must believe you did right by them."

He waited for an answer. There was thirty seconds of dead silence.

Richard Picking was still stapling Hunter Davis' card to the file folder and removing the staples. He threw all of the papers on the floor and stepped on them. Then he walked over to the window and looked down again. The street was empty. Not a soul. Not even a taxi. It was an omen.

"Yeah, that's a good idea," he said finally. "I'll call up someone I helped adopt a baby." One of the many babies located and stolen away from its birthparents by Hunter Davis. And him. Co-conspirators. "Thanks."

"Hello?"

Picking had hung up on him. He did the same. The man was becoming a lunatic. If his guilt and depression did not subside after the New Year, Richard Picking would have to be reckoned with. Maybe he needed to see a psychiatrist. Obviously, he had never resolved the deaths of his wife and child. It was tough, but eight years had passed. You had to go on with your life, meet someone new, remarry, have more kids. Leave the past behind you.

For a city ravaged repeatedly by hurricanes, earthquakes, fire and flood, Charleston was still one of America's most beautiful and historic places. It was a survivor. Its eighteenth and early nineteenth century buildings — those not demolished by natural disasters — were held together by nails, mortar and metal rods. Bronze markers proclaimed triumphantly that it would take more than wind, rain, tidal waves and a flaming inferno to defeat Charleston, "The Holy City." The town was here to stay.

Richard Picking wished that he had stayed in Charleston, his birthplace and home to generations of Pickings. Most had moved away, to smaller cities in the Carolinas. A dearth of male offspring had resulted in the virtual disappearance of the Picking surname. His brother, Daniel, the black sheep of the family, still lived in town. Richard prayed Dan would never marry. It was better for the name to die than to be carried on by *his* children. Dan had tried every line of work, from carpentry to real estate to house painting. In the end, he was an incorrigible. A drinking, smoking do-nothing whose most ardent desire was to inherit a vast sum from a family member, part of the reason most had relocated. Dan owed his brother Richard about four thousand dollars, written off at the time of the "loan."

Charleston. Poe's "Kingdom By The Sea." With its diverse ethnic mix, a Southern city without a homogenous Southern accent. Its cobblestone streets along its glorious and bountiful waterfront, Civil War cannons still lining its peninsular battery. Its fabulous churches, museums, pedestrian marketplace, restaurants and other cultural and social attractions. Its renowned horse-drawn carriage rides, usurping motor traffic and announcing symbolically every day that *the past must not be forgotten.* And, of course, its unsurpassed architecture; its row houses and antebellum mansions, its Post-Victorian and Pre-Revolutionary statements of wealth commemorating yesterday's most powerful families.

Had he never left Charleston, Richard told himself, he would now be happy. Or at least content, occupying his correct place in the universe. Instead, here he was, in New York City of all places. A Yankee stronghold he once vowed he would never visit, much less live in. New York, where he had found true love and in the blink of an eye lost it. Appropriately, the place where he had been seduced into committing the very worst sin of his life: tricking two desperate people into making a deal with the Devil. And he was the Devil's messenger, God forgive him.

Picking sat down at his desk again, tired and defeated. He reached down and slid out a drawer. Underneath a pile of unopened envelopes from creditors he found his father's handgun. The trigger felt tight. In his mind, someone else put the gun against the side of his head and fired it. A soldier at Fort Sumter, in Charleston Bay, at the start of the War Between The States. Not him. His last thought was that God would grant him salvation and that he was about to be with Pat and Billy. He could hardly wait to kiss them.

Before Hunter Davis could try Picking at the office or at home, hoping he was somewhere else, his telephone rang. It was the New York City police. They had found his business card on the bloody floor, next to the suicide victim.

After his initial shock and disbelief Hunter Davis explained that he was an old friend of the deceased. Picking had called him only a few hours ago to tell him of his despair and depression. No, he had no idea the man was considering suicide. No, he did not recognize any of the names on the files. No, he did not know who they should contact as the next of kin. He wasn't that close.

Detective Schoenfeld gave Davis some details. The doorman had notified the police when no one in 1406 answered his standard 5:00 PM reminder call. An order was given to kick in the door when someone thought they smelled smoke. There was no sign of a forced entry, no struggle, nothing disturbed or stolen. Just the crumpled remains of Richard Ellis Picking, whose death would be declared self inflicted by the Medical Examiner. After taking photos, the blood was wiped from Uncle Clarence's desk and the nicely framed family pictures were tossed into a cardboard box.

Chapter 19

❦

"REVELATION"

"Nice shot, Steve."

While Steve McDermott leaned forward, bracing his arms against his thighs, Jamie scooted down the long driveway. The basketball had bounced and rolled almost to the street, lodging in mom's impatiens, crushing quite a few. Saying it was an accident would not be accepted as a valid excuse. She might, however, show some compassion for her son's careless and obnoxious wrestling buddy when she saw his taped ribs. On the other hand, she might not when she heard why he was in bad shape.

Mickdee straightened up, painfully, and said he was sorry. The same thing he had told his dad after the accident last Thursday, exactly a week ago. On his way back from a hiking and smooching day trip in the Bear Mountains, he had attempted to pass a slow-moving vehicle on the Palisades. To his misfortune, Steve suddenly discovered that at 95 miles per hour, everyone else on the road is moving slowly. After sideswiping the Chrysler Minivan, hitting the back of the Lincoln and then getting rear-ended by the original slow-moving car, he was lucky to be alive. The BMW, completely demolished, ended up sideways on the median, Steve McDermott pinned in his seat and his girlfriend unconscious, neither wearing a seatbelt.

They were admitted to the Emergency Room at Englewood Hospital where Steve was released the same day. The passenger, amazingly, had only suffered a minor concussion and a broken arm. Far less than what her father would do to Mickdee, or her, should he ever find them together again.

"So your car was totalled?" Jamie asked.

"Totalled," answered Steve. "Gone. I mean . . . gone! You can't believe what it looked like. The insurance company took pictures."

"Don't show them to me." Jamie sunk a layup. "I hope you're gonna drive carefully from now on. This is why my dad bought me a Volvo."

Steve grabbed the ball and dribbled it slowly, then held it to his midsection, momentarily unable to move. "Yes, Big J. After a near-death experience, one does tend to value one's life a little more." Gasping for air, Steve dropped the basketball. "Hey, I have to sit down. This is killing me."

They sat under a large maple, a shady spot.

"I take it you'll be driving a new car shortly. Another Beemer?"

Steve smiled. "Hell, yes. My dad was p.o.'d at first, but after I promised to mend my evil ways, he gave in. As soon as we collect the insurance, I get to pick a new color." Jamie doubted that Steve, or his father, had learned his lesson.

"Let's go watch a video," Jamie suggested, feeling the warm,still August air on his glistening golden skin. "My Dad gets them free from a client. He's got all the killer movies: Arnold, Bruce Willis, Steven Segal . . . "

"Help me up." Jamie pulled his outstretched arm. "Ow! Not so hard!" They walked through the kitchen, snatching two bags of chips enroute to the media room. "The inner sanctum," Steve remarked, as Jamie popped *Casablanca* out of the VCR.

After about half an hour of grown men kicking each other's faces off, and exploding car hoods sailing into second story windows, the two aficionados of celluloid violence were interrupted.

"So this is where you've been hiding," said Diane Randolph. "I didn't know if you guys were out or not." Diane looked quickly at the TV screen, saw a head turned into hamburger, looked back. "Nice movie."

"It's Dad's video."

"Oh, yes, I forgot. His two favorite flicks are *Casablanca* and *Night Of The Living Dead Part Three* . . . " Steve laughed, coughed, held his chest.

"Steve! What happened to you? And who trampled my poor flowers?"

"It was an accident, Mom. The basketball got away." Jamie stood up, put his arm around Mickdee. "Mr. Indianapolis Five Hundred, here, wrecked his car on the Palisades. But don't worry. Daddy's buying him a new one."

Steve removed his friend's sarcastic embrace.

"I didn't do it on purpose, Mrs. Randolph. This old lady was clogging up the right lane. I tried to pass her . . . "

"At ninety-five," injected Jamie.

"Save it," scolded Mrs. Randolph. "Just drive carefully from now on." Diane donned a pair of grey gardener's gloves with thin red stripes. "You know, when I was your age . . . " She heard what she was saying and stopped herself. The classic words of wisdom from the older generation. Kids' ears were deaf to it.

"When you were our age," Jamie joshed, wrapping his arms around her waist, "there weren't any cars!" He kissed her neck. "I love you, Mom."

Diane twisted free — Two points for Mom! — and tickled her chunky son. She knew just where to go, between his underarms and his pecs, to bring him to his knees. The same ticklish spot since he was two years old.

"Mom! Stop!" he screamed, escaping between chairs. Mickdee howled.

"I love you, too," she said. "You're next, Steve."

"No, please, don't!" Mickdee raised two palms, like a cowardly bandit. "Really! My ribs. You'll hurt me."

Jamie bolted towards him, double-fisted. Laughed and backed off.

Diane started to leave, then remembered something.

"The reason I came in here, by the way, is to tell you that you just got a call from that Mrs. Davis you met in Memphis. She says it's important. That's the lawyer's wife, right?"

Steve was surprised. Jamie hadn't said anything about going to Tennessee.

"Memphis? I thought you were in Florida with that babe

from Fort Lauderdale?"

Jamie's friends did not know about the inheritance.

"Who said I was in Memphis?" he asked. "This is a lady I need a reference from, for school. She just moved."

"Oh," said Steve. "Well, I gotta meet Eddie and some girls over at Friendly's. You wanna come?" Jamie wondered what Mrs. Davis had called about.

"I'll meet you there," he said. "I have to make a couple of calls."

"Eleanor?" Steve winked, clicking his tongue suggestively.

"Who?"

"The girl from Florida."

"Delaney. Not Eleanor."

"Delaney. Whatever. Can I borrow your car?"

Diane Randolph's eyes bulged. "No way!"

"Mom, I was gonna tell him that. Thanks for your vote of confidence."

Diane picked up her spade. "I'm going to rearrange the Impatiens," she explained. "Please keep your basketball at the top of the driveway." The family dog was standing behind her, nudging her leg. It was time for his lunch. "Or I'll tell Grover to eat you guys instead of his Purina." Grover snorted, brushed his wide skull against the lady of the house. "Okay, okay," she said, pulling off a glove. "Come with me, Steverino. I'll drop you off at Friendly's. Just let me feed Grover."

Before driving into town to meet his friends, Jamie returned Mrs. Davis' call. Marna, her housekeeper, told him that she was out but a good time to reach her would be about seven thirty. Hunter, Jr. and his children were coming for dinner at six. "Don't call during the meal," Marna warned him.

After supper, Jamie first made his daily call to Delaney.

"Hi, there!" he greeted her. "It's your handsome boyfriend."

"Which one? I have so many."

"The one with the big . . . " He waited.

"The big what?" she asked playfully.

"The big blue eyes!" he laughed. "Boy, do you have a dirty mind."

"What's new, boyfriend?"

"Oh, nothing much. I played a little basketball with my

friend, Steve. You know, the guy who crashed his car."

"Yawn, yawn," said Delaney. "Sounds like an exciting day."

"Oh, it was," Jamie responded. "We ate chips and watched a killer movie. How was your day?"

It had only been seven days since their departure on separate flights from Los Angeles. Not long enough to really miss somebody, especially a person you only knew for two weeks. But that was how Jamie felt. He thought she did, too.

"Florida's dead in August," she reported. "I'll be going back to Boston in three weeks. Will you miss me?"

"I miss you now."

"That's sweet." Delaney noticed her message counter flashing a call she had forgotten to erase. "Oh, Daddy called today. He hired a man to check up on that plastic surgeon, Dr. Goldman. He wants to talk to you next week. The guy owns a huge house in a place called Benedict Canyon. It's about four miles from Beverly Hills. And they expect to get his income tax returns any day."

Jamie was all ears. "What else did he find out? Anything about Hunter Davis?"

"He didn't say. You'll talk to him soon. Ask him yourself. Hey, I was just about to take a shower when you called. Can I call you back later?"

Jamie pictured the two of them in the shower.

"Sure. Or else tomorrow. When am I going to see you again?"

"Soon," she answered.

"If I had one of those video phones, I could see you now. Are you naked?"

Delaney teased him. "Yes, I'm running my hand up and down my thigh," she said, breathing hard. "Now I'm touching my . . . breasts . . . just the way you did."

"Is this a obscene phone call?" said Jamie. "You're under arrest."

"Now I'm putting my fingers in my mouth . . . Oooh! Oooh!" She began to imitate her favorite actress, Meg Ryan, from *When Harry Met Sally.*

"I'm sorry," said Jamie. "I just realized my mother is

listening in."

"That's funny, big boy. My shower's running. Gotta go."
Kiss-kiss. Click.

It was about seven thirty. Jamie called Memphis. Marna
said, "Hold on."

"Jamie?"

"Hi, Mrs. Davis. Does your son know I'm talking to you?"

"Yes, he does. In fact, he's sitting right next to me. My
grandchildren are here tonight. They're eating chocolate
Ninja Turtles, for dessert. Of course, I bought the wrong
thing. I'm supposed to get . . . Powder Ringers?" Hunter
corrected her. "I'm sorry. They're called Power Rangers."

Jamie laughed, then listened to a description of her
grandchildren, the cutest, smartest, most wonderful little
darlings on the planet.

"My mother said you have something important to tell me."

"I do." Jamie waited patiently. "What's your birthday?"

"May 13, 1977."

She repeated the date to her son. They were in his father's
office, the murder scene.

"That's what I thought. Now, listen to me very carefully,
young man. And don't interrupt me. I have something that is
difficult for me to tell you. When you were here two weeks ago,
I had in my possession a safe deposit key that I think belongs
to you. It says J. Randolph on it and your birthday." Charlotte
covered her lips with her fingers. "I . . . apologize for not
bringing this up during your visit, but I wasn't sure what to
do. I found this key several years ago in my husband's
upstairs den. It was taped under a desk drawer, and I never
saw it until we decided to give the piece of furniture to my son.
He was redoing his office and I thought he would like his
father's desk. We took out the drawers to make it lighter, and
there it was. The police never inspected any room in the house
besides Hunter's downstairs office. That lady detective made
a pretty thorough search, but she never found the key."

Charlotte took a sip of water. Her son held her hand.
Jamie listened eagerly.

"Anyway, by the time I found the key, my husband was
dead ten years. The case was closed. I didn't want Hunter,

Jr. to get upset. Things were going well in his life. So I called the bank about the safe deposit box. I asked them if I could come down and see what was inside. I was afraid of what I might find, but I wanted to know."

"What was in the box?" asked Jamie.

"I don't know," she said. "I couldn't get into it. The box is not in my husband's name. It's in your name."

"My name? How is that possible?" Jack Randolph walked into Jamie's room.

"Because the box is owned by your trust. There is a letter on file with the bank stating that the contents of the box are *your* property. The rent on the box has been paid in perpetuity, that means forever. My son has confirmed that you can get into the box now that you are of age. He's made arrangements with the bank. We've told them you'll be coming in."

Jamie was flabbergasted. "This is great news!" he said, making his father sit down on the bed. "Let me talk to my parents. I'll be down as soon as I can."

"I'm really sorry," Charlotte reiterated. "I didn't want to keep this a secret from you, but I was . . . I'm still worried about what's in the box."

"Why?" asked Jamie. "What could be in there?"

"Who knows?" said the older woman, her voice quivering, handing the phone to her son and leaving the room without warning.

"Hello? Mrs. Davis?"

Jamie waited.

"This is Hunter Davis. Jamie? Don't hang up. Let me tell you what's happening here. I'm sorry, too, for the way we treated you. My mother is extremely upset at herself. It's possible we could have got in touch with you about this five years ago, but she never said anything to me. It's even possible we could have opened the box with a court order, claiming it had to do with my father's murder. We talked about doing that. But it belongs to you."

"I'm not mad," Jamie assured him. "I appreciate your calling me. Maybe this will give me the answer."

Hunter coughed into his hand. "You could be my brother," he ventured.

247

"What?"

"That's the other reason Mrs. Davis is unnerved." The lawyer pictured his father. "You see, you look like my father. You have the same color hair and eyes, you're big and muscular. And . . . " It was hard to say. "And we have reason to believe that my father might have other children out of wedlock."

"That's impossible," Jamie said. "I was born up north. Your father never knew my mother. What the hell are you talking about?"

Jack Randolph whispered a question to his son: What was wrong? Jamie couldn't answer yet.

"I'm just telling you what my mother thinks. I agree with you. I don't know how this is possible, but my mother has no idea who my father met on his business trips years ago. You say they didn't know each other and I hope you're right. But who left you the money? My father was a rich man. He made lots of deals for cash. And why did he establish a safe deposit box in trust for you? Unless he was your father."

Jamie Randolph was speechless. He did not believe what Hunter Davis was suggesting, but the questions remained unanswered. If he could live eighteen years of his life without knowing that he was conceived in-vitro, anything was possible. Had Jack Randolph, the person he called Dad, lied to him? Was Hunter Davis really his father? He did resemble him. But Hunter Davis' sperm had been tested at the fertility clinic. Supposedly, he couldn't father children. Or was that someone else's sperm? The possibilities were endless, the confusion disturbing, the deception mind-boggling.

"That's why you have to come to Memphis," Hunter said. "We all need to know what's in the box. Good or bad. It may even shed light on the murder. Oh, incidentally, this is Elvis Week in Memphis. There may not be any hotel rooms. You can stay at Magnolias with us."

"I'll be there." Jamie looked into Jack's eyes. "I'll call you back tomorrow morning."

"Call me here. We're all living at my mother's house for a while. I'll be taking some time off from work. What time will you call?"

"Early."

Jamie disconnected Davis. He turned to his . . . father.

"You'll be where?" asked Jack, smiling. A smile that no longer looked exactly like his son's.

"Memphis," Jamie answered. "I have to go back."

"When?"

"I don't know. Monday, I guess. I made some plans for the weekend." Plans? he thought to himself. Something more important than getting to the bottom of this horrible, you-should-be-grateful multi-million dollar inheritance mystery, once and for all? There was nothing else on his agenda that couldn't be put on hold. Maybe he would leave tomorrow, on Friday.

"What's going on?" his father inquired. "And what does this have to do with your mother?"

"That was Charlotte Davis. And her son, the lawyer."

"The lawyer who warned you about talking to his mother? What changed?"

"They found something."

Jack saw the sorrow in Jamie's eyes. He was concerned.

"What did they find? You look unhappy."

Jamie faked a smile.

"They found some boxes. Hunter Davis' personal files from 1970 to 1978. Actually, Mrs. Davis knew about them all along. She just didn't want to show them to me when I arrived unannounced." Jamie didn't like lying to his father; maybe Jack hadn't liked concealing certain facts from him either. "They said I can go through the files in their house, for a couple of days. Provided I don't tell anyone what I find, unless it's about me. I think Mr. Davis did a lot of business in cash." He elaborated on the fabrication. "They told me I can't make copies of anything, that someone has to watch me so I'm not tempted to steal any of the papers . . . and after this I can never see the files again. They also said that Mr. Davis might have done business with Mom."

"No way," said his father. "If that were true, I'd know him, too."

Jack found the story plausible in the scheme of things. He got up from the bed, walked to Jamie's bookcase and picked up the book Jamie had folded open to the middle pages.

"New book?" he asked. "Religious?"

"No. I've been trying to finish that book for weeks. It's about a guy from upstate New York who gets kidnapped by aliens. Maybe I'll take it with me on the plane."

"If you can wait a few days, we can all go," Jack suggested. "It's quiet in the office right now. Your sister will be back from Cape Cod with Aunt Ellen on Monday. I don't think your mother would mind. We've always wanted to visit Graceland. Let's go ask her."

Jack replaced the book, searched for Jamie's eyes.

"I don't think so." Jamie stared at his poster of the San Francisco Forty-Niners, next to Van Gogh. "I'd rather go alone."

The devoted father and lawyer was at a rare loss for words. His son's sudden unwillingness to share his problems with the family had surprised him. He tried to think of what Humphrey Bogart would say but there was no son in *Casablanca.* He ran his fingers across Jamie's books. Quite a few were about UFO's and visitors from outer space, but many were environmental books — save the oceans, clean the air, recycle — and psychology books. Until this recent obsession with the money, the boy had been an avid reader, a well rounded scholar and athlete, a down-to-earth teenager with his head screwed on right. He was still a good boy. Jack trusted him implicitly. Enough to let him go back to Memphis, by himself, even if he felt like putting a Full Nelson on this impetuously independent new person. They had raised him right. In the end, he would not disappoint them.

"No problem," Jack said. In his mind's eye, he (Bogart) stepped forward, breath-smelling close to Jamie, and told him: "Get outa here, kid. If there's one thing I can't stand, it's a loser. And you wanna know why you're one? It's because you don't realize that you've already got it all. It can only go downhill from here. So go on, get out."

Jack reached for one of the books on the top shelf. A children's book. There were boxfuls in the attic, saved for the grandchildren, but Jamie's favorites were still in his room. "The Five Chinese Brothers," first published in 1938. A great lesson story about five identical brothers, one of whom (the brother who could swallow the sea) had accidentally killed a young boy trying to be nice to him. When sentenced to death, each night a different brother secretly took his place. All of the brothers had special death-defying abilities and none could be executed. Like the brother who couldn't be burned. Or the one with the iron neck. Finally, the judge decided that if the brother (he thought there was only one) couldn't be killed, he must be innocent, and set him free.

"You remember this book?" Jack asked, recalling the excited eyes of his six year old son.

"I remember it, Dad. Dad . . . This is something I have to do." Jamie put his arm on his father's shoulder. "Really," he said. "It's almost over. If there's nothing in these files . . . "

"Let's go tell your mother." Jack shoved the book back in place. Right between "Where The Wild Things Are" and "The Velveteen Rabbit."

⚜

The second time Jamie Randolph came to the impressive gates of the Davis estate, they opened automatically, as the hood of Hunter, Jr.'s Cadillac nosed slowly through.

"Elvis Week is crazy," the young man observed, exiting the car. He took the front steps two at a time, caught his balance without dropping his suitcase, then stood still. "Where's the dogs?"

"Mother put them in the pen." Davis slammed his door. "Figured they might not recognize you until they tore off a leg." The lawyer laughed. "The way you jump around, I wouldn't blame them. They're trained to attack strangers. Well, first they hold you at bay. It's only if you try to escape that they attack."

"I'll keep that in mind," Jamie said.

"Tonight is the Reunion Concert," Davis told him. "That's where performers and musicians who worked with Elvis get together again. Guys like J.D. Sumner. Tuesday night is the Candlelight Vigil. Thousands of Elvis fans from around the

251

world carry a candle past the gravesite on the evening before August 16th. This is the eighteenth anniversary of his death."

Eighteen years ago, Jamie reminded himself, he was born.

"That's if Elvis is really dead," he said.

"Oh, he's dead," said Davis. "You've been reading The Enquirer, haven't you?"

The door opened. A large white woman in a gray and white uniform held it for Charlotte Davis with one arm. It was a stifling, humid afternoon, just like New Jersey. The shade trees helped but nothing beat air conditioning.

"Welcome back," said the lady, stepping out, fanning her neck and retreating to the cooler air. "Come inside, you'll live longer." A Jewish expression, funny coming from Mrs. Davis. To Jamie's surprise, she kissed his cheek. Oh God, he thought. Don't let her turn out to be . . . related to me. I don't fit in.

The elegant entrance hall led to a grand living room. All of the ceilings were tall. On the way, Jamie felt his valise pulled away by the female wrestler type, good old Marna. He recognized the voice. After a brief tour downstairs, and some small talk in the great room, he was escorted to his bedroom. He showered in the luxurious marble bath, not as outrageous as the one in the Ritz-Carlton, but pretty cool.

Before returning to his hosts, Jamie leaned over the pedestal sink and stared at his face in the mirror. He felt like he was looking into someone else's eyes. Back to Charlotte.

"Your home is beautiful," said Jamie, saying what his mother would say. The massive fireplace mantel was carved with symbols of the Confederacy: flags, crossed swords and military emblems.

"Thank you." Charlotte smiled at him. Indoors, she was even more attractive.

"Where are your grandchildren?"

"They're out with their mother. Be back shortly. After we talk."

Jamie noticed a coloring book and a box of Crayola crayons on a an antique pie crust table.

"Tomorrow, you can go to church with us if you like," said Hunter.

"That would be nice."

"And Monday morning, first thing, we're off to the bank."

Charlotte scanned the room to be sure Marna was elsewhere. Jamie looked up at an oil painting of Charlotte and Hunter. It was life size, surrounded by an ornate gold-leafed frame that probably cost more than his Volvo.

"I've speculated on what might be in that box for a long, long time," said the poised Southern lady. "But if for some reason it has nothing to do with me, I will respect your privacy."

"The bank knows you're coming," injected her son. "You have plenty of ID?"

"Of course he does, Hunter. Be quiet a minute." Hunter played with his ear, a little boy following Mommy's orders. "Now, Jamie, this is important. Before we go, I want you to promise me that if there is information in that safe deposit box that I should know, you will tell me. I do not want you to try to spare my feelings by withholding facts about my husband that may seem unpleasant. I hope that is not the case, but if it is, do you promise to tell me the truth?"

An image of Hunter making passionate love to her appeared briefly in Charlotte's mind. She had never actually pictured him with another woman.

"I promise," said Jamie.

"Good. Because if, as Hunter suggested to you, you are somehow a member of this family, it will be made public. That is, unless you don't want your family to know."

"Mother, let's not put the cart before the horse."

"Of course, you're right. I'm jumping to conclusions. It's much more likely that we'll find something related to Mr. Davis' death. You know, Jamie I have never believed that my husband's murder was the result of a robbery. He was murdered, in my opinion, over a very controversial matter that the police covered up. Probably involving sex. We're hoping that there's a letter in the box. A letter of explanation, however painful it might be, even after sixteen years."

"If it's there, I'll give it to you," Jamie said.

Charlotte then revealed the unauthorized investigation conducted by Detective Darlene Flood from 1979 to 1982, the year she retired. Flood was now married, with one child, and still lived in Memphis. They had kept in touch but had not spoken about the crime in years. She had never been told about the safe deposit key.

"She gave me copies of all the police reports," said Charlotte. "And she offered to continue working for me after she quit the force, but I didn't see the point. She wasn't getting any cooperation, and frankly I was afraid of what might come out while Hunter and his sisters were growing up."

"We never found out a damn thing," Hunter explained. "Nothing about the gun. Nothing about the stolen jewelry. Nothing, period." He shook his head.

"What jewelry?" asked the guest.

"That's not important," said Charlotte. "My husband kept some valuable gold and diamond jewelry in his safe. It was stolen with his money. We didn't care about getting it back. We were hoping it would turn up somewhere so we could trace it. Well, we would have liked to recover the cuff links. They were handed down to Hunter from his great-great Grandfather John Davis, who served as a colonel during the Civil War. A Rolex watch, you can always buy another."

Jamie was starting to get the feeling that Magnolias was a shrine to the War Between The States. In addition to the fireplace mantle and cuff links, he had seen two paintings of Confederate Officers (perhaps one was Colonel John Davis), two Confederate flags and a small cabinet filled with Civil War mementos.

"What did the cuff links look like?" the boy asked, out of curiosity.

"Confederate flags," said Hunter, Jr. "Daddy let me wear them once."

Jamie checked his watch. Three-fifteen. Almost forty-two hours until the bank opened. Yesterday, he couldn't wait to fly to Memphis. Now it seemed like he would be unable to carry on a conversation with the Davises for two days without embarrassing himself or making them uncomfortable. Unless all they talked about was Elvis Presley and the Civil War.

꧁❀꧂

"I don't know what to do," said Ira Goldman, adjusting his trousers. "I told you that guy was a reporter. For the goddam National Enquirer yet. Who knows what he's up to?"

As usual, Leonard Stein was the calmer member of the pair. It was he who had called the Los Angeles Times, pretending that Sid Morrison had contacted him as a Times reporter. No, they said. There was no such person on their staff. But an investigator for another publication by that name was currently in Beverly Hills. Morrison had been assigned to the O.J. Simpson trial early in the year, was still in California as far as they knew. Maybe on his own time now. The National Enquirer in Lantana, Florida would not confirm Morrison's whereabouts unless the caller gave his name and phone number. Never mind.

"Why don't we just wait and see what happens?" Stein recommended. "He hasn't been back here. How is he ever going to find out what we do? You'll see. In a couple of weeks they'll send him off on a new story. King Kong found. Adolf Hitler owns The Empire State Building. You know that newspaper."

Goldman didn't find anything funny about the Morrison situation.

"I'm not paranoid," he said. "How do you think the guy found us in the first place? It wasn't by sheer chance. He lied about Hunter Davis. He knows we did business with him. I wouldn't be surprised if he knows everything."

Stein was adamant in his opposing viewpoint.

"If he knew, then he'd print the story. You think The Enquirer cares about double-checking their facts? They just go for it. They could care less if they get sued."

"That's what they want everyone to think."

"Okay, so maybe he suspects that the kid is the world's first test-tube baby. I don't see how that is possible, since you're a plastic surgeon. But let's say that's what he thinks. If he can't prove it, no one is going to pay any attention to him."

Goldman shrugged.

"If he prints my name in the paper, I'm going to pay attention. And so will you. People are going to start showing up at our doorstep. Then what?"

"It will never happen," said Stein. "You're imagining things."

"I think you should take a little trip to Memphis, Leonard." Goldman looked at his vanilla Yogurt. He pushed it away. His weight was down to around one hundred and forty-three pounds. Thirty pounds less than his smaller assistant. He needed to gain weight but he was never hungry.

"And what would I do there?" asked Stein.

"You figure it out. That's where Morrison got his information. We know that. What we don't know is why."

Leonard Stein was not in the mood for travel. Whenever possible, he preferred to wait until the last minute before taking action. Usually, things got better by themselves.

"How about we wait another week?" he said. "If we don't hear from this guy again, he's probably dropped us. If he's already set the wheels in motion, it's too late to do anything. But I have a feeling he's hit a dead end."

"One week," agreed the scientist. "I hope you're right."

Chapter 20

꧁꧂

"RETURN TO SENDER"

The safe deposit room of the Merchants Bank of Memphis opened promptly at 9:00 AM. Waiting at the door were Charlotte Davis, Hunter, Jr. and Jamie.

"Good morning, folks!" said Floyd Henderson, the wiry, talkative vault attendant. "Guess you people heard about our big Summer Sale?"

"What are you talking about?" asked Hunter.

"That's a joke. I'm just not used to people being so anxious to get in here." He slid the polished steel door aside.

Jamie had the key to Box 331. Hunter handed Henderson his business card. The man read it and smiled.

"I knew your daddy, son."

"You did?"

"Sure did. I've been working here since 1966. This is only my second job."

No one was all that interested in his first job. But the man in the short-sleeved white shirt described it anyway.

"I started out running the elevator in this building, back in 1959. I was fresh out of high school. Had a full head of black hair then, like Elvis. My salary was $56 a week. It was one of those old Otis elevators. You know, the kind with the wheel and crank like you see in the movies. Had a good time with that job till they offered me $70 to hang around the dungeon here. I can't believe I've been doing this for twenty-nine years. I could retire if I wanted to, but I don't know what else I'd do. Go fishing, mostly." He paused for oxygen. "So you're a lawyer like your daddy?"

"Yes sir. And that's my second job, too."

"Don't need to hear about the first one. Work to do," said Henderson. "Who's got the key?"

Jamie had a tight grip on it in his right hand. He dropped it into the attendant's open palm and waited for further instructions.

"Okay folks, sit over here a second. I just have to get out the signature card."

Jamie was too excited to sit. Hunter and Charlotte sat down on a comfortable old sofa set at a forty-five degree angle in one corner of the small office. With space at a premium, the sofa belonged flat against a wall, but apparently Floyd's third job would not be an interior decorator. The walls were covered with black and white photographs of the bank the day it opened in September, 1922.

There were four small tables in the office, backed to the walls, each with its own ash tray, a note pad, a ballpoint pen and a black wire wastebasket. The pens were attached to the tables with twisted elastic bands screwed in place. Three rows of long fluorescent bulbs covered a good part of the ceiling. The room was lit up to a near-blinding level. Just the way Floyd liked it.

Within thirty seconds the signature card had been located and centered on the gigantic oak desk. Henderson had an envelope in his hand, from which he removed two documents. One was a notarized letter from Hunter Davis dated June, 1977. The other was a certified copy of a New Jersey birth certificate dated May 13th of the same year.

"I need one Jamie Randolph," said Floyd. Jamie stepped up to the desk. "Ain't got no signature on your card, Jamie, since this box was opened just about the time you were born. How do I know you're really you?"

Jamie produced the original of his birth certificate, along with his driver's license and two credit cards. Henderson examined the items slowly, compared addresses and asked Jamie to sign the card, then returned his ID.

"Is this here good-looking young man Jamie Richard Randolph?" he asked the Davises.

"No doubt about it," responded Hunter.

Mrs. Davis nodded in reply and raised her eyebrows. Floyd nodded back.

"Okay, I guess I can let you in. Who's going into the vault, just you or all three?"

That was the cue for Charlotte and Hunter to stand up.

"We're leaving," Charlotte announced. "This is a personal matter for Jamie to handle."

"Okay, boy, let's go dig up the coffin."

Charlotte shuddered at the thought. Jamie shook hands with the Davises and said good-bye.

"If you need anything, call us," said Charlotte.

"Thanks, Mrs. Davis. Mr. Davis. Thanks for everything. I'll call you later."

Charlotte and Hunter, Jr. left the vault.

Inside the claustrophobic cubicle, Jamie hesitated before opening the safe deposit box. He pried up the clip with his thumb, lifted the lid halfway, and peeked inside. There were several envelopes and a sturdy six inch wooden box. The top of the box was fastened down with screws. Jamie removed the envelopes and laid them out on the counter before him. They were labeled #1 to #6 with a blue magic marker. He shook the wood box. It did not rattle.

He opened envelope number one.

Had he been given a thousand guesses at what was in the first envelope, none would have even come close. Inside was a *1933 United States $10 Gold Piece* with an Indian Head design and a copy of the very first issue of *Captain Marvel* comics. Both were in protective holders and in mint condition. An invoice from 1976 on Excelsior Stamp & Coin Company stationery in New York was made out to Elvis Presley. No address. The price was $43,000 for the pair, marked "Paid in cash."

Jamie opened the second envelope.

Inside was a hand-written letter. After reading the first two lines, he felt excited and fearful at the same time. It was a greater adrenaline rush than wrestling or making love, the equivalent of winning the lottery, being elected President and marrying Miss America simultaneously.

The letter to him from Elvis read:

June 5, 1977

Dear Jesse:

I know your legal name is Jamie Richard Randolph. I saw you and held you in Englewood Hospital the day after you were born, May 14, 1977. Your parents met me disguised as a Priest. I haven't seen you again yet but I hope to visit you soon and on your birthday every year. Maybe I'll come as a clown next time, or Mickey Mouse.

The reason I'm writing to you as "Jesse" is that I believe you are the reincarnation of my twin brother, Jesse Garon Presley, who died while I was being born. I know it wasn't my fault but I have always felt guilty about the life I had and you didn't. I have prayed to God for many years that you would be "born again" someday. I visited you and spoke to you at the Priceville Cemetery, and I know you heard me. Because we were identical twins I sincerely believe that your soul has returned to earth. I've read a lot about these spiritual matters.

Many people do not believe in reincarnation but earlier this year I met a lady at Graceland named Ellen Marie Foster who I feel strongly is the spirit of our mother. I gave her a ring Mama gave to me twenty years ago.

If I am alive when you turn 18, I may give you this letter in person. Otherwise, I am leaving it with my attorney and very close friend, Hunter Davis, to decide if and when to give it to you. I have sold many personal possessions to make this dream possible and to be certain you can go to college and take care of any medical problems you may have. Mr. Davis will work out all of the financial details. You can trust him.

I guess you have found the Gold Coin and the comic. I wanted you to have the closest American Gold Coin to our birthday in 1935. This was the last Gold Coin made in the U.S.A. except for a 1933 $20 Gold Piece which is illegal to own. As to the comic book, when I was a kid I loved Captain Marvel. Some people think I tried to look like Captain Marvel, Jr.

Anyway, I'm sure you know something about me from my records and movies but if you're reading this letter without me, that means I'm probably dead. (Or else a sixty year old hermit.) If all you can go by is my public image, please let me tell you about the real Elvis Presley, your (twin) brother.

I was called a loner and to a certain extent that was true. I didn't always fit in. But I liked people, and I loved being an entertainer. Unfortunately, my life just seemed to get out of control. I was okay until I hit thirty. It all came naturally and easily, and I was feeling great, mentally and physically. Millions of people loved to see me perform, and I loved singing for them. Then I started to worry about everything. The Beatles were getting all the hit records. They stole all the attention I had coveted as my birthright. Someone once called them "the four Elvis Presleys" and that made me jealous. I prayed to God not to think what I was thinking, but I guess God has his own plan for me.

I am not proud to admit that I have neglected my wife Priscilla and my daughter Lisa Marie. I have become obsessed with recapturing fame and fortune which have always been like an aphrodisiac to me. I may be successful in becoming a "Super Star" again, judging by some of my recent hits and all the concerts. But I am fulfilling the dreams of the Devil, not the Lord. Jesse, remember this. You've got to love God and your family first, before money, before houses, before cars and jewelry and any kind of material wealth. For as Jesus said, it is easier for a camel to pass through the eye of a needle than for a rich man to enter the Kingdom Of Heaven.

That rich man, I am sorry to say, is me. Although after all the money I have spent I don't really know if I am as rich as everyone says. My only redemption may be the fact that I don't really care about keeping the money. I'd like to give more of it to charity than I do, especially to help children, but I can't seem to find the time. I hope you will be generous, too.

Talking about Jesus, I sincerely hope that you have accepted Him as your Lord and Saviour, and that you read the Bible often. Every time I read it, I learn something. Like in the story of Passover in The Old Testament. I realized that I am like Pharaoh. Why did it take all ten plagues to convince him to free the Jews? How many more warnings do I need to change my ways? Hunter says eleven!

I'm just a few years younger than the age of our beloved mother Gladys when she passed away. Sometimes I feel like I am going to join her soon. I doubt it, but you never know. After all, I fly a lot so I could die in a plane crash like Buddy Holly. And my health is not very good. Next year I would like to get away from it all, live alone in the mountains for a year or two and get into hiking and health food. But to tell you the truth, I will most likely never change. Luckily our family comes from strong English stock and maybe I can survive my own terrible habits.

After Priscilla divorced me four years ago, I did not know if I could go on. I suddenly realized that my musical talent and all my "success" had not brought me happiness. Just the opposite. I got through it somehow but I have wished for a long, long time that I could live my life over. If I could, I would never choose to be a singer or even a movie star. So many famous people are miserable. Look at what happened to Marilyn Monroe and James Dean, just to name a few. I would have a normal life, and it doesn't matter if I was a doctor, or a carpenter, or a used car salesman. Just as long as I was totally committed to my family. That's what counts, Jesse.

I have tried to imagine what my life would have been like if no one had ever heard me sing. Truthfully, I can't even imagine it. And why should I care when it isn't possible? It's just depressing. And the worst *thing is I can't stop doing what I am doing. If someone said I could go back in time and do it over, I feel like I might say no. Because I love my fans as much as they love me.*

Then I found out about a medical breakthrough that seemed like the answer to my prayers. With the help of Hunter Davis, we tracked down this scientist in Beverly Hills named Dr. Ira Goldman. He says he is a plastic surgeon, but really he does research on evolution and diseases. He's worked for all kinds of important people including the President. But we think he's caught up in something illegal that has to do with cross-breeding animals. I don't really want to know what he does and I'm glad I never met him. But when we found out he could create babies from your blood, we decided to risk doing business with him. It's called "cloning" and by 1995 (when you're 18) Goldman says it will be a common thing that everybody does. We tried to have this procedure done at a reputable fertility clinic in New York, Chicago, Atlanta, The Mayo Clinic and a place in Beverly Hills but no one could do it. So Goldman was our only choice. I strongly suggest that you stay away from this guy as Hunter warned me that he could be very dangerous. Hunter hates him. But Goldman has no idea who you are.

The bottom line is we paid him a small fortune to make a clone of me. Since I do not seem to be capable of fathering a child the normal way at this time, maybe due to stress, it was amazing that there was another option even though it sounds pretty weird. By the way, my only other child is Lisa Marie, although lots of people claim to be raising my son or daughter.

Anyway, Hunter Davis contacted a lawyer named Richard Picking in New York. Together they located a couple who couldn't have children of their own but who we all felt would make great parents for you. That would be Mr. and Mrs. Jack Randolph, your Mom and Dad. I don't know exactly how they did it but my blood was collected on Christmas two years ago. Goldman did his thing with it, and your mother got pregnant through what they call "in vitro." I think that means in a test tube.

Jesse, I am truly sorry to tell you that the Randolphs are not your real parents when it comes to the sperm and egg. If I could, I would apologize to them although I believed having a baby would make them happy. I don't think you should ever tell them the truth now as it would undoubtedly hurt them. They love God, and they believe you are His gift to them. They share no knowledge or blame in this whatsoever. I also think it would be a good idea for you not to tell anyone else where you really came from. At the very least this might make you a "freak". As the son or brother or reincarnation of Elvis Presley, I am sure people would only exploit you. And if you were "lucky" enough to be accepted as the real Elvis Presley, because you are my exact duplicate, take my word for it. You will not be happy to be the idol of millions of loyal fans. They will love you, but they will love you to death. It can be the most wonderful feeling in the world, but being an "idol" is not what God wishes for us. And the Devil will gladly arrange for your own self-destruction, just as he did mine.

I hope you have grown up in the kind of loving home Hunter and I envisioned for you. I also hope that somehow you are smarter than me and will go to a good college and become something important, but not famous. Jesse, it is my only hope that you will become the person I wish I was. And I hope I have watched you grow and helped you from the sidelines in every way I can.

But you have to make your own decisions. For that is what makes you a man.

That is why in case you ever decide to tell the world who you are I am leaving you the proof. Hunter has had vacuum sealed samples of my blood put into three slots in a special wood box you will find with this letter. Each one is numbered and my initials and fingerprints are on the tape wrapped around the samples. There is a letter inside signed by me and Hunter (we are the only ones who know everything) attesting to where the blood samples were taken and that it is my blood. According to Dr. Goldman, in a few years they will be able to do new tests to match the blood to the person it came from. Or his twin. You must give this matter a great deal of thought before you make your final decision. You know where I stand, but only you know the person you want to be.

Legally, Hunter does not know if you would be entitled to any part of my estate when I die. In fact, he doesn't want me to ever tell you about our relationship, or if I do he says to wait until you are much older. In the hope of encouraging you not to reveal your true identity for money, I have left you enough money to live a good life. But you are not in my will. Please don't be mad. I have also left you a Star Of David to wear with your Cross in case that might help you get into Heaven. I wore both myself. I put a Star Of David on Mama's grave stone for the same reason. Good luck, Jesse. Joy and health to you and your family. I hope we can be friends someday. I hope you will live a very happy life, get married and have many wonderful children. It will probably be safe to tell them who you are when they grow up. Thank you for understanding what I did for you and me. I love you with all my heart.

Your brother,
ELVIS ARON PRESLEY

P.S. No matter which path you choose to take, my prayers and hopes are with you.

To say that Jamie was stunned was an understatement.

After opening Elvis' time capsule, he did not know what to think or feel. He looked through the other four envelopes quickly. One contained a book called "Elvis In Hollywood." Another the film "King Creole." In the fifth envelope he found copies of all documents associated with his trust and his birth. Power of attorney letters, a file on the Randolph family, Chemical Bank's papers and photostats of cashier's checks made out to Richard Picking for nearly $800,000. Plus additional cashier's checks to the Internal Revenue Service. In the final envelope was a photo of Elvis, Gladys and Vernon, and a Gold locket with their pictures inserted. A note explained that this was a gift for Gladys purchased shortly before her death. Elvis had kept it as a remembrance. Now it was Jamie's.

Strangely, the young man found himself touching his face without knowing why. When he realized it was because he was questioning his own identity, he stopped. He was Jamie Randolph, of Tenafly, New Jersey. Not Elvis or Jesse Presley of Tupelo, Mississippi. Just because you looked the same as another person didn't make you that person. Even identical twins were different, sometimes totally different. Or were they? Being a "clone" — what a creepy word, (he would look for a synonym, "twin" was better) was a prospect he had never considered. What were the consequences of being a human reproduction?

Were Jack and Diane Randolph still his parents? The thought hit him like a fist as he closed the lid of the safe deposit box, leaving a second key inside. Of course they were his parents. Who else could be? Elvis Presley? A man he had never met, who had died three months after his birth?

However, no matter how logical he tried to be, he still didn't feel like himself. He didn't feel like Elvis Presley, or the clone of Elvis either. But he didn't know who he *did* feel like.

The good news was that at least his parents had not lied to him. If he was a victim in all this, so were they. So the three of them still shared something, if not the same blood.

Or perhaps Elvis was lying. After all, cloning human beings was considered science fiction in biology textbooks. Well, not exactly science fiction, but a technique that had not yet been perfected. Except with frogs. And frogs were hardly the same as people.

But why would Elvis lie to him? And how else could Elvis know so much about him? Why would Elvis leave him a million dollars? The new questions were worse than the old ones.

Jamie called Charlotte Davis from the airport. He had taken his suitcase to the bank and planned to return to New Jersey that day. He expected to go home and talk to his mother and father about getting ready for college. Now he was unsure of what to do next. It was like finding out you had one year left to live. Were you better off knowing or not knowing? Dad had told him to just take the money and be happy. Everyone had told him that. Why hadn't he taken their advice?

He wondered what would have happened if Charlotte had gotten into the box five years ago and he had learned the truth (if it was the truth) at age thirteen. Hunter Davis was right. Elvis should have withheld the information, or kept it a secret for another eighteen years. Too late for that now.

Jamie told Charlotte that what he had found in the box had nothing whatsoever to do with her. He was not the son of Hunter Davis. His father's uncle, he claimed, had hired Richard Picking to set up an anonymous trust. No one knew the man was rich and he wanted it to stay that way, to keep peace in the family since all the money had gone to Jamie. Picking, in turn, had hired Hunter Davis as an out-of-state attorney to further confuse any investigation and Davis was supposed to tell Jamie the truth in person when he turned eighteen. The safe deposit box, he told Charlotte, was only there as a precaution in case of Davis' death. The ill-fated events that took the lives of Picking and Davis proved that the box was a wise move. Otherwise, the mystery could never have been solved.

"It's complicated," Jamie said. "But it's the truth."

Jamie debated telling her about Goldman. The man Hunter Davis "hated," and whom he considered "very dangerous." *Maybe his murderer.* But such a conclusion was highly subjective without evidence. If he found out more later, he would keep his promise to tell her the truth about Goldman. As far as he knew, nothing else he had seen was of importance to the Davis family.

Instead of boarding his plane, Jamie took a cab back to the $45 a night Days Inn.

Chapter 21

"CONFESSION"

Billy Crystal and Meg Ryan. Tom Hanks and Meg Ryan. Interesting. In two of her best movies, Meg Ryan's co-star was an ex-comedian who had either hosted the Academy Awards or won two of them.

Delaney Morrison laughed halfheartedly as Billy Crystal tried to convince his passenger that attractive men and women can't be "just friends". Indeed, asserted the neo-Freudian philosopher, there is an uncontrollable sexual force that will inevitably pull attractive males and females together no matter how hard they resist. Delaney recalled Jamie trying to concentrate on playing the piano; without warning, he suddenly kissed her. And wanted more. Just like Billy Crystal.

Then why hadn't she heard from him in four whole days?

It was Tuesday and she had called in sick. No one really cared if she was there or not. She didn't work on breaking news or hot rumors. As a features writer, or trainee, you were given very liberal production deadlines. For some journalists, one or two great stories a year was enough. You weren't paid by the story — that is, preferential staff writers were not, or the daughters of "family members" like The Superstar — as long as you came through over a period of time. Once, Sid had delivered only one significant piece in eighteen months. Fortunately for him, the story was about Michael Jackson, it was true, and it scooped every other paper in America. After that, he was on a roll, exposing "inside stories" on Johnny

Carson, Carol Burnett and Frank Sinatra within a month. Two out of three turned out to be factual, and long-term circulation gains out-performed the lawsuit. Right now in 1995, Sid was "cold".

Soon Delaney would be back at school, so there was little pressure to crank out the one last article she had promised. Her pay was mediocre, and they were not about to fire Sid Morrison's prodigy over small potatoes. Morrison claimed to be onto something big. His all-expenses-paid vacation in Beverly Hills was coming to an end. One of these days, he would strike oil again and be back on top. It always worked out that way for Mr. Lucky.

Delaney picked up the phone on the first ring.

"Jamie?" So much for playing hard to get.

"Delaney?"

"Daddy! It's nice to hear from you."

Sid Morrison threw his naked feet onto his girlfriend's lap. She bit his toes.

"I'll bet," he said. "I guess you haven't heard from Mister Universe?"

"I don't know where he is. Daddy, I'm worried about him. He said he would call me every day."

"I tell women a lot of things I don't really mean," Sid replied.

"That's you, Daddy. Jamie's not like that."

"Thanks a bunch, sweetie." The woman's fingers climbed his hairy chest. "That's like the scene with Steve Martin in *Father Of The Bride*: He's like you, Daddy . . . only he's brilliant!"

"Sid, this is serious. His parents won't tell me where he is. All they say is he's out of town. Out of town where? He's not in Beverly Hills, is he?"

Sid checked his messages. "I haven't spoken to him since you were here. I have something very important to discuss with him."

"What?" Delaney asked. "In case he calls me first."

"It's about Dr. Goldman. We've discovered some very unusual things about him. Like, he hasn't actually practiced plastic surgery for fifteen years. All of his income is from selling experimental drugs to pharmaceutical and biotech companies. Yet he is still a board certified plastic surgeon. And he has an ad in the classified for face lifts and tummy tucks." Sid sipped his Marguerita. "Not enough salt," he whispered, and his beautiful nude maid scampered off to the kitchen.

"You're drinking at seven in the morning?"

"Or how about this? He owns a four million dollar mansion in the hills, but he drives a 1988 Toyota."

"Maybe he keeps the Bentley in his ten car garage."

"I'll let you know," said Sid. "We're taking a look tomorrow night."

"Who's we?" asked Delaney.

"Me and the private investigator I hired. Don't worry. We know what we're doing. If I've learned anything from history, it's not to wind up like Richard Nixon."

Delaney gasped. "You're breaking into his house?"

"Did I say that?"

"Daddy! That's bad. Even for you. I don't want you to go to jail," his daughter admonished.

"Relax," Sid assured her. "We're not breaking in. We're using the latest high tech surveillance equipment. Laser night vision scopes. Special cameras. The works. This guy charges $3,000 a day. He doesn't want to get arrested any more than I do. I've seen a demonstration. He's got these virtual reality headsets connected to binoculars. You can walk through someone's house, room by room, without opening a door. You can see what's in the refrigerator. It's unreal."

What her father told her did not make her feel any better. This was probably the kind of thing he had been doing for years but she had never asked before. Sometimes you were better off not knowing certain things.

"We park about a quarter of a mile away," Sid continued. "We're inside a blackout van the whole time. If the police show up, we're taking night photography for an art magazine. This guy's work is on display at two museums. And get this. If he has an answering machine in the house, we can play back the messages."

"You're kidding."

"I'm not kidding."

Delaney was in a state of shock. "Daddy! This is like that book, 1984. Big Brother is watching. I mean, you are still breaking the law. And you're violating his privacy. How would you like someone to do that to you?"

"All's fair in love and war," Sid retorted.

"I don't know. You'd better be very careful."

"That is the plan," Sid said. "Listen, Delaney, maybe you'd better not ask me any more questions. I just need to talk to your boyfriend about something."

"I'm already an accessory to a crime."

"I see you've learned something at The Enquirer!"

"Very funny. What do you want to talk to Jamie about? There's more?"

Sid tasted the stronger Marguerita. He licked his lips. The woman ran the tip of a fingernail along his spine. He put down the drink and touched her breasts. "I'll be off the phone in a minute," he promised. "Close the blinds."

"What *about* Jamie?" she asked again, louder.

"Oh. I just wanted to ask Jamie about the Davis family, since he's spent some time with them."

"You think he's hiding something from me?"

"I'll tell you later. First let's see what we find at the doctor's house. We're also checking out his assistant's home. He has a condo in Santa Monica. And I'll tell you something else. Not only do I feel in my bones that Dr. Goldman is involved in criminal activities. I really believe that Elvis Presley is going to turn up in this story."

"You do?" Delaney asked, surprised to hear the name again.

"Absolutely. But I don't think he's Jamie Randolph's real father. My theory is that Elvis was seeing a plastic surgeon about changing his face. Hunter Davis was the cover. Davis looked something like Elvis. I think they wanted to experiment on Davis first. See how good a job Goldman could do."

Delaney's surprise turned into the fear that her father was losing his marbles.

"This is just for the story, right Daddy? You don't really

believe it?"

"I don't know," he answered. "Like I said, that's why I want to speak to Jamie and get into Goldman's place. Maybe I'm off base." Maybe? she thought. "On the other hand, there's no doubt that something very abnormal has been going on out here for twenty years. I spoke to a number of other plastic surgeons. And people at the drug companies Goldman deals with. No one has done business directly with Dr. Ira Goldman since the eighties. They all meet with Leonard Stein, that musclebound guy who works with him."

"What does that prove?"

"I can't answer that just yet." Sid pulled Yvonne's hand from his pants. "Oh yeah, one last thing. That guy Stein. He doesn't look the same as he used to."

"What do you mean?"

"He's had *extensive* plastic surgery on his face. A lady doctor I spoke to says she remembers him from Berkeley. She thinks he's had a *couple* of different faces since he went to work for Goldman. And he used to be short and fat."

"I don't get it." Delaney walked to the kitchen for a snack. She had skipped breakfast. "How do you get taller?"

"I don't get it either. Does he have a brother? Are there other assistants who have been given the same face? This would make a good science fiction movie, wouldn't it? But the best part is about Elvis changing *his* face. *Imagine if Elvis is still alive with a different face!* And they buried one of Goldman's clients in Memphis! I love it. And so will millions of readers. I just need a few more facts."

"I can see why you and Mom got divorced," said Delaney. "Who could take your craziness?"

"This is the kind of story The Enquirer wants," answered Sid. "That's what they pay me for. I thought this is what you wanted to do, too."

Delaney couldn't tell him the truth. Sneaking around at midnight trying to create a phony Elvis Presley mystery was not her idea of good journalism. There were too many important issues in the world that needed to be publicized.

"After I graduate," she said. "That's years away."

"Call me when you hear from Jamie," Sid requested. "And

don't worry about me."

Delaney prepared a hearty bowl of Cocoa Puffs, picturing her and Jamie on the floor watching *Sleepless In Seattle*. Meanwhile, in Memphis, Jamie had just consumed six Oreo cookies and a quart of milk.   On TV, Elvis Presley was frolicking in Seattle in his 1963 movie, *It Happened At The World's Fair*. Between catnaps, Jamie had been overdosing on Presley flicks since Monday afternoon. Elvis movies ran continuously at the motel. So far, they hadn't shown *King Creole*, generally considered his best movie.

He had not spoken to his parents, or Delaney, since leaving New Jersey. Now that he knew the truth, he was no longer irked at Dad. Every few hours he picked up the phone to call home, or Florida, but changed his mind. When he looked in the mirror, he still saw Jamie Randolph. But every time he watched Elvis on the tube he felt like he was in a trance. No matter what proof he had found at the bank, it just didn't seem possible that he was a carbon copy of The King Of Rock 'N Roll. Was this a dream? No. But it did explain the twin brother dream he now recalled more vividly from his childhood. The dream in which he meets a young boy who seems to be his twin, they shake hands and hug, then the boy starts shrinking and turns into a mouse. The dream he had experienced again last night, for the first time in about ten years. Why a mouse? His subconscious knew, but he didn't. He was gravitating toward calling Mom and Dad, so he did the opposite.

"Delaney? It's me."

"It's about time!" she said angrily, out of character. "Where are you? I've been calling your parents since you supposedly left town. Are you back in Tenafly?"

"No," he answered. "I'm at the Days Inn in Memphis."

"Memphis? I thought Memphis was a dead end?" She remembered her conversation with Sid. "Does this have anything to do with Elvis Presley?"

"I can't tell you on the phone," said Jamie. "But I need you to come to Memphis. There is something I have to share with you. It's really, really important."

"This was the second man in her life Delaney feared might be cracking up.

"Give me a hint. I just spoke to Sid. He wants to talk to you."

Jamie sounded very emotional, a different Jamie than she knew and . . . liked.

"I can't give you a hint. I need to see you. Right away. Can you come?"

Just up and fly to Memphis? I don't think so, she said to herself.

"I'll be there tomorrow," she told him.

"Thanks." He was relieved. "Thanks a lot. You're the only person I can talk to about my . . . problem. What's new with your father?"

She told him what Sid had learned about Dr. Goldman, about his surveillance plans, about wanting to ask Jamie about the Davises.

"What could I possibly tell your father that would incriminate Goldman?"

"I don't have a clue," replied the girl. "But Daddy is very resourceful."

Now Jamie had another reason to see Delaney. To warn Sid about Goldman. That he was not someone to mess around with, in the words of a man who might be dead as the result of doing precisely that. As well as to ask Sid to drop the whole story, at least until they had taken the time to sort everything out.

"So I'll see you tomorrow?"

"First available flight," she confirmed. She would call in sick again.

⸎

That evening Jamie participated in the annual Candlelight Vigil at Graceland. After a brief ceremony, almost twenty thousand Elvis fans carried a candle through the grounds and past the gravesite in quiet tribute. The Meditation Garden, which had become the final resting place for Elvis, Gladys, Vernon and Vernon's mother, was a solemn and peaceful refuge. Also in the garden was a bronze tablet in memory of Elvis' twin brother, Jesse, whose body remained in Tupelo. It occurred to Jamie that if the letter was true, and if he was the reincarnation of Jesse, then the roles had been reversed. He, Jesse, was now the living twin visiting the grave of Elvis. Tomorrow he would stop by the garden with Delaney, as part of the Graceland Mansion Tour. Before that, he would tell her what he knew.

When he returned to his room, he wondered how so many people could have been deeply touched by a rock star. So infatuated with him that they would travel to his grave every year as to a Mecca. Without removing his clothes, Jamie fell asleep. He did not have the twin dream, and he slept like a baby.

At five to eleven Wednesday morning, Jamie was awakened by a knock on his door.

"Rise and shine, sleepy eyes!"

The beautiful young woman stood like an apparition. Backlit by the sun, he could not see her face as he leaned against the door squinting.

"This place is a dump," she said, pushing past his hulking form. "And you look like shit. Ready to sing a few bars of Blue Suede Shoes?"

"How did you know?" He shut the flimsy door, turned on a lamp.

"Know what? That the money belonged to Elvis Presley? You told me the first day."

On the plane, she had tried to guess what this was about. Just the fact that he had returned to Memphis suggested a link to Elvis. The really important problem, she figured, was what to do about the money now that he had somehow discovered it should have been part of the estate of Elvis Presley. Obviously, they didn't know about it. Legally, it was in his name. Morally, who was to say anyone else deserved it more than he did?

"I think you should keep the money," Delaney said. "How did you find out it wasn't meant for you?"

Jamie pulled off his polo shirt, kicked it away. He needed a shower.

"What are you talking about?" he asked.

275

"The money. The inheritance. The million dollars!"

If he had lied to her about inheriting a million dollars, she was not pleased.

"The four million dollars," he corrected her. "It started out as one million, but it's grown over the years." He removed his own soap from his valise.

"Oh my God," she said. "That hurts. It's bad enough to have to give back one million . . . "

"Give back?" he asked. "Why on earth would I want to give it back?"

"Then what's the problem?"

"Sit here," he said, taking her hand. They plopped down on the disheveled bed, as Elvis sang "Can't Help Falling In Love With You" in *Blue Hawaii*. They looked into each other's eyes and Jamie kissed her. "I missed you."

"I missed you, too. I was afraid you were in trouble."

Jamie held her chin. No matter who he was, he knew one thing. He loved her. He hoped his feelings were reciprocal.

"Listen to me," he said, softly stroking her cheek with the knuckles of his hand. "What I'm going to tell you is *unbelievable*." She smiled, happy to see he was all right.

"I'll believe anything you tell me."

"I don't know about that."

"Try me."

He turned her face straight toward his.

"First you've got to promise to keep this a secret."

"Okay. I promise," she said, brushing against him.

"No, I mean it." He let go of her and worked his hand into a tight pocket. "I guarantee you that you've never heard *anything* like what I just found out. It's changed my whole life. And I have to confide in someone. Somebody else has to know."

"You haven't told your parents? Why me?"

She hoped he would say the words.

"Because I know I can trust you," he answered. "And because I'm in love with you." He hoped she wouldn't laugh at him. He was only eighteen. They knew each other for such a short time.

"You are?" Her eyes lit up. "So am I. Thank God you said

it first."

They kissed again, just like in a Meg Ryan movie, or in *Casablanca*. Only this was real. For about a minute, time really did stand still for both of them. They opened their eyes, hardly knowing where they were, and he caressed her. Despite the great power in his hands, Jamie's grip was tender, caring. He held onto the moment, trying not to return to reality. His relationship with Delaney was the universe. There was no Dr. Goldman, no Elvis Presley clone, no unsolved murder of Hunter Davis, no question about whether to attend Dartmouth in September or check into a lunatic asylum instead! No blood samples, no Elvis letter, no safe deposit box key . . .

"See this key," Jamie said. "Read what it says on the envelope." He showed her his name and birthday in Davis' handwriting. "Hunter Davis wrote that in 1977. He opened a safe deposit box in trust for me the year I was born."

"You looked inside?" He nodded. "What did you find?"

"Promise me you won't tell Sid."

"It's that bad?"

"It's not bad at all," he replied, pulling loose his leather belt. "It's not good or bad. It's just crazy. But it is a great news story. Page one."

"Okay, I promise," she said. She crossed her heart while holding her Gold Crucifix and Star Of David. "May God strike me dead if I ever tell another living soul what you tell me now! There. Is that good enough?"

"I am honestly the son of Elvis Presley," he said, matter-of-factly.

She watched his face, waiting for the punchline. She leaned forward, putting her hands on his knees.

"That's not a joke?"

"That's not a joke." He held up the key. "In this safe deposit box is a letter to me from Elvis Presley. Written in pen in 1977. I read it. I'm his son."

Delaney tried to treat this revelation objectively.

"You can prove it?" she asked credulously.

"I've got blood samples for a DNA test. I'm sure a handwriting expert can verify the letter." He stood up, putting

277

his hands on her shoulders. "I'm telling you, I am the son of Elvis Presley. I can't believe it, but it's true. Can I take a quick shower and tell you the rest of it on the way to Graceland?"

She looked up at him. "I guess so." She lay back, gazing at Elvis playing Chad Gates in Honolulu, listening to the sound of spraying water and Jamie singing "Yesterday."

They ate lunch at the Rockabilly's Diner, a 1950's reproduction eatery complete with black-and-white checkerboard floor, blue neon lights and a round top multicolored Juke Box. It was straight out of "Happy Days," lacking only Richie and The Fonz. Mounted on the wall in each turquoise and white booth was the old-fashioned page turning hit record selector. The hits did not feature The Beatles.

As he finished both the story and his second juicy hamburger, the New Jersey wrestler sensed that his listener had become more convinced.

"I'm not excited about the word clone either," said Delaney. "It makes you sound like a biological experiment."

"That's what I am, right?" He licked the ketchup off his fingertips.

"No you're not!" she begged to differ. "You're flesh and blood. Like me."

He laughed. "I know I'm not the bionic man. I'm just saying that the reason I'm here with this particular set of genes has to do with the whims of a singer, a lawyer and a scientist, not my parents, and certainly not God."

Delaney winced. "You make it sound so . . . "

"Experimental?"

"So cold and calculating. Like . . . Frankenstein," she laughed.

"Oh, thanks!" Then he reached across the table and attempted to grab her by the throat.

"Very funny," she said, pulling back. Jamie vacuumed up the last drops of Coke with the straw in his special Elvis Presley paper cup.

"Are you ready for the tour?" asked Jamie, checking his tickets. "I can hardly wait to see my room full of Gold records. Think they'll let me take a few home to show my friends? Maybe I'll drive back in my pink Cadillac."

Graceland was an interesting place to visit, whether or not you were the genetic duplicate of The King. It wasn't huge by current standards, or compared to the massive rooms of the Davis home. The all-white living room was only twenty-four feet long and seventeen feet wide. As a boy, Elvis had vowed to buy his parents the finest house in town someday. He made good on that promise on March 26, 1957 when he bought Graceland for $100,000. The original owners, Dr. and Mrs. Thomas Moore, had built the house in 1939 when 13.8 acres of the 500-acre Toof family farm was subdivided.

The tour began in the dining room, the same size as the living room, where a guide explained that Elvis' dinner was usually served around 9:30 PM. Elvis and Priscilla's Noritake wedding china, she said, now resided in California with Priscilla. The dining room colors were blue, gold, white and dark grey, the decorating here and elsewhere closer to Liberace than Martha Stewart. Jamie felt very little emotion in most of the house. The Jungle Room which Mrs. Davis had described as "hideous" did nothing for him. Neither did the TV and Pool Rooms, correctly labelled "seventies hip" and not his taste. Everyone noticed the rip in the blue felt top of the pool table. "Some time in the mid-to-late seventies," reported the nicely dressed young lady, "a friend tried a trick shot that did not quite work out." No one knew why it was never repaired. Perhaps for authenticity.

Jamie felt an uncomfortable "presence" throughout Graceland, but it was only when he approached Vernon Presley's office that this grew more intense. He remembered this feeling the day John Porter, the claims attorney, had spoken to him. Now he knew why. This was the room where Elvis, Davis and Picking had made the deal to create him. He sensed it — knew it — just as surely as he knew he loved Delaney, but he did not say anything. A kind of tranquility came over him, the same type of peace he felt in church, or asleep in his room at home. He knew instantly that he would never have to return to Graceland, except as a tourist. He had found himself. He *was* Jamie Randolph, physically the double of Elvis, but psychologically *a victim* of Elvis and his cohorts, a pawn who had been manipulated for eighteen years but who was now, finally, in a position to choose to be the master of his own fate. Today, on the eighteenth anniversary of Elvis' death, he had at last been born.

The tour continued in the trophy building, through the Hall Of Gold, an 80-foot long room lined with Gold and Platinum records. During his career, Elvis (not Jamie) had recorded eighteen Number 1 singles; ironically, the number was eighteen, his exact age, not seventeen or nineteen. Overall, *a billion* Elvis records had been sold worldwide, more than any other singer, ever. His awards and accolades were numerous, but not too numerous to mention. Statisticians had calculated every detail of Elvis' illustrious if tragic climb to the top. Graceland guides recited paragraph after paragraph of memorized verse. They knew by heart the time of his birth (4:35 AM on a Thursday), the price of his first guitar ($12.95), the date he graduated Humes High School (June 3, 1953) and, of course, the day he died: August 16, 1977. Ninety-five days after the birth of his only son. Of course, that last statistic was something they didn't know. Even though it was right under their noses.

The tour of Graceland ended at the Meditation Garden. Jamie and Delaney did not spend much time there. Instead, he was ready to leave.

"What do you feel, standing here at his grave?" she asked, squeezing Jamie's hand.

"I feel sorry for him," Jamie answered. "He had a rough life. Let's go."

On the way back to the motel, Delaney asked Jamie to sing an Elvis song.

"I don't really know any," he said. "I know The Beatles, The Doors . . . I do a great rendition of 'Blowing In The Wind' . . . "

Delaney found it hilarious that Elvis Presley's clone did not know all the words to a single song.

"How about *Hound Dog?*" She started singing it. "You ain't nothin' but a hound dog . . . "

"That's a silly song." He held her hand tightly as they crossed Elvis Presley Boulevard. Cars zoomed by. "I've got one," he blurted out. "*You Were Always On My Mind.* I know the words from Willie Nelson's remake but I've heard Elvis sing it."

The Jamie Randolph version of the two-time hit by Elvis and Willie was not very good. The young man had a beautiful voice. The song just had no life to it. And he sounded nothing like Elvis.

"You need practice," said Delaney. "Before you go on stage."

"I guess singing the blues isn't genetic," he responded. "It's a state of mind."

"You don't really look like him either." She studied his features. "I mean, you do and you don't. Maybe with Ultra Black hair and big sideburns . . . "

"With black hair and sideburns, everyone looks like Elvis," he mused. "You know, even Elvis didn't look like his public image. Did you see those pictures of him with my color hair? I'd never recognize him as Elvis the way he looked at thirteen. Or even at seventeen. There's a lot of people who look alike, not just twins. I mean, how many different faces can there be?"

"I guess that's one reason nobody ever suspected the truth."

"Not to mention that I don't have a Southern accent and I weigh about thirty or forty pounds more." He flexed his arms. "Solid muscle, of course."

Jamie put his room key into the lock. It was baking hot outside. He hoped there had not been another power failure. The door swung open and a gust of cool air coated their faces.

"Well, there's one good thing about this crazy mess," Jamie said.

"The four million dollars?" She tickled him.

"No . . . you! In a way, Elvis brought us together." A chill ran down her spine because she knew exactly what he was going to say next.

"We'd never have met if it wasn't for Elvis," she said first.

"That's right. If not for the anonymous inheritance, why would I have gone to The Enquirer?"

"That's true," she said, then added, "But you could have just kept the money. Never looked for the truth. Maybe that's what Elvis would have done."

"I don't think so."

"Maybe not. Still, this was your decision. It wasn't pre-programmed, like your musical ability. And you weren't emulating Elvis. You didn't even know."

It was true. No one had forced him to spend his entire Summer vacation following wild goose chases from New Jersey to Tennessee to Florida to California and back to Tennessee. If Steve McDermott or any of his upper middle class friends had received the same good news, their first thought would have been which new car to test drive. Not to question a fantastic, mysterious gift.

A gift so cleverly arranged that a major New York bank, the Internal Revenue Service and the chief Claims attorney for the Presley estate could not identify the benefactor. A gift shrouded in such mystery that even now the widow of the lawyer who had set up the trust did not suspect what her husband had done. A plan so secretive that the only living participant, Dr. Ira Goldman, couldn't fit all the pieces together. Yet he, Jamie Randolph, with pit bull tenacity and the strong moral values of Jack and Diane Randolph, had persisted against the odds of getting to the truth. Until he eventually arrived at the point where the only remaining question was *what to do* with the truth. The ridiculous truth that he was, or so it seemed, the son of Elvis Presley.

"So where do I go from here?" he asked his good friend, and the latest in a long line of Elvis Presley secret-keepers. "Should I tell anyone?"

"You told me," she reminded him. "You said in the letter Elvis asked you not to tell anyone at all. I suppose you've already spilled the beans to one person too many."

"You can't tell Sid," he reiterated.

"If he'd even believe me." She saw Jamie's troubled face. "I'm not telling Sid. I promised. Not Sid, not anybody." Delaney picked up the phone.

"Who are you calling?"

"9-0-2-1-0."

"Beverly Hills? Your father? Why?"

"Don't panic. Just sit there." Jamie popped an Oreo into his mouth.

"Tell him to stay away from Goldman. He's dangerous."

"Stop worrying." The phone was ringing. "He must be out . . . I'll call him . . . Hello, Daddy? Hi. It's me. Yes, I'm still sick. I may not be going in tomorrow either. No, I don't have any fever. Yes, I checked. It's just a stomach virus or something. I'm much better now. I'm eating chicken soup, what else?"

She gave Jamie the eye. Now they were both lying to their fathers. She covered the phone with her hand and whispered to Jamie: "He wants to know if I've heard from you?" Jamie shook his head no. "No, Daddy, I haven't. I'm sure he'll call soon. Daddy, I have a favor to ask you. A big one. Can you listen to me very carefully, please? You're not playing tag with what's – her – name, are you? Yes, Yvonne. Oh, she's resting? Good. She needs her beauty sleep."

Jamie put his hand over the phone. "Goldman," he said. "Don't forget."

"What's the favor? Well, Daddy, first you have to promise me that you'll keep this a secret." Jamie hovered over her. She had promised not to tell Sid. "That's right. A secret from everyone in the whole world. It's just between me and you. Do you promise?" What the hell was she doing, Jamie wondered. But he sat back and kept silent. He had to trust her. "Okay," she said. "You promised. Here's the secret. The money doesn't belong to Jamie. It belongs to Elvis."

Sid was not gullible. It would take more than a brief statement to make the story stick.

"What kind of bullshit are you giving me?" asked Sid.

"It's true, Daddy. He told me last week. Jamie has evidence that Elvis and his lawyer, that Davis guy we were checking out, were hiding money."

"Why?"

"He doesn't know. He doesn't want to know. Once he found out that something was wrong, he decided to stop looking. He's afraid that the money might be illegal, but it's been so long — eighteen years, and everyone's dead — that why should he worry about where the money came from. What he doesn't know won't hurt him."

Sid Morrison didn't buy it for a second.

"He already knew that might be the case before he met you.

Why didn't he just stay in New Jersey?"

Jamie was laughing his head off. There was no way Sid believed a word she was saying.

"Daddy," she said. "It doesn't matter what you think. I just want you to drop the whole thing." She began to cry. Jamie couldn't tell if it was real. Neither could Sid. "Daddy, I'm in love with Jamie Randolph. And you're going to hurt him if you write a story about him. True or not true, it doesn't matter."

She was bluffing, Sid thought to himself. Probably faking the tears.

"You're asking me to kill the biggest story of the year? Maybe of my whole career? Because you've fallen in love with an eighteen year-old guy with muscles who looks like Elvis Presley? Delaney, get real. This is my job. This is what I do."

And now, the closing argument.

"Daddy, you once told me that nothing is more important to you than your family. That you would do anything for me. If you meant what you said, then you'll do this. Don't make fun of me because I'm only nineteen. I'm a real person. And these aren't fake tears . . . " Mind-reader. " . . . and I'm really in love. Can I promise you that I'll be in love with this . . . very affectionate, caring young man from New Jersey in twenty-five years? No. But I think I'm going to marry him someday . . . "

Jamie couldn't believe what she was saying. He felt a lump in his throat.

"Are you serious?" asked Sid.

"I *am* serious. I think Jamie is the man for me. At least I hope he is. And if you ruin his life, just to try to prove that you're still numero uno at The National Enquirer, just to make a lot of money that you don't really need . . . well, it's wrong. And I'll never feel the same about you again. Please, don't do this. I don't care what Dr. Goldman is doing. I don't care if he's a murderer. I don't want you to get hurt. And I don't want Jamie to get hurt. Please, Daddy. Please drop the story. Please."

She was begging him. For Jamie's sake. His faith in her was restored. Now he felt guilty for doubting her. He realized how much she meant to him. How much love they could share for the rest of their lives if only they could get through this together. His entire life had been condensed into a few weeks, a few days . . . his head was spinning . . . he closed his eyes and took deep breaths . . .

"You'll do it?"

Jamie opened his eyes.

"You know," said her father, "I've been trying to be a hero all my life. But I've never felt like one. And I don't feel like one now. Everybody knows I'm the best in the business. I don't have to prove it anymore. Someday, next month, next year, whenever . . . I'm gonna stop being the best. That's a fact, too." He was becoming inspired. "Like Elvis," he went on. "He was on top, and he wanted to stay on top forever. Unfortunately, you can't. But I can be your Daddy forever . . . as long as I'm still alive. So the hell with the story. Who needs it? Me, but who cares? I'll find another story. A lot easier than finding another daughter. Delaney, I love you. I do. And I want you to be happy."

Now she was really crying. Tears of joy.

"Thank you, Daddy."

"Even if he's the goddam son of Elvis Presley," said Sid. "There's no story."

"Thank you. Daddy, I'm tired. Can I call you back later?"

"Sure." Sid took a bite out of a candy bar with his $35,000 implants. "Call me later, baby." He swallowed a gob of chocolate and caramel. "Oh," he said. "You can tell your boyfriend over there, that I'll be keeping an eye on him. You're still my little girl. See ya."

Delaney filled Jamie in on the other half of the conversation. But he already knew. He thanked her, and took the phone to let his parents know he was coming home.

Sid Morrison was not into playing games with slinky models today. As he had promised his daughter, he had every intention of dropping the story about Jamie. But he had no intention of ignoring Dr. Ira Goldman. The man was a possible threat. To him. To Delaney and Jamie. To the Davis family. Perhaps to a lot of other people he didn't know. In any case, he would have a better idea what to do about Goldman after tonight. He picked up his electric stun gun and put it with the other equipment. If the police caught him outside Goldman's house, first he would offer them two thousand in cash.

Chapter 22

⊱✾⊰

"ASHES TO ASHES"

The silver Mercedes 600 crunched along the winding gravel drive leading to the impassable front gates of Dr. Ira Goldman's Benedict Canyon estate. Set high on a rocky hill overgrown with jagged terraces of natural landscaping, the white multi-dimensional structure was the perfect retreat for reclusive millionaires. No traffic. No nosy neighbors borrowing sugar or sharing cozy stories at the invisible wooded property line.

With only a few large western exposure windows to capture the majestic vista and a dozen skylights for daytime visibility, no adjacent homeowners, or adventurous tourists, could see the interior at all. A walled courtyard pool and patio was equally hidden from public view.

Sid Morrison was sorry he had lied to his daughter about not breaking into Goldman's house. That crap about the sophisticated surveillance stuff was partly true. His hired hand, Elliot Mustapick, did charge three grand a day for his technical arsenal. The electronic gates rolled aside on their well oiled tracks at the press of a code-searching button. Next, the ex-cop used his scope to locate the central security box. It, too, was disarmed with a microwave transmitter. Actually, all zones of the alarm system were "bypassed", including the motion detectors. Tiny red lights throughout the rooms continued to flash, unable to sense intruders.

The sports car circled a fifteen foot tall red iron art-fountain with water spraying in all directions. Morrison turned on his windshield wipers after the vehicle came to a halt on the black brick driveway. The fountain needed adjustment.

"Don't have time to fix that today," Mustapick joked. "What do you think those large flowering plants are around the fountain?"

He was referring to the clump of white petalled Crynum Lilies, an exotic, odorless floral secimen that required no gardening attention.

"Who do I look like?" asked Sid. "Mr. Green Thumb? They're *flowers.*"

In less than a minute, the man with the small blue bag had unlocked the front door and was using some kind of testing device inside.

"Everything's fine," he said. "No gas. No life forms. You're welcome to look around. I'll be back for you in an hour."

"Where are you from . . . Star Trek? No life forms? Did you check the closets for Klingons?"

"Hey, you never know. Sometimes these people have a Doberman or two upstairs asleep when you first walk in. That's not something you want to find out after I'm gone. Do you have your C-58?" Morrison felt the stun gun in his pocket. "And the pager?" It was there. "Good. *Don't* use the phone. That could be hooked up to the alarm company. If you need me, just press the pager once. It's got a message screen if you want to talk to me. See you at seven."

Mustapick unfolded the inflatable "Safe-T-Man" from the trunk and propped it up in the passenger seat. Just in case anyone had noticed *two people* driving up the hill. He headed back toward town, whistling "Love And Marriage" and watching the oscilloscope which kept track of Dr. Goldman's Toyota Camry. Goldman and Stein always worked until at least nine on Wednesday. However, if they left early tonight, he would know instantly and the car engine would be disabled for twenty minutes. Enough time to get Morrison out. There was only one car to watch. Stein's Infiniti J-30 was in Goldman's garage, right next to the Rolls Royce and the Jaguar.

Every morning, Stein left his car at Goldman's house and drove them to work in the Toyota.

Sid took in the aura of the spacious, scantily furnished living room. Only three colors were represented: white, black and red. Just like outside. To his left, a white marble staircase led to a blank wall. A construction error or an architectural statement? Who could tell? To his right, below a wide, irregular-shaped window affording no downstairs view except the sky, was the only wall decoration. An original abstract painting by Klee. From where he sat, Sid couldn't read the signature. It was worth about a million dollars.

Goldman had purchased the four acre residence in 1984 for $2.6 million from the builder who had gone belly-up creating his hard-to-sell masterpiece. The broker had told the plastic surgeon that there was almost twice that invested in the house and that the furniture went with it. Since he had bought it, Goldman hadn't changed a thing. The painting in the living room had been there, too. It was an interesting piece to glance at occasionally but the scientist had no idea of its value or he would have sold it.

Once again, Sid contemplated his discussion with Delaney. He was still convinced that the man who owned this house — this museum or mausoleum — was fair game. What was he hiding? Unless his instincts were faltering, there was some clue in this ten or twelve thousand square foot box. Something that would tip him off as to what the plastic surgeon had been doing in Beverly Hills instead of plastic surgery.

In a way, this cold, ultra-modern habitat brought back memories of the house at Sloan's Curve in Palm Beach. That first day, when he, Claire and their eight year old daughter had inspected the just completed building, it had also felt very impersonal; empty, unfurnished, awaiting kitchen and bath cabinetry. Theirs was the last unit in a row of tract oceanfront mansions. Regrettably, they had not enjoyed Goldman's good fortune to be the only buyer. According to Claire, future Palm Beach Platinum Club broker, they had overpaid about $40,000 in a bidding war with two other contestants. But at least they were able to pick out the finishing touches that make a house a home. Striped and floral wallpaper, natural oak floors and green marble vanity tops, pickled maple cabinets, a glassfront Traulsen refrigerator and a new front entrance with a spider web window. Unlike this . . . warehouse.

Now is not the time to be a romantic, thought the hard-boiled reporter as he rummaged through the knives and forks.

In fact, what the hell am I searching the kitchen for? Sometimes, Sid Morrison liked to reminisce about birthday celebrations, beach parties, trips to Maine, Delaney's Sweet Sixteen. But daydreaming was a bad idea. All the good times were on video tape, back in Florida, to be indulged in when he didn't have to count the minutes. He looked around for the master bedroom. Or better still the office or library.

⚜

Goldman turned on the centrifuge.

"Lower the temperature," he instructed Stein. He was not talking about the air-conditioning but rather the incubators, which kept jumping to 105 degrees. It was amazing that anything was alive when they came back in the morning.

"These are not the best thermostats, you know," said Stein.

"I've already ordered new ones. Even though these are only a year old." Goldman walked along the aisle of fresh embryos. "It's a good thing I'm rich," he said. "In our line of work, mechanical failure is intolerable. We keep a lot of people in business upgrading our equipment. If I had the time, I'd build it all myself."

"If I had the time," mumbled the assistant, "I'd go skiing in Vail."

"Did you say something?" asked Goldman, leaning over a glass tank, inspecting the four-limbed creatures floating in a medicated saline solution.

"I said, there's never enough time."

"You're right about that, Leonard." Goldman wiped his fingerprints off the glass compulsively. "But we've been making progress lately. I'm very hopeful about this latest group. Did you freeze all of the specimens from last month?" He wiped the glass again.

"Of course," answered the well trained Stein.

"Good. Then un-freeze them. I need to examine some organs under the microscope. Liver problems." He tapped his stomach. "Enzymes in the liver. So many billions of combinations. It's a wonder human beings have survived this long."

289

Progress. Breakthroughs. According to the good doctor, they were always on the verge of making evolutionary history in their subterranean hideaway. Meanwhile, not one new animal had sustained life for more than three months, except for the brain-dead chimp. Nor had they published a single damn article in any medical journal in more than twenty years. Progress? The word had a hollow ring to it in light of the actual results. True, Goldman had, in the process of trying to create higher life forms, inadvertently invented (and patented) about thirty-five new drugs. Not one of which had received FDA approval, even for experimental human use. But others in the field had been only too eager to purchase the rights to these highly controversial genetic catalysts for vast sums. In total confidence, of course, with no possible mention of Dr. Goldman's name. Fine with them. If anything worked, they wanted all the credit anyway. And the profits. He simply retained the right to use the drugs privately.

Stein did as he was told, removing the stainless steel trays from the icy storage shelves while wearing special insulated gloves. Touch this liquid-nitrogen-cooled organic material with your bare hands and watch your fingers fall off! And since there was no known technique yet for regenerating "compatible" human body parts — even *here* where surplus hearts and lungs were available in Zip-Loc bags by the hundreds — Stein was not anxious to test Goldman's cloning theory with his own arms or legs. Indeed, there were a pair of Goldman and Stein duplicates "in progress", but the middle aged lab technician preferred to "go second" when it came to transplanting his head onto a younger version of himself.

Had Goldman the omniscient paid attention to the advice of his underling, Leonard Stein, things might have been different. Stein had no doubt that the man he had devoted his life to was a genius. There was ample proof of that. The question was, why couldn't he bring himself to collaborate with others? As a two-man operation, their limitations were severe. They couldn't work round the clock, although often they did. They spent thousands of dollars on materials used only once. Despite computers, there was no way to organize all of their research properly, since they were constantly involved in starting or monitoring new studies. In cooperation with the right organizations, to be selected from among more and more daring hospitals, universities, biotech companies or even cyronic societies, true progress could be multiplied greatly. But Dr. Ira Goldman, being in his words pragmatic as opposed to stubborn, insisted that working with others would tie his hands. All of the time saved through group interaction would be nothing, he claimed, compared to the bureaucracy. Nor could they trust another assistant, or a secretary. There was no use discussing it. And they hadn't in several years.

But enough was enough. Stein had never had a real life. His mother was dead. His father had disowned him, calling him a kook, remarrying and moving to Philadelphia. He hadn't had contact with anyone in his family since 1979. Like many people, Stein wished he could live his life over, an unrealistic option that bothered him immensely whenever he dwelled on it. So he didn't. He just did his job and watched the pages of the calendar turn. Once in a while, he wondered what year it was.

"Where are the specimens?" Goldman called from his table, adjusting his powerful electron microscope. A recent six-figure acquisition.

"I'm defrosting them," Stein yelled back. "This isn't Domino's Pizza!"

Goldman hobbled back to the centrifuge and turned it off. He had just created the perfect plasma for transplanting seven monkey livers or, if the machine had been running too long, he had about two quarts of gooey red paint.

⤜⊛⤛

Sid Morrison was in Goldman's office. There was a library, too, but it was empty. The bookcase in the office was filled with medical and science books. He had already gone through the desk, finding only a personal checkbook, paid bills for house maintenance, and some X-rated magazines. He was surprised to learn that Goldman paid $360 for his monthly landscaping, the same as he did. So far he hadn't seen anything even remotely illegal. Being a sexual pervert wasn't news unless you were a superstar. And not necessarily then either.

He thumbed through the books. A couple were about plastic surgery, but most had to do with genetics, biology, diseases and evolution. So the man had a hobby: science. Maybe he was even a "mad scientist." That wasn't against the law, unless he was stealing bodies from the graveyard and bringing them back to life. Sid thought about it. That, too, was probably legal nowadays.

A book protruding slightly from the rest caught his eye: "The Book Of Man," a new hardcover about the Human Genome Project and "the quest to discover our genetic heritage." The cover design showed a baby swimming underwater surrounded by what appeared to be the clear blue ocean. He read the first line of the flap of the dust jacket: "Our destinies lie in our DNA." The summary went on to explain that the Human Genome Project is a scientific study aimed at uncovering the 100,000 genes that control human development. The blurb ended by calling genetics "the fledgling science that will soon change all of our lives." Heady stuff, thought Sid. Controversial, too. Genetic engineering. The science of eliminating birth defects or creating an army of Hitlers. Something that could change our lives? Yes, he agreed. Possibly an understatement. But again, perfectly legal.

Morrison flipped through the book looking for pictures. There were very few. On page 39, a photo of the discoverers of the structure of DNA, James Watson and Francis Crick. Mostly there were line drawings of such stimulating subjects as *hybrid mouse cells* and *cancerous gene mutations*. On page 56, a sketch of "the art of cloning."

Throughout the book passages were underlined in red, with Goldman's notes in the margins.

"Bullshit."

"Valid point."

"We proved this in 1981."

A small sheet of paper, intended as a bookmark, escaped from between two pages and fluttered to the floor. Morrison picked it up. It was an invoice from a company in Switzerland, Guenther Lefferts Labs, typed in English. Dated only a few months ago, this was an order placed by Dr. I. Goldman in care of a post office box in Hollywood. The investigator tried to decipher the abbreviations. Goldman had purchased two sets of eighteen somethings, one male, the other female. Animals? Imported from Switzerland? What kind of special order animals came from that country? The price was $280 per unit, or $10,080 total. Plus shipping and handling for Registered Mail. They must have been very small and expensive animals, thought Sid, to put in a box.

Under "Description" was the term "hap. gam." Followed first by "Male" and then "Female." What in the world were eighteen *Hap Gam Males*? At the bottom of the bill, under "Remarks," was typed: "This order conforms to your individual specs as to height, weight, color and African origin." It was a real brain teaser. Not that he expected to be able to arrest Dr. G. for purchasing three dozen African Hap Gams, unless you needed a special import permit. Or the Hap Gams had entered the country without getting their shots or being quarantined.

Sid looked for a dictionary. There it was. "Webster's New World Dictionary." First he counted the words that started with "Gam." There were sixty-seven. He then turned to "Hap." Only twenty-two entries. Without his reading glasses, he had to hold the dictionary out in front of him with two hands. "Hap." "Haphazard." It was probably a Swiss word anyway. "Haploid." What was a haploid? The definition was: "Biology. Having the full number of chromosomes normally occurring in the mature germ cell or half the number of the usual somatic cell. A haploid cell or gamete." He then looked up gamete: "A reproductive cell that is haploid and can unite with another gamete to form the cell (zygote) that develops into a new individual."

In layman's terms, Goldman had purchased eighteen specimens of male sperm, and eighteen female eggs, all somehow tested and certified to have the full number of chromosomes. From Africa. Goldman was interested in creating eighteen African babies? That was the secret? The ex-plastic surgeon was breeding black children in Beverly Hills? For what reason?

In seconds, Sid had a new theory. Dr. Ira Goldman, student of genetics and biology, was running an unlicensed fertility clinic — a black-market counterpart of the Beverly Hills Fertility Clinic — for people who wanted "special" kinds of babies. In this case, he might be selling genetically superior, perhaps genetically "improved" black embryos to wealthy African-Americans. Maybe he was going even one step further and implanting the embryos into the mothers via an in-vitro procedure.

What other explanation could there possibly be for importing African sperm and eggs through a Swiss broker? Just as there were white people who wanted strapping blond-haired, blue eyed sons, or daughters who resembled Elizabeth Taylor, there had to be rich African-Americans who wanted the best of *their* original ancestry. And were willing to pay exorbitant amounts of money for the product. Probably $100,000. Maybe twice that. A much better business than doing nose jobs. Eighteen babies at that rate came to between $1.8 million and $3.6 million. Off the books, since no such fees had been reported on his tax returns. If this was something he could do three or four times a year, the untaxed income was staggering. Since 1975, Goldman could have cheated the government out of $40 million!

What a headline! "BEVERLY HILLS PLASTIC SURGEON CHEATS I.R.S. OUT OF $40 MILLION SELLING BLACK-MARKET BLACK TEST-TUBE BABIES!" It was a winner.

But, it was only a theory. After checking out the rest of the house quickly in his remaining fourteen minutes, Morrison would move on to Stein's condo, and last but not least to the lab itself. He stuffed the Swiss invoice into his front pants pocket and replaced the book about genes and DNA. It would not take more than the short amount of time he had left to complete his search. There wasn't much in the house, unless he wanted to start slashing open couches and mattresses. Morrison found it odd that a television set, the staple of the American home, was conspicuously absent. In the basement he found boxes of old clothes. They were not worn. He figured that Goldman had gained weight over the years. Actually, the man had lost weight. He snapped a few photos, just to hang on to. Time was up.

In the car, Mustapick driving, Sid Morrison claimed that he had found nothing. He wasn't paying this guy to sell his story to a rival publication.

"Did you re-set the alarm?" he asked.

"Everything is the way it was," said Mustapick, scratching

his groin. "Want some gum?"

"No thanks."

As they hoped, Stein's place did not have an alarm. It was protected by three deadbolt locks, which took the expert about thirty seconds each to open. He then set off the car alarm by remote control. Headlights flashed and sirens blared for about ten seconds, a long enough diversion for Sid to enter Stein's home without being seen. Mustapick then drove off, back in an hour at eight-thirty.

Inside, Stein's duplex was the antithesis of Goldman's house. There were signs of life, and lifestyle, in every nook. A cereal bowl with a quarter inch of milk and a ring of soggy Corn Flakes sat in the sink, an unwashed spoon nearby. A sweaty green sweatshirt was lying on the sofa in front of the TV. A glass-topped cocktail table was pushed aside and a pair of heavy dumbbells lay askew on the carpet. Several exercise videos were left out on the table. A mix of men's workouts and programs by supermodels intended as much for men to drool over as for women to utilize. There were two unopened cans of non-alcoholic beer which had warmed up and made puddles. They already knew that Stein was allergic to dogs and cats. There were no pets in the house.

Stein's bookcase was filled with mysteries and romance novels. In addition, a pile of books on bodybuilding, travel and hairstyles. All of the books were unevenly stacked, with the bottom shelf so jam-packed that pulling one free would have created a book explosion. Morrison was not tempted to search for anything stuck in the pages. Again, he looked for an office and went to work on Stein's cluttered, disorganized desk. If Goldman's possessions had been too impersonal, his assistant's were too personal. He read Stein's diary for five minutes, learning that Stein was sick of his job, starved for affection and threatening to run off to Europe or South America "one of these days." Six months earlier he had pledged to write a biography about Woody Allen. A few weeks ago he had said he intended to look for his father "and possibly kill him." Sid suspected that Leonard Stein was disturbed. Who else would work for Dr. Goldman all those years? Nothing specific about his work was recorded in the journal.

Stein's bedroom was the neatest room in the house. His

bed was made, with hospital corners, and Sid laughed when he saw the frayed-nose teddy bear on a pillow. Closet organizers held clothing, shoes and accessories in tidy compartments. The uninvited guest stuck his hand into a few pockets to see if anything strange surfaced. Nothing. But the photographs on Stein's dresser, and hanging on the wall above, were more than strange. They were all pictures of him taken in Goldman's reception room over the years. And, as Sid had heard, the man had changed dramatically. In his younger photos, he was chubby, with a most unattractive face full of pocks and pimples. As the years passed, his face, and his body, improved. In fact, he had at least three or four completely different faces over time, while his physique seemed to grow increasingly muscular, possibly larger. It was logical to assume that this was the doing of Dr. G., using both plastic surgery and experimental drugs. It might be bizarre, but it was once again within the bounds of the law to alter someone's physical appearance with their consent.

Morrison cringed as his ungloved hands moved aside the man's socks and underwear seeking hidden objects. There were a few odds and ends in the drawer. A digital watch. A pair of cuff links. A deck of cards. He closed the drawer, then reopened it to take a better look at the gold cuff links. Stein didn't look like a formal dresser. He picked them up. They had a raised flag design. The Confederate Flag! Sid turned them over. The cuff links were dated and initialled. "J.D. 1863."

Against his better judgment, Sid Morrison confiscated and wrapped the cuff links in the Swiss invoice and put them in his pocket. The antique jewelry was out of place among Stein's belongings. Why would a Jewish boy own Confederate Flag cuff links? His grandparents, or their grandparents, were probably living in Poland or Russia in 1863. He didn't seem to be a Civil War buff. And nothing else in his home pre-dated the 1970's. Thus, Morrison concluded, they were either stolen or given to him by a friend. If he had any friends.

When Mustapick tapped him on the back, Sid almost had a heart attack. He fell back on the tight green blanket and tried to regain his equilibrium.

"Did you have to do that?" He sucked in extra air, felt

lightheaded. "It's not even eight o'clock."

"I hate to be the harbinger of bad news," the detective explained, "but the doctor and his pal have left the office."

"I thought they work till at least nine tonight."

"Usually," replied Mustapick. "People are inconsistent. That's why God invented tracking devices."

"Damn. I just wanted to check two other places."

"Not a good idea. Goldman is probably on the way to his house first, so Stein can pick up his car. But they could be coming here for some reason. Or Stein might have taken a taxi. All I know is the Toyota pulled out three minutes ago."

"I thought you could make the engine break down?"

"You really want me to do that? That was only for an emergency. They might get suspicious."

"You're right," said Morrison. "Let's get out of here." He snapped two quick shots of Stein's photo gallery.

The two men headed for the door.

"Wait," said Mustapick, handing Morrison sunglasses and a hat. "Put these on. I can't keep setting off the car alarm. I parked around the corner. No one will recognize us."

After Mustapick put his gear in the trunk, Sid asked him to wait in the car for a second. He hid the cuff links under the spare tire, got into the car and readjusted the driver's seat. "Here's your money, Elliot." He gave the man an envelope.

"Thanks. I figured the money was back there somewhere."

"I only hire really smart people," said Sid sarcastically. Schmuck. The envelope had been under his shirt the whole time.

They circled the block until Stein pulled his J-30 into the garage, one of the places Sid had wanted to explore. It was more important to get into the downtown office, if they could. That was the next stop.

⚜

This time they left the car five blocks away. Walking two different routes, they met across the street from the grey building. The man with the bag surveyed the area, aimed a transmitter at the front gates and waited. He turned a small knob, aimed again and said, "That did it. We're in."

"The alarm's off?"

"No. We're just in the front door. I have to see what else they've got. I spoke to the guy who monitors the system, but they've modified it. There may be a completely independent back-up with heat sensors. I assume you want to spend an hour in there."

"Maybe more."

"Okay. Then let's get into the office and see what they think is foolproof."

"You can short-circuit anything?"

"Anything," confirmed Elliot Mustapick. "Even handprints and voiceprints. As long as I'm not in a rush."

They crossed over and entered the corridor to the office. The gates locked behind them. After covering their faces as they passed the security cameras, they had to take the risk of possibly setting off an unknown feature of the alarm system in the first room.

"I can't tell anything from the hall," said Mustapick. "Chances are, there's only a contact on this door. If I'm wrong, we're out of here."

"How will you know if a silent alarm is tripped?"

"I can tell. I just won't know why it happened." He paused. "Get ready to run." The electronics expert pressed another magic button.

The door opened and they walked in. Mustapick looked at a meter. It was safe. Within ten minutes, the elevator was off the alarm system. In ten more minutes, Sid was informed that it was all clear. He could roam about freely once the doors were unlocked.

"Let's unlock them," said Sid.

"They're all on an enter-exit clock," he was told. "According to my calculations . . . " Mustapick ran his hand along a wall to the right of the elevator. "Yup. See this box? It looks like a thermostat, but it's a lock timer." He flipped open the hinged plastic door covering three small wheels with twenty-four hour cycles. Digital times flashed on and off as the wheels turned very, very slowly. "You don't touch the wheels . . . " he began.

"Like I give a crap. Just unlock the doors."

Another ten minutes passed.

"We're all set," Mustapick announced. "The joint is yours. Let's see. It's twenty after nine. How about if we do this? I've got a sandwich in the car. Page me at five to eleven if you want me to pick you up at eleven. Otherwise, I'll be back at eleven thirty. That's over two hours. You can stay longer, but it might not be a good idea."

"Why not?"

"Because after two hours, the car might look suspicious."

"A Mercedes? In Beverly Hills? Drive around for awhile."

"Hey, it's your ass. Just don't forget whose plates are on the car. Yours."

Sid was already rifling Goldman's desk.

"Okay, Elliot. I'm sure two hours is enough."

"And don't forget. I'm only watching Goldman's Toyota. If the doctor comes back here in a different car, or if Stein comes back, we're in trouble. You're gonna have to whip out the C-58." Mustapick zipped his bag. "Remember, I won't be right across the street. The faster you get out of here, the better."

"I understand," said Morrison. "I'll probably see you at eleven."

First he took the elevator upstairs, which appeared to house a small, well-equipped hospital for performing plastic surgery. It only took five minutes for Sid to determine that this was a set-up. The layout was what one would expect to find in Dr. Goldman's office. Hopefully, there was something more unpredictable *downstairs*. Morrison re-entered the elevator. With foreboding anxiety, he pressed Lower Level.

⚜

Ira Goldman and Leonard Stein were on their way back to town in the Rolls. As planned, they would eat a late dinner at Luigi's, after which they would check the incubators. Goldman was ready for a full day of surgery tomorrow. A week's work would go drown the drain if the specimens died.

"I'm starving," said Stein, cruising by the Silver Mercedes parked inconspicuously one block from the restaurant. "I think I'll order Linguini with white clam sauce."

"Is food all you ever think about?" asked the scientist.

That did it. "I'm off duty!" said Stein in a loud voice. "How come we can never have a pleasant conversation? You're always bossing me around. Lighten up!"

"Off duty?" Goldman queried. "There's no such thing as off duty to me. I'm on the job twenty-four hours a day three hundred and sixty-five days a year. You think *Jonas Salk* went off-duty at five o'clock? When you're on a mission . . ."

Stein slammed on the brakes and gave the car to a valet.

"What mission?" he asked, stepping up to the exquisite front entranceway of Luigi's "Venice In Beverly Hills." Luigi was on his way over to greet them. "Tell me, Ira. I want to know. Is the mission to prove that you're the greatest evolutionist since Charles Darwin? Is that the mission?"

"Keep your voice down."

They were escorted by the owner through the main dining room out back to a private garden area with only four tables. Candles and gas lanterns provided light to eat by and a true South European ambience. Leonard Stein loved Luigi's. Goldman found the food tasteless but he did enjoy being treated like the Pope. Luigi served them menus, described the specials, smiled and walked off. They were two of his best customers, always leaving the waiter an excessive tip.

"No, I'm sick of your holier-than-thou attitude, Ira. We both know you're the doctor, you're the scientist, you're the brains of the operation, and I'm . . . what am I? The doctor's little helper? The one who does the dirty work, like defrosting monkey corpses?"

"Will you be quiet, please. I apologize, Leonard. You're much more than my helper. Without you, the project would not be as far along as it is."

"Oh, really?" Stein ordered a bottle of red wine and two salads. "And how close are we to actually achieving anything? Not one of the transgenic animals has grown to maturity. None has even lived more than a couple of months. How are we supposed to reproduce them if they can't stay alive?"

The scientist shook his head disparagingly. "I thought you understood," Goldman said. "You know, we've done over two hundred thousand experiments since you came to me. Two . . . hundred . . . thousand! And in the process we've learned more about the relationship between man and his forerunners than anyone else on earth."

"Yes," Leonard whispered. "We've learned that you can't cross a man and a monkey and get the . . . creation . . . to live a normal life."

"That's not true, and you know it. If all I wanted to produce was a half man, half-monkey, I could raise a thousand specimens a month. But that wouldn't prove a thing. It wouldn't prove that man *evolved* from apes."

The waiter brought the wine and salads, plus a plate of fresh garlic bread smothered in melted mozzarella cheese. Leonard looked like he had just been served the Holy Grail. He snatched a slice of bread and bit it in two. Goldman tried to ignore the pungent aroma.

"And you honestly believe we're getting closer to the proof?"

"I do," said Goldman, eating lettuce without dressing. "We're getting very close. I realize that maybe it doesn't look that way right now, but I'm telling you, another six months, maybe a little longer."

"And then what?"

Goldman sipped the wine, pursed his lips, and put the glass down.

"And then we'll be done. It will just be a matter of editing all of the videos and writing the book from our notes. And then we'll go public. We'll be famous. *You and me.* Not just me. You'll get credit for your work. You will."

"And will the world be a better place to live? Will I be able to have the life I never had? Or will we both wind up in jail?"

Goldman frowned.

"Leonard, listen to me. I know it's been a long time. I've tried to make up for that by giving you the face and body you always wanted. The growth hormones are also keeping you young. You'll probably live an extra twenty or thirty years, all the time you lost on the project. You'll get it back. And I will, too. As soon as we start the book, I'm going to begin taking the drugs myself. Do you think I like looking like this? I'm weak, run down, old. It's got to end. Soon."

"When? You really expect me to believe this will be over in less than a year?"

The waiter took their order. Linguini for the gentleman. Plain pasta for the other gentleman, with the tomato sauce on the side. Very good.

"It should be no more than a year."

"You're dreaming." Leonard wolfed down his third piece of bread. With wine.

"I'm telling you the truth. Leonard, listen to me. Once I get just one animal to survive to the point where the liver functions, we're almost finished. Every other organ works perfectly now. It's only the liver. And I've isolated the problem in those last specimens from Africa. That was part of the answer. The evolution from lower life form to higher life form, from ape to ape-man to man, originated in Africa. That was the key. We're now coupling monkeys and humans from the exact same environment. That's why their hearts are stronger. I've added two new steroids to the daily injections. And it's working. It really is."

Leonard drank some more wine. His tolerance for alcohol had quadrupled.

"You told me the same thing four years ago."

"I told you the same thing about brain chemistry. But that problem had to do with the spinal column. When we adjusted the genes that control curvature of the spine, so the monkeys would be able to stand straight, the brain stem separated from the top of the spinal column. Hence, brain death. Now that the animals have a longer spine, it stays intact."

"You could convince me of anything, Ira. Seriously. For all I know, this project could take a hundred years. A thousand."

Goldman was trying to be patient with the imbecile. He was telling him the simple truth. Why was he being so negative?

"One year," said the doctor. "Leonard. Pay attention. I want you to know what's going on so you can maintain the stamina to see it through. All I have to do is get one healthy specimen and I can clone as many as I need. Then I can mutate the fertilized eggs in vitro, let them split, mutate them again and so on. All by natural selection. We don't have to wait millions of years for evolutionary change. With our computer and the gestational catalyst I sold to the Hyperion Corporation, *I can create 4,000 generations of human life in one day!* That's almost a million and a half generations a year. Even if you figure a lifespan of only thirty years, we can duplicate *forty-four million* years of human evolution in one year. If we also grow some embryos from the latest generation once every eight days, we can see how life has changed every million years. Can you imagine what I'm describing? Every week we can see what happened to man in a million years!"

As Stein shoveled twisted forkfuls of Linguini into his new and improved mouth, he fully grasped the significance of what Dr. Ira Goldman was explaining. Theoretically, it was possible to *prove* Charles Darwin's now accepted but still controversial theory of the evolution of man by demonstrating it in the laboratory. Prior to the work of the two men from Beverly Hills, that would have taken forty-four million years. Now, if Ira was correct, it could be speeded up to only one year. Like a genetic time machine. All you had to do was create 4,000 generations of human life per day *in a test tube.* No pregnancies, no childbirth, no actual human lifetimes. Just a lot of chemical reactions which would cause the same kind of mutations in eight days that would have taken one million years. Then, pull out all the relevant specimens and let them mature. Neanderthal Man. Cro Magnon Man. The whole run of Prehistoric Man categories deduced from fossils. It was brilliant. It was possible. In fact, it was more than possible, it was inevitable. Someday, it would be accomplished. But not necessarily by Dr. Ira Goldman within twelve months.

"If we had the time, we could grow embryos every day, Leonard. Then we could have a record of human evolution based on intervals of only 100,000 years."

At the moment Stein was more concerned with the delicious bits of chewy clams.

"And you become God," he said to Goldman.

The doctor's eyes lit up.

"Funny you should say that. Because in a way, it's true. Little by little, as man discovers the secrets of the universe, he does become God. Let's face it, Stein. The odds of a supreme being creating the universe are infinitesimal. Because in order to have a God, he had to be created in turn by a Super-God, and so on and so forth. It is much more logical to assume that man is slowly but surely evolving into God. See, if you define God as an all-knowing, all-powerful force in the universe, it is only a matter of time until man achieves that status. And then he will be his own God. As a leader in this progression, it is not wrong to suggest that I am unquestionably a major factor, a human link, in the creation of God. In that sense, yes, *I am becoming God.*"

Leonard watched God pick at his spaghetti. And wondered what was going to happen. The only thing he knew for sure was that this would not continue for another two decades. And that his egotistical boss, who had strung him along with promise after promise of fame and fortune, was not on the verge of giving birth to the missing link right around the corner from Rodeo Drive.

❧

Sid Morrison could not believe his eyes. The terrifying, paralyzing, sick scene he had been trying to comprehend for an hour had jumped right out of the pages of a novel by Robin Cooke or Stephen King. In his long career as a reporter, Sid had seen a lot. Accident victims. Wounded soldiers. Children maimed by terrorists. Before entering Goldman's lab, he did not think there was much that could shock or frighten him. As he photographed the sick and dying animals secured by clamps in their incubators, his opinion changed. Alone in this very large room of spotless stainless steel and whimpering primates, he was too appalled to let out his true feelings. He was enraged, at a doctor who could go home to a mansion every night while hundreds of living creatures suffered to serve his wishes. But Sid held in his empathy, his desire to weep and the awareness that he was not far from a total panic attack. There was a job to be done, and a story to be written.

To be the only human in an underground prison confining hundreds of innocent victims was bad enough. But to see the deformed embryos floating in a yellow solution, the hearts and kidneys and brains wired to video screens, gave him a chill. He took his photos sparingly; there was only one roll of film. It was important to document everything, to be sure a judge would okay a search warrant. He took a shot of the bank of morgue-like roll out drawers. With trepidation, he opened one, snapped a close-up of the dead baby gorilla, and closed it quickly. He felt a shiver.

What in God's name was this guy doing down here, he

wondered? How long had it been going on? Since the day of Hunter Davis' visit in 1975? His mind was racing. After photographing several weird-looking machines he had never seen before, Sid abandoned the theory of a black-market baby service. There was nothing in this . . . torture chamber . . . to suggest the birth of perfect, happy, expensive infants for sale. He could more easily believe this was Nazi Germany, if not hell! In fact, the only other room in which he had ever felt this unsettled was one of the actual gas chambers his parents had made him visit at Auschwitz.

Goldman and Stein strolled past Morrison's Mercedes again. The office was only a few blocks away and the younger man needed to clear his head. His belly was full, and he was also slightly inebriated. Five or ten minutes of fresh air would put him into a more sober state. Once they had checked the equipment and walked back to Luigi's, it would be safe for him to drive. They slowed down to glance at a window display of diamond bracelets, then crossed the street. Neither the scientist nor the reporter were aware of how close they were to one another.

Goldman opened the gates easily with his key. Locked them behind him.

"Are you sure we need to go in?" Stein asked. "If I know you, we'll wind up working here all night. I really need some sleep."

To Ira Goldman, Stein was like the child he never had. Well, since he had never *wanted* children, maybe he was more like a nephew. An immature, always complaining nephew whose most valuable attribute these days was his ability to lift heavy objects. Recently, Goldman had been informed of the boring fact that Leonard Stein could now bench press over three hundred pounds.

"You'll be home in an hour, Leonard. I just want to make sure the temperature is right. I thought you wanted to see this project completed?"

"It'll never be completed," said the petulant boy. "Not in our lifetime."

"Still doubting my talents, I see." Goldman rubbed his slender, bony nose and adjusted his glasses. They got into the elevator, first de-activating the alarm. "You know what this project is like?" Leonard stared at the ceiling. "It's like General Motors."

"What?" That got Stein's attention. You had to break these big concepts down into simple terms, for simple minds.

"That's right. It takes G.M. twenty years to design and perfect a new car. But then it only takes them one year to build millions." The perfect analogy.

"Bullshit," said the fake nephew. "This isn't like building cars. It's like building a spaceship to Mars."

"Maybe we'll do that next," jested the scientist. The hell with him. Just do your job and shut up already.

When the elevator door receded, Goldman and Stein both tried to exit first. Like a pair of bungling comedians, they got stuck in the doorway. While they freed their shoulders, Goldman ultimately pushing himself out into the laboratory ahead of the dumbbell, Sid Morrison removed the film from his camera. He handed it to his friend at the all night One-Hour Photo with a twenty dollar bill. The usual bonus to get the pictures developed in half the time.

"Come back at a quarter to twelve, Sid," said the clerk in the blue O.H.P. jacket.

Morrison returned to his car, put down his bagel and cream cheese wrapped in wax paper, and redialed The Enquirer's secret hotline. He had dropped off Mustapick at a garage.

"The National Enquirer. How can I direct your call?"

"Stephanie, this is Sid Morrison again. Did you find Calder?"

The girl was ticked. It had only been five minutes. In Florida, it was 2:15 A.M. Mr. Calder was asleep at a friend's home. If she woke him up needlessly, she could lose her job.

"I left a message," she said. "Can't you talk to someone else? Why do you have to speak to the Editor-In-Chief?"

Sid tried not to blow his cool, but he was too emotional.

"Goddammit!" he said, losing it. "You didn't call him! Listen, you stupid schmuck! This is a matter of life and death. I am about to ask my attorney to phone a Los Angeles judge at midnight. Now, either you call the man, or give me his private number wherever he is. Otherwise, I'm going to personally kick your ass through the wall." Sid waited a few seconds. "Oh, by the way, I apologize for my language."

Stephanie gave him the unlisted telephone number of Donald Trump's house in Palm Beach, where her boss was spending the night.

⚜

To Goldman's surprise, the incubator temperatures had stabilized. However, he noticed some fingerprints on the embryo tanks.

"Wipe these prints, Leonard. And keep your hands off the glass. You know my policy about cleanliness." According to God, it was next to Godliness.

"Those aren't mine," said Stein. "They're yours."

"No way," returned Goldman. He then put his prints to the right of the unidentified Morrison smudges. Stein pressed his grimy fingers to the left. They examined the three sets. Clearly, the hands of three different people had left their impressions. Goldman, Stein, and who else? No other person, to their knowledge, had ever been here.

"I can't believe it." Stein was shaken.

"You know it's him," said Goldman. "That bastard broke into the lab tonight. Get the videodisk."

The assistant did as he was told, removing the video from one of two hidden cameras which continuously recorded everything that transpired in the room. There were thousands of dated disks locked in a storage closet behind a one-way mirror.

"Some things were moved around in my house," Stein reported. "I thought it was my imagination." He shoved the laser disk into the thin horizontal slot and searched back one hour. Sure enough, there he was. Morrison. Taking pictures.

"I told you we should have gotten rid of him." Goldman turned on Stein, pulling his shirt collar. "Look at this!" He shouted. "He photographed everything."

"I'm sorry," cried Stein, trying to get the man's hands away. Goldman held on tightly, then loosened his grip.

307

Strong hands for this shell of a man.

"Sorry doesn't cut it," said the boss. "Maybe there's still time. Where's the gun? You know where he lives. Chances are he doesn't know that *we* know. It's late. Maybe he's not going to do anything until the morning."

Stein adjusted his shirt. "You want *me* to kill him?" he asked succinctly.

"Who else?" Goldman glared at the video, watching Morrison contaminate his sterile equipment. "And while you're at it, you might as well find the boy, and the girl. Kill them, too."

Stein slid the old German automatic out of the box in the storage closet. It was still loaded, three bullets shy of a full clip, the silencer in place. Untouched since 1979.

"Who else should I kill?" he asked, politely. "Mrs. Davis? Obviously, she knows too much. The rest of her family? She might have told them the whole story."

Goldman realized what Stein was implying. The truth was, once you started murdering people, there was no stopping point. Anyone who knew the person you killed might also know the secret. Charlotte Davis was probably living off the $500,000 her husband had never paid him.

"Let's just start with Mr. Morrison," Goldman advised the powerful helper. "As long as we can get the film from him, that might be the end."

"Let's just start with you," said Stein, grabbing the scientist by his throat, lifting him off the floor the way Hunter Davis had lifted him those many years ago.

"Are you crazy?" squawked a choking Goldman, his face turning purplish red. "Put me down, you idiot! You're hurting me." His long, bony fingers tried frantically to release Stein's grasp, tearing the skin off Stein's forearm. He needed to think fast. "Look at the computer," he said. "The book. I've already started it. It's called . . . ugh!" He twisted his neck to get some air. "It's called 'The Genetic Blueprint Of Evolution' by Goldman and Stein. Look it up. I'm telling you the truth!"

Unfortunately for his former master, Leonard Stein was no longer interested in the truth. He stared at the bulging muscles and veins in his bloody forearm, then at the bulging eyes of Dr. Ira Goldman. A temporarily relieved Goldman hoped that Stein's violent temper had subsided when the man untensed his arms. Stein then flung the old man across his desk and onto the white tile floor, where his once bushy haired skull cracked like an egg. Stein looked Goldman directly in the eye as he pumped two bullets into his forehead. No more commands. No more dead monkeys. No more worrying about going to jail for a murder he had never wanted to commit.

From the time Stein simultaneously pressed the two red buttons labeled "Emergency" and "Exit", he had sixty seconds to change his mind. If he did not cancel the order in less than one minute, he could no longer leave the locked room. And everything within the 180,000 cubic foot area, from wall to wall, floor to ceiling, would be incinerated by microwave radiation and fire. Including the contents of the freezers. For the last minute of his life, Leonard Stein tried to remember what he used to look like.

Chapter 23

"ALL MEN ARE BROTHERS"

It was a good thing Sid Morrison's Los Angeles lawyer had gone to bed early, leaving his answering machine on all night. Had he spoken to a judge about the contents of the private lab, while it was burning to a crisp, he would have had a big, big problem, with criminal consequences. Right off the bat, Morrison would have been arrested on suspicion of arson. His request for a search warrant denied.

Sid received word from his buddy, Elliot Mustapick, at half past five. His naked girlfriend, Yvonne, rolled over to give him the phone and accidentally bopped him on the head with it.

"Morrison," he said, rubbing his skull.

"Sid? Elliot. Do you know what happened to Goldman's office?"

"Tell me."

"It's history. Someone torched it around midnight. It wasn't you?"

"Hell, no."

The Los Angeles papers were publishing the story in the morning edition, but not as a front page headline. The National Enquirer's attorneys in Lantana, Florida were already trying to figure out how to release the "Inside Story" — including The Superstar's exclusive photos — without risking criminal prosecution. The headline had already been typeset. They were just waiting for the go-ahead from Calder, who was having breakfast with his general counsel.

Calder was not in the mood to be extradited to California over a technicality. The caption read:

CRAZED BEVERLY HILLS PLASTIC SURGEON BREEDS MUTANT APES — DIES IN FIRE!

With the publication of this story, Sid Morrison would be back on top!

At six-thirty, after four cups of coffee, two Dunkin' Donuts and a roll in the hay with the energetic model, he could wait no longer. He phoned Delaney, got her machine, then watched the local news on cable until she returned his call. Firemen were standing in the street in front of the Goldman building. Hoses were curled around barricades and through the white metal doors. A firefighter with singed hair and an ashen face holding an ax, who had been on the scene since two a.m., was telling the TV reporter about the fire.

"We broke in about five o'clock," he said. "Actually, the fire seemed to be contained by extra-thick reinforced walls. I'm not sure it was ever in danger of spreading."

"And what do you think caused the fire?" The reporter pushed her microphone into the man's chin.

"The police say the fire may have been set on purpose. The arson squad is in there now. We won't know anything for a while."

The reporter nodded into the camera.

"I understand this was the office of Doctor Ira Goldman, a respected Beverly Hills plastic surgeon. Can you tell us whether there was anyone in the office at the time of the fire? Have the police or fire department spoken to Dr. Goldman yet?"

"I really don't know," answered the fireman. "The place is a total disaster, it's practically melted. It'll be a while until we can sort through the debris." Someone across the street waved him over. "Sorry, I gotta go."

"Okay," said the well-groomed thirtyish lady in a blue suit. "And that's the latest from here, Rob. No one knows at this time exactly what happened early this morning in downtown Beverly Hills. It is possible that there might be some victims inside, but we'll have to get back to you later. From the scene of the strange fire in a doctor's office, this is Denise Rinkerhaus . . . "

Delaney was planning to fly back to Florida after lunch. By the time she awoke in Jamie's arms, it was ten. She had meant to get up an hour earlier to call in sick again. By now, they would have assumed she was not coming in on Thursday, two days in a row. She checked her messages long distance with a remote code.

"Daddy called an hour and a half ago," she told the young man with thunder thighs. She pulled her leg loose from under his and looked for her hair brush. Jamie picked the morning dirt specks out of the corners of his eyes. "He thinks I'm in Palm Beach. I'd better call him."

Sid was still home, concerned with legal matters, when Delaney dialed his number.

"Are you all right, honey?"

"I'm fine, Daddy. I'm just resting up one more day. What's new?"

Morrison filled her in on the situation in Beverly Hills. Jamie sat up, holding her around the waist and rubbing his nose in her soft hair. As she repeatedly uttered the phrase "Oh, my God!" Jamie handed her a pen and note pad. She wrote: "Goldman Lab Burned Down." Jamie's lips formed the words, "Oh, wow."

"By the way," asked Sid. "Can you get to those Elvis photos today? The ones you showed Jamie."

"Why?"

The photos were in Florida.

"I want you to take a close look at the one outside Goldman's office. The picture with the man Jamie identified as Hunter Davis. Get a magnifying glass."

"What am I looking for?"

"I want to know if he's wearing cuff links."

Delaney told Sid she would call him back later. When The Superstar hung up, Yvonne had the jewelry in the palm of her long, photogenic hand.

"These are beautiful," she said. "They're really old. Who's J.D.?"

"Jimmy Durante," kidded Morrison.

"Who's Jimmy Durante?" asked the twenty-six year old.

Delaney put down the phone and kissed Jamie. "You smell good," she said.

"What happened?" he asked, his fingers tracing the line of her jaw, from her chin to her ears. "Goldman burned his place down?"

"I didn't get all the details. Daddy wants me to examine that photo we found with Elvis and his lawyer. He wants me to use a magnifying glass."

"What for?" Jamie flexed and stretched his arm and chest muscles.

"This is nutty," she told him. "He wants me to see if Davis is wearing cuff links."

The wrestler felt his adrenaline flowing again.

"Cuff links?" he asked curiously. "Could you see that clearly in a photo?"

"Sure. With Alonzo X's black and whites, you could blow up a button to three feet tall."

"That's interesting, Dee." Jamie remembered his stay at Magnolias. "Mrs. Davis mentioned her husband's cuff links to me a couple of days ago."

"She did?"

"Yeah. She told me that Mr. Davis had a pair of Confederate Flag cuff links. They were stolen the night he was killed. The police never found them. Could you call me after you look at the photo and talk to your father?"

"No problem. Well, Jamie, I think we ought to take a shower and eat lunch at the airport. My plane takes off at twelve twenty-four."

"That's two hours."

"I know," said Delaney, snapping the elastic band of Jamie's briefs. "But we have some important business to take care of first." She jumped up and bit him.

"Something's been bothering me," he confessed, holding her, stifling her advances.

"What?"

They sat down on the bed again, faces close.

"I have to ask you a question. Okay? Don't get mad. It's

313

about us."

"Ask," she said.

Uncomfortably, Jamie brought up the thought that had troubled him since that first night at her home.

"I'm not the only guy you ever made love to, right?"

She grinned at him.

"Don't laugh," he said. "Please. This is serious. I need to know."

"Whether I've slept with lots of guys?" He turned red. "And what about you?"

Jamie looked at the beautiful young woman in bed with him. Her face was innocent, childlike.

"I've touched lots of girls. I mean, I've done a lot more than just touch them."

"But you never had sexual intercourse with them?" she asked.

"We've done other things," he admitted. "Just not that."

"That's what I figured." She was teasing him.

"What about you?" He tried to look into her eyes but looked away. "I couldn't take it if . . . I mean, I've told you everything. I really do love you. I just don't know what I'd do if . . ."

"You're adorable, Jamie Randolph," she said, hugging him. Her petite hands turned his big, lightly whiskered face toward her. "You sure you want to know?"

"I have to."

Delaney observed Jamie's body language as he waited for her answer. He shifted back and forth like a mountain lion, muscles taut, ready to pounce.

"You're the second," she said. "I promised myself, and my parents, that I would try to wait for the man I married someday. Which, if it turns out to be you, won't be next year. I'm graduating first. That's definite."

He liked what he was hearing. And he liked her hands on his face.

"Me, too," he said. "Even if I'm rich, I want to *be* something."

"Good. So we agree on that."

"Who was he?" Jamie asked, his eyes on hers.

Delaney answered without hesitation.

"His name was Mark. I met him in Boston. He was a senior. I thought we were in love. He told me he was in love with me. We only knew each other two months." She was sorry, but not ashamed. "It just happened. Now it's over . . . "

"*We* only knew each other one day," Jamie reminded her.

"I knew it the first minute," she said, holding back her tears.

"Me, too." He kissed her eyes, tasting salt. "So I guess you believe in love at first sight?"

"I believe in you," she responded.

"Me, too."

"I'm sorry I didn't wait. Do you forgive me?"

He took her in his arms once more, feeling happy and safe. He was a man in love. Whatever obstacles were before him, he knew he could overcome them. And whatever he had to lose in the struggle, internally or externally, would not include Delaney. That he knew for certain. She melted into his embrace.

After lunch at the airport, he walked her to the departure gate.

"Thanks for coming to Memphis," he said, kissing her good-bye.

"It was a trip," she said, making fun of the lingo of the sixties and seventies. "Good luck with your decision. I'll call you tonight. I'll tell you more about the cuff links. And don't worry. Your secret is safe with me."

The line of passengers moved toward the plane.

"Fly carefully," Jamie called after her. "And watch out for UFO's!"

Not exactly the best thing to yell to someone at the airport.

❦

The cab dropped him off at the Graceland Visitor Center where he overheard a mother telling her two children she had misplaced her wallet.

"Daddy will pick us up in two hours," she explained to the

disappointed youngsters. "But we won't be able to take the Elvis tour today. I'm sorry."

Jamie walked over and handed the woman some money and his father's business card. Over her half-hearted objections, she agreed to mail him a check.

"I trust you," he said. "The kids have to see Graceland."

"Thanks so much," she replied. "This is our last day in town and I gave them my word. Elvis is a national institution. Thanks again."

Jamie watched them board the Graceland tour bus, and waved. He then walked across Elvis Presley Boulevard himself and stopped at the Music Gates designed by Elvis in 1958. He thought about going in again but decided against it. He had seen enough to know that this wasn't his home. But it was the home of the man who had arranged for him to be born. The man whose blood ran through his veins, or at least whose DNA comprised the cells of his body. The man whose desire for a son, and a religious miracle in the form of the resurrection of Jesse Presley, had changed his life eighteen years after that same man's death.

And where was this man, this "national institution," on August 17, 1995? Was he just a box of decomposed flesh and bone up the hill in the Meditation Garden? Were any of the "Elvis sightings" around the country true? He doubted it. In her book "Elvis And Me," one of several Elvis books he had skimmed through in the past two days, even his own ex-wife, Priscilla, acknowledged that The King was gone. It wasn't likely that she would participate in such a grand fraud if Elvis was still alive. No, he had to believe that the man who had wished to watch him grow up was dead.

As Jamie Randolph leaned against a tall street pole, one knee bent up, he stared at the two guitar playing figures decorating the protective gates. Each figure was a mirror image of the other, like twins. He wondered if they were intended to represent Elvis and Jesse, or whether they now stood for Elvis and him.

There were so many more questions that would never be answered.

Drawing upon all of his powers of imagination and creativity,

Jamie envisioned one of the musical figures on the gates turning into a living, breathing Elvis and jumping down to have a brief conversation with his son.

"What do you want to know, boy?" Elvis asked. The superstar was much older than his metal caricature. From photos, it was easy to conjure up a forty-two year old overweight, worn out Elvis Presley with wide, untrimmed sideburns.

"How could you do this to me?" questioned the younger version.

"Listen, Jesse . . . "

"The name is *Jamie*. I'm not your dead twin brother. I'm Jamie Randolph, and I had a perfectly normal life going for me, just like you wanted. That is, until I got the letter. Not to mention the four million dollars."

Elvis snickered.

"I said I was sorry in the letter. Damn, boy! You're as stubborn as I am. Well, what should I expect? You *are* me."

Jamie saw himself losing his temper, taking down the rock 'n roll idol with a quick movement, wrestling him into submission. But the man was past his prime, and not healthy. What would it prove?

"Okay, forget the letter. What's done is done. Only what am I supposed to do now? Just pretend like it never happened? Take your advice and keep my mouth shut? Easier said than done. I know who I am. Why should I have to go through my whole life, or even the next twenty years, keeping your secret, not mine?"

Elvis took off his wrap-around sunglasses, sucked in his gut.

"Telling the truth will only hurt people. Your parents. My daughter, Lisa Marie. Maybe even you. Why can't you just be happy? I would have been happy to have your life."

Jamie gave him an answer The King was not expecting.

"Do you know how much your estate is worth these days? When you died, you were in hock up to your ears, even though you made seven million dollars a year. They almost mortgaged Graceland! Now," he said, "thanks to Priscilla, the estate is valued in the hundreds of millions. You're worth more dead than alive."

"I always knew Priscilla was dynamite," said Presley. "*Hundreds* of millions? That's cool. But what does all that money have to do with being happy?"

"They say money can't buy happiness. But if I declare that I'm your son, don't I get half of the estate? Or better still, if I'm legally you, being your exact duplicate, maybe I get all of it."

Jamie felt like Barbara Walters, the dream interview she never had with Elvis.

"That's why I left you the money. So you wouldn't have to worry."

"Oh, I'm not worried," answered Jamie. "I just want what's rightfully mine. I could give it all to charity, like you said you would."

"Nothing is worth the price of fame," warned Elvis. "Suddenly, you don't have any time to yourself. You can't go out of the house without a bodyguard. You're not *you* anymore."

"I'm not myself anyway. I'm you. Remember?"

"You know what I mean."

"Who says anyone will care?" asked Jamie. "I'd be news for a few months, maybe a year. I could write a best-seller, get on all the talk shows, have a hit record . . . but after that, who would care? There are a thousand Elvis impersonators who sound more like you than I do."

Elvis smiled, a snarling putdown expression.

"I doubt you'd just be an overnight sensation. Look at me. I died almost twenty years ago, and you said it yourself. I'm bigger than ever. In fact, Elvis Presley is bigger than life! Don't you see? I went from being a person to being an image. The same thing would happen to you. Because you're not just another Elvis impersonator. You're the genuine article. Even if you're Jesse, you're me."

"That's only a theory," argued the young man. "It's what you want to believe. If you really cared about my life, you'd have left me alone."

"Just a theory? It's time for a reality check, son. If Priscilla made all that money you were talking about, people must have exploited the hell out of my name, my image. You tell me. How did she make the money?"

"People bought a lot of your records. And Graceland is a museum. Over half a million visitors pay ten million dollars a year to see your house."

"Where'd the rest of the money come from?"

Jamie hesitated. "Souvenirs," he said. "And licensing."

"What kind of souvenirs?" asked The King, wiping the sweat off his brow.

"Ashtrays," Jamie began. "And pillows. Books, postcards, bumper stickers. Christmas tree ornaments, key chains." He recalled the items stacked on downtown shelves. "Wall clocks, watches, statues, belt buckles, pen knives, mirrors. I've seen them all over Memphis."

"I'll bet they're not just in Tennessee," ventured Elvis. "And if they sold off my ranch in Mississippi, I imagine some wise-ass broke it up into little pieces and made millions."

"Actually, they sold seven-inch pieces of the fence. Your cousin, Billy Smith, signed certificates of authenticity. I was offered one at the airport today."

Elvis laughed. "I knew it." His face grew stern. "They didn't try to dig my body up, did they?"

"Vernon had you moved to Graceland. The Meditation Garden."

"Good idea," the star commented. "I guess he's there, too, by now."

"He died in 1979."

"Rest in peace," said the child of Vernon and Gladys. "The point, Jamie, is that if even my corpse is in demand, how can you believe you'll escape the life I tried to save you from? Elvis Presley isn't a man. He's an obsession. I saw it while it was happening, and I couldn't stop it. You'd be as powerless as me. We can't change history, son. All we can do is learn from it."

Jamie was as confused as when the imaginary conversation started. Finally, he came up with the solution.

"I could test the waters," he said. "I could find out if it was safe or not before I told the world who I am."

"And how would you do that?" Presley asked.

"I'll think of something," said the A-student. He looked at the aged entertainer, garbed in a shiny white and gold outfit with a highback collar.

"Don't do it," advised Presley. "I'm telling you this for your own good."

"Why not? You said you were happy until you were thirty. Maybe I can stay happy."

"Because once you start, you can't stop. I can see already that you want a taste of the fame. Next, you'll want to do a duet with Willie Nelson in Las Vegas. Believe me, it never ends. If you don't get on the roller coaster, you don't have to fret about how to get off. Listen to me. I'm your . . . friend."

Some friend, thought Jamie. You've turned my whole life upside down. I'm already on the roller coaster. And you're right, I don't know how to get off.

"You've been standing here quite a while, son," said the big Graceland guard. "If you want to take the tour, tickets are across the street." The man studied Jamie's handsome face, but showed no sign of recognition. "Otherwise, I'll have to ask you to move along. Don't want you to get hit by a bus, and sue the estate."

"No, we don't want that ," agreed Jamie." I'm done for the day."

The son of Elvis walked up and down the street for about an hour, grabbed a burger and returned to Days Inn.

By the time Jamie had unlocked the door to his room, the phone had stopped ringing. He dialed Delaney's home number, figuring it was her.

"I've got the photo," she told him. "We lucked out. Davis is wearing the Confederate Flag cuff links."

"That's interesting," said Jamie. "Because I already know about the cuff links."

"You know Sid has them?"

It was one surprise after another. Jamie scratched his head.

"How could he have them?" he asked. "They were stolen in 1979."

"They were in Stein's condo in California."

Jamie realized what she was telling him.

"That means . . . "

"That Stein or Goldman murdered Hunter Davis. Probably

Stein, Daddy thinks. He doesn't know why, but he says it doesn't matter any more."

"Why not?"

"Because he thinks they're both dead." She read her scribbles. "The cops found Goldman's car a couple of blocks away. The two of them ate dinner at an Italian restaurant late last night. Just before the fire. The burglar alarm company says they were in the building around midnight."

"They might have escaped." Jamie hoped he was wrong. As soon as he got off the phone, he planned to call the Davises with the news. It would help them cope.

Delaney continued to explain. "There was only one way out," she said. "The elevator. But it was still downstairs in the lab, sort of melted. The police think the elevator cables were disconnected. It looks like whoever was down there died."

"When will they know for sure?"

"Daddy's supposed to call me back. He knows you want to tell Mrs. Davis the truth. You can have the cuff links, he said. To give to her. He doesn't care about solving the Hunter Davis murder. Don't tell anyone," she whispered. "Sid has photos of the laboratory before the fire. No one knows. The Enquirer is going to publish the story in a day or two. Sid wouldn't tell me what he saw, but he says this is big. And it has absolutely nothing to do with you, or Mr. Davis."

Jamie was glad for Sid Morrison. He deserved another fifteen minutes of fame. The answer to Jamie's own question of fame still eluded him.

"How was the flight back?" he asked, remembering his manners.

"Fine," said Delaney. "The lady next to me kept looking for flying saucers. Why did you have to say that?" They laughed.

"I'll call you later."

"No, I'll call you when Sid tells me more." She heard the sound of her Fax machine, an ear-piercing electronic whistle. "I gotta go," she said. "I love you."

After supper, Delaney confirmed that Goldman and Stein had perished in the blaze. Their charred remains had been dug out of the rubble and were on their way to the forensics lab. Reporters were promised more information within a week. Long after Sid's story had hit the newsstands.

Jamie called Charlotte Davis, who was with her son. She could not believe what he told her. They had finally found the cuff links, and the murderer.

"Thank you," she said. "I needed to know."

"No one will ever know why they killed your husband," said Jamie. "It could have been money. It could have been anything. This guy Goldman was just a terrible person. There will be a story about him in the newspapers soon."

Charlotte had some ideas about why Hunter had been in contact with the Beverly Hills doctor, but she did not pursue them. The truth about his death was sufficient. And to know that the murderer was dead.

She called her friend Darlene Flood, who had been helping her with this for sixteen years. Darlene needed only to know that the case was closed. She would show her the cuff links, Charlotte thought, but would never reveal where they came from.

Now there was only one mystery left to solve.

Whether or not to take the advice of Elvis Presley and keep quiet.

CHAPTER 24

"AN ACT OF FAITH"

After many interruptions, Jack Randolph finally managed to escape to his private screening room to watch the end of *Casablanca*. Humphrey Bogart is still undecided about what to do with the stolen Letters Of Transit that will allow two lucky people to depart from Morocco to the free world. On the surface, Rick remains neutral about all of the good and evil going on around him during the Second World War.

"I don't like disturbances in my place," he tells a French and German soldier, breaking up a fist fight between them. "You either lay off politics or get out."

A short while later, Ilsa is waiting for Rick in his office above the bar. She tries to convince him to give her husband, Victor Lazlo, the exit papers. She tells him that he should help fight for the cause.

"I'm not fighting for anything anymore," claims Rick. "Except myself."

This was Jack's favorite part of the movie. Every other line is a classic. Bogart is sheer poetry. Rick tries to leave the room when Ilsa suddenly pulls a gun on him. She demands the papers. Rick has already told her he plans to die in Casablanca. "It's a good spot for it," he says. When he won't hand over the letters, Ilsa is challenged to kill him. He steps close enough to feel the gun barrel.

"Go ahead and shoot," he suggests. "You'll be doing me a favor."

Jack stuffed a handful of salt-free popcorn into his mouth

323

as Ingrid Bergman admits that she still loves Rick. They kiss, and what other romance might follow is left to the imagination of the viewer. (In 1942, films were suggestive, not graphic.) After whatever happened is over, Rick is still neatly attired in a white suit and black bow tie. But now Ilsa doesn't know what to do. She loves both men.

"I don't know what's right . . . " she laments. "You have to think for both of us."

In a surprise ending, with many twists and turns, Rick leads everyone to believe that he is leaving Casablanca with Ilsa, abandoning her husband and the fight for freedom. However, at the dark, damp, smoggy airport, Bogart tricks the Moroccan Police Captain, shoots the evil Nazi officer, Major Strasser, and gives Ilsa and Victor the exit papers.

"We both know you belong with Victor," Rick says, dressed in his trenchcoat. "If that plane leaves the ground and you're not with him, you'll regret it . . . Maybe not today, maybe not tomorrow, but soon . . . and for the rest of your life."

"What about us?" she asks, Rick and Ilsa speaking where no one can hear them.

"We'll always have Paris," he answers. The greatest single line in any movie, ever.

Paris, of course, was where Rick and Ilsa had a love affair when, unknown to Rick, Ilsa thought her husband had been killed in the war. Rick has now learned the truth, and in this sensational black and white film whose theme is clearly about right versus wrong, Rick chooses right. He tells Lazlo the falsehood that he and Ilsa are no longer in love, and wishes the couple well.

Of course, in the grand finale, even the Police Captain exonerates Rick, lying to his men that someone else shot the Nazi officer. In the very last scene, Rick and the well dressed cop disappear into the fog as they begin to make plans to take a stand in the war.

"Louie," says Bogie. "I think this is the beginning of a beautiful friendship."

THE END

"Pretty good flick," said Jamie, sitting up straight. "For the forties."

"I didn't know you were back there. Boy, you're quiet. How long have you been here?" Jack screwed the cap off a bottle of Diet Coke.

"About twenty minutes. You couldn't hear me because you were making so much noise eating all that popcorn." Jamie moved to a closer seat. "Can I have some?"

It was Saturday afternoon.

"Here, you can finish it off," Jack said. The bag contained about ten fluffy kernels of corn and half an inch of scraps that stuck to the bottom.

"I can't see why you're so in love with that movie, Dad."

Jamie polished off the ten good pieces, then stuck his tongue into the bag.

"Here, give me that!" Jack snatched the bag, just as he had taken away objects that were too dangerous for his son at two or three. "Would you like to know why *Casablanca* is, by far, the best American film ever made?"

"According to you."

"According to anyone with a brain. You're eighteen now. You have a brain. So I'll tell you." Jack looked at his son. He was a really good kid. "*Casablanca*, my young friend, dramatizes the eternal confrontation between right and wrong within ourselves. Rick, as the protagonist, constantly reminds us that we have to make moral decisions in life, whether we like it or not."

Jamie understood that much just from seeing the last twenty minutes.

"What's so exciting about that?" he asked.

"Well, compared to star cruisers blasting the hell out of inter-galactic armies, nothing, I guess. But in real life we are always faced with small scale situations like what to do in Morocco during the war."

Jamie took a bag of M & M's from the refrigerator.

"The way I see it," he said, "it was an *easy* decision for Rick. He knew if he ran away with the girl, in the end she'd never love him. And he'd feel too guilty about leaving the other guy in Casablanca. What other choice did he have?"

Jack smiled. "A lot of people would run off anyway. You see what's going on in the world today. All the violence. All the divorces. People don't always worry about the consequences of their actions. Live for today. That's what kids your age thought in the sixties and seventies." Jack reached for some candy. "You also have to remember that Rick Blaine made his decisions during a war in which people were afraid they might die any day. In other words, his long term outlook was exceptional. For all he knew, the three of them only had a week to live. And he gave it up anyway."

"That's true," said Jamie. "I never thought of that."

"But Ilsa's husband was willing to do more than Rick. He told Rick to leave him in Casablanca, if that was the only way to get his wife out. So Rick knew he could never love Ilsa more than her husband did."

"I think you're reading things into the story, Dad."

"Maybe, Jamie. But sometimes you've got to make a tough decision if you really love someone."

Jamie thought about the decision he still had to make. Was it selfish to want to tell everyone who he was if it hurt his parents? Or would they understand that it was torture to hold in the truth? Right now all of the pain was his alone to bear. If even just the family knew, at least they could share the burden. And wasn't that what family was all about: sharing?

"Home movies!" yelled Diane Randolph, flinging open the door and heading straight for the VCR with a box of tapes. Olivia and her friend Lori came in behind her. "I just transferred the early ones from Betamax," said Mom.

"What's *Betamax*?" asked Jamie.

"I know," said Olivia. Her brother gave her the eye.

"What is it?" he dared her.

"It's a different kind of videotape than VHS. Sony used to make them. Now people can only watch VHS, so they have to convert all their old Betamax to VHS. Right, Mom?"

"That's right, Livvy." Diane popped out *Casablanca*, which was rewinding. "Watch this. It's 1979!"

Without warning, Jack and Jamie's philosophical discussion had shifted into a lighthearted trip down memory lane.

"Look," said Livvy. "That's me!"

Mom was holding a chubby little baby, flanked by a blond-haired Jack and a white-haired Jamie. They were in the back yard with a Calico cat.

"We had a cat?"

"For a little while," Diane told Jamie. "Her name was Spunky. She got hit by a car."

"Hey, where's my baby movies?" asked the older sibling.

"That's you," said Diane. "You were about twenty-one months old. Look at you. Those skinny little legs. Those pouty lips." Her eyes were misty.

Jamie studied himself clinging to his mother's dress. Although he couldn't remember 1979, it was clear as a bell who his real mother had always been. When the camera zoomed in, his face reflected total adoration for Diane.

"No, I mean when I was a couple of months old, like Liv."

"Oh," said Diane. "Those are still on regular film. I forgot to bring them in and get them put on tape. I'll do it this week. I promise."

"Who took the movies?" asked Livvy.

"That's a good question. Who did take the pictures, Jack?"

Jack thought about it. "I got it. Stan Long."

"Our neighbor across the street?" said Jamie. "Mr. Long? The guy who's always complaining that Grover made doo-doo on his lawn? The guy who used to examine my bicycle tires whenever some kid rode on his property?"

"We were good friends with Stan until you started to do better than his son in sports," Jack reminded him. "He's a very competitive person. Always trying to prove that he makes more money than me, plays tennis better, and so on. The only thing he could ever beat me at was Scrabble. I used to kick his butt at chess!"

"How about wrestling? Did you ever pin him, Dad?"

"No, but I often felt like it." They laughed.

"Jack, be nice." Diane inserted a new cartridge.

"Oh, my God!" shouted Olivia. "You're naked!"

Lori, who had always wanted to see Jamie without his clothes on, gaped at the screen. Of course, he was only four, diving into the pool and climbing out with his swimming trunks missing. But it was better than nothing. Olivia constantly told her friend that she would outgrow her crush on the handsome athlete, but she was determined to hang onto her hope until he was married.

The nostalgic tapes evoked feelings in the family, and especially in Jamie, that had been dormant for a long while. It brought them closer together as they re-lived the baseball games ("Randolph" and "7" on his pin-striped back), Livvy's ballet and ice-skating performances, the trips to Massachusetts, Jack's surprise 40th Birthday bash, then Diane's . . . all the experiences they had participated in as a family unit. There were lots of tapes to watch.

"That's enough," said Jack, after about ninety minutes. "I'm getting hungry. I feel like Chinese." He stood up and yawned. "Let's take a vote. Who wants Chinese?"

Nobody responded.

"Then it's Chinese!" announced the head of the clan.

No one disagreed. Lori called home and said she was eating out with Livvy for a change. *Fine.* Then they might take in a movie. *No problem.* Just be home by twelve. And no rides with anyone who was drinking. Don't forget what just happened to Steve McDermott. And he was sober. Lori agreed to the rules, and together the best friends would obey them. Their personalities blended well, Livvy's exuberance counterpoint to Lori's more passive daydreaming; they kept each other stimulated, and out of trouble.

While the girls were getting ready, Jack strongarmed Jamie in the kitchen. The boy was looking for a pre-dinner snack. Jack shut the refrigerator door with a whoosh.

"We've got to talk," Dad said. "Frankly, I don't like the way you've been treating me since Mrs. Davis called. I don't know if your mother has noticed, but I have. You've been very cold to me, and I don't like it."

Jack waited for an argument.

"You're right, Dad." The tone of voice was contrite, not cocky. I've really been obsessed with this inheritance thing. I've been blaming you for not telling me the truth."

"I can't tell you what I don't know."

Jamie now knew that his father was not holding back.

Aside from what he had uncovered, he could see it in Dad's eyes. To his knowledge, the man had never lied to him. Like Humphrey Bogart, there was a time when Jamie believed Dad might have lied to protect him, but Jack had nothing to hide. He was a good father. The best.

"I'm sorry," said Jamie, lowering his head. He didn't know what else to say. If fact, he didn't know what was going to come out of his own mouth. "When I was in Memphis with Charlotte Davis . . . "

Jack cut him off. "Oh! Mrs. Davis called. I spoke to her for an hour." Obviously, Dad had accepted his weak apology.

"You did? When?"

"This morning. Before you got up." Jack opened the refrigerator again and allowed Jamie to reach inside for the peanut butter. "That's why I was watching the end of *Casablanca*. It's always inspirational to me."

"What do you mean?" asked his son.

"Well, Mrs. Davis called for two reasons. First, she told me she was sorry you never found out where the money came from."

Charlotte Davis had lied to Jack. Jamie had revealed to her, although lying himself, that the money had come from Jack's uncle. Somehow, she had sensed that Jamie was not going to tell that story to his father and had given him support for whatever he wanted to say. She certainly wasn't dumb. He wished he had met her husband.

"What else did she say?"

Jack wondered how his son could swallow a tablespoon of peanut butter without choking. Even in his hey-day, he could never do that.

"She said to tell you thanks for the cuff links," Jack answered. "She said they were beautiful. I take it they were for her son."

"Yeah," said Jamie, watching the lies multiply and hating it. "When I was in Memphis, I saw this really neat pair of Confederate Flag cuff links. They told me their family was very patriotic during the Civil War. I didn't know what else to get them for their hospitality. I mean, they're rich. They have everything."

"Did you buy Mrs. Davis something, too?"

One more lie, coming right up.

"I bought her a book about Elvis Presley," he said, thinking it was such a stupid thing to say the second after he said it.

"That was nice," said Jack. "Did she like it?"

"She loved it. Everyone in Memphis loves Elvis. He's . . . like a God."

Jack gagged on a fingertip of Jif Creamy. He really had a yen for spare ribs and shrimp with lobster sauce. Peanut butter was a distant second choice.

"You know, I'm glad to hear you admit you've been exhibiting some rather bad behavior, son. I didn't say anything because I wanted you to have every opportunity to get to the bottom of this money thing. And I'm not going to question you about everything that happened. When you're ready, you can tell me about it. I'll respect your privacy. But I am glad you've come to your senses and decided to accept your good fortune and move on with your life."

Jamie wished that was the case. He was still thinking about the public's reaction to the secret son of Elvis.

"Thanks, Dad."

"The only thing I wanted to ask you about was Elvis Presley."

Jamie felt the peanut butter stick to his esophagus.

"What about Elvis Presley?" he sputtered.

"You remember that theory we came up with," Jack said. "About Elvis and his lawyer putting the money in a trust in your name. And then passing away before they could take it back."

"Oh, yeah."

"Well," Jack asked. "Did you ever disprove that theory?"

It was time for another fabrication.

"The truth," replied Jamie, finding it ever more difficult to tell the difference, "is that I couldn't prove or disprove anything. It's just been too long. No one remembers what happened, everyone is either dead or mentally incompetent, the names have disappeared . . . "

There was a grain of truth in that last statement. Except for the Elvis letter, it was a blind trail.

"I'm not surprised. I'm just sorry that you had to waste your whole vacation barking up trees. You would have had a much more interesting time in my office. We had a real estate closing last week where the seller showed up in his long johns." Jack slapped his knee. "This young couple bought a historic house in Saddle River. The owner had been living there without electricity for the past year and a half. A beautiful piece of land. If it was me, I'd knock it down, but you know kids. They're all like you. Idealistic. They want to restore the house."

Jamie just wanted to restore his life.

"Sounds great. Sorry I missed all the fun. Maybe next year."

Jack laid his heavy hand on Jamie's shoulder.

"You're still going to college in two weeks?" he asked nervously.

"That's the plan, Dad." Jamie put away the jar of peanut butter. His stomach was starting to palpitate.

"I mean, you're not planning to live off your inheritance?"

"No way," said Jamie, meaning it. "If there's one thing I learned from all this, it's that you need a sense of self-esteem. It's great to have a couple of mil for emergencies, but I have to prove that I can make it on my own. I'm not saying I'm going to be a doctor or a lawyer. I might turn out to be a baseball player or a stock broker. Or even a rock star." Jack shrugged. "But first I want to get a good education."

Jack was relieved to hear Jamie's renewed dedication to his college career.

"And when will we be meeting this girlfriend of yours?"

"Delaney?" Jamie saw her cute smile and felt better. "Oh yeah. I meant to ask you and Mom if she can stay here for a day or two on her way to Boston. I promised her a tour of New York. Not that I'm more familiar with it than she is. But her favorite movie is *Sleepless In Seattle* and she's dying to go to the top floor of The Empire State Building."

"Sleepless In Seattle?" Jack pondered the title. "That's the movie based on *An Affair To Remember*, isn't it? With Cary Grant and Deborah Kerr?"

"I guess so," said Jamie, vaguely recalling details of the film while a clear mental image of himself and Delaney making love appeared in his mind's eye.

"Yes, that's the one. Your mother loved that movie. Both of them, actually." He thought of *Casablanca.* "No comparison to . . . never mind. Yes, of course, Delaney can stay with us for a few days. We'd love to get to know her. How serious is this?"

Jamie saw himself walking down the aisle with her. Or was he waiting up front with the minister while Sid walked her down to him? Whatever.

"I really like her," he said. "She's something else."

Suddenly, Jamie remembered that Elvis had claimed he had met Jack and Diane the day after his birth, disguised as a priest. He almost started to ask his father about the event, but realized there was no way he could know about it. This was the kind of mistake he would have to struggle to avoid if he chose not to divulge his genetic heritage. How long before he slipped up? Could he keep the secret for five more years? Ten? Was it really worth the effort? Maybe after dinner . . .

"I'm starving," Jack said, tapping his back pocket to make sure he had his wallet. He took his car keys out. "How about you?"

"I guess you're driving?"

"No. You are." Jack handed Jamie the keys to the Mercedes. "You'll probably be driving a Mercedes in a couple of years when you get the money. You might as well start practicing."

Jamie felt proud and guilty at the same time.

When the three pretty ladies entered the room, Lori, who had preened herself for Livvy's brother, said to him: "You know, Jamie, you remind me of that guy in the movie your father always watches."

"Humphrey Bogart?"

"I guess so. The guy who owns the bar in Morocco."

"Oh yeah?" He took it as a compliment, which it was intended to be. "Why?"

"Because you always try to do the right thing." Livvy poked her in the ribs. "I mean it," she said. "I can see why all the kids in school idolize you."

"Thanks, Lori. That's a nice thing to say." Jamie grabbed his mother's arm as Jack twisted the door knob hard enough to snap it off. "Let's eat!"

Jamie eased the car back out of the garage, past the '64 Mustang, braked gently and steered toward Mom's flowers. He backed up again, closed the garage door electronically and drove slowly down the driveway to Woodland Avenue. The street was empty, not a single car parked along the road where there had been fifty on the Saturday of his birthday party three months ago. Still, he looked both ways, twice, out of habit, before pulling off the curb and accelerating gradually from zero to thirty-five. Just the way Dad did it. The way Dad had taught him to drive six years ago.

While the big Labrador Retriever slept peacefully on the living room rug, dreaming of better days and of Jamie's soothing piano playing, the young man began to make his final decision. If he kept the secret, he could always change his mind later on. How much worse would it be to come out of the closet in a year or two? But if he defied Elvis' dire warning, he could never go back and undo the harm. Like Bogart in Casablanca — more like Mr. Spock in Star Trek — it was logical to wait.

That was the decision for now. On Sunday morning, Jamie Randolph read the Bible for two hours, an hour before church and an hour after.

Chapter 25

THE RESURRECTION

The *20th Anniversary* of the death of Elvis Presley.

A sellout crowd of 15,000 has flocked to the M.G.M. Grand Hotel in Las Vegas, at $350 a head, to see the one-time performance of "Elvis Lives!" Including Pay-Per-View television, it is estimated that nearly two billion people are watching the event, dwarfing the 1997 Super Bowl and far beyond everyone's original expectations.

Across the United States, youngsters, teenagers, adults and young grandparents — plus thousands of news anchor persons — anxiously wait to see who will come on stage. It is a fabulous media sensation, advertised as "More Magical Than David Copperfield," and only a handful of insiders know who will be giving "The First Real Elvis Concert Since 1977."

Superstars line the first three rows, roped off as the "V.I.P. Zone." Fireworks have been exploding outside continuously for over an hour, showering the sky above the seven block traffic jam with waterfalls of colored light.

"For Pay-Per-View, this is Oprah Winfrey, your co-host of 'Elvis Lives!'"

The live audience and TV viewers did not need to be reminded of the name behind one of America's most familiar faces, still ranked the number one talk-show personality.

"Actually," she continued, "Even I don't really know for sure who is backstage. The producers of this fantastic promotion are claiming that they have the genuine Elvis Presley, who is going to sing here tonight. We recently did a

334

survey that shows that as many as 50% of all Americans believe that The King did not die twenty years ago. In one new book, the author claims that Elvis has been kept in the Witness Protection Program because he was a federal agent appointed by Richard Nixon. That last part is true, I checked it out. But I still can't promise that Elvis Presley is warming up to do *'Hound Dog'* or *'Love Me Tender.'* I just don't know. So don't ask me, honey!" She turned to the man beside her. "What do you think, Phil?"

Her famous silver-haired colleague scratched his scalp with the patented bent forefinger. It was that quizzical Phil Donahue scratch suggesting that even if he knew the truth, he wasn't sure if the public would believe him.

"Well, Oprah," he said finally, the crowd reacting with ferocious shouts. "If you asked me, would I bet my life savings on Elvis being alive, and being here tonight, I'd have to say no." The people booed. "But . . . I've got a sneaking suspicion that we're in for *one hell of a surprise* in Las Vegas. And, by the way, I'm not crazy about this one hundred and ten degree weather."

Behind Oprah and Phil the amphitheater stage was draped with a huge curtain advertising Coca-Cola. It featured the now popular logo of Elvis drinking a 1950's bottle of Coke. Below the drawing, the humorous slogan: *"Elvis Used To Drink Coke! Maybe He Still Does!"*

"Ladies and Gentlemen," announced Oprah (above a chant of "We want Elvis! We want Elvis!" being suppressed by hotel security.) "No matter what your opinion of this show is, and I really do hope Elvis is with us tonight, one thing is for certain. Nothing is going to top the mystique of the man himself. The renaissance began in February, 1995 when Life Magazine published its all-Elvis pictorial collector's issue, after which the books and documentaries eventually over-shadowed the O.J. Simpson murder trial. Then, in 1996, Elvis mania spread so fast we all thought it was 1957 again. Who ever would have guessed that *'Heartbreak Hotel'* would turn out to be the biggest hit single of the year? I guess, like they say, what goes around . . . comes around!"

"And," Phil injected, waving his finger, "How many movie

buffs expected Elvis Presley to be honored with a posthumous Oscar at last year's Academy Awards ceremony?"

"I feel like this is Oscar night," remarked Oprah.

"So do I."

Then, suddenly, without warning or introduction — after six trying months of hype and wonder — all of the lights went out and there was dead silence. A few moments later, an instantly recognizable deep Southern voice filled the room.

"Good evening, everybody. It's me. I'm back . . . and I'm here to stay. But before we turn the lights on, I just want to ask y'all one very important question . . . " The performer hesitated, then sang, slowly . . . "Are you lonesome tonight . . . ?"

The voice of Elvis Presley was absolutely unmistakable, as was the musical talent of the producer of those immortal four words, sung as only one man could ever sing them.

Yes, there were endless expert Elvis impersonators. One had warmed up the crowd before the show. It was not unusual for men to look, dress or even sound like the real McCoy. However, there was a strange and wonderful feeling that only the voice of the man from Memphis could instill. And this was the voice of that person. You could feel his presence, his spirituality, his awesome power. *This was no hoax!*

When the lights returned, fifteen thousand Elvis fans felt the same shiver at the same time. Now the face of Elvis Presley joined his voice. When he swayed his hips, hundreds of spectators passed out! The president of one of the major Elvis fan clubs had to be carried from the auditorium.

Then two cross-spotlights focused on the head and shoulders of the star of the night.

"See, I'm for real!" he screamed, doing a little dance.

For the first time in their careers, Oprah Winfrey and Phil Donahue were totally speechless. Had their microphones been turned on, they honestly could not have said a word. No one knew what to say.

For the man before them, dressed in tight black pants and a tan short sleeved shirt, was not a 62 year-old Elvis. Instead, the Las Vegas audience which had paid a grand total of more than $5,000,000 hoping to be in the same room as their idol for two hours, stared in utter disbelief at the image of a muscular young man around twenty years old. Equally mesmerized, via satellite, was the vast international network of those who had shelled out literally billions to see the return of The King.

What they were all seeing was impossible, and yet it was right before their eyes. The tired, overweight yet charismatic Elvis Presley last seen at age 42 had somehow, miraculously, been transformed into an earlier blond-haired version of himself. Instead of aging twenty years since 1977, he had grown twenty years younger! And it was not an optical illusion. To his left and right, people who had known Elvis intimately stared wide-eyed at the handsome and happy entertainer. Priscilla Presley gave him a kiss.

"I'm going to sing for *you* tonight," said Elvis, smiling at the beautiful older woman. "I think you've waited long enough. But first, I'd like to introduce some very special people to you." He laughed, threw his head back, fixed his hair. "These are the guys and gals who have temporarily replaced me as what you-all call superstars. Ladies and gentlemen, Mr. Paul McCartney!" The ex-Beatle stood and took a bow. "And next to Paul is my old friend Jerry . . . Jerry Lee Lewis! Jerry, please stand up, but stay away from my piano! Man, that boy can burn up your keyboard!" Seated beside Lewis was Michael Jackson, who was not introduced as The King's son-in-law. "I can't believe how you move your feet, Michael," said Elvis, with true admiration. Next to Michael Jackson sat Madonna, then Bruce Springsteen, then Prince, Willie Nelson, Michael Bolton, Whitney Houston, John Mellencamp . . .

One by one, Elvis introduced the 62 top music stars of the fifties through the nineties as "the cream of the crop". A few first choices had refused to show up. Numerous second choices were highly insulted that they hadn't been named first choices. Overall, the array of big names was spectacular and the audience responded well.

Elvis sang hit after hit. Teddy Bear. Blue Suede Shoes. Jailhouse Rock. Don't Be Cruel. Suspicious Minds. My Way. Can't Help Falling In Love With You. He *wrestled* Willie Nelson up onto the stage and did a duet with him of "You Were Always

On My Mind." It brought the house down. Every song was performed with gusto, with the intense emotion and unmatched vocal virtuosity reminiscent of the Elvis Presley of the fifties and the 1968 tour. Plus, this Elvis appeared to be physically stronger.

And then, at midnight in Vegas, it was over.

As quickly as he had appeared, Elvis disappeared. No interviews, no good-bye, no standing ovations. The lights were increased to maximum brightness, the band departed, and life was back to normal.

Again, there was stunned silence and some minor confusion before Oprah and Phil regained control of the situation.

"Damn!" squealed Oprah. "That white boy can sing!"

"Yeah," said Phil. "But who *was* that white boy?" Phil scratched his head in a different manner.

Oprah took his arm. "Phil," she said, tilting her head and batting her lovely eyes. "You are not a true believer. You don't think that young man was Elvis Presley? Then who do you think he was?"

Phil Donahue shrugged his shoulders. "Oprah . . . I really, really don't have the slightest idea who that young man was. Elvis Presley? Maybe. *A clone of Elvis Presley?* Got me. An incredible look-alike? Someone who had plastic surgery?"

"To his vocal cords?" asked Oprah, laughing with the crowd.

"I don't know," said Phil. "All I know is, I'm in shock!"

Television reporters were scurrying to find the singer's agent for an interview. But there was no agent. They searched for Priscilla Presley, who had left five minutes before the show ended. They would talk to anyone who could boost their ratings.

⚜

Meanwhile, in a soundproof media room in a pretty Colonial home in Tenafly, New Jersey, Jamie Randolph pressed "Stop" on his dad's VCR. They had recorded the $29.95 show.

"Did that guy look like Elvis or what?" he asked the family, including his fiancé.

338

Delaney squeezed his hand.

"Jamie Randolph," she said. "That guy was a fraud and you know it. You look more like Elvis than he does. Elvis impersonators are a dime a dozen."

Jamie chuckled.

"What's so funny?" Delaney asked. Mom and Livvy smiled at Delaney. They loved her.

"Well, I was just thinking how hard it would be if you really were Elvis Presley." He took a deep breath. "I'm glad I'm not Elvis. Let's get some Edy's chocolate chip ice cream and watch *Casablanca*. I'm starting to appreciate Humphrey Bogart."

Jack Randolph grinned.

"Here's looking at you, kid," he said.

Jamie smiled back, his lip curling up unintentionally, looking exactly like Elvis when he was young and happy.